MAGGIE MASON

The Fortune Tellers' Secret

SPHERE

SPHERE

First published in Great Britain in 2023 by Sphere

13 5 7 9 10 8 6 4 2

A CIP catalogue record for this book is available from the British Library.

ISBN 978-1-4087-2816-1

Typeset in Bembo by Hewer Text UK Ltd, Edinburgh
Printed and bound in Great Britain by Clays Ltd, Elcograf S.p.A.

Papers used by Sphere are from well-managed forests
and other responsible sources.

MIX
Supporting
responsible forestry
FSC
www.fsc.org
FSC® C104740

In loving memory of Kathy Dobson, a dear friend, who I met through my books and came close in my heart. Miss you, dear lady. RIP

PART ONE

Unfulfilled Dreams

1922

ONE

Trisha

The June sunshine streamed through the windows as Trisha stood in front of the long mirror that she'd bought from Second-hand Lil's shop especially for today – her wedding day.

Turning this way and that, she sighed as she looked at herself in the beautiful ivory gown. Sweeping the floor as she moved, her wedding gown had a sheen that caught the light, making it shimmer. The style – fitted, then spraying out at the hemline – suited her slender body. *Eeh, lass, it's like you're a queen*, she told herself, then shook her head. *Me second wedding, and still not a bride in white, but then, me first were a shotgun wedding!*

This thought filled her with pain for a moment as she remembered the violence Bobby used against her and how it ultimately caused her to lose their unborn child.

The bedroom door opened, and her five-year-old daughter Sally came bursting in.

'Look at me, Ma! I'm a princess!'

As she watched Sally dancing around the room, Trisha felt so grateful to her future husband for accepting Sally as his own. And for loving them both.

Walter's love was full of kindness, and thoughtfulness. He was always romantic, bringing her presents and complimenting her, calling her beautiful, when she knew she wasn't. Attractive, yes. At least, when she smiled, as then her long face became more rounded, and her hazel eyes lit up. Her mousy-coloured hair was nothing special, though it did shine, especially in the sunshine when golden strands were picked out. And she loved her new bobbed hairstyle. It suited her – cut to chin-length and with a fringe.

She sighed as she thought that for all Walter's loving ways, he'd never made love to her since he'd become her man two years ago. Many times she'd wondered why. It wasn't as if she was a virgin. And why the long wait to marry her? Sometimes she'd thought he would never ask. And yet he was caring and kind in how he treated her and her little Sally.

They'd met when he'd tended her first husband Bobby in his last days. A specialist doctor, Walter's handsome face was marred by him having to wear bottle-bottom glasses, as she thought of the thick lenses that gave Walter sight.

'Ma, Ma, you've gone inside your head again!'

'Ha! I knaw. It's a day for doing that as memories keep visiting me ... By, me little lass, you do look like a princess!'

Sally gave a twirl. Her long pale blue satin dress floated around her.

'Aw, lass, I need one of your hugs.'

Clinging on to her child – the saviour of her and the light of her life – Trisha took this moment to shrug off the past, though she allowed her beautiful long-departed ma and da to stay with her. The rest she let go of, determined to look to the future, which, to her, looked full of happiness.

Releasing Sally, she asked, 'Where's Aunty Martha and Bonnie?'

'They're in me bedroom. Oh, Aunty Martha looks like a princess, like you, Ma, and Bonnie looks like me!'

Trisha laughed at this as she thought that it wasn't possible for her to look as beautiful as her adored friend, Martha, with her lovely long red hair that hung in ringlets, and her beautiful green-blue eyes – all-seeing eyes, as Martha had inherited her gypsy ancestors' ability to see into the future. Known as the Fortune Teller, Martha had helped so many people, and yet knew secrets that gave her pain as she saw what was to befall those she loved. Though sometimes she blocked these, as she said she can tell fortunes but not change people's destiny.

As if these thoughts conjured Martha up, she came through the door. 'Oh, me darling Trish, it is beautiful that you are, for sure.'

Trisha laughed as she went into Martha's open arms. 'Will I do, lass?'

'You will, me darling.'

The hug dispelled the last traces of the fingers of sadness that had clung to Trisha, despite her trying to brush them away. Life was going to be different now. Walter was different. She had no need to be sad any more. Memories could be made of good things, they didn't always have to be dwelling on the bad.

As they came out of the hug, Martha stood back. 'I'm for saying meself, so I am, but that frock is for sure the very best garment I ever made in me life! You truly are for looking beautiful, Trish.'

As they looked into each other's eyes Martha's clouded. Then, there it was, the shudder that told Trish Martha didn't like what she'd seen with her mind's eye.

Not wanting to know, Trisha laughed out loud. 'Now, don't be having ghosts walk over your grave today, Martha. It's the best day in me life.'

'It is, me darling, and I see nothing but happiness for you.'

Trisha doubted this, but whatever would be, would be. She just wanted to be wed to Walter. To know that it was true that such a man wanted her – a Blackpool lass who'd never had much until the day Martha, fleeing from the Troubles in Ireland with her granny, came to live next door to her in Enfield Road and changed her life.

As from that moment, they had supported each other through the loss of loved ones, the war years, and having daughters out of wedlock. But they'd won through.

Martha had given up telling fortunes on the promenade and they'd set up a business together making and selling baby layettes.

'Come on, me darling, Josh is waiting downstairs. It is that he is looking handsome in his black suit, and I'm for falling in love with him all over again!'

'I didn't knaw you'd fell out of love with him!'

Martha's lovely tinkling laughter filled the bedroom. 'No, to be sure, that will never happen.'

Joshua, Martha's lovely, gentle husband, stood at the bottom of the stairs as Trisha went down from the flat above their layette shop, where she'd lived since losing the home she was born in, in Enfield Road, his smile lighting up his handsome face. 'My, you look beautiful, Trisha. Walter's a lucky man.'

Taking his arm, Trisha could only grin. It was she who was the lucky one, she thought. She'd never dreamed she could love again, or be loved, but here she was about to begin an exciting journey, if only her nerves would settle, and she could stop worrying about fitting in and not letting Walter down.

Today was going to be the first time she'd met Walter's parents, which she felt was unfair, and couldn't understand – unless Walter really was ashamed of her. Though he'd said it was because he couldn't get enough time off to take her up to Cleator Moor in Cumbria where they lived, and where Walter had been born.

And yet, there were many times that he went alone to Manchester to meet up with friends he'd made whilst training at a hospital there. Her heart quickened as they were another reason her nerves were on edge – she would meet them for the first time too. What would they think of her?

Suddenly, with these thoughts, Walter seemed like a stranger to her, and what lay ahead – the intimate side of marriage – made her nerves jangle even more. It had been such a long time since a man had made love to her. The last time was with Bobby.

Changed after the loss of their child, he'd been gentle and loving, instead of rough and demanding, whilst she'd been cold and unforgiving of his violent past, pretending to enjoy it for the sake of peace.

What would it be like to be made love to by Walter? He'd only ever kissed her and hugged her – she couldn't even remember him caressing her. And yet she loved him with all her heart and so wanted to be his.

Sensing her distress, Martha touched her arm. 'Sure, everything is going to be all right, me darling.'

With this, Trisha knew a confidence to enter her. Everything would be fine. Men brought up how Walter had been – posh school, then university and medical school – would always behave gentlemanly, wouldn't they?

'Ready, love?' Joshua smiled down on her. 'The trusted Arthur awaits you outside with his carriage to take you to your future husband. And he's a very lucky man.'

Everything happened in a whirl after that. The sound of the horse's hooves as they trotted along the promenade, the Blackpool visitors waving to her as she passed and shouting 'good luck', and then a smiling Walter, who greeted her at the altar, clutching her hand to reassure her.

Before she knew it, she'd said her vows and listened to Walter affirming his and was gliding down the aisle of the Sacred Heart Catholic Church, Blackpool, only yards from the seafront.

Once outside, Trisha gasped as a braying of donkeys could be heard vying with the church bells.

'Eeh, Walter, ain't that a sight, eh?'

Walter looked on astonished as Trisha, closely followed by Sally and Bonnie, ran towards her beloved donkeys congregated at the church gates with their owner, Benny, who Trisha had loved working for on the beach, before her and Martha's shop really got going.

Shelley, the gentle, timid donkey, was nearest to Trisha. She nuzzled her nose into Trisha's hand. Everyone laughed, but to Trisha, it was a 'hello' and 'please protect me from this crowd'.

Sally seemed to sense this too, as she gently stroked Shelley in a reassuring way.

As Benny drew her away, he said, 'We just wanted to wish you luck, Trisha, love, and to let you knaw we'll allus be waiting for you, if he don't treat you right.' He winked and grinned at Walter, who laughed out loud.

'Ta, Benny. It's made me day seeing them.'

Just before they left, Daisy, the granny of the troupe who was lazy and often refused to budge no matter how you tried to coax her, came over to Trisha and looked up at her. To Trisha, she seemed to smile, her large eyes shining in the sunlight. Trisha smiled back. 'Off you go, old girl. I'll come and see you soon, eh?'

Daisy nodded her head, nuzzled Sally and made her giggle, and then ambled off at her own pace, resisting Benny trying to pull her rein to make her go faster.

'What a delight, my dear.'

Trisha felt immediately on her guard as the tone of voice these words were said in, by the woman she knew

9

to be Walter's mother, made her feel that her new ma-in-law meant exactly the opposite to what she was saying. Her expression showed her distaste as her eyes followed Daisy.

When she turned back to Trisha, she masked her feelings for the donkeys with a tight smile. 'I'm Beth, Walter's mother. He told me how you used to work with the donkeys and then rose to own your own business! I'm impressed. Quite a rise.'

Again, Trisha felt an underlying implication. Her nerves jangled but she managed to say, 'Pleased to meet you ... Ma.'

'Call me Beth, dear. Even Walter does, and has done since he was a boy!'

'Eeh, that don't seem right but if you're sure?'

'I am. And is this little Sally? Oh, she's a pretty little thing.'

'I'm pretty an' all!'

'Oh, you are, and what is your name?'

'I'm Bonnie.'

'Oh dear, it is sorry that I am. The two of them are often rivals, but they love each other as sisters, so they do. I'm Martha, Trisha's friend.'

'Oh, the one who can see into the future.' Beth lowered her voice and, meaning for Martha's ears only, said, 'Well, that power seems to have let you down, dear.'

Trisha felt a moment's trepidation as Martha answered, 'No, I knew me lovely friend Trish was going to meet a handsome, kind and caring man, and it is that she has!'

10

The last bit she said as if in triumph and Trisha relaxed and turned towards Walter, who was waiting to introduce his father.

Glad of the interruption, but wondering about how the man who looked so like Walter, even to the thick-lensed glasses, would be with her, Trisha fixed a smile on her face. But her new father-in-law was a charming man, who asked her to call him Cyril. 'Father is too formal, and we aren't formal at all, my dear. I'm so pleased to meet you at last.'

Trisha's nerves settled with this welcome and the short hug Cyril gave her.

Feeling as if everything would be all right, and that it was natural for a new ma-in-law to be wary of her – her first had never been friendly – Trisha looked around the small crowd gathered to celebrate with them. She was startled when she caught a glimpse of a man looking at her as if he hated her.

Walter squeezed her hand, bringing her attention back to him. 'Well, that's the first ordeal over with, darling. And you handled it well.'

Although he smiled as he said this, Trish had the feeling she was taking some kind of test.

When they moved into the church hall for refreshments Walter introduced her to his Manchester friends. The staring man was the first.

'Pleased to meet you, dear.' His eyes said otherwise. Then he nodded, and looked at Walter. 'She'll do.'

His mocking laugh made Trisha snap.

'I ain't part of a line-up, lad. You don't get to pick if I'll do or not.'

Walter looked appalled.

Well, Trisha thought, *so am I.*

Picking up the hem of her frock, she flounced away with as much dignity as she could muster. Tears stung her eyes, but she wasn't going to let them fall. How dare Walter allow her to be humiliated in that way?

One of the group, a young woman with black curly hair, came after her. 'Patricia!'

Trisha stopped and looked back. It seemed a day for being called by her given name. She would have so liked to have been asked, 'Trisha, do you take Walter?' It would have sounded right to her. Now it seemed she was to be Patricia all day!

When the young woman caught up with her, she looked flustered. 'I'm sorry. I'm Freda . . . Look, Carl can be such a beast at times but he's all right, really. Please don't let him spoil your day.'

'Why are you all so judgemental? You knaw nowt of me, or me life. Why can't you accept that Walter loves me, and I'll do me best to make him happy?'

Freda looked down at the floor. 'I'm sorry . . . We behaved badly. It's a "we were all students together" thing. Hard to understand unless you've formed such friendships. It's very cliquey. We should be more grown-up and are, when not with each other – we're all medical staff. It's stupid and we should change. I'm mortified that we've upset you.'

'Ta, love, I ain't blaming you all. I knaw I ain't what you expected and you can't see me fitting in, and you're right, I won't. I ain't had no education and cannot think why

Walter chose me. I won't try to be one of you all, but Walter will still come and see you like he allus has done as that makes him happy.'

'You're a lovely person, Trish. I like you. You're honest and have no side. I wish I was more like you instead of being like a sheep following the crowd. May I come to visit you sometimes? I love Walter and would like to spend time with you and him. I can see why he chose you. Never put yourself down, Patricia.'

'Trisha. Call me Trisha, and aye, I'd like that. You seem different to them lot.'

'Different is good, and I'm going to carry on being so. You've taught me a lesson today, Trisha. I wish . . . Anyway, I won't hog your time, see you soon, eh?'

Wondering what it was that she wished, Trisha just nodded and moved away, seeking out Martha.

'Eeh, Martha, lass, I've proper let Walter down.'

'Oh? Well, it is that he is smiling. Look, he's coming over. He's not for looking like a man who's been let down, love.'

Trisha turned, ready to apologise for her behaviour, but Walter's lovely smile stopped her.

'Well said, darling. You really put Carl in his place, and he is getting a good dressing-down from Freda now. You've made a friend there.'

'Eeh, but I'm sorry. He's your friend.'

'He deserved it, he showed bad manners, and I hate that. Like Freda says, they all need to grow up. They aren't students any more.'

Trisha relaxed. Martha took hold of her hand and squeezed it. She had no need to speak. They'd always been

13

able to convey what they wanted to say to each other by a touch, a gesture or a look.

Feeling comforted, Trisha regained her confidence as Walter took hold of her other hand and together they watch the antics of Sally and Bonnie, playing in the centre of the hall.

Trisha's love for her child swelled, but once more her happiness was marred by the thought that she would never be able to give Walter a child. She'd suffered greatly after giving birth to Sally and had to have an operation to take her womb away.

With this thought, her love for Walter increased as she looked up at him and thought how lovely he was to accept this and her little Sally as his own.

Suddenly they were surrounded by Walter's friends from Blackpool Victoria Hospital, some of whom Trisha already knew. How different they were. Funny, welcoming and including her.

As they did Cilla when she joined them. A gypsy cousin of Martha's, and Trisha's friend, Cilla had taken over Martha's fortune telling business on the prom.

To Trisha, she looked beautiful today in her traditional gypsy clothes – long black skirt hemmed with sequins, teamed with a red silk puffed sleeved blouse. Her long dark hair she'd caught back with a black band, which was also threaded with sequins that caught the light as she moved. She drew many a glance and sideways remark – now she seemed to have become the object of mirth to the 'horrid lot', as Trisha had named the Manchester crowd.

Trisha held her breath as Cilla excused herself and boldly went up to the horrid lot. She only spoke a few words, but it shut them up and their expressions showed fear as she left them. A good moment.

At last it was time for her and Walter to climb up onto Arthur's carriage and be driven to their beautiful new home on St Anne's Road, just a few doors down from where Martha and Joshua lived.

As they waved to everyone before climbing into the carriage, Carl came up to them and, without looking at her, said, 'Don't forget who your *true* friends are, Walt.'

Walter blushed, then laughed as he put his arm around Trisha. 'I won't. Take care and wish us luck.'

'Oh, I do. You will need it!'

With this and not even acknowledging Trisha, he turned and went back to the others in the clique.

Martha came over and hugged them both. 'Oh, it is that you are going to be so happy. We will see you tomorrow when we will bring Sally to you.' To Trisha, who she held for longer, she said, 'Beware of those friends from Manchester. They ... I – I mean, don't be taking any notice of them. Sure, you won't have to be seeing them often, if at all.'

'I've never met them before or even heard their names and don't ever want to see them again. I can't understand why Walter asked them to come today. Surely he knew they ain't happy with him marrying me?'

Martha looked deeply into her eyes. Trisha knew for certain she had a secret she wasn't sharing, but then, they had always said she shouldn't as it would be like directing her life for her. They were friends – the closest friends ever – and loved one another. Martha didn't work as a fortune teller any more, but that didn't stop her having visions of future happenings, but she would never presume to read Trisha's future. For that, she had to go to Cilla. But she'd never done that. Maybe this time she would.

This feeling passed as the anticipation of her new life as Walter's wife took over when he once more pulled her to him. 'Everything will be all right, my darling. Don't let them worry you. I rarely see them. They insisted on coming today.'

His parents came over to them then. Beth hugged her. 'Patricia, please make sure that this son of mine brings you up to see us as soon as possible, and bring little Sally. She is adorable.'

'I will, but you can come to see us at any time, can't they, Walter? We have a guest bedroom.'

Trisha felt excitement grip her as she said this. Never in her wildest dreams did she think that she, a girl from Enfield Road, two up, two down terraced houses, could ever live in a large house with a garden and a guest bedroom.

As Walter's mother went to hug him, she whispered something about doing his best to be a good husband. Trisha only caught this and her saying, 'This is your chance to live a normal life, darling.'

What she meant by that, Trisha assumed, was that he didn't have to live in hospital accommodation any longer, but in a proper home. She smiled and nodded, but Walter looked annoyed at his mother's words.

There was no time to dwell on this as after a quick goodbye to his father, and a massive hug for each of them from Sally and Bonnie, they were climbing onto the carriage and it pulled away, leaving them laughing together at the sound of the tin cans clattering on the road. Who tied them to the carriage they had no idea, but it added to their enjoyment and relaxed them both.

TWO

Martha

As they drove home in the brand-new Austin 7 that Joshua had recently bought, Martha was unsettled by the feeling that something wasn't right. This left her unable to enjoy the freedom of the roof being down and the feel of the wind on her face, even though she loved the sensation of travelling in the car.

A third-generation descendant of the ancestor who broke the gypsy code and married a gorger, Martha had been gifted with the ability to see into the future. But today she wouldn't allow her 'guiding spirit' – what all the gypsies called the means of them getting their information – nag her into wanting to accept the knowledge of Trisha's future.

Trisha had made her promise that she would never tell her what was in store for her, so Martha would rather not know. Besides, she'd never wanted to be gifted. Had fought against being so, until she'd been forced to earn her money helping her lovely, late gran to tell fortunes on the promenade, hoping their palms would be crossed with silver.

But since she'd handed over to Cilla and taken up needlework, opening the layette shop on the promenade with Trisha, she'd so wanted to leave all of that behind.

Sighing, she thought how difficult it was for her to stop bad news coming to her and how it was such news that had been the means of her knowing she had the gift in the first place.

Her mind went back to the little cosy kitchen of the cottage she was brought up in on the outskirts of Dublin. And she saw again the first vision she'd ever had, of her mammy and pappy, supporters of the uprising, being shot.

Her whole body shuddered with the pain of how that had become real.

'Are you all right, darling? Are you cold?'

She could only shake her head in Joshua's direction.

His hand came on hers. She managed to smile up at him. But her troubled mind wouldn't let that smile touch her heart as she so wanted to save Trisha from all she had to face, but always she had to listen to what her gran had taught her – that they can inform if asked to do so, but they must never try to change a person's destiny.

Martha was of the same mind and was glad that it wasn't possible to see her own future, but she could consult the tarot cards to get any answers she wanted and meant to do so to ask if she would have another child – Joshua's child.

With this thought, Peter came to mind. Bonnie's father. She shook the thought from her – helped unwittingly by Josh, as he went from being quiet to suddenly talking about anything and everything. A tactic he often used to distract her, if he thought her troubled by her spirit.

'I took some lovely photos today, darling. I can't wait to get into my darkroom tomorrow.'

'It is that I saw you clicking away. It is lovely that Trish and Walter will have the photos to keep, so it is.'

'They may find there's more of you than them, my darling, you look so beautiful in that colour. And you said pale blue wouldn't suit you.'

'Ha, it is that I cannot wait to get it off! Satin is for being the hottest of fabrics.'

'I can't wait either. I'll help you with it, if you like.'

His grin showed his desire.

Martha's muscles in her groin clenched, but she shushed Josh and glanced back at the children. Glad to see Sally had nodded off and Bonnie wasn't taking any notice, she brought her attention back to Josh.

His desire showed in his expression, adding fire to her own. She knew her voice conveyed this as she said, 'The children are tired, Josh, darling. I think it is that I'll be putting them to bed for an afternoon nap when we reach home.'

'Good idea, darling.' The husky voice he used told her that he'd read her meaning.

Bonnie's petulant 'I don't want to go to bed, Mammy. I ain't a babby, you know!' made them both burst out laughing but didn't break the spell that sizzled between them.

'Maybe it is that you will feel differently once we are for being home. Sure, Sally is fast asleep already.'

'Aunt Trisha says she's a sleepy head.' As she said this, Bonnie showed her love for Sally by stroking her hair.

Seeing this gesture warmed Martha's heart.

'Ah, but to be sure, those who rest now can be finishing the day with a walk along the promenade and a fish and chip supper out of newspaper. Me and Pappy are going to rest to get ready for that treat, isn't that so, Pappy?'

'It is, and if Bonnie doesn't, not only will she miss the fish and chips, she'll be alone downstairs with no one to talk to while we rest.'

'No, I don't want that, but Mammy, if I go to have a rest, can I stay in Sally's bed and lie next to her?'

'I think that is for being a good idea as then it is that when Sally wakes and she isn't for being in her own bed, she will have you and won't be feeling lost.'

'I always look after Sally, Mammy.'

'I know, it does me heart good to see you and Sally care for each other.'

'That's because I love her, and she loves me.'

Martha smiled and as she turned back to face the front, she caught a wink from Josh that rekindled her desire and sent a warm feeling trickling through her. With it the thought came to her that maybe this time it would happen.

They'd been married for two years and had been blissfully happy. Both had grown their businesses, especially Josh, who now owned a printing firm alongside his photographic and film developing business. But the one thing that marred that happiness and success was that she hadn't become pregnant. She couldn't understand why and blamed herself, thinking that her sin of having a child out of wedlock had come home to roost and that maybe Bonnie's birth, although easy and over very quickly, had somehow damaged her.

21

Peter, Bonnie's father, came to mind once again.

Peter belonged firmly in her past – but did he? One day she must face up to him being part of Bonnie's future.

Inwardly she rebelled against this. She wanted Josh to always be pappy to Bonnie and for her never to know the truth, but she knew that wasn't fair. She and Josh had promised Peter that when Bonnie was older, they would tell her who her real father was. He'd been willing to wait so as not to disrupt Bonnie's tender years, so she couldn't break that promise.

For the umpteenth time she wondered how different her life would have been if Peter, who she'd fallen so completely in love with, hadn't walked out not to return for many years – years in which she'd met and fallen more deeply in love with Josh.

It helped to know that Peter didn't walk out in a casual way having had what he wanted from her, but that trauma from his experiences in the Great War caused him to have episodes of complete loss of memory.

She'd been happy to learn that he'd married one of his nurses and had a child himself, but even happier that he hadn't wanted to disrupt Bonnie's life and intended not to be a part of it until she was much older.

To this end, they had regularly sent Peter updates on her progress and photographs as she reached each birthday.

The car turning into their drive gave Martha a happy release from these painful thoughts as Josh squeezed her knee once more just as soon as they came to a halt. His look immediately flooded her with the thrill of anticipation.

She didn't have long to wait, with Sally not waking from her slumber and Bonnie already yawning as they climbed the stairs.

Feeling impatient to be with Josh, it was a relief to see Bonnie close her eyes as soon as she lay her head on the pillow next to Sally.

Now that the moment was on her, all the anticipation burst into a raging need inside Martha as she opened the bedroom door.

Josh, already naked, took her in his arms and kissed every part of her as he undressed her.

'My Martha, my love, oh, my darling, I love you deeply and want you so much.'

When they lay on the bed, frantically kissing, touching, moaning their pleasure and giving their all to each other, Martha thought she would die with the intensity of the waves of ecstasy that washed over her.

Then it happened. His fondling and caressing of her brought her to the height of sensation that she could hardly bear. She cried out his name as she became one with him and knew the sheer joy of being a woman loved.

When he stiffened, she was ready. She held him close as his cries and hollers of sheer pleasure filled the space around them.

Soon after, he lay beside her, cradling her in his arms. She was where she wanted to be, always and for ever.

After a moment, Joshua leaned over her, kissed her brow and looked into her eyes. 'Does your crystal ball say that we have made a baby at last, my darling?'

She giggled. 'It is that you know it never speaks to me of me life.'

'What about mine? Can you tell my future?'

'I refuse to.' As she said this a great sadness came over her. She clung to Joshua, feeling the strength of him, wanting some of that for herself as fears she didn't want to take heed of gripped her heart.

After a moment, she relaxed again. Joshua didn't remark on her action. He knew by now that when she was visited by strange spirits, she would talk about them if she wanted to. Instead, he surprised her by broaching the fear she'd never spoken of to him.

'Darling ... I've been thinking a lot about how it is that you don't become pregnant, and I think we ought to look into it ... I mean, well, it might be something simple that can be sorted out for you.'

'You mean, if it is that something is wrong with me, it could be put right? To be sure, if that is so, Josh, then it is that I will do whatever it takes. I am wanting to give you a child more than anything in the world, so I am.'

'Oh, Martha, really? Even if it means an operation?'

Martha didn't like the sound of this, but she nodded her head. 'Is it that you are for knowing for sure things can be done?'

'Well, not for sure, but Walter was telling me that he has a friend who works at the Manchester hospital. He's a gyno ... something or other ... Well, you know these doctors, they like to have long names for their speciality but as I understand it, he is an expert in reproduction problems.'

'Then it is that I will make an appointment with him. Oh, Josh, sure, it will be wonderful if this doctor can be putting things right for me.'

'It will, darling . . . Well, as long as whatever he comes up with won't cause you a lot of pain.'

'I'll gladly go through it, me love.'

Joshua pulled her closer and kissed her hair, then giggled, a pleased kind of giggle, as he said, 'This could be a turning point for us, darling. I'm going to put my order in now: I want five girls and five boys, please!'

'Holy Mary, Mother of God! Is it you're for being mad? Haven't Bonnie's tantrums put you off?'

'Ha, she's getting better now. Anyway, I think it's because she's frustrated.'

'About what? It is that she is but four years old!'

'I know, but she has the intelligence of a much older child and spending her time playing isn't enough to stimulate her brain. I think we should look at putting her into school soon. She needs knowledge. She seeks it all the time with how she is so full of questions and doesn't accept things as they are but wants to know the reason for them.'

'So, it is that we've gone from wanting ten more babies to getting rid of the one we have! To be sure, it is a daft idea. The wee mite is too young.'

'No, of course not, you goose. But you must see she is ready, and that's what counts. I think Elmslie Girls' School would be ideal. The Brodie sisters have moved the school into Elms House and renamed it from Elleslie. They have an excellent reputation. And besides, it isn't fair to say I want to get rid of her. Nothing is further from the truth. I want to help her to progress. Already she shows she has spirit. If we encourage her, educate her, who knows what she can achieve.'

Part of Martha agreed with this, but to let go of her little girl now would be a wrench. Though she had to admit Josh was right. A lot of Bonnie's tantrums were born of frustration as if she had so much more to give ... But to go to school!

'Look, what if I talk to Walter about sending Sally to Elmslie too? He may already be thinking about it as she is due to start school in September.'

Martha didn't know what to think but nodded her head. 'To be sure, it is that you need to let Walter enjoy his honeymoon first.'

'Ha, that won't be long. He was telling me he's going back to work on Monday.'

This shocked Martha. She knew it would upset Trisha, who was hoping they would have at least a week together. She'd been talking of days out with Sally and taking Bonnie as well.

The worries Martha tried to deny came back to her. She shook them off. There was nothing she could do about the vague feeling she had that not all would be right for her dear friend. For this reason, Martha wouldn't let herself delve into it to find out more. *Just go away and leave me alone, I don't want to know!* she told her guiding spirit. Then, as if to really ward it off, she moved out of the circle of Joshua's arms and threw back the covers. 'I'll put the kettle on and be making us a nice cup of tea.'

Joshua looked at her with an expression that said he'd noticed her sudden discomfort but as he didn't say anything this time, she knew he'd decided to leave her to deal with what was troubling her. Sometimes she detected that he feared this side of her. She didn't blame him. Seeing into the future was a scary thing.

As she dressed, she asked, 'Why is it that Walter has so many friends from Manchester?'

'Oh, he trained there, I believe. You know, when I knew him at school, I never saw him becoming a doctor. He was always so timid ... and, well, bullied because of his thick glasses. I used to champion him and got myself a few beatings for it.'

'That's nice to hear, so it is ... Not the beatings, but that you looked after him.'

'I liked him and still do. He's a very interesting man to talk to and I love to listen to him. He knows something about everything. I can't understand how he has become part of a crowd like those he invited today, especially that Carl. He gave me the creeps.'

Martha understood this. She'd felt more than the creeps; she'd had a feeling that she had to warn Trisha to beware of all of them, but truly, she had meant Carl.

The act of making the tea and taking a cup up to Joshua took Martha's mind off future happenings. Always a relief when this happened, she set about laying out clothes for the children. Trisha had packed an overnight bag for Sally, and Martha was glad to see it held outdoor shoes and leggings. Even in June the sea breeze could chill you.

*   *   *

Blackpool was alive when they walked down to the promenade, a fair walk which was made easier for the children by Joshua giving them turns to ride on his shoulders. They both loved this and were very good at waiting their turn, though Bonnie amazed her by knowing exactly when it was each of their time to get down and let the other be lifted up.

When asked she said, 'I can see Pappy's watch. Ten minutes each, Pappy said, and that's what I'm timing, Mammy.'

Martha didn't comment but knew this to enforce what Joshua had said earlier. Her mind settled on agreeing and asking Joshua to make an appointment with the Brodie sisters – besides, they sounded as if they had Irish ancestors, with such a name, and that boded well with her.

'Mmm, I can smell the fish and chips! Who else can?'

'Me, Pappy.'

Sally, who was clinging on to Joshua's head, nodded her own. Martha hadn't noticed how fearful she looked perched up so high.

'I think it is that we can all walk now, me wee ones. Come on, Sally, I'll help you down.' Sally looked relieved and though she didn't say so, Martha tried to show her with a hug how brave she thought her.

'Shall we have a ride on the big wheel first?'

Martha looked at Sally as Joshua suggested this, wondering if it was a fear of heights that had made her look so scared on Joshua's shoulders, but her face was lit up and she clapped her hands. Only then did she tug Martha's arm and the cause of her distress came to light. Her jigging about

28

was because she was desperate for a pee. Laughing at her antics, they ran along the prom and dived into Macie's café.

'Eeh, Martha, lass, I ain't seen you in a while. And Joshua, how are you?'

'I know, it is that I don't often get down this end. We're fine, but please, Macie, can the little ones be using your lav?'

''Course they can, love. Come on, me lovelies, this way.'

When they came out, Martha told Macie, 'It's grateful I am, Macie. Ta. Oh, but I do miss your fish and chips. We'll be back in a wee while, so we will, as it is that we've promised the wee ones they will 'ave some tonight. They were for being the best of bridesmaids today.'

'I knaw, lass, I shut up shop for half an hour and nipped up to the church, but I don't think any of you saw me for them blinking donkeys. Whatever were Benny thinking of?'

'Ha, they were one of Trisha's highlights! She is for loving them donkeys.'

'I knaw. She's as daft as Benny over them. So, where you off to, me little lasses?'

Bonnie piped up. 'The big wheel! We're so excited. Did you know it was built way back in 1896?'

This astonished Martha, but Joshua smiled at Bonnie. 'Good girl for remembering. I told you that over a week ago.' He looked at Martha as he said, 'You're a very clever little girl, Bonnie.'

Bonnie beamed at Macie, who told her, 'Aye, I did, little lass. I were about fourteen at the time and remember it being built. It was a wonderful sight and rivalled the Tower, which had opened two years before. By, they were exciting times.'

'So, the Tower opened in 1894, then.'

'That's right, lass. Eeh, it's like Joshua says, you're a clever girl and you're only . . . let me see . . . four, aren't you?'

Martha held her breath, then coughed, as she desperately tried to attract Macie's attention, afraid she was going to let out that Josh wasn't Bonnie's father, but Bonnie saved the day by retorting, 'It's me pappy, not Joshua.'

Macie looked up at Martha, read the plea in her face. 'Aye, of course it is, silly me. But you knaw, I've known your pappy since he were knee high to a donkey and he'll allus be Joshua to me, lass.'

Bonnie giggled. 'I like that saying. Am I knee high to a donkey, Mammy?'

'Well, you're for being a little bigger than that, Bonnie. Think about it, if it was that you were stood next to a donkey, you would be reaching his hind quarters.'

'Ha, I'm bottom high to a donkey!'

She and Sally fell around giggling as Sally chanted, 'Eeh, Bonnie, you said a rude word.'

Martha joined in, as did Joshua, and she could see that he was as relieved as she was that the moment had passed.

'Ta, Macie, love. We'll see you in a wee while.'

It was a relief to get outside, and to see that nothing had registered with Bonnie or Sally as they skipped along, holding hands.

Both loved the big wheel, though Martha wasn't so sure when they were at the highest point and the wheel stopped to let on more people. The carriage they were in began to sway in the wind and her stomach turned over. But Joshua kept the children amused by pointing out landmarks as far

30

away as Barrow on sea, which was visible due to the clear night.

As they sat on a bench eating their delicious fish and chips, Joshua whispered, 'That was a near miss in Macie's. It made me realise how easily the truth could come out.'

'I know, I've been for worrying about that meself. Or even if one day, with how quick it is that Bonnie is with remembering facts, she will be for putting two and two together herself.' At that moment, the girls ran off after scattering the pigeons that had landed on the promenade.

'Don't you be going too far, now.'

Both girls called back to Martha that they wouldn't. But them being out of earshot was a relief to be able to talk openly and to answer Joshua.

'I know what it is you are saying, Josh. And though it is that she knew you from birth, she was almost two already by the time we married. It was then it was that we taught her to call you Pappy.'

'That changes to Da at times as she plays with Sally who always calls Walter Da.'

'I'm not for minding that, she's a Blackpool lass – a Sandgronian, as those born here are for being called – so it is fine if it is that she wishes to speak in the Lancashire way. But I am feared that she will find out the truth before we can be telling her ourselves.'

'Maybe we should?'

There was trepidation in the question.

Martha shook her head. 'I am agreeing with you about going to school, and know that it is that I've been blind to

31

how she is ready. But no. I am not thinking that we should tell her. She is for being too young to understand the truth of her parentage.'

Joshua nodded. He screwed the newspaper up that he'd been eating from and threw it with accuracy into the bin attached to the nearest lamp post, before he looked at her and gave her a reassuring smile. 'I'll stand by your decision, darling. And I will speak to Walter about Sally attending Elmslie. But whether or not they decide to send Sally, I think we should enrol Bonnie.'

Martha agreed. And as Joshua's arm came around her and pulled her towards him, she snuggled her head into his neck. Her happiness swelled her heart, but suddenly it was as if a cloud was on the horizon of their future. She silently prayed, *Please, Holy Mary, Mother of God, don't let anything be spoiling me happiness.*

But she knew no matter how hard she prayed the cloud wouldn't lift. Her heart thumped loudly, seeming to give her the message that whatever was to be was her destiny and she couldn't change it.

THREE

Trisha

As Trisha arrived in her new home, bought by Walter but furnished to her liking, she had looked around her, unable to believe that this was truly her home now. She loved every part of the house, with its huge kitchen with light oak dresser, long oak table and six chairs, its range with two ovens, a large hotplate, besides three small ones, its deep pot sink and draining board, which had the red with white daisy patterned curtain hanging around it that she had made, as she had the matching ones hung at the window above it. All was set off beautifully by the polished red slate tiles of the floor.

Trisha couldn't wait to cook their very first meal. She'd planned that that would be tonight and for this purpose had asked Joshua to light the range for them this morning.

When she'd gone upstairs to their room to change out of her gown, she'd asked Walter to come too, to help her with the many little buttons.

With this done, Walter had caught hold of her, sending a thrill zinging through her and the thought that the time was on her. But she'd realised with a sinking heart that he didn't intend to as he said, 'You looked so beautiful as you walked towards me, darling. I love your hair like that,' then sighed, 'I'll leave you to it and see you downstairs. I'll make us a cup of tea.'

She'd longed for him to stay and had offered her lips, aching for him to hold her. But he'd kissed the tip of her nose and left.

When she'd gone downstairs, he was out of his morning suit and wearing a short-sleeved shirt and grey slacks.

'By, how did you manage that? You never came back into the bedroom, lad.'

He laughed at her. He always loved her calling him 'lad'.

'No, I put most of my things in the wardrobe I had fitted on the landing and used the guest bathroom. I thought that a good idea for when I'm on nights, or early shifts at the hospital. I needn't disturb you then.'

This reassured her that he did mean to sleep with her. She sighed with relief. She so wanted him to make her his.

'Aye, I like me sleep, so that's a good idea, but ...' Something stopped her from saying that she'd wanted him to stay with her in their bedroom and to watch him undress, to have him stop her from dressing, and to make love to her. It seemed the natural thing to have happen and something she so wanted.

He looked at her quizzically. She felt herself blush.

'Trisha, darling, I – I, well, I have something to tell you ...

I – I should have done before, but well, we never discussed anything like … well, you know.'

Tears welled up in his eyes and he slumped down onto one of the chairs around the table.

'Eeh, whatever is it, love?' Trisha dashed to his side and held his head against hers.

'I'm so sorry, but I can't … well … I can't make love to you.'

'What?' Shock vibrated through Trisha. She stood straight, looking down on him. 'I – I don't understand. Don't you fancy me, is that it?'

'No. I love you with all my heart, and Sally too … I want to be with you, more than anything, darling, but … Oh, I should have said, I should have been honest … You see, well, some men cannot get an erection. I – I am one of those.'

Trisha could only stare at him, unable to think for a moment what he meant.

'I'm sorry, truly sorry … I thought, well, hoped that how we have jogged along these last two years could continue. I – I mean, after the problems you experienced in your first marriage, and then the ordeal of finding you were pregnant after you were raped and then having to have everything taken away after Sally's birth, that that side of things didn't bother you now. After all, you are unable to have any more children.'

Still Trisha couldn't react. Though she felt the sting of his last words, and how they seemed to dismiss her as a woman with feelings and the shame of her lie of how she was raped. But then, hadn't Walter lied by omitting to tell her the truth and keeping her waiting in anticipation?

'We ... we have been so happy ... I thought we could carry on being so. That nothing would change ... Please, Trisha, don't look at me like that, I can't bear it.'

More tears streamed down his face. His shoulders bent over, he took off his glasses, rested his head in his hands, and sobbed ... 'I need you, Trisha, so very much, and love you with all my heart. Please forgive me.'

His hand reached out to her, his head lifted and he looked into her eyes – his bloodshot and pleading; hers, she knew, reflecting her disbelief.

'Is there nowt that can be done for you?'

'I – I think so, but research in these fields is still so very much in its infancy ... I – I will look into it, I promise. Please be patient with me, darling ... As well as me not wanting you hurt, I do know that stress can make my problem even worse.'

His eyes looked deeply into hers. The appeal she saw in his touched her heart. But she couldn't help herself from wanting to understand further. 'Have you never ... I mean, have you, well ... ever done it?'

He shook his head. 'There's never been a woman in my life. It – it's not that I didn't want ... I mean, well, look at me. No one has ever looked beyond these glasses to see the real me, until you came along ... Oh, Trish, I do love you, don't give up on me.'

These words pulled at her heart strings. It came to her that if she was patient, maybe as his confidence grew, things would happen.

Besides, she'd lived for years without having sex and never had she been as happy as she had these last two years, since Walter had asked her to be more than a friend, and they had started courting. And how she'd missed him when he went away, mostly to Manchester where he'd told her he was attending further training in his field as a urologist.

Well, now they were man and wife, promised to each other through sickness and in health. She supposed this condition that he had spoken of was some kind of sickness ... and yes, she knew she could do this for him. She had done it while she lived in the flat, for all this time, and she could carry on doing so.

'It don't matter, love. Like you say, we ain't done owt to date, and been happy. I do wish you'd have told me, though.'

'I feared losing you, Trisha. I wanted to show you happiness of a different kind, built on strong feelings and friendship, kindness, understanding, and ... and, faithfulness.'

'Aye, you've done that. I ain't ever been as happy as I have since you told me you loved me, and Sally ain't known the happiness she knaws now.'

He got up and held her close. Not in the way a lover would, but as a loving friend. Trisha liked the feeling. She'd been used by men, beaten by them, had so much expected of her by them, and treated as if she was nothing. Walter had never treated her like that and had made her happy and at peace. To her, this was a gift to rival any sexual feelings, and she would take it with both hands.

'I love you, Walter, and always will, lad.'

His lips came on hers in a gentle, undemanding love. 'My Trisha. My darling. I love you. Thank you.' He lifted her and swung her around, knocking over the chair.

'Hey! Watch what you're doing, you daft ha'peth!'

37

They fell about laughing once he'd lowered her, then went into a hug again, and Trisha knew that though she'd have her times when she really wanted to be made love to, she had so much with Walter's love, and she had another best friend in him. A loving friendship that would see she and Sally were looked after and given the best of everything, where they would know respect and kindness. Surely that counted for a lot, didn't it?

She felt at peace now as she'd managed to quieten the anticipation she'd built up since becoming Walter's girlfriend, but for how long, she didn't know.

It was while she was preparing their evening meal that the enormity of it hit her and tears flooded her cheeks. And now, her speciality, meat and potato pie, added to her distress as she suddenly felt sure that it wasn't the kind of food that Walter had been used to. She had no idea what he liked – how could that have happened? How could she have let these past two years drift by, never having eaten a meal with Walter, never knowing his likes and dislikes?

Oh, they'd had fun times, but none of them had involved them really getting to know one another, otherwise she would have known about the intimate problem he had hit her with earlier. As this knowledge dawned on her, she felt at a loss. Walter suddenly felt like a stranger.

Hearing his footsteps, she quickly wiped her face with the tea towel.

'Mmm, something smells good. Can I do anything, darling?'

Taking a deep breath, Trisha turned towards him. 'I – I don't knaw if you're going to like what I'm cooking for you. I ain't got a clue what you like and what you don't.'

He hurried over to her. 'Darling, I will love it. You are cooking our first meal on our wedding day ... Oh dear, that doesn't seem right now. I should have booked us a table somewhere, sorry ... so sorry.'

'Naw. I wanted it like this. We've had folk around us all day. I wanted it to be just us. But I just got worried that you won't like meat and potato pie.'

With this, the tears came again. She knew it wasn't all down to meat and potato pie, but a lot to do with her unfulfilled dreams. Oh, how she'd dreamed of this day – this night.

'Oh, my dear! I love meat and potato pie. We're served it all the time in the canteen and always the others will say, "Your favourite today, Walt."'

'Walt?'

'Yes, I'm known as that.'

Another thing she had no idea about, but she was in the circle of his arms and that made things better. 'Eeh, I like that. I'm going to call you that. Walter's so formal. But you're not just saying it, are you? You really do like meat and potato pie?'

'Love it, and I know yours will be much better than any I've ever tasted.'

'Oh, Walt, ta. I feel better already. And I've red cabbage to go with it an' all. We allus have red cabbage with pie.'

'Delicious, and what's for dessert ... I mean, pudding, then?'

His slip of the tongue seemed to highlight the gulf between them, but Trisha didn't dwell on it. 'Ha, I cheated there as I baked a few jam tartlets at the flat and got Martha to put them on the cold slab for me. I didn't want to be standing cooking for hours. And I bought some Nestlé condensed milk for us to pour over them. I can pop them in the warming oven when we sit down to our dinner, and we can have them hot.'

'Sounds wonderful. Oh, darling, thank you for marrying me. And thank you for being understanding. It's a condition that little is known about. There is research, but it seems to be more leaning towards it being a condition of the mind, not the body. I haven't asked colleagues' opinions about it, but I will. I'll do anything. I'll pretend I'm asking for a patient.'

Trisha hadn't thought a doctor would be embarrassed about anything, but then, these were his mates he would have to ask and that couldn't be easy for a man.

'By, me love, don't fret about it. If it ever happens, then it'll be lovely, and all of me dreams would be realised, but if it don't, I knaw I'm going to be happy just being with you . . . I love you, Walt, with all my heart.'

He took her into his arms then, and like always, it was a lovely hug. But now Trisha knew the truth, she also knew that his hugs were truly just like Martha's, given by a friend who loved her, and not how a lover would hold her. She so longed for him to hold her like that. But something told her he never would.

With a heavy heart, she turned back to the stove.

'I'll lay the table, darling. I can't cook, so I can't help with making the dinner, but I can do all the other things needed.'

As he worked, he hummed a tune. This made Trisha relax once more and begin to enjoy finishing off cooking the meal, her first for her new husband, and so far, everything was coming along perfectly.

When they sat to eat, Walter was very complimentary, telling her that her pie was far superior to the one in the canteen and he was really enjoying it. From this came some tales about his work and he soon had her laughing fit to burst as he related tales of hospital life – a patient presenting with a spot they thought was the beginning of something awful, but having it squeezed and being sent home, and how they'd given one who was forever at the hospital an enema and had never seen him since! And how one of the trainee nurses made a patient swallow a suppository, thinking it had to be taken by mouth, and they'd had to pump out his stomach to save his life!

Trisha, too, had a few tales about the goings-on in the shop, so all in all, she began to relax and really enjoy their first evening.

It was when it was time for bed that things became awkward. Which to Trisha was ironic as she imagined that any bride would have these feelings about going to bed with a man who'd never made love to her, but hers were for something she never dreamed possible – a man who couldn't make love to her.

They were sitting chatting in their new front room. The only room they'd disagreed on, with Trisha wanting reds and golds, which she thought fitting for such a grand house and Walter wanting blues and creams. Now, Trisha was glad she'd gone along with Walter's choice as the room was elegant and had a restful feel.

But the feeling was unsettled when Walter stretched his body, and mid-yawn said, 'Well, my dear, it's been a long and lovely day, and I for one need my bed.'

His bed? Does he mean he won't be in my bed? She hated this thought. What was the point of marrying just to live together as if brother and sister? At least they should share a bed, then maybe ... Hoping against hope, she told him she was tired too. 'I allus take a mug of cocoa to bed with me, love. Do you want one an' all?'

'That sounds wonderful. And I always like to read a while before I sleep, so I'll drink it in bed while I do ... I'll go up and get ready while you make it – it's no good me offering, you'd end up with something like ditch water.'

This lightened the moment, making her giggle. 'Eeh, Martha's used to be the same till I taught her how. I might have a go at teaching you one of these days.'

'Ha, well, you'll need a lot of luck and patience. I can just about boil an egg in the kitchen ... No, that's not true, I once made Carl ... I ... He and I bunked together when we were students ... Look, I know he wasn't very kind to you today. I'm sorry. I don't know what got into him. I couldn't bawl him out in front of everyone, but I will speak to him and tell him how much he embarrassed you and hurt me, by behaving like that with my new wife.'

'Ta, love, but there's no need. When folk are ignorant enough to behave like that you ain't going to change them. As long as I never have to be in his company again, I'll be happy.'

'You're a very wise lady, Trisha. Sometimes the best thing is to let these things drop to save any further antagonism.'

Trisha felt miffed that he agreed with her. She'd have rather he'd said he'd bop the stupid, spiteful Carl on the nose!

As she made the cocoa, she prayed Walter would be in their bed when she went upstairs, but he was still in the guest bathroom. Determined not to give him a choice, she placed his steaming mug of cocoa on the side table on the other side to where she would lay.

When she came out of their bathroom wearing a short cotton nightie, his cocoa had gone. Her heart dropped. But then her temper flared. How dare he treat her any other than his wife! He'd married her, hadn't he?

Storming along the landing, passing Sally's bedroom and then Walter's study opposite and coming to the guest bedroom and bathroom opposite each other, she opened the door. Walter was just about to climb into bed. He looked at her red-faced and obviously uncomfortable.

'What are you doing, Walt? You're me husband, not a guest.'

With this, she burst into tears.

Walter stood, his stance showing his indecision, his too-thin body clad in blue silk pyjamas and his sandy, curly hair unruly-looking as though he'd run his fingers through it, and she just wanted to hug him.

'I – I didn't think you'd want me next to you when . . . well, you know.'

'Well, I do. I ain't going to be lonely again. I love you, Walter. I want to be with you.'

'Of course, but you know how things are with me.'

'Aye, I do. But that don't make no difference, we can still be loving and close. Otherwise, why did we even bother to marry, just to live together as friends, or brother and sister? That ain't what I had ever dreamed of. And if it's what you want, then you should have just carried on living in them hospital quarters. You had enough friends there!'

With this, Trisha's tears increased. How could her dream of being married to Walter have crumbled and soured so quickly?

'Oh, my dear, our wedding day and I've made you cry. I'm sorry. That's not what I dreamed of happening either. I'm sorry.'

He was by her side, one arm over her shoulder in the way any friend might comfort her. To Trisha, it seemed to mark how her life was going to be. His live-in housekeeper, his cook, his friend, but never his lover.

He kissed her cheek. 'Please don't cry, Trisha, I feel such a cad. You don't deserve this . . . I . . . feel as though I'm only half a man . . . I want to be like other men, but I can't. But I love you. I truly love you so very much.'

'C–come to me bed, then. Be a husband to me, not me employer.'

'What do you mean? I never saw myself as that. Oh, darling. My Trisha. Come here.'

As he took her into a proper hug, her whole body cried out for more. She raised her lips to his, thrilled when he kissed her in the way he had done many times – gently, not passionate, but loving. She craved being loved more than anything. And she did have Walter's love, she knew that.

When they parted, he wiped the last of her tears with his thumbs. 'I'll seek help from research and colleagues. I promise. Someone might have a solution. Come on, let's go to our marital bed.'

The feelings that had taken Trisha increased as the bed took his weight, and he lay next to her. But drinking their cocoa and Walter reassuring her that everything would be all right in the future soothed her. It would happen one day, she was sure of it. And she had Walter for her husband, a lovely home, and a safe and loving environment for Sally. *I must try to make meself content with that, I must!*

They lay in each other's arms for a while, until Walter said, 'Well, darling, I'll just read a couple of pages. I just don't seem to sleep without doing so. It's as if the characters in the book take over from all the things I need to think about and help me to relax instead of mulling everything over.'

'I ain't never read a book.'

'Oh, you should try, darling. It's relaxing, educating, and like I say, transports you away from your own troubles. I love reading over any other pastime.'

'I don't knaw what to read. Though I loved it when me teacher read us a story. And, aye, it did take me to another world.'

'We'll go to the library together and you can browse and see if there's something that catches your fancy.'

This was the last conversation Trisha thought she would have on her wedding night. She felt so miserable and yet hopeful too. All the things she'd told herself she had were good things to have and she could find happiness. She just had to find a way of quieting the fire raging inside her.

Sighing, she made the excuse that it had been a long day and she was tired.

As she turned away, she said, 'I'd like that, and it'd be good for Sally an' all, we could get her reading.'

'We will, most definitely. She loves me to read a story to her now . . . Goodnight, my love.'

Saying goodnight and snuggling down on her side with her back to Walter, tears of loneliness of a kind she'd never known trickled down her face. This was a loneliness within a loving environment. One that made her feel shut out and less of a woman than she'd ever felt.

Sometimes it felt that she was always to know pain from the men in her life. Though this wasn't comparable, as it was a different kind of pain. Her mind went back to all she'd suffered at the hands of Bobby when he beat her, or what Ralph Stretton had inflicted on her, after having his way with her, and promising her everything, leaving her with child to face Bobby and the world, with the lie that she'd been raped.

Only later when Bobby returned from war, riddled with disease, did she find out he'd caught it by going with other women.

This time, she'd thought she'd found true love. A love that would be fulfilling and beautiful. And yet, on her wedding day, the day she'd longed for, she'd discovered the cruel truth.

FOUR

Martha

The second week of July was on them, and the day had dawned for their trip to Manchester. Martha dreaded the outcome, knowing that whatever they were told of why they were childless would change their lives for ever. She tried one more time to stop it happening.

'Is it that the examination will be painful, Josh?'

'Walter assured me that it wouldn't be, darling. He has consulted in-depth with his friend, John Bird, who he told me we are to call Mr Bird because of his status. Apparently, he only lets his closest friends call him John, not even his acquaintances.'

'To be sure, he sounds a horrible man – a pompous idiot. It is that he already reminds me of the English men who were for stealing our land and caused me so much pain. I'm feeling afraid just thinking of him.'

'Oh, Martha, we won't go then. I can't bear you to be afraid.'

If only Joshua knew that my fear isn't about pain. Not the physical kind anyway, but what the revelations of why we are childless may do to us.

Now she'd been taken into Josh's arms, and he was kissing her hair, it felt as though her fears were unfounded. That the premonitions that came to her were wrong. They had been in the past, as some unforeseen happenings had changed the course of what she had seen.

'It is that we must go, Josh, for as you have said many times, it could just be a simple thing that could be put right, and we can be having a babby of our own.'

'I was your babby once, Mammy. So why do you want another?'

'Bonnie! Where is it you came from? You should be with Aunty Trisha. Sure, she will be ready to go to the shop and so it is that you should be.'

'I forgot my book. I can't go a whole day without my book.'

'Come on, darling, I'll take you back.' Scooping Bonnie up, Joshua swung her onto his shoulders. 'And of course you were our baby once, and as you are such a bundle of joy, we wanted another one for all three of us to look after. Wouldn't that be wonderful?'

'It would, Da. I could change its nappy – not the stinky ones, though.'

They were all laughing and this increased when Bonnie asked, 'So, are you going to Manchester to buy another baby, then?'

'Ha, no, but maybe order one.' Joshua grinned at Martha. Then asked her, 'Will you be ready when I get back, darling? The time is getting on. We don't want to miss the train.'

That's just what she did want to do, Martha thought as they disappeared out of the door – Joshua having to almost bend double so as not to send Bonnie flying.

By the time he came back, Martha had her hat on – a small imitation of a bowler hat, in a pale blue, with a darker blue soft feather sewn to the side of it, looking as though it was held there by the ribboned bow, also in a darker blue, that adorned the brim. She placed the hat at an angle on the side of her head and quite liked the effect. Blue had featured more in her wardrobe since the bridesmaid's dress that she'd worn for Trisha had attracted so many compliments, especially from Joshua. Usually, she would choose browns, creams and greens as they were said to complement her red hair but soon after they had returned to work, she'd visited Lisa Mathews' haberdashery stall on the promenade that had always been their main source of material for their baby layettes.

The lovely blue linen had caught her eye, and she had set about making a pattern for a costume that imitated the one Lady Rebecca – the lady from London, who first set her and Trisha off in their business – once wore. Martha had never forgotten it. With its fitted jacket falling to her hips and straight skirt, it had been elegant in its simplicity. The costume had turned out perfectly, and Martha had been thrilled to find the hat that was an almost exact match.

To complement the powder blue of the costume and hat, Martha had chosen a navy blouse. She'd never been to Manchester and felt sure that all the women would be the height of fashion so was determined not to let Joshua down.

Once ready, she did a twirl, enjoying the feel of her skirt around her calves. Both she and Trisha loved the shorter fashions, feeling liberated not to have their frocks at ankle-length. They often giggled at how they would be seen as hussies if they'd had their ankles on show a few years ago, and now they exposed as much as five inches above!

'Ready, darling?'

'Yes, it is that I am.' Martha donned her navy gloves and picked up her matching handbag.

'You look lovely, not a bit like a lamb to the slaughter as you did earlier. Now . . . you are sure about this, aren't you, my darling?'

'It is that I am as sure as I'll ever be. Let's be for going, before it is that I change me mind.'

As the cab Joshua had hailed when they'd come out of London Road station drove them up to the hospital on Oxford Street, Martha thought it a beautiful and yet imposing building with its central dome and two tower-like buildings flagging the entrance.

Once inside they were introduced to Mr Bird. To Martha, he so resembled his name, with a pointed face that wouldn't have looked out of place with a beak. This thought made her giggle. Mr Bird looked at her over the top of his half-glasses as if she was mad.

'It is that I am nervous and always tend to get the giggles at such times.'

'You're Irish! Well, well, my mother was Irish too, from Cork . . . A lovely, gentle woman whom I miss greatly.'

'It is sorry I am at her passing, sir.'

'Thank you . . . Ah, such fond memories of Cork when I was a boy going to see my granny. I must return one day. Anyway, tell me in your lovely lilt what is troubling you.'

Feeling relaxed, Martha told him, 'It is that though I have had one child, not fathered by Joshua, I cannot seem to be getting pregnant again, and for sure would so dearly love to give Joshua a child.'

'Hmm, that doesn't happen often. But it may be that there is a blockage of some kind. I am researching into these things all the time ... Hmm, interesting case. How old is your other child?'

The questions went on and on, some of them making Martha blush, though she didn't find Mr Bird at all like she'd imagined him. He was a very pleasant man who cared deeply about his work and his patients, so by the time he wanted to examine her she was relaxed and happy to do as he asked of her. Though she hadn't expected to strip from the waist down and have her legs held apart by a contraption that had stirrups dangling from it to put her feet into! Even Joshua was embarrassed at the sight of this, and Martha was mortified.

And then, though she hadn't thought it could, her embarrassment deepened when Mr Bird started prodding her with all manner of instruments as well as his finger. Not that he hurt her, but the whole experience left her feeling humiliated.

'Well, everything seems to be in perfect working order to me. I can feel that everything is where it should be, and from what you say about your monthly cycle not being painful and as regular as clockwork, I would say the problem doesn't lie with you, my dear.'

Martha couldn't look at Joshua as she donned her knickers, suspender belt and stockings once more. For now, Mr Bird was saying, 'So, if the problem isn't with Mrs Green, it must be with you, Joshua. And that isn't simple to detect. I think it best that Mrs Green sits in the waiting room while we have a chat.'

'It is that I want to stay with Josh. We were for promising we would support each other.'

'It's all right, my dear, do as Mr Bird says.'

Martha could hear the fear in Joshua's voice. She wanted to hold him, to drag him out of there, to tell him that it didn't matter that they couldn't make babies and that their love was enough. But he encouraged her to go, so she left the room, praying that if their childlessness was down to him, it was something small that could be put right, and that she need never know of.

But when finally Joshua came out, his face looked like thunder. Martha had rarely seen him angry. She didn't try to soothe him but walked beside him until they left the hospital. Once outside, he spat out the word, 'Poppycock!'

'Is it for being something you want to talk about, me darling?'

'No! It's ridiculous! Whoever heard of it being the man's fault when a couple are childless? Having babies is all down to the woman, not the man. He can only do what he does and I'm a normal man with a normal functioning body! The man's mad — a mad scientist with mad theories that cannot possibly have any basis in fact!'

'Tell me, please, Josh, what did he say?'

'I – I don't think I can. He insulted me, made me feel abnormal. I can't and won't believe his theories! Nor will I take any more of his bloody tests!'

Martha felt a bit annoyed at this. Yes, she felt sorry for Joshua, but he'd led her like a lamb to the slaughter. He hadn't thought at all that it was a ridiculous notion that it was her fault they hadn't conceived a child.

Pulling herself up, she thought that it wasn't anyone's fault. How could it be? Neither of them had caused anything to be wrong with their body. At least Joshua hadn't. There may have been some justice if she'd been the one who had a problem – after all, she'd had a child out of wedlock.

'Don't even be for thinking about it, me darling. He is what you say, a mad scientist, coming up with theories out of the blue. Sure, it is that he cannot tell that I am all intact by prodding me in the way he did. It is that he would need to be able to see inside of me, and he didn't take an X-ray, so how can he be so sure it is not me who is for causing this?'

'Exactly. The man is an idiot. A waste of money. We're no further forward than we were ... Oh, I'm sorry, darling. I felt so much for you when he was examining you. I wanted to punch him on the nose!'

'It was for being one of the worst experiences in me life.'

This seemed to calm Joshua. His hand came into hers. 'I should never have put you through that. Did he hurt you, my darling?'

'No, it wasn't for hurting but I hated it. I was for wanting to scream at him ... Having said that, it was that I liked him more than I thought I was going to.'

'Ridiculous man! There was nothing to like about him. I'm furious with Walter for sending us to him.'

Martha thought it best not to say any more. Joshua was worked up by whatever Mr Bird had said or done to him, or both, and she thought to calm him by changing the subject. 'Is it that we are still to go to tea, darling? I saw a lovely tea shop on the way here.'

'Would you mind if we didn't, my dear? I just want to get home. He's made me feel dirty – I'm disgusted with his methods. I wish I'd never put us through it.'

With this, Martha wondered what on earth Mr Bird had done to Joshua. She'd never seen him like this before.

'Well, I will need to be buying something for supper then. High tea was going to be our evening meal after having such a large breakfast. Trisha is giving Bonnie her tea as I was for telling her we wouldn't be home till around seven.'

Joshua didn't answer. He seemed to have gone into his own world. Not a happy one by the look on his face.

Martha's fears came back into her. Was it to be that this day was to change their happiness and leave a scar that would never heal? *Please, Holy Mary, Mother of God, don't let it be.*

But as the weeks went by, Joshua became more and more withdrawn, till Martha felt that she was living with a stranger.

Their lovemaking wasn't anything like as wonderful and joyous as it had always been, but a quick release for Joshua, leaving her frustrated and so longing for the feelings he used to give her. Sometimes she felt them building, but then he would speed up, and bring it all to an end before it happened for her.

Unhappiness crowded Martha. And she was sure it did Trisha too. Though she never said anything was wrong, Martha could tell there was.

It seemed as though the tension between her and Joshua had spilled over into her friendship with Trisha, as throughout their days working together, they hardly ever laughed, just got on with what they had to do and only spoke about what was necessary to discuss. So, it pleased Martha that as they sat busily working on an order they had to get out, Trisha seemed more talkative.

'Eeh, I ain't much for Sally going to the posh school, you knaw. I'd have taken a stance if it wasn't for Bonnie going.'

'It is that I felt the same. I was for making Josh promise he wouldn't go ahead with putting Bonnie there unless Sally was going too. I'm not wanting her out of her depth.'

'Aye. They'll be all right together, and them Brodie sisters seem nice. Anyroad, I've bought a couple of the recommended frocks for Sally to wear to school. I just couldn't be bothered to make them. We do so much sewing, it seems like a chore now. I have made two pinafores each for them, though. I'm pleased with them an' all. I hope you like them. I've sewn pockets into them, so they don't have to hitch up their frock to get their hankies out of the pocket in their knickers. Eeh, I've never liked that. I used to hate having me hankie there when I were a kid.'

Martha laughed. 'Ta, Trish. I haven't been able to get around to doing anything, yet. It is that I will go to the shop they told us of. And it is that I'm glad you thought of the pocket, as I hadn't been liking that idea, and haven't ever had a pocket in me knickers!'

'You were lucky then, lass.'

'I think it is that I need to accept it's happening and get on with kitting Bonnie out. But it was that I saw her going to the local church school, and am finding it hard to get me head around it, so I am.'

'It's good that they'll be getting a good education, though. Lasses have more chance in life now. You never knaw what they'll turn out to be.'

'That's true, so it is. Wasn't I reading just the other day about a woman doctor!'

'Aye, there's a few of them now . . . I wish I knew one. Eeh, it would be lovely to chat over your problems with a woman doctor, wouldn't it?'

Taking her chance to find out what was wrong with Trisha, Martha asked, 'Is it that you have a problem, Trish, love? Is it for being anything that I can help you with?'

Trisha looked up from the hem she was sewing of a baby girl gown. Martha could see her bottom lip quivering.

'Oh, Trish, me darling. Tell me. It is that we aren't sharing our pain how we always used to.'

A tear plopped onto Trisha's cheek.

'Look, I'll be for closing the shop. It's quiet anyway. Then I'll put the kettle on, eh? It is that we need to chat . . . I – I am so needing to chat to you, me darling.'

'Oh, Martha, I knaw as things ain't right for you either. I – I just didn't want to bother you with me troubles, but I feel I'll burst if I don't share me worries, lass.'

Martha got up from her bench. Her back ached from treadling her sewing machine for most of the day. But they had an order that they needed to get on its way.

It had been Lady Rebecca, the lovely lady who'd visited Martha to have her fortune told when she worked in her tent, who had helped them so much to get up and running. And it was she who suggested they have a mailing service. Now it was the biggest part of their business, keeping them busy most days with fulfilling orders.

It worked by them advertising in magazines that reached from the south to the north of England. To any enquiries they sent out a brochure that Joshua produced for them. He would photograph their latest stock, and design and print the brochures, making a lovely job of them – even recently producing them in colour!

The thought of Joshua made her heart feel heavy. Sighing, Martha went to the door and dropped the catch, turning the card that declared them open or closed to the closed position after looking up and down the prom and seeing it almost empty of people.

They were only a few days off being in September, a time of year when visitors to Blackpool dwindled until Christmas time, when they enjoyed a few days of the prom bustling with life once more. Though for her and Trish, she sometimes wondered if they would have a business at all without their postal service to all over the country as the busy summer months of shoppers weren't long enough to keep them going. She sighed. How often she'd heard how different it was before the war when the illuminations lit the piers. People flocked here then, when most seaside seasons were over, to see what Trisha had told her was a spectacular display. She'd been glad to hear lately that there was a proposal to bring them back soon.

By the time she had everything closed up, the kettle was already whistling.

'Here you are, lass. I got on with it. And I checked on the girls. They're still napping upstairs, so we won't be disturbed ... Eeh, Martha, I've longed to talk to you. I so need the comfort I knaw you'll give me. And I'm here for you an' all as I knaw all isn't right with you and Joshua and ain't been since you came back from Manchester.'

Martha sighed. Her problems seemed difficult to talk about, even to Trish.

'It is that I feel you are in the most need, me darling. What is it that troubles you?'

Never did Martha dream to hear what Trisha told her. And yet, she shouldn't have been surprised – it seemed her visions were starting to come true.

'It ain't Walter's fault, but eeh, Martha, I feel like I'm a leper like them as they spoke of when I used to go to Sunday school as a kid. And I feel bad as I thought I could cope with it. Walter's so loving and kind in every other way, but ... Aw, you'll be thinking me a loose woman who just wants sex, but it's, well, it's so frustrating ... Sometimes, I feel like I'll go mad.'

'Oh, me darling, I had no idea this was happening. You seemed so happy until recently.'

'I knaw. I thought it would all come right, but it ain't, Martha, and I can't cope ... Am I a hussy, lass?'

'No, it is that you are a normal woman with normal feelings. Why is it you haven't spoken of this before?'

'I was all right with it, I was, honestly . . . but . . . Oh, why can't I still be?'

'No one would be, it's not just you, me darling. But it is that I have no answers. Sure, it is that Walter is a doctor, why is it he doesn't be for seeking help?'

'We did talk about that and I said that I loved him enough to stand by him despite this. And he says that . . . Eeh, Martha, he says that he can't understand me. That I can't have babbies, so why is it that I need that which makes them?'

'That's for being cruel. I can't believe Walter can be so callous. My poor Trish.'

They came together in a hug. Something Martha needed too. But the feel of being in Trisha's arms undid her and she sobbed.

'Martha, eeh, Martha, lass, what is it?'

Trisha listened in amazement. 'By, I can't believe how selfish men can be. Even the decent ones. They think of us as having no needs of our own, but only being bloody baby machines – there, and that's me swearing!'

'It is that you are right. Didn't we always be saying that they take what they want and then leave the woman with the consequences and walk out on us? . . . Oh, Trish, I thought all of that was behind us.'

'Me an' all. By, they were hard times, Martha, me having had a fling with someone I thought cared for me, and you falling in love with Peter and then both swines walking out on us. Well, Peter didn't, bless him, but where is he now, eh?

59

He said he'd keep in touch with you after he came back, but does he? Naw. You ain't heard nowt of him for ages.'

'Well, he isn't for being very well. Maybe it is that he is having another episode of losing his memory.'

'Then why doesn't his wife contact you? ... Eeh, what am I on about? They're blokes from the past. It's them we have now that are the problem.'

They sat down again and held each other's hands. To Martha, it seemed that their dreams had shattered and were never going to come true. How was it that they had got to this, after being shown happiness beyond all they'd dreamed of and being taken out of poverty – some of it through their own efforts, but also by meeting two lovely men who wanted to take care of them? Was that all to go wrong, never to come right again?

She squeezed Trisha's hand.

Trisha smiled a watery smile. 'At least we've still got each other, lass.'

Martha nodded. 'Always, me darling. It must never be that we become like we've been these last weeks. I am needing you, Trish. You're me best friend and I love you like me sister.'

They hugged again, but nothing lifted Martha's heavy heart and she knew it was the same for Trisha, too.

FIVE

Trisha

When Trisha and Martha stood in the corridor of Elmslie school, Trisha felt as though her heart was being ripped out as she watched Sally and Bonnie walk hand in hand into the classroom. They turned and waved. Both looked excited, though Trisha knew Sally was afraid, but Bonnie geed her along.

Martha's hand came into hers. Her sigh told of her anguish.

'I reckon we should go and leave them now, lass. I don't want to but there's naw other mothers here.'

'No, it is that most had a carriage to drop their wee ones off. How frightening that must have been for them to have to walk into the school on their own.'

They walked back to where Arthur waited for them, his horses shuffling nervously.

'This pair ain't used to the motor cars. I'm breaking them in gently as there ain't so many about this early.'

As they climbed up, Arthur surprised them by telling Trisha, 'I've bad news for you, Trisha, lass. Benny's ailing. He don't look well at all.'

'Aw, naw. Poor Benny. It ain't serious, is it?'

'He ain't said it is – well, not directly – but I think it is.'

'Eeh, but how is he managing? Who's looking after the donkeys?'

'The lad he set on a while back. Benny said as he loves them and takes care of them a treat, so don't you go worrying about them, lass. They were on the beach as usual this morning, though why the lad bothered, I don't knaw. There's naw one around.'

'And there'll be even less with schools opening. I'll have a word with him when you drop us off and check on the donkeys.'

'Benny'd like to see you an' all, Trish. I can take you up to his cottage if you like?'

'Aye, when you pick me up to fetch the girls, eh?'

'I reckon you should go afore then. Benny seems agitated about sommat and is asking for you.'

Trisha turned to Martha. 'Have we got time, lass?'

'You have, love, but it is that I need to complete those baby gowns I'm making . . . Will you be dropping me off, Arthur, and then it is that you can take Trish to see Benny?'

Arthur donned his cap.

It wasn't long before they were pulling up outside the shop. Trisha thought it looked lovely with its window dressed in lemon – the most popular colour for those expecting their babies as it was a safe bet for them.

'Can you wait a mo, Arthur, lad? I just need to pop inside.'
A sudden urge to pee had taken Trisha and she jigged about as Martha fumbled with the keys. Once she'd managed to open the door, Trish rushed towards the back door, pulled the bolts to unlock it and dashed through to the lav.

She could hear Martha laughing. She was always telling her to go before she came out.

When she went back inside, the shop bell clanged – always loud enough to waken the dead, and though she was used to it, it made Trisha jump most times.

A man walked in – not their usual customer; hardly any men ever used their shop unless they were with their wives, and then they took little notice of anything, just settled the bill once a layette was chosen.

Both she and Martha stood and stared at him for a moment. He coughed. 'I would like to speak to Martha Green, please.'

'It is that I am Martha. How is it that I can be helping you, sir?'

'I've come with a message. It's from Mrs Jenny Reynold.'

Martha stiffened. Trisha racked her brains as to who Jenny Reynold was, but then it dawned on her that it must be Peter's wife. She moved closer to Martha, sensing this wasn't going to be good news.

'Oh? Is it that there is something wrong with Peter?'

The man sighed. A tall man with dark hair, he had a very serious face.

'Yes, there is. He is back in the clinic. But it's Jenny who is the worry. I'm her brother. I'm in the Navy and . . . well, my sister isn't well . . . She's dying.'

The man seemed to crumble. Martha ran to him and took his arm but shock held Trisha still for a moment.

'It is that he is in need of a chair, Trisha.'

Bringing one over, Trisha looked at the gentleman's pale face. 'Eeh, lad, you gave me a fright.'

He sat down heavily. 'I – I'm sorry.' He looked from one to the other of them. 'You see, Jenny is my only sister – only sibling . . . and there is no other family.'

'It is sorry that I am to hear this . . . You are for saying you have a message for me?'

'I'll put the kettle on, lass. Would you like a cup, Mister . . .'

'Jack. Call me Jack. And thank you. I would love a cup of tea.'

'I'll just go and tell me cab to come back for me. I won't be a mo.'

'Trish, it is better that you close the shop for a wee while when you come back in.'

Trisha nodded at Martha. She could see the emotions assailing her dear friend. To hear that the wife of Bonnie's father was dying and that Peter was in his no man's land, as his episodes rendered him, knowing nothing and feeling nothing, had come as a shock. She smiled, trying to reassure Martha.

As she came back in and closed the door, she heard Martha say, 'Oh, it is that I don't know if I can . . . My husband will have to be consulted . . . I – I'm not for knowing if he will allow it.'

Trisha felt her stomach muscles tighten as she filled the kettle. She could sense the anguish in Martha, and her indecision over whatever it was that Jack had asked of her was worrying.

She didn't have long to wait to find out why, as taking the tea in to them, she heard Martha say, 'It is that me heart wants to take the wee mites in, but I will have to be letting you know.'

'What is it, Martha? Eeh, lass, you've gone very pale.'

'Jenny has sent Jack to ask if I'll take her and Peter's boys on and be looking after them and bringing them up! She is for saying that they are brothers to Bonnie, and she has no one else. She's not thinking that Peter will recover this time. It was hearing the news of her illness that has sent him over the edge for it is that trauma of any kind will, and hearing this news is for being trauma of the worst kind for him.'

'Eeh, lass. Two boys!' Turning to Jack, Trisha asked, 'How old are they?'

'Jack, named after me, is four and known by his second name, Johnny, to save confusion, though I call him Boxie … I know, a funny name, but he's like a Jack in the box, always fidgeting and popping up when you least expect him to.'

Jack smiled fondly. Trish felt a lump in her throat. 'Aw, bless him. Such a young age to lose your ma.'

But then she wished she could take her words back as a look of pain creased Jack's face. But he managed to carry on. 'Joseph is just six months … It was his birth that started everything. Jenny haemorrhaged and … well, it's cancer.' Again, he lowered his head.

Martha seemed to have turned to stone. Trisha's heart went out to her.

'How long … I'm sorry to ask, lad, but how long has Jenny got … ? I mean, it's just so we can sort sommat.'

65

'You will help then?'

'I don't knaw. We're both married and have our families and our husbands to consider, but if we've to get them to agree and if we can make enough time, we could maybe work sommat out.'

Trisha was thinking that she'd take the boys in. They'd be the distraction she needed – caring for them would fill some of her lonely hours.

'The doctors say only weeks. She is fretting over the boys. We have no one. Peter has no one and he isn't well enough to care for them. I am terrified they will land in an orphanage as I can't get out of my commitment to the Navy for a long time.'

'That isn't going to happen. I – I will be sure not to let it. It is like you say, that Johnny and Joseph are for being the brothers of me little Bonnie. And it is as Trish is saying, we will sort something out for them.'

Trisha put her arm around Martha. 'I'll help, lass. Aye, I knaw as we might have objections at first, but my Walter and your Joshua are decent men. I can't see either of them letting these young 'uns go into an orphanage when they can offer them a good home.'

'If it is that Josh refuses, you will have to understand, Jack, that it will be because these are the children of the man who fathered me own child. It may be that this is for being too much for him to take. But I am thinking that if Trisha will take them, Josh will be for coming around to the idea after a wee while. But whatever it is that happens, I'll be taking care of them with Trish.'

Jack nodded.

'Look, love, can you come back tomorrow, eh? Give us time to talk this over. Eeh, it's a massive thing you're asking of us.'

'I know. I understand. I'll drop in tomorrow if you like.' He got a card from his wallet. 'This is where I'm boarding for a few days in Hornby Road but I have to report back for duty soon. Anyway, I'll say good day, and . . . Well, I hope with all my heart that you will take the boys for us. I'll do everything in my power to support them. I won't leave it all to you.'

Trisha got up and let him out. In a quiet voice, she told him, 'Don't worry, lad. Sommat'll sort out, you'll see. We won't see them little lads stuck. And though we ain't said owt about your sister as the shock of what you've asked of us took the wind from our sails, I'm sorry to the heart of me to hear how ill she is. Poor lass.'

'Thank you, that means a lot.'

His voice caught in his throat as he said this. The sound made Trisha determined that she and Martha would find a way of taking the little lads in.

As she turned back to Martha, she didn't know what to say as she realised that they'd practically committed themselves to a massive undertaking that neither of them knew how they were going to do. 'Eeh, Martha, we're in a hole now, lass.'

'It is that we are . . . I keep thinking that our situations are powerfully different to a few weeks ago. Then, I wouldn't have hesitated and would have known Josh would be for taking the boys, no question, but . . .' She let out a massive sigh. 'Josh isn't Josh any more.'

'I knaw. And Walter ain't Walter. He's getting more and more difficult to live with … I feel like he wants to tell me sommat. And, well, as you knaw, he only came back from Manchester for two nights last week. I just don't understand it.'

'I thought I hadn't seen him. What is it he does in Manchester? Isn't it that he is needed in Blackpool Victoria Hospital?'

'I don't knaw.' Feeling herself close to tears, Trisha changed the subject. 'Aw, I'd better go. I'll pop over to the beach and see the lad, then I'll find Arthur. More than likely, he'll be in Macie's having a mug of tea. I'll be back as soon as I can, love … And, Martha, don't worry too much. Sommat'll sort out, lass.'

As she crossed the road, Trisha wished she could believe her own words. But more than that she wished that this huge problem hadn't landed on their doorstep, and especially that Jenny wasn't so ill.

The donkeys spotted her first and came trotting over to her. The lad Arthur had been speaking about was having a job to hold on to them.

'You must be Trisha. Benny told me about you and how the donkeys love you. Eeh, he ain't wrong. I thought I had a stampede on me hands then. I'm Dickie, by the way. I'm new at this job. I only left school at the back end of July, and I were glad to get work, I can tell you.'

Trisha smiled. There wasn't a great deal of work in Blackpool for a strapping young lad like Dickie.

'Pleased to meet you, lad. And by the look of the donkeys, you're doing a good job.'

'I've allus loved them. I live in Marton near to Benny, and I've known him, and hung around the donkeys when they're in their paddock, all me life.'

'Well, I can see they're in good hands. Look, I'm only at the shop over there during the day if you want owt. Have you got plenty of water for you and the donkeys?'

'I have. I put a yoke over Billy, and he carried two bucket-fuls down. He's a strong lad that one, and a proper lad, always got an eye for the ladies.'

Trisha laughed at this. 'Aye, how he knaws is a mystery, but I've seen him many a time shove his nose under a lady's skirt when we wore them long, and lift the hem then make that laughing sound they make.'

They both giggled at this, and Trisha thought what a lovely lad Dickie was and felt relaxed to know he had the care of the donkeys. She trusted him to do a good job.

'Well, I'm just going up to see Benny now. I'll give him a good report.'

'Ta. Though I think he knaws that I'm all right with them. He said I was the best since you, and nearly as good as you, so that says sommat.'

Trisha grinned again. But then became serious. 'Is Benny very ill, Dickie?'

'Aye. I'm right sorry, but I don't think he's long for this world.'

'Eeh, naw. Not Benny.'

'Well, he's ailed this good while. But I knaw what you mean. The bottom'll drop out of me world when owt happens to him. He's been like a da to me ... Me own da copped it at the Somme. They say he were a hero and he's going to have his name on the memorial when it's built.'

Trisha could hear the pride in Dickie's voice.

'That's grand, lad, and a fitting tribute to him. We owe a lot to them as fought in the war, and them as lived, 'cause they did good an' all and have a lot to live with.'

'I hadn't thought of that. But aye, I suppose we do. There's a bloke lives in our street, and he's never been the same since. I remember him as a lovely man, allus had time for us kids. Now, he hardly speaks, and I thought of him as having turned into a miserable old sod, but you've made me think on.'

'Aye, so you should. Don't be calling him names but try a bit of understanding. Most of them were only your age when they went. Anyroad, you won't have to face the same. They say that was the war to end all wars. Now, I've to go and fetch Arthur from Macie's as he's giving me a lift.'

'I'll go if you like. Benny gave me a halfpenny to get a few chips with for me dinner. I can get them at the same time . . . that is if you wouldn't mind watching the donkeys for me?'

'I'd be glad to, lad. And ta, you'll save me the walk but ain't it early for your dinner?'

'Naw. I'm allus hungry.'

He laughed as he went, and Trisha suspected he hadn't yet eaten today.

When he'd gone, she sat down on the wall that divided the prom from the beach. She was glad that there were few people milling around and especially that there were no kids wanting rides. Her head was bursting with everything.

But mostly how her little Sally was faring at school. Such a strange environment for her, and one that Trisha thought would be so alien to Sally, who loved to sing and dance around. She imagined her feeling restricted in the classroom.

Sighing, she let her mind go to the problem Jack had presented them with. She somehow knew that Walter would welcome her having something to occupy her every minute and wouldn't object – besides, he seemed to want to be away more than he wanted to be at home. She wasn't convinced that all of his time in Manchester was taken up with studying and felt a pang of jealousy and a hatred of his friends who were seeing him more than she was – or so it seemed.

With these thoughts she began to wonder what it would be like to look after a tiny baby, even to hold one as she'd not thought she would for many a year with how things were for herself and Martha. She smiled then as she remembered one of Martha's predictions that she would have a daughter who would have loads of kids! *Eeh, Sally, lass, I reckon we'll have our hands full of babbies then.*

Her thoughts became serious once more as she knew how difficult it was to accept that you'll never have any more children and how much harder that must be for Martha, knowing that there was nothing wrong with her.

But then some pity entered her for Josh. A lovely man who would make a wonderful da – was already to Bonnie, even though she wasn't his. It must be breaking his heart, and aye, hurting his pride to think of himself as less of a man.

71

She felt sorry now that she'd shown her anger at Josh and wondered why it was that he couldn't father kids. She'd never heard of a man being like that in her life. Though she knew a few women who wouldn't have minded their men being like it!

She grinned at this thought as Ted, the boy from Enfield Road, came to mind. Ted used to run errands between her and Martha when Bobby came home from war and was ill.

Ted came from a family of ten kids, and she'd seen his poor ma recently with her belly up again. The war had been a respite for women like her.

She remembered the pride Ted had in his ma and thought how he was a good lad, and she'd like to see him again.

A cold wet nose nudged on her leg, making her giggle, as she realised the donkeys were all surrounding her and looking at her expectantly. 'I suppose you're hungry, me darlings. I'll just see what there is in Benny's box. I'm sure Dickie will have kept it filled.'

Lifting the lid of the wooden box that Benny had constructed, she saw there was plenty of straw in there. The donkeys must have smelled it as they nudged her out of the way and vied with each other to get at it. Trisha laughed at them. She so loved them.

'I'm back, Trisha. Arthur's waiting across the road for you.'

'Ta, lad. Eeh, I envy you spending your day with the donkeys. Ta for treating them right, lad.'

With this she ruffled his sandy-coloured hair. He blushed but gave her a lovely grin.

'Right, I'll see you later. I think me little lass and Martha's will deserve a ride when they finish school. They come home at three, and they love the donkeys. You'll still be here then, won't you?'

'Aye, I reckon there'll be a bit of trade about then.'

'Well, I'll make sure that I pop over now and again each day an' all, to see as you're all right. But ta-ra for now, lad.'

Trisha was shocked when she went into Benny's cottage to find him sitting in a chair looking so ill. 'Eeh, Benny, what's to do? Have you had the doctor?'

'Aye. But I'm glad you came, love, it's grand to see you. Sit down.'

'Naw, I'm going to make you a drink and tidy up a bit for you. Your lips look parched, and you can't sit around in this mess.'

'Ta, love. I couldn't stomach a tea or owt, but I'd love a sip of water.'

When she handed him the tumbler of water, his hands shook so violently that most of the water spilled onto him. Rescuing the glass, she held it to his lips, then worried as he coughed and spluttered.

'When did the doctor last come and see you, Benny?'

Between catching his breath, he told her, 'It's been a week since. I don't like bothering him. I know I'm for curtains this time.'

'Naw, you're not going to die, Benny, love. We'll get you to the hospital. They'll take care of you.'

'Naw, lass. I don't want to die in hospital. I want to be here in me little cottage near to me donkeys. Dickie ... he brings them to the door every evening ... It ... it's good to see them. Ha, Daisy ... she came in and right up to me chair ... She ... she were saying goodbye as she didn't come to the door again. Dickie said she refused.'

A tear plopped onto Trisha's cheek. It seemed to her that the bottom was dropping out of her world, what with how things were with Walter, and poor Martha so unhappy, them little lads needing a home, and now it looked like she was losing Benny.

On an impulse she took hold of his hand. 'Eeh, Benny,' was all she could think of to say.

'It's all right, lass. I've had a good innings and a good life with me donkeys. I never married ... I never went anywhere to meet a lass ... and, well, I ain't an oil painting.'

Trisha looked into his round and pudgy face, a lovely face with lines that showed how much he'd smiled all his life.

'The kids riding me donkeys were ... a joy to me. I've had all I wanted out of life ... But there's just one thing I need to do ... Will you see as one of them solicitors comes to see me, lass?'

Wanting to ask him what would happen to the donkeys, but not wanting to upset him, Trisha nodded her head. 'Aye. Walter will knaw one. Now close your eyes a while and I'll potter around. Have you had owt to eat?'

'Naw. I'll just have a bit more of that water, eh?'

As Trisha held the tumbler to his lips once more, she saw how blue they were and this made her heart drop. Her lovely Benny really was dying. She didn't want him to. She wanted to save him but felt helpless as to how.

While she'd tidied and cleaned his room, finding dust lying in layers on every surface, a plate with an untouched meal on it and newspapers strewn around, besides shoes and his cap and coat, Trisha thought to herself that she would take care of him in future. She'd come every day and do what she could. She stood a moment looking down on him. His breathing was steadier now he was asleep, but she feared he really was near to his time.

Without thinking, she bent and kissed his forehead. He opened his eyes and smiled up at her. 'I – I love you, lass. You're a good girl . . . But eeh, I can see you ain't happy . . . Is it owt I can help with?'

'Naw, Benny. No one can help me situation. But I'm all right. I've a kind husband, naw money worries and, best of all, me little Sally.'

Benny shocked her then as he shook his head. 'Eeh, lass. You ain't lived in the outside world . . . I ain't much, but I knaw things. Men talk about different stuff to women . . . you knaw, your Walter . . . well, he can't help being like he is . . . He, well, he shouldn't have married. But that said, he's made your life better, lass, and little Sally's, so try to make yourself content with that . . . and . . . just in case . . . I – I, well, I need to see that solicitor, lass. Will you go now and find one, eh?'

Trisha couldn't understand half of what Benny had said but knew a fear over what he'd told her about Walter. What did he mean that Walter should never have married? How did he know that Walter couldn't make love, or did he?

Confused, and seeing Benny's agitation, Trisha decided to ask Arthur to take her to the hospital so that she could ask for Walter's help. But when she ran outside to him, he wanted to know how things were and if she wanted him to fetch a doctor. When she told him it was a solicitor that Benny was asking for, he looked at her with astonishment. 'A solicitor? Look, I'll pop in and have a word. Hold on a mo.'

When Arthur came back out after a few minutes, he looked different. Determined, and yet his expression held sympathy. 'Right, lass, I knaw the very bloke to go and see.' He hesitated a moment. Then he coughed in an awkward manner. 'I didn't knaw everything weren't all right with you, lass. I'm sorry ... Look. Benny intends to look after you so don't you worry about a thing, and I'll allus look out for you an' all.'

Trisha felt herself colouring from the neck upwards. How had it come about that these two men knew her situation? She just couldn't think. She hadn't said anything about Walter not making love to her, nor would she. Mystified, she didn't answer.

'Now, you go back inside and stay with Benny, and I'll fetch that solicitor for him. I've a lot of contacts, and this lad I'm thinking of owes me a favour as I helped him out a lot when he was trying to fund his way through college.'

By the time Arthur came back, Trisha had helped Benny to freshen up and made him more comfortable as she'd stripped his bed and put fresh linen on and then helped him to get up the stairs and into it. She thought that the sheets and pillowcases she'd taken off must have been on for months. Guilt entered her at this. She'd known Benny was struggling, and she had asked him many times if he needed any help. Often, she'd looked after the donkeys for him for a couple of hours and loved doing so, but she had no idea that his home life was so chaotic. She'd been wrapped in her own world. Well, that would change, and she'd make sure she came every day to care for him.

How she was going to do everything, she had no idea, but she would cope somehow. She had to.

SIX

Martha

When Trisha came back to the shop Martha could see her distress. Listening to her as she related all that had happened, Martha knew her fear for Trisha to deepen.

'It is sad that I am that you found dear Benny in such a state ... But how is it you will manage? I have been worrying all day about you and about Peter's boys ... How is it we can take them on? And yet, how can we not?'

'I knaw. Everything's getting on top of us. But Benny's been a good friend and he needs me. I have to help him, Martha.'

Martha sighed. Sometimes she felt like suggesting they sell the shop. They were both financially secure, but always she held back, knowing, and yet not fully knowing, that sometime in the future, they may need the security it gave to them both.

An idea she'd mulled over came to her, and now she felt the time was right to suggest it.

'It is that I am thinking that we should be taking on some staff to help us.'

Far from Trisha objecting, she surprised her by saying, 'Aye, I've thought that for a long time. We could teach them the skills needed, though many might already have them. Most women can knit and crochet and a lot can sew.'

'I am for thinking the same. But even if it is we just get the simple tasks done – the hems and the stitching together of the knitted garments – it would be for freeing up a lot of our time.'

'Aye, and maybe someone to serve in the shop and run the errands? Going to the post office takes many trips a week for one or the other of us. We never did replace Cilla once her fortune telling business took off.'

'Oh, it is glad I am that you are of the same mind.'

'I am. And you knaw, I've been thinking about Ted. We ain't seen him for a while, but if he came after school, he'd have time to take any post we have before the post office closed. It would give him the means of earning some money an' all.'

'Oh, that's for being a really good idea. Such a lovely wee lad and one it is that we know we can trust.'

Now they were talking about employing help, Trisha was surprising her with her ideas as she said, 'Aye, he is, and you knaw, I don't see why them as'll be helping with the garments need to come and work here. They could work in their own homes, then that would give them women with young 'uns a chance of earning a bit.'

'Yes, I would love to help those women, so I would, Trish. Ooh, it is that I'm feeling relieved already.'

With this, Martha did what she'd wanted to do from the moment Trish returned: she opened her arms to her.

As they came out of the hug, it seemed they had a solution for one problem – freeing up more of their time – but still there was the huge one of tackling their men and getting them to agree to letting them take the boys in.

It was Trisha who once more came up with an idea of how to do this.

'I reckon we should all be together when we tell our menfolk. It'll be harder for them to say no, then.'

'That's for being another good idea. You're full of them today. Is it that Walter will be home tonight?'

'Aye. He promised me he'd be back as he's working at the Vic today. And he wants to be there for Sally to see how she got on.'

'The Vic' was a fond term that most Blackpool folk used for their pride and joy – the Victoria Hospital.

'I am excited to see them both meself, and it is glad that I am that that Josh's mammy is for picking them up at this very moment.'

'Aye, and it ain't right that we ain't there to greet them as they come out. But I'm glad that she's bringing them here first, so we can see them. I'm thinking of taking them over to the donkeys for a treat.'

'They will be loving that. Sheila can be watching the shop and we can keep an eye on it from the prom.'

'You know, I reckon the first member of staff we get must be a shop assistant; someone we can leave to lock up.'

They agreed on this and as Trisha tidied up, Martha wrote

out a note to put into the window. It simply said, *Shop assistant required, must have needlework skills*.

When she'd done this, she helped Trisha refold all the baby blankets that sat on a shelf near to the window, but back a little to stop them from fading. 'Is it that you and Walter could be having supper with us?'

Without having to think about it, Trisha said they would.

Martha felt the pity of this as from how Walter was always away and what Trisha had told her, it seemed that Walter welcomed anything that meant they weren't often left alone together. Her heart broke for her dear Trisha, and she could see that tears had welled in her eyes. Her own were pricking and threatening to spill over as she thought, *How could it have all gone so wrong for us all? How is it I now feel wary of asking me lovely Josh something?*

The bell clanging brought her out of these thoughts.

A joy-filled squeal met her. 'Mammy, Mammy, oh, Mammy, it was wonderful! I loved it and didn't want to come home!'

'Ha! Now, that's for being a two-headed statement, for it is that I am pleased you loved school, but I am sorry you didn't want to come home.'

Bonnie threw herself at her. 'I did miss you, Mammy. So much. Especially when we had lunch. I felt me head flopping and wanted to be on your knee.'

Martha gathered her into her arms, conscious that a divide in their status was already showing. What the posh folk called lunch was dinner to them and their dinner was tea to them! But she didn't comment, just relished having her Bonnie snuggled into her.

Sally was quiet as she snuggled into Trisha. This worried Martha and she wondered how the wee child had fared with her Lancashire accent, when she imagined that most of the other pupils probably spoke posh. Bonnie adapted to any situation easily, she wouldn't have had problems. She often came out with Lancashire sayings but could just as soon string a whole sentence together that would give the impression that she'd always been privileged.

Sheila, Josh's mammy, broke into these thoughts.

'By, the teacher said they'd both been model pupils and it were a pleasure for her to meet them.' Then, as if she thought it important, she voiced Martha's thoughts. 'She loved Sally's accent, being a Blackpudlian herself. But eeh, lass, she asked me if I'd ask if you'd mind very much if they taught her to speak the King's English. A bit cheeky, I thought, and sommat she should have taken up privately with you. I had the same when Joshua went to school, mind. I've never regretted giving me permission as he can fit in anywhere.'

This shocked Martha. She couldn't ever imagine her Josh speaking like Trisha, but then, his mammy did, and his pappy slipped out the odd word, so she should have been wondering the opposite really.

Sheila was a real mixture of a strong Northern spirit in a frail body. To hear her you'd think she'd take on the world, and Martha was sure she'd try, but she ailed badly at times with arthritis. Always, though, she was cheerful and would stand the corner of justice.

'Aw, you'll cope, won't you, me little lass?' Trisha ruffled Sally's hair. 'Anyroad, be nice to speak properly with you going to such a nice school. You've got prospects, me Sally. So, you're to try to talk more like Walter, eh?'

'Ain't Walter going to be me da any more?'

''Course he is, love.'

'Well, das are allus at home, Walter ain't.'

Seeing Trisha looking at a loss as to what to say, Martha jumped in. 'Ah, but it is that das like Walter, who have a special job, must be looking after sick people everywhere, so they do. Ain't that for being grand to have a da like that?'

Sally smiled. 'Aye, me da is special.'

The relieved look on Trisha's face with Sally reverting to calling Walter her 'da' settled Martha, until Bonnie ran to Sally and put her arm around her. 'I wish you had a real da, like me, Sally.'

Martha felt her heart drop. Why had they lied to Bonnie, but worse than that, how were they going to tell her now? And with her half-brothers coming to stay, will they know? Will they tell Bonnie?

Sally telling Bonnie not to worry stopped these panicky thoughts. 'Me proper da were a hero, anyroad, and he lives in heaven, so Ma said I'm lucky . . . though, I wish I'd have known him. So, you're lucky really, Bonnie.'

Both Martha and Trisha were at a loss. Sheila stepped in. 'You're both lucky to have such wonderful men to look after you and you should allus be grateful for that, no matter what. Now, shall we get you home?'

'We're wanting to take them for a ride on the donkeys first, so we are. Is that for being all right with you, Sheila?'

'Eeh, and leave me with the shop?'

'Sure, it is that you will be fine. We can see the shop and will come back the moment we see anyone come in.'

'Aye, all right then.'

They made a happy, giggly party as they ran across the road. Both children loved the donkeys and relished any time that they could have a ride and were soon in the saddle and trotting off.

'Ha, look at them! Isn't that a sight to please your heart?'

'Aye, it is, love . . . Don't let them trot too fast, Dickie.'

'Eeh, you're asking sommat of me there, Trisha. They're off already and with me only just lifting the last of them on.'

'Ha, Trisha! Is that you fussing like a mother hen, now? Sure, they can both handle the donkeys as if it were they were born on their backs.'

They giggled at this as they watched Bonnie and Sally trotting into the distance. The other donkeys, except Daisy, had followed.

'By, you get lazier, Daisy, but then you're entitled at your age, old girl.'

Daisy nuzzled Trisha, and Martha thought how natural they were together, and how much Trisha loved the donkeys.

It was then that the thought came to her that maybe Trisha was in the wrong job and that it had been her who'd always been the driving force behind the shop, not Trisha. A feeling took her that her own ambition had taken Trisha's real calling from her. With this thought, guilt washed over her.

'Are you remembering that you once said that you'd end up buying the donkeys, Trish? Why don't you broach the subject with Benny? Sure, it is that Walter could be affording them for you.'

'Huh! Where did that come from, you daft ha'peth? Benny'd never part with the donkeys. Not while he has breath in his body he won't.'

'But what about after he goes to his rest?'

'Aw, I ain't wanting to think about that, Martha. Now, stop worrying. Aye, I love the donkeys and working with them were me dream job, but me and Sally would have starved but for the shop. And I love that an' all, so there ain't need to make changes.'

The few moments they'd spent with the children had been a blissful respite from their cares, Martha thought, as an hour later she went into the back hall to lock the door and collect her and Trisha's handbags. But now, all her troubles were flooding back into her. She allowed the tears to flow for a moment as she prayed, *Jesus, Mary and Joseph, make everything right for us. Help me lovely Josh to come to terms with him not being able to father a child and make it that he loves me again.*

With the prayer came the pain of the knowledge that Josh had fallen out of love with her. That in finding out he wasn't the man he thought himself, he was for thinking he wasn't worthy. For just this week he'd been to see his own doctor who'd told him that not having children was always something he might have to face as he'd had a very bad bout of mumps as a child, and it is that this can cause infertility.

So now, he was angry with his parents too, for not telling him that they had been told this at the time. *But how is it*

*that I can be helping him come to terms with it all? And now, I
could make things worse for asking to take in Peter's children.*

Sighing, she brushed away the tears.

Thinking of Josh's parents gave Martha a warm feeling.
She loved them both, and they added so much to her life
and to Bonnie's. Poor Trisha hadn't even got that comfort
as her parents-in-law seemed indifferent to their own child,
let alone Trisha. Though, strangely, they wanted to be in
Sally's life and had asked if they could come down to stay
so as to get to know her.

This had made Trisha nervous, and glad that the right
time hadn't presented itself.

Once home, tiredness crept over Martha and, to make it
worse, Sally and Bonnie were playing up. She guessed they
were tired and probably hungry too.

Even Sheila, who had the patience of Job, snapped a
little. 'For crying out loud, finish the milk I poured for you
both, or it will waste and we ain't made of cows, you knaw.'

With this, they all burst out laughing. Sheila was so funny
with her sayings. But the tension broke, and Martha relaxed
a little. Though would she ever relax completely? It didn't
feel like she would. There were so many questions left
unanswered, and so many secrets, and untruths, that sometimes she thought she'd go mad.

After Trisha left, taking Sally and Bonnie with her to
play together for an hour, and saying she would give them
tea and bring Bonnie back at six thirty, Martha found that
she had Sheila to herself for the first time since the awful
revelation that had all but wrecked her marriage.

'Is it that I can talk to you, Sheila?'

'Eeh, lass, of course you can. But if it's about me and Joshua's da not saying owt about Josh having mumps as a lad, I can only say it was a decision we took, just as you've taken a decision, Martha, about not telling Bonnie about her real da.'

This stumped Martha. It was that she knew the pain of trying to tell a child something that would hurt them. Not that being told there was a possibility you couldn't father children would have been devastating to a boy, but it must have been to Sheila and George.

She'd found it difficult at first to call Mr Green, Joshua's father, George, as until she'd married Josh, she'd only ever known him to be her estate agent in charge of the shop's lease and now he was her father-in-law – and such a lovely one, helping them all he could and welcoming her and Bonnie into his family.

'It is that I was going to mention that, but you are right, I am for knowing how difficult these decisions are.'

'Me and George were allus of the mind that you should have told Bonnie about her real father from the beginning. She's a clever child. She'd have handled it, but now. Eeh, I reckon you've made a rod for your own back, lass, just like we did ... But that's not all that's troubling you, is it?'

'No ... Oh, Sheila, everything is for changing. We were so happy.'

'I knaw, lass. And now I wish we'd have been straight with Josh, so he grew up knowing, but it were only told to us as a possibility, not a definite ... Still, it wouldn't have come as a shock, and he wouldn't have been so adamant that not having children together was down to sommat wrong with your ability to have more ... For that, I'm so very sorry, lass ... Come here and let me give you a hug.'

She went willingly into Sheila's arms. It didn't happen often that they hugged as it caused Sheila pain, but though it was a gentle hug and felt lovely and loving, it didn't alleviate her worries.

'Look, love, has Josh told you his plans yet? I mean, well, it ain't my place to, but you ain't said owt about what he's up to.'

'Plans? To be sure, I am not for being aware of any plans. Oh, unless it is that you mean how he intends to expand his business?'

'Oh, he has told you. That's good. I've been worrying me socks off that there was no communication between you ... Eeh, lass, it will work out. This move might be the making of you. I'm glad you're for it.'

Although a little mystified as to how any plans to expand Joshua's business could be the making of them, other than to secure their financial positions, Martha couldn't think. But then it hit her. The feeling she'd had lately that Josh was going somewhere – this is what Sheila was trying to tell her. Always she was blind to what was going to happen in her life, or ignored her guiding spirit trying to get through to her about her own fate ... But she couldn't bear it if this revelation was true. 'Jesus, Mary and Joseph, is it that you are telling me that Josh is planning to work away?'

'Eeh, you didn't knaw! Aw, lass, I'm sorry. Look, me and George will be here to support you while you're on your own. You'll manage. Only this is a chance of a lifetime for Josh.'

Martha thought she was going mad. How was it that it had come to this? Josh planning things, discussing them with his mammy and pappy, but not saying a word to her. Seemingly not even thinking how such a thing would affect her! She wanted to scream and throw things; her anger and hurt cut so deep.

All of this must have shown on her face as Sheila looked afraid. 'Eeh, lass, don't tell him that I told you ... Though I did intend to, I had an inkling you didn't knaw. But with how it's affected you, Josh was maybe waiting for the right moment ... Try to look on it as a good thing, Martha, lass. Sommat that might bring you back the happiness you had. Often a break from being together all the time can do that.'

Martha took a deep breath. How was she to cope with everything?

SEVEN

Martha

Closing the door on Sheila, Martha leaned against it. It almost felt as if she'd thrown her lovely mammy-in-law out of the house, though they had hugged again before she'd left, and Sheila had said that she understood as she'd told her, 'It is a wee time alone that I am needing. And soon it is that Josh will be for coming home and Trisha and Walter will be here for tea.'

Sheila had stood her ground for a moment and told her then that she'd already put the lamb in the oven for her, and that she'd be willing to stay and help all she could.

Martha had felt the desperation in these words but couldn't change her mind. She'd shook her head. 'It is that I'm sorry, Sheila, but ta for starting me tea.'

Now she could only focus on the hug as that told her all would be all right as she sat down at the kitchen table and tried to make sense of what she'd been told. How could this be? How could Josh have been planning and putting into action working away?

She didn't have to ask what he was going to be doing. He'd held an ambition for ever to work on one of the national newspapers as a photographer. Had he found a position? Would he really go to live and work in London and leave her to fend for herself, only coming home now and then? Her head shook with disbelief, and yet, she knew it was a truth. The thought of the loneliness ahead, the not being with her Josh, him not holding her, sent a wave of misery through her. Why did this have to happen to them? Why?

Busying herself helped. Something she loved to do was to cook, and Josh always loved anything she made for him. She'd planned a roast lamb dinner and had cut rosemary from the garden this morning and left the lamb joint marinating on the cold shelf with the fresh, delicious-smelling herb scattered over it, and a note to ask Sheila to pop it in the range oven for her. All she had to do now was to peel some potatoes and prepare veg, and roast these around the joint. The meal would be ready for seven. The children would have had their tea.

An anguished feeling clutched at her. This had been Bonnie's first day at school, and she hadn't asked her anything about it, not even what they had had to eat at dinnertime! Her worries had been such that she'd let her child go without even thinking about the wee one's day. Tears that were full of pain tumbled down her cheeks.

Through misted eyes she looked around her. Everything felt alien to her, even the kitchen she loved, and had made hers, since she first arrived. Adding personal touches to the furniture she and Josh had chosen – displaying the beautiful china tea set that Sheila and George had bought them on the painted white dresser and regularly adding fresh fowers to sit in the middle of the huge pine table. The rugs she'd lain on the polished, red-tiled floor and the fresh curtains in red gingham around the sink and at the windows.

Now, it was as if all the love it had held and all the happiness, joy and laughter was crumbling around her feet.

She didn't hear the back door open and was shocked when Josh said, 'Martha? Martha, darling? What is it?'

Never had her temper boiled like it did at that moment. She stood, her stance defiant. 'It is you – you and your constant punishing of me for something I cannot control, or was not for having a hand in. You, and your spoiling of the beautiful marriage we had. You, and your having secrets, plotting, planning to leave me, it is for being more than I can take. My love for you is turning to hate!'

He stood there, his mouth open, shock trembling through his body. 'Martha ... darling ... I – I didn't realise!'

'Is it that you care so little for me that you are not seeing me any more? That you are not detecting me frustrations? Are you for being so callous that you can satisfy yourself on me, and leave me unloved, unfulfilled and alone?'

He stepped forward.

'Don't! Don't be for touching me! I cannot be bearing your deceit.'

'Please, Martha. Please let me speak. I love you, my darling ... I'm sorry. I didn't know. I've been in such a bad way in my mind ...Yes, I have been seeking to further my dream of becoming a photographer, but I haven't finalised anything. I was just doing it as a distraction. I wouldn't have taken that step without you, my darling. I – I just couldn't talk it over with you. I wasn't able to withstand your hurt when it was just an idea, but even if I do take the position, I'll only have to stay away a couple of days a week.'

'So, it is that you have applied, and you are for getting the job – that doesn't sound like someone just making enquiries to distract you from something that none of us can alter . . . Why is it that the first time you are feeling pain you are for shutting me out, making me life hell, and ruining everything we built up together?'

Josh sat down. 'I – I don't know . . . I didn't mean . . . and what you said about . . . us in bed . . . Oh, Martha, I don't know why, or what drove me . . . Help me, Martha, help me.'

His plea shocked her. Was he really suffering? Had she not seen this in the man she loved? Had she taken all the hurt onto herself and been oblivious to all he was going through? She bent her head. Wasn't it said that women could talk of their pain, but for a man to, it showed weakness?

Suddenly, Martha realised that she was as much to blame. That she had failed him as much as he had failed her.

Standing, she went and stood in front of him. 'Oh, Josh, me darling, what is it that is happening to us? I'm sorry to the heart of me. I didn't think of how you were suffering. I thought it was that you were blaming me.'

'The guilt isn't all yours, or all mine, darling. I should have said how I was feeling, but like I said, I couldn't deal with it. I felt less of a man. A nothing. I'd been so sure it was you who had the problem, I'd badgered you into going through that awful examination, humiliated you, and hadn't stopped to think that our childlessness was anything to do with me ... I'm so angry at Mum and Dad. Why didn't they tell me?'

'I was for being angry, but Sheila threw it back at me, as she pointed out that I too am holding painful things back from me own wee child.'

'Hmm, put like that I understand a little better ... May I hold you, my darling?'

'Oh, Josh, my Josh.'

They clung together, and Martha thought that some of the pieces of her world were coming back together, but still she had a bombshell to drop. How would Josh take the news that she wanted to care for Peter's boys?

This worry faded, too, as they healed a little, spoke words of love and so wanted to make that love a physical thing, but made themselves content with making that a promise to come true later.

Coming out of his arms broke the spell a little and Martha sought to distract them further. 'It is that I must hurry to change, we are for having Walter and Trish around for tea. We need to find out how it is that Bonnie and Sally got on at school and then once they are in bed, we can be discussing everything while we eat.'

'Hmm, that all sound ominous. Are you plotting something, darling?'

'Not plotting. It is just a couple of things that were for taking us by surprise. The rearranging of our working day, for one.'

'Well, I'm all for that. You go up first as I daren't come with you. I'll ravish you on the bed despite who might walk through the door.'

Martha laughed at this, when she'd thought she wouldn't laugh again. Josh joined her, and she thought it was such a wonderful sound that it seemed all her cares were lifted or weren't going to be a problem at all.

That changed when the children were in bed, having told them what felt like every detail of their first day at school, as then Josh turned to her and asked, 'So, what are all these changes you are talking about, darling?'

Jumping and not ready to tell him, Martha rose. 'It is that I must serve supper out now, or it will be for burning. Once it is we are seated, we will be telling you both.'

Josh looked mystified. Not wanting him upset, Martha turned when she reached the doorway to reassure him further, but then gasped. It was that Josh looked beautiful to her as the last of the evening sun beamed through the window onto him. A premonition shuddered through her. Their lovely front room in pale greens, rose and creams suddenly looked like a prison, for she'd seen an empty space where Josh sat, and herself weeping and wailing.

'Martha? Martha, darling, what is it?'

Shaking the sight away from her, Martha laughed. 'Ha, I was for seeing the little people dancing on the rug and wondered how it was they were coming from Ireland.'

Josh laughed with her, but she knew he hadn't believed her. But the tension broke and Walter, who'd sat stiffly watching her, relaxed back in his chair.

When she and Trisha were out in the hall, Trisha asked, 'What did you see, lass?'

'It wasn't for being anything specific, and nothing that is to do with your life, me darling. Visions can give confusing messages, so they can. Josh was for promising me he wasn't going to leave me, I am just being silly.'

'Leave you? What? He hadn't thought of doing that, had he?'

'I'll be telling you all about it as you are laying the table for me, love.'

Trisha was shocked at Martha's latest turn of events. 'Eeh, Martha, I'm scared of that happening to me. I mean, Walter has been loving and kind as always, but he said he had to go away again for a few days next week. I just don't understand why, or how it is that he don't have to be at work in the Vic!'

'Well, it is that you must confront him. I was for doing that and everything came right – though how it will be when we tell them what we are planning . . . I'm not looking forward to that.'

'Well, I don't see a problem for me in that. I think Walter would be glad if I took the boys.'

'I know, but it is that they are half-brothers to Bonnie and should be living here. Though I will be needing all the help you are able to give me, so for sure, it will be a joint undertaking.'

They had no time to say more as they heard the menfolk coming towards them. Martha looked heavenward. *Jesus, Mary and Joseph, if it is you never be for helping me again, help me now. Make it possible that I can be for taking care of Peter's boys and be keeping me Josh happy too.*

When the door opened and comments were made about the delicious aromas, Martha's tummy flipped over. She looked towards Trisha, who, for all her bravado, looked like a scared rabbit, frozen to the spot. Martha's heart went out to her. It was that she was hanging on to a slim thread of the love that Walter had for her. How Martha wished she could magic that to being a thick cord of strength.

But it was her who needed that, as all she and Josh had built earlier splintered when she told them, and Josh stood up and glared at her.

'Well! You don't do things by halves, Martha! How can you expect me to accept this?' His eyes filled with tears. 'I – I understand the situation . . . I mean, these are just children who need a home and we have been asked to take them in, but they represent so much more to me.'

Martha's feeling of concern for Trisha changed to crest-fallen heartbreak as she now faced a broken Josh, and an embarrassed silence clothed them all.

After a moment, she found her voice. 'It is that I am for knowing that, me darling. But we are being put in a position. These little boys are half-brothers of Bonnie. Sure, I cannot deny them a home and I was for thinking that you wouldn't either.'

Josh didn't answer. He just turned to Trisha and Walter, apologised and walked out of the kitchen.

As Martha went to follow him, Walter caught hold of her arm. 'Sit a moment, Martha.'

As all the fight in her left her, Martha did as Walter bid.

'I must counsel you to be patient, Martha. I have seen the kind of mental stress that Josh is under . . . I know it doesn't seem reasonable, and it isn't, least of all to him. But he took it hard when he learned he could not father a child of his own. It sent him off track for a while. You have suffered too, I know. That is the problem with illnesses of the mind. They consume the person and affect everyone involved with them. And it isn't anything a patient can get better from on their own. Josh needs help. What you are presenting him with, and forgive me for speaking bluntly, is to take in the children of the man who has proved that he can father children and has done so with you, his, Josh's, own wife! It is a horrendous thing to ask of him at this moment. Before he had the shock of his own infertility as a man to deal with, he wouldn't have thought twice, but now, those boys represent all the pain he is going through, and you, the woman he loves, wants to inflict that pain onto him.'

Martha couldn't find the words to answer, nor could she take in all Walter had said.

Trisha came to her side, her own heartache forgotten.

Martha felt Trisha's arm around her shoulders, needing the comfort, as it seemed to her that Walter had more to say.

'If I was you, I would forget for now that these boys are related to Bonnie and treat them as any little boys who need a home. Let Trisha have them and you help to care for them ... It's the best solution. Trisha will have company and something to keep her busy while I am away, and Josh can get used to them at his own pace.'

Trisha's arm dropped from Martha's side. 'You're going away an' all? You mean, for longer than you do now?'

The fear in Trisha's voice was tangible. To Martha, it shuddered alive the fears she'd always had for Trisha, and she knew the crumbling of her dear friend was beginning and she could do nothing about it. Now, her heart was truly broken.

EIGHT

Trisha

It was as if the world had come to an end. Trisha stared at Walter. Had she heard right? But there had been no mistaking Walter's words.

'Darling, I will only be away weekdays. I – I've tried to break you into the idea slowly while I was on a three day a week trial, but now, with this proposal of you caring for these potential orphans, as they will be if their father never recovers, you will have so much to occupy you that I felt that at last I could tell you.'

'Eeh, but to have already left the Vic!' This had astounded her. 'And without a word, and you in a post in a Manchester hospital that'll be a full-time consultancy Monday to Friday – I can't take it in. I can't.'

Almost light-heartedly, Walter replied, 'I'm sorry, darling. It just seemed like the ideal time to tell you.'

Questions tumbled through her mind, but all that came out was, 'Where will you live? Eeh, Walt, you ain't going back into hospital digs, are you?'

Still, he remained calm, but his answer gave her hope. 'No, darling. I have found a flat to live in.'

'So, I can come and stay with you, then?'

Walter coughed and shifted uncomfortably. For one dreaded moment, Trisha thought he had a mistress! The idea shocked her to the core. Could it be that he couldn't make love to her but that he could to someone else? It seemed to be the only explanation as it was obvious that he didn't want her to go to Manchester to stay with him.

'I don't think that a good idea. You will have the boys and Sally to consider, darling. And your business. Rearranging all of that will be a lot for you.'

His tone, that she'd thought kindly, suddenly felt patronising. Trisha had the overwhelming urge to spit in his face. To her, he was using the boys to salve his conscience in leaving her alone.

'Trisha, please don't look at me like that. This position I have taken is a massive step up in my career, I need your support to help me. Please, Trisha, darling.'

'Eeh, it's all worked out for you ain't it? Well, go! And don't bother to come home at weekends. I've managed without you most of the time anyroad . . . By, we ain't been married six months and it's come to this . . . You married me under false pretences, Walter. False pretences!'

She knew her voice was rising. Knew that at any moment she was going to scream and scream out her frustration, but Martha stood and took her into her arms and held her.

As she trembled, unable to take in all she'd heard tonight, a sob came into the silence. Her Walter was crying!

Trisha's heart melted. She untangled herself from Martha and went to Walter's side. 'Aw, Walt, Walt, I don't knaw what came over me.'

He stood. She went into his arms and thrilled at how tightly he held her, his words full of apologies. His love for her pouring from him. Each word putting the pieces of her heart together again and making her strong.

'I'm sorry an' all, lad. Sorry to the heart of me ... Eeh, we'll find a way to jog along. We've got a deep love between us and that must count for sommat.'

Walter squeezed her and then let her go and turned to Martha. 'I apologise, Martha. How I have behaved in telling Trisha and upsetting her like I have whilst a guest of yours is unforgivable ... You see, we all have our crosses to bear. Not all people are the same, not in make-up or in how they have been nurtured. You and Trish have come up the hard way. You've taken knock after knock, till you have the strength to weather anything. Me and Josh? Well, we've been cushioned all our lives, and now the knocks of life are coming to us, we don't have the tools to deal with them ... We can only do our best. And hope the love of the women we married will help us to get through everything.'

Martha came around the table to him and opened her arms. 'I am for understanding, Walter, and ta for helping me, as now I am knowing my Josh far better for your words and it is that I won't hurt him further. Nor will I try to clip his wings. I am knowing he wants to progress in his field, I won't be for holding him back. And if you, Trish, can be finding that you can take the boys, we'll care for them together, without us causing more pain to me Josh.'

Trisha couldn't believe this speech, or quite grasp what was going on. She only knew that folk she loved were changing in front of her eyes, and yes, that she too had been made different in some way. For now, she understood Walter, and loved him all the more. She was ready to support him in the path he'd chosen for his career just as Martha had said that she was for Josh.

'Aye, I'll take the boys in and gladly. And we'll take care of them as if they are our own. Won't we, Walt?'

Walter nodded and managed a smile. 'With Martha's help we will. Between us they will get all the love in the world and a good home. Josh will come round when he has healed, you'll see ... Now, my love, I think you and I had better leave Martha to it.'

With this, he hugged Martha again. 'Ask me anything, Martha, I know I won't be here as often as I should be, but I will be at the end of a telephone – once I get one installed, that is. And Josh will heal, I promise you.'

Trisha took this moment to run upstairs to check on Sally. Finding her fast asleep, she decided not to wake her, but to be here first thing in the morning and to carry her home then. At least, she thought, as she looked on her sleeping angel, she was happy at that posh school. She had Bonnie to look after her, and in her little world everything was fine. *Eeh, I shouldn't be asking for more than that. And if I can give the same to Johnny and Joseph, then that ain't a bad thing to achieve, is it?*

As they were about to leave, Trisha felt a tug on her arm. Martha took hold of her, and they clung on to one another as if their lives depended on each other until Walter gently put his arm around her and guided her out.

The chilled air hit her as Martha's door closed behind them and Trisha thought how strange life was. She'd never felt so loved in all her life, but had never felt so alone and lost either.

'I'll make the cocoa, darling. You go up, you look exhausted.'

'Eeh, I ain't drinking the ditch water you make, Walt. Ha, that would put the tin hat on a rotten evening.'

Though she was joking, Trisha wished she could take the words back. Walter sank onto one of the kitchen chairs. His look showed fear as well as remorse.

'By, lad, I didn't mean it.'

'I know, but I've hurt you badly, darling, and have since we married. I don't know how to make it up to you.'

'I ain't been hurt all the time, Walt. And you've given me a lot. I – I feel loved ... Aye, it's in a different way to the love a husband usually gives, but then I've had that and it didn't allus come in a nice package ... It's the loneliness more than anything in our marriage.'

Walter brightened. 'Well, having the boys will help with that then, won't it?'

Trisha looked at him. He hadn't a clue. He didn't seem to see that she could be lonely even when with him and especially in their bed together. For all him being a doctor and understanding others' problems, he didn't see hers.

'Aye, they will make a difference. You go up and I'll bring the cocoa.'

As they sat up in bed, Walter seemed to want to talk and talk about anything and everything other than their immediate future.

They talked over the predicament of Jack and how sad Peter's case was. 'Eeh, the war had more casualties than were counted. Life's a living hell for a lot of lads and their loved ones after the so-called victory.'

'It is . . . And it isn't just those injured in mind and body. Financially, the country suffered. I know we are coming out of the slump, but I want you to think of securing your future. It could all happen again.'

'You mean, we might have money worries coming to us?'

'Yes, I do. Everything's going at a pace now recovery is happening. People are throwing caution to the wind. It's important that you and Martha go steadily with your plans for the shop. I mean, don't put all of your eggs in one basket, and don't overstretch yourselves. Always have a good reserve.'

Trisha felt at a loss as to what he was talking about but didn't want to say so. She often felt inadequate in matters that he knew so much about.

'Anyway, Josh is a businessman and will always advise you . . . but, I wonder if he is preparing. I mean, wanting to get another job – a paying job, whilst he still has his business to run. Maybe he's thinking that if the bubble does burst again, he won't be reliant on his business, so won't be so hurt financially, if it crashes.'

Trisha still felt out of her depth, but asked, 'We'll be all right, won't we? You're in a job that ain't going to lay folk off.'

'Yes, dear ... but, well, if anything happened ... I mean, we have to be ready for any event as none of us know what is around the corner. Then, it is better that you have a stable income. I'm just cautioning you to go steady with all these changes you are talking of.'

'Aye, we have plans, but we ain't going to do them all at once. We just need to free up some of our time. The girls need us more now they are at school. We can't just give them sommat to amuse them in the corner of the shop or workroom while we stitch away, or see to customers. I knaw they're from under our feet more, but there's stuff to do to get them ready for school every day, and they're to be picked up an' all, and that happens in the middle of our afternoon opening hours. Then we'll have the boys to consider. They ain't been used to sitting and being good while their ma gets on with sommat. And they're only little.'

'Having them couldn't have come at a better time, as they will help you not to be lonely, and yet couldn't come at a worse time, as I won't be around to take some of the load off your shoulders.'

'Naw. And I ain't got over that shock yet, Walt. You've got to learn to include me in your decisions – talk stuff over with me and see how I feel about it. I should matter in these things. When I don't, that contributes to me loneliness. I begin to wonder just what I am in your life. Even a friend would expect you to discuss things with them, let alone a wife!'

'I'm sorry, darling. I thought you had enough worries. And I was torn as I knew what I wanted to do was a huge step – both for me and my career advancement, but more so for you. I think I buried my head in the sand.'

'Promise me you won't do that again, eh? And while we're on, don't forget me all week, will you?'

'Of course not, darling, I will miss you. I'll speak to you every day on the telephone, I promise. You can give me all the news on Sally. And I can chat to her about her day before she goes to bed. And I want to hear all about the shop and, when we get them, the boys and their progress. The week will fly by, you'll see.'

He put down his mug on his side table and turned towards her. His warm body was close to hers; his arm came around her. Trisha felt the familiar trickle of anticipation in her groin, tried to suppress it, but felt it increase as he lay his head on her breast. She wanted him so badly. To feel him inside her.

His lips brushed her shoulder, fully lighting the fire of her desire. She stiffened, her breathing quickened. But she daren't respond. Doing so knowing his problem would make her feel dirty.

But then his hand brushed over her breast. Shock zinged through her with the thrill it gave her, and yet, she couldn't detect any sign in him that he was getting aroused. The thought made her release a deep sigh as she tried to control her feelings.

But that proved impossible when his hand cupped her breast. She stretched out her arm and put her own mug down then turned towards Walter, her silky nightgown allowing her to almost slide into his body.

His kisses over her face and in her hair thrilled her as his fingers gently squeezed her nipples. Was it going to happen?

Her body screamed out for it to, making her forget caution and put her arm over him, pulling him towards her, wanting to touch him – wanting to try to get some response by using her hand. But when she'd done that once and nothing had happened for him, he'd ended in tears, so she just held him, caressing his firm and surprisingly muscly body. It felt so good, she wanted to strip off her nightie and his pyjamas and snuggle into their nakedness. But another shock came that had her almost gasping for breath as his hand gently opened her legs.

She was lost. Lost in the wonderment of being touched for the first time in so long that she couldn't remember when she had last felt this hunger, this desperation.

Then it happened. As if he'd always been doing this to a woman, Walter found the exact spot that shivered feelings though her she'd almost forgotten.

Giving herself up to the pleasure of his expert caresses, it wasn't long before her whole body was gripped in an exquisite spasm she didn't want to end, and yet could hardly bear. She cried out his name and her love for him as he held her to him.

When it was over, Walter asked, 'Was that good, darling?'

'Mmm, delicious.'

'Ha, I've never heard it described like that before!'

This seemed to be a funny thing for him to say. How could he have heard anything about having an orgasm? A new word for her, one that Walter had explained the last time he was home. He'd asked her if she was all right when they were in bed and she'd cried and told him she did miss a lot about making love, but she was all right.

108

He'd asked what she missed, and she'd tried to explain. It was then that he'd told her what it was called. He said he'd been reading up about it. Now she wondered if he'd prepared himself for tonight.

'Have you never had the feeling, Walter?'

His coughed in that certain way he had when he felt uncomfortable.

'Lots of lads have a go at themselves from when they're thirteen or so – didn't you ever do that?'

'Oh, Trisha, I don't want to talk about it tonight. I've done my best to give you what I can. I – I'm sorry it isn't more, darling.'

'Naw . . . naw, I weren't meaning that. It were lovely, and I can't believe it happened. I just suddenly felt sorry that I experienced such a feeling and you didn't. It seemed sad.'

'Don't worry about me. I loved getting you there. I should have done this a long time ago. I've been selfish, but now we have found a way to keep you happy. And me too, as watching your expression of sheer joy and pleasure was enough for me. I don't know why, but I just don't feel the need for any of it myself.'

'Oh, Walter. Surely there's sommat that can be done? Have you ever researched it?'

'Please, darling, shall we just accept it tonight? I just don't want to talk about it. And you should be wallowing in the after feelings and the relaxation it gives you. The feeling of release, not worrying about me.'

This again felt strange to Trisha. How could Walter know about all of that if he'd never experienced it? Or even worry about her and do what he did – finding out how he could help her and then doing it to her, if he'd never known that urge and how desperate you feel to have it satisfied? But she didn't ask any more as these thoughts brought the question to her mind that had visited her earlier . . . Did he have a mistress? *Oh, God, I couldn't bear it.*

Turning her head, she looked at Walter. Thought what a handsome man he was without his thick glasses. His lashes were long and the sandy colour of them matched his hair. His eyes were sort of mystical as if he was seeing everything through a beautiful haze, and his lips – his kissable lips – were plump and perfect to her. Oh, how she loved him. Leaning over and kissing his nose, she told him, 'Ta, for loving me, Walt. I love you with all me heart, you knaw.'

'I know, darling. You wouldn't put up with me if you didn't. And I love you. You're my saviour in more ways than you can ever dream of.'

'Aw. That's a lovely thing to say.'

Walter yawned, showing his beautiful white even teeth. 'Well, darling, I need to sleep now. Are you all right?'

'I am, me darling, I'm feeling all sleepy meself.' She wanted to giggle as she felt so relaxed, and had never dreamed Walter would do what he'd done for her. Somehow, the future didn't look so bleak now – on one front anyway.

'Well, I'll just slip out to the bathroom. You get off to sleep. I won't disturb you.'

She heard the tap start to run and wondered if he was scrubbing his hands. Had he hated the thought of where they'd been?

But then, for some reason the question came to her if he was just making a noise to cover himself getting his own release, something she'd tried to do once, but he'd turned away from her, leaving her feeling very down. She'd been hoping to stimulate him.

Walter was a mystery to her. One her tired brain wouldn't let her try to unravel. Nor did she want to at this moment, as still she was reeling from the sensations that he'd given her, and she wanted to hang on to the last thread of them as she went to sleep. They'd reassured her that she was a woman, a young, sexual woman, and not just a body that couldn't function how women's bodies should – to be able to bear children.

This thought made her think of poor Josh. She understood his feelings more than most, but at least she'd had two children. Her lovely Patricia who cemented herself into her heart in the few seconds she had her for and her adorable Sally. Josh would never know that joy. She could cry for him, but mostly for lovely Martha, whose life had changed since the revelation. With all her heart Trisha wished that Josh wasn't dealing with the shock he'd had in such a way as to want to run. But at least she and Martha would have each other – no one could take that from them.

With this thought Trisha felt herself drifting off. She didn't resist but allowed the sound of running water to soothe her and to send her into dreamland.

NINE

Martha

It felt to Martha that her legs were made of wood as she climbed the stairs. It was as though she was burdened with something she couldn't understand.

Yes, she'd seen traumatised men coming back from war and behaving strangely – Peter, for one, and how it affected him, sending him in to a world where he forgot everything and lost a sense of who he was to protect himself from all he'd seen and been through. But that this could happen to her Josh, over finding out he couldn't father children, Martha found unfathomable.

It wasn't men dying around you, or seeing their limbs being blown off. It was just a result of a childhood illness that had left him a little different to other men. Why couldn't he deal with that? Trisha had dealt with what had happened to her to prevent her ever carrying another child. Were men so totally different to women? Or was it like Walter said, that he and Josh had been protected from bad things happening all their lives?

Whatever it was, she had to face it – her lovely, strong Josh was suffering mentally and she had to be his strength.

Josh was lying face down on the bed, his head turned towards the door, staring at it as if he didn't recognise what it was.

Martha knelt beside the bed and touched his cold arm. 'Josh, darling, it is that I am here for you. I am understanding your pain a little better now. Walter has been for explaining to me what all of this is doing to you. We need to get you well, me darling.'

His hand reached out to her, his fingers feeling like ice as he clung to her, clamping his hand on hers in a grip that was painful.

He eased his hold when she winced in pain.

'Martha. Forgive me, I can't seem to master this demon inside my head. It makes me angry at you . . . You were right earlier. I have been punishing you . . . Oh, Martha, I – I've even used your body to vent my frustration on with no regard to your feelings . . . your needs. I – I so wanted children . . . a family, with you, me, Bonnie and the sons and daughters that I dreamed of fathering. I had so many plans for them – they lived, really lived, in my imagination. It was the best dream and one I had constantly with me – as I worked, as I went about daily life, and yes, as we made love. Each time I thought would be the start of my dream, but it never was. Then it became that making love was just an act – a means of relieving myself. I began to look on it as meaning nothing other than that – that there would be no end result from it, not

113

ever. I've been such a pig to you, my darling. How can you ever forgive me?'

Martha gently brushed his hair from his sweating brow.

'It is that Walter has explained that none of the behaviour you are describing was your fault, me lovely Josh. We can be unwell in many ways, and you are in your mind right now. Sure, it is only for being a temporary state, caused by you having your dreams shattered and feeling that it is yourself to blame. Some of what you have been for doing is the right thing to do – filling your life with distractions – and sure, it is for being right that you seek different goals to replace those you've lost. But it is that until now you've been for doing this on your own. You have no need to now, me darling, as it is that I am ready to support you. It is right that you should be following another dream you've been for holding since you first became interested in photography – to work on a national newspaper.'

With her thumb, she wiped away a tear that had lodged on his nose. He stared at her as if he couldn't believe what he was hearing.

'But . . . well, I do want to, but we will be separated often and sometimes for long periods of time, if I am sent abroad to cover a story. I may even be assigned to an area that will mean constant travel. Paul – my old friend who you haven't met – covers a lot of foreign politics and he has a job lined up for me. He goes to America for ages at a time, or countries in Europe. And he sometimes covers a royal tour abroad and was away for weeks when our King and Queen were the Duke and Duchess of Cornwall and York and went on a tour of Canada.'

'So, sure, it is that on top of what you are for already suffering, you have this conflict between doing what is your calling and being a good husband to me. But it is that you can do both, me darling. My heart will ache for you when it is that you aren't here, but I will be for knowing you are happy following one of your dreams.'

Josh sat up. His eyes, swollen from crying, held love for her. His arms reached out for her. His look showed a wonderment at her understanding.

'Me love ain't a chain locking you to me, so it isn't. Sure, it is that it does have a chain, locking you into me heart, and that will never loosen, whether it is that you are by me side, or off on your travels being a renowned photographer . . . Oh, me Josh, I love you, and if it is that I can have you back – the real you – then it is worth the sacrifice of being apart, so it is.'

He slid off the bed and snuggled her into him. His hands caressing her, his lips seeking to kiss her face, her neck and her hands.

Martha wasn't aware of them undressing, or of getting into bed. All happened while she was floating on a fluffy cloud that she never wanted to disintegrate, but to take her deeper and deeper into the place she wanted to be – at one with her Josh.

When it happened, her cry was almost agonising as her longing and need collided and she knew complete fulfilment of herself and the love she had for Josh.

Lying in his arms afterwards, Martha couldn't believe that at last everything was coming right once more. Josh had made love to her. Real love, not a satisfying of his own hunger, but a passionate loving that had taken her to heights that had released her and exhausted her.

She prayed that this marked the beginning of his healing – a healing of them both. She prayed too that she would have the strength to follow through with her resolve and take the path she was being led down – to lead a different life to what she'd known, a lonely life without Josh always by her side.

Up early and with the sound of the birds busily tweeting their songs, and sometimes sounding as though they were deep into an argument with each other, Martha shivered from the cold as she opened the window to throw them some breadcrumbs, then jumped at the sound of Trisha's voice. 'Morning, lass. I've come to check you're all right and thought Sally might wake early with how excited she is about her new school.'

'My, it is that you are up with the larks and looking as chirpy as they sound. Is it that all has been resolved with you and Walter?'

'Eeh, Martha, it's more than resolved, love. I'll come inside to tell you, though, as this wind has a real nip to it.'

Martha's mind was racing as to what Trisha would tell her but she had an inkling as she looked so happy – the happiest she'd looked for a long time.

It didn't take long for Trisha to enlighten her. As soon as she came in the door she said, 'Eeh, lass, it happened – well, not proper, like, but Walter made what he called "alternative love" to me . . . By, me lovely Martha, I'm that happy.'

Martha laughed. She could guess what this alternative love was as she knew herself there were things that Josh did that gave her that special feeling and a release without entering her.

'Oh, it is that I am so pleased for you. Walter should have been for loving you in this way this good while. Sure, as a doctor, he would know of such techniques. It is as we have said many a time, menfolk just don't recognise that it is that we women have our needs and our frustrations as much as they do.'

'Aye, and I take it by your happy expression that normal service has been resumed for you an' all, lass.'

Martha felt her colour rising – more from rebound pleasure at remembering than embarrassment. She just grinned and nodded, and then found herself in Trisha's arms.

This was a different Trisha, a relaxed Trisha, a truly happy Trisha. And Martha was glad.

The kettle whistling and demanding attention parted them.

'Is it that you have time for a cuppa? I was for going to have one on my own. Josh is sleeping like a baby. Bless him, it is that he has spent many sleepless nights, so this is for being a good sign.'

'It is, Martha. By, we've been put through the wringer once more, but we've come out the other side, none the worse. I really felt sorry when Walter said last night that he and Josh weren't able to deal with upset like we were.'

'Well, it is that we have had to. At least until now, as it was that there was never anyone to pick us up but ourselves.

They have never been for falling, until now. But we will do the picking up of them, and that is what they are for learning.'

'Me an' all. I never thought me Walter would need supporting, but he does, you knaw, and more than I do. He needs a mother. And I can be that . . . well, with perks.'

Trisha grinned, and Martha laughed out loud. It seemed that Walter had at last woken up to the perks needed by Trisha. His life should go smoothly from now on.

The thought shuddered through her that Walter could now pursue whatever it was he'd found in Manchester, and he could do so with a restful conscience knowing that he'd found the key to Trisha's happiness – well, it was only the next best thing to being made love to properly, but it did give her a release.

Martha suspected it was more the feeling for Trisha that she was desirable, that her needs were considered, and that the love Walter had for her did mean a love for a man to a woman.

'So, is your life to change an' all, Martha, love?'

'It is. Josh is to follow a dream he's had since his pappy first bought him a camera, so he is.'

'How are you feeling about that, lass?'

'Strange. Not looking forward to it, to be sure, but willing to make the sacrifice, whilst it is that I will be hoping this is just a passing phase – something that is for helping me Josh to heal.'

'Aye, I knaw what you mean, love. I'm the same. I married a man who has ambitions in medicine, as he puts it, and not the usual fisherman, market trader, miner, or labourer that the class of folk I belong to marry. It means that I'm out of me depth at times, but that I ain't counting the coppers, or taking a beating on a Friday night, when me old man has a skinful and has spent his earnings in the pub instead of giving me me housekeeping. So, now I'm to learn different rules, a different way of living and thinking, but it all comes with a love, kindness and security that makes it worthwhile.'

'It is that you have woken up a wise woman this morning, Trish, me darling.'

'I knaw. I felt it happening last night. I felt us both changing – learning a lesson, if you like. It was strange, but it were like you and me had truly grown up.'

Martha nodded. 'I couldn't put it better meself, so I couldn't, for that is a good way to describe the acceptance we are for both finding ... I think that it is that we are going to be much happier in the future, once we are for adapting to it all, Trish.'

'I think that an' all ... So, this new me wants to get on with sorting out our business to make it more manageable, and Walter was just saying this morning it will probably be more profitable as we could expand our range and maybe one day have a factory! My, wouldn't that be grand, eh? Though he also cautioned me. He said to make sure we kept our security in mind at all times and not to take risks as he thinks this boom will change again one day.'

'My, that's a powerful statement, but the factory is something that has been in me mind for a time. We could be for taking on machinists. For it is now that our little ones are growing, we could be making clothes for their age group too. But always be mindful to keep enough of our capital, just in case, so we should.'

'Eeh, the sky's the limit, lass. By, I wish we could still call on Cilla to help. She could turn her hand to owt.'

'Yes, but it is that she has stepped up her fortune telling business and now is busy going to the houses of the rich and famous to do readings for them, just as I predicted years ago that she would ... It is happy I am for her. And for her little sister, Sunita, as it is that she is enjoying telling fortunes from the tent for the holidaymakers, just like Granny and me used to.'

'I knaw. We hardly see Cilla now. We ain't seen her since me wedding day.'

'Ha, it was that she turned a few heads that day, for sure.'

They both laughed at this. Trisha became serious first. 'The reason I'm pushing on getting our plans into reality is not only our need to free up time to be around for the girls after school, and to have time to take care of Johnny and Joseph, but that Benny needs me. I want to visit him every day and make sure all is all right with him ... You knaw, I can't see him recovering, bless him.'

'I'm sad to hear that, so I am. Benny's for being a good chap. But yes, I agree. We are going to need a lot more time to devote to all of the children. And it is that it will be a joint effort – you, me and Jenny's brother, Jack. And Peter, too, when it is that he recovers ... Well, what I'm trying to say is, that though they will be having a bed in your house, they aren't for being your sole responsibility.'

'Aye, I knaw that, love. And I've been thinking an' all that we're to tell Sally and Bonnie about them yet. What are we going to say? They're going to think it funny, us just taking on two lads they've never heard of.'

Martha thought for a moment, then came up with the idea of telling them that Jack, an old friend of Trisha's, came to find her as he knew she was settled now, and his nephews were needing a home. 'It is for being a bit of a tale, but if we all stick to the same story, then I think it is that they will be happy with it. Especially if we are for telling them that Johnny and Joseph will have no one if it is that we refuse them a home and will be for going into an orphanage.'

'I'm happy with that, but one day, Martha, you're going to have to tell Bonnie the truth. Look at Sally, she accepts that Walter isn't her real da, but she loves him as though he is and calls him Da.'

Martha felt the pain of this, and of hers and Joshua's deceit most days of her life. And now wished with all her heart that she'd been truthful from the very beginning.

'Is it that Sally thinks that Bobby is her father, or Ralph? I – I mean, that wasn't for being a spiteful question, but it is that I have always wondered. You see, me keeping my secret is for being tied to the fact that Peter is still alive, and he was an affair – a sin, as it was that I was an unmarried girl. I was thinking it would be easier as you were married.'

'I understand, lass, you don't have to get your knickers in a twist. You're holding back because you are thinking of the shame that you'll bring on Bonnie, that she'll think less of you. But it weren't any easier for me, as I told Sally the truth. Kids can take a lot more than you think. They accept things as they are, they don't think like us. Though one day, it may dawn on Sally that what her ma did was wrong, but she'll be used to it by then . . . And I had a head start as she was of an age to understand there was only me and her and to ask why she hadn't got a da. Bonnie hasn't known another life without Josh.'

'How was it you told her?'

'I just said that I had been lucky and known two loves, but was sad as both died because of the war. I told her that Ralph looked after me while the other man I loved was away fighting and that he gave me her . . . ha! She asked, "Did he put me in your tummy?" Eeh, I was that embarrassed, but I just said yes and that she grew inside me and then came out and I've loved her ever since, but her da could never visit as he'd been killed – that he was a hero and now lived in heaven. She just accepted it all.'

'I think you were for doing the right thing and wish with all me heart we had, but . . . well, it wasn't just me feeling like a sinner, but Peter is still alive, and it is that if she knew, she may have wanted to go to him.'

'Well, we all have to do what we have to do. And lass, when we get the boys we have to prepare ourselves for Peter getting better and wanting them back. He's got better before, you knaw.'

Martha sighed as she thought of how complicated life had become. But was glad the conversation ended there as Trish said, 'Well, I'd better get Sally up and take her home to get ready for school . . . You knaw, thinking about Ralph and the family he must have come from, it makes me glad that his daughter is getting the education he would have given her and that she's learning to be a lady. It's fitting somehow that she should have the upbringing he would have given her.'

Martha just agreed with this, but inside her stomach was churning and her head was full of indecisions and contradictions.

The bustling about getting breakfast, tidying after and getting an excited Bonnie ready for school made Martha's doubts take second place and then fade as her joy at restored family life took over from any misgivings.

When Josh was finally ready for work, having caused pandemonium by chasing Bonnie about and tickling her till she begged for mercy, Bonnie went up to him. As she kissed him, she clung on to his neck and asked, 'Where did you go, Da?'

It seemed she'd set her mind on Josh now being Da and not Pappy, but the question mystified them both.

'Do you mean when I was away for a few days? I went to see a friend. Da's going to have a new job that will mean I have to go away, but I know my two girls will look after one another.'

'No, I mean, you were a different da, like you were living in your head, and you didn't know I was there.'

'Oh? I always knew you were there. I – I had a lot on my mind. But it's all sorted out now. Come here and give me a hug before I go.'

Bonnie seemed happy with this as she hugged Josh and told him she loved him.

As she went scampering off, happy now, Josh took

Martha into his arms. 'You were right, I was spoiling our beautiful marriage. I'm so sorry, darling.'

'Hush, it was that you weren't well. And Walter said that it is that it will take you time to recover.'

He grinned and winked at her. 'Well, I think I've made a good start.'

She laughed at him as he went off waving to her. But that laughter turned to tears as she leaned on the door and the thought came to her, *Yes, together we have made a good start, but recovery will take my Josh away from me for long periods of time. How am I to bear it?*

It was as if for her and Trish, it would always be that their dreams would forever remain unfulfilled.

TEN

Trisha

Trisha stood with Walter, holding his hand beside the open grave, looking down on Benny's small coffin. It being as small as it was surprised her as Benny had been a tallish man, but as he'd become sicker, he'd shrunk in size.

The day was a typical October day with the sun shining and leaves scrunching beneath their feet as they walked.

The past six weeks had been tough, caring for Benny, watching him deteriorate, knowing she was going to lose him and worrying over the donkeys. Though she'd been able to rely totally on Dickie for their care, with Benny now gone she didn't know what would happen to them.

Besides this, the activity at home, getting ready for the boys – changing Walter's office into a bedroom for Johnny, as Walter had wanted to keep the spare bedroom as a guest room, and getting the cot and pram around from Martha's attic, assembling and cleaning them ready for Joseph – had been stressful on top of all the changes she and Martha were trying to put into place for their business. Funny, she'd thought many a time, how they'd gone from calling it their 'shop' to calling it their 'business', but exciting too, as that is what it was turning into, a proper business.

As the priest droned on, Trisha's mind went over how her life had changed so quickly and how it was to change even more.

She'd coped well with Walter being away all week, better than she'd thought, but this she put down to knowing his reasons for going, and supporting him to further his career – something she thought wives of men like Walter did, and she was proud to be that kind of wife to him now, instead of questioning him on why he was always away and if he didn't love her enough to want to be with her. All of that had gone, as had the awful feeling of not being a proper wife. For now they did make love, even though it wasn't complete and Walter didn't get or want anything out of it. But he gave her a lot and was forever telling her it was all he needed – to see her happy and fulfilled. Though she'd never be that; she didn't tell him, just made herself grateful for what she had.

Reports of Jenny were that she was holding on. Jack had been given compassionate leave to be with her, and when he last visited them he had brought with him the most beautiful letter from Jenny that had made them all cry, Walter and Josh included.

Josh had continued to get well, though had never said he would have the boys, but that he would be a good uncle to them. And as he was home a lot more than Walter, he would be a father figure too.

Walter nudging her brought Trisha out of her thoughts. The priest was handing her a small silver plate of soil. She took it and scattered a handful onto Benny's coffin.

The noise of it hitting the wooden box resounded around, making birds in a nearby bush take fright and tweet angrily at being disturbed. For Trisha, it brought home to her that Benny had truly gone, and unlocked the tears that had knotted her throat. Walter pulled her close to him. She loved the feel of his herringbone coat against her cheek, and of the love he surrounded her in, so much so that she reluctantly came out of the circle of his arms as Martha opened hers to her.

In Martha's hug was a shared sadness, for a man they had both known and loved. A kind man. A jolly and gentle man. Benny was all of those things.

With the service over, the solicitor that she'd seen at Benny's and who had been standing with Arthur stepped forward and had a word with Walter. Walter looked surprised as he glanced at her, then came nearer and told her, 'It seems, darling, that you are the main beneficiary of Benny's will. The solicitor has asked us to go back to his office with him.'

'Eeh, Walter, what does that mean?'

'We'll find out, darling.' Turning to Martha, he told her, 'We will see you both back home. We'll come as soon as we can.' Martha nodded.

They'd been glad when the funeral had fallen on a Wednesday, as they had decided a couple of weeks back to make that a half-day. It was the day that Elmslie had any extra activities on, and so far they'd been to watch the younger children painting and admired a gallery of their work – mostly splodges of colour, but they'd been amazed at the work of the older girls, which to Trisha had looked like it'd been done by professionals.

They'd also spent an afternoon watching a sports day, and so enjoyed that as Bonnie, cheered on by Sally, had won a gold cup for winning a race against older girls. All of them had swelled with pride at this.

Today, luckily, there were no activities that they need attend as dance classes had begun – something Sally loved – and they all wanted to surprise the parents by them seeing the show for the first time when it was performed before the half-term break.

Sitting opposite the solicitor in his neat office, with a huge desk and shelves lining the walls, heavy with files and thick large books that had what Trisha knew to be Roman numerals on the covers and tiny titles she couldn't read, they waited while the solicitor looked through some papers.

'Good afternoon to you both.' Looking at Trisha, he asked, 'You are Patricia Kenning, formally Rathbone, and formally of Enfield Road, Blackpool?'

'Aye, I am.'

'Good.' He passed her a form and a pen. 'Would you write your name and your address and then sign this, please.'

This done, Trisha was feeling impatient as to what all this was about, and she felt hot in her black wool costume she'd teamed with a white blouse. But somehow, she didn't want to ask if she could remove her jacket; she didn't know if such a thing was done in this formal setting. Neither of the men had removed theirs.

She reached under the desk for Walter's hand. He took hers and squeezed it reassuringly.

'May my wife have a glass of water, please, Jeremy?'

This surprised Trisha. She didn't know that Walter knew the solicitor, let alone enough to call him by his first name. But then, she was always finding things out about Walter.

The water was cool and refreshing and served by who Trisha assumed was the secretary. It came on a silver platter, holding a jug and two glasses. Walter poured them both a glass and drank his own in one go.

'Now we have established you are who I need to talk to, I have to tell you that Mr Benjamin Cuncliffe has left his entire estate to you, Patricia, after a small legacy to a Mr Richard Bardwin, who here he has specified in brackets is known as Dickie to you.

'The estate consists of property – a cottage, a barn and a stable. Besides, a paddock and five donkeys, and his licence to trade on Blackpool Beach, which will have to be trans-ferred to your name. As well as this, he has left you the sum of sixty pounds.'

Trisha gasped.

Beside her, Walter gave a sigh that sounded like he felt relief. She couldn't understand this but imagined it might be because the solicitor hadn't given her bad news about the donkeys, as neither of them would ever have imagined her coming into everything Benny owned. His solicitor had said that first time she'd fetched him for Benny that Benny intended to make sure she was well set up in the future – but all this!!

For a moment, Trisha couldn't take it all in. That was an enormous sum of money, the like she'd seen only as a total of their three months' takings, and then only as a written figure as most of it had gone to pay the rent and for new stock, though they were building up a nice capital sum.

She couldn't speak as gradually it registered with her. She owned the donkeys! The lovely donkeys. They would be safe. She'd worried about them so much. But then it occurred to her to wonder how she would take care of them all, and what she would do with the cottage. It came to her that she could sell it, but then the solicitor stopped her thoughts.

'There is a clause to go along with the cottage and that is that it is not to be sold or rented out for a minimum period of ten years.'

'Really? Why would Benny put a clause on it like that? What am I to do with it then?'

Walter shifted uncomfortably. Trisha looked at him wondering why, and why the sigh. But he just smiled at her.

The solicitor took their attention once more. 'Mr Cuncliffe hasn't said. People are always leaving these clauses. They have their reasons but they are often unfathomable to the beneficiary.'

Again, Walter shifted in his seat, then put his finger into his shirt collar and ran it around as he often did when too warm.

Trisha knew there was something troubling him but couldn't think what. Though Benny's words did flash into her mind, something about making sure she was all right, and that men like Walter should never marry. But she couldn't connect any of it together to make any sense.

130

When they were outside, Walter said, 'Shall we go and have a look at the cottage, darling? I've never seen it. We have time as Martha said they would pick the girls up from school if we were delayed for long.'

'Aye, I'd like that. It's a lovely place, and in a nice setting. I can't believe I own it.'

'Yes, I find it strange. Benny must have been very fond of you, darling.'

'He said sommat about wanting to protect me, but I hadn't a clue what he meant.'

Walter cleared his throat. 'It's an old-fashioned notion, I expect. Don't worry about it. But it is a lovely gesture. Shame he had no living family. I wonder if he was ever married?'

'Naw, he told me once that he hadn't. He did say he served in the forces as a young man – a sailor, I think – but he didn't talk much about himself or his life.'

When they got to the cottage, Walter looked around him. It stood well back from the road with a field next to it that had a gate connecting it to the cottage garden.

'That must be the paddock, but we would have to look at the deeds to be sure. It's a fair bet, though, as look, there are the stables.'

'Aye, I'm sure it is as I've seen the donkeys in it.'

'That alone is worth a lot of money. And structurally, the cottage looks sound.'

Trisha stood and gazed at the lovely cottage. She loved its slated roof, and how it came down at one side to just above the window, which she knew was the living room window. How its walls were rendered and painted white, though some of this was flaking off.

Sadly, the small garden was overgrown now, but it was once cared for as there was a lawn with grass around a foot high and flower beds with rose bushes and shrubs in, which all looked healthy, though some were not in season.

The inside was small and yet had room enough and would have a lot more if it didn't have so many boxes about, and such huge furniture that had long ago seen better days. The kitchen was square, but again cluttered, so difficult to see what it could look like. Upstairs they found two bedrooms and a box room. The lav was outside and there was a tin bath hanging on the outside of the lav wall.

'Well, all in all, I think you have a good little property here, darling, but what you're going to do with it, I have no idea. I wonder if the renting out clause covers letting it out for holidays?'

Somehow this didn't appeal to Trisha. 'Naw, I think I should use the money to do it up, and just look after it. I've the donkeys to consider an' all. Dickie, who cares for them, is trustworthy. I could make him a kind of manager of them and the gardens. He won't be going to the beach soon with them, so he can do jobs to get this place ship-shape. Then I think I'll just come to be here on some of the days you're away. It'll be wonderful for the kids to play around here.'

'Like a second home, you mean?'

'Aye, sommat like that. Mind, I'll have to sort through all of them boxes before I start on owt else.'

'We can take a couple home with us if you like. We can put them in the garage and then you can sort through them at your leisure. No doubt some of his things will tell us more about Benny.'

'Aye, I'd like that, ta, love. I do have some lonely evenings, when Martha can't come around. It will keep me busy.'

'Oh, I'm sorry, darling. You've made a huge sacrifice for me.' He pulled her to him and held her. 'Thank you. I do appreciate it. I have always aimed to be a senior consultant, and it is quite a feat at my age that I have achieved that.'

'I'm proud of you, love. I'll be fine once we have the boys, though I hate saying that as Jenny won't have them then and will be gone. It's so sad.'

'I know. In my work I see so many sad cases and that is why I spend many evenings researching. We know so little about so many conditions. But we will make break-throughs . . . Anyway, darling, I think we should get back and try to absorb all of this over the next few days. You can think about what you would like to do to modernise it. One suggestion from me would be to make that small spare room upstairs into a bathroom. I'd help out with cost if you find your money getting low.'

'Eeh, Walter, you're so good to me. I do love you.'

'And I love you, very much. You're my perfect wife.'

He kissed her then. Since he'd been making love to her, if she could call it that, his kisses were more those of a lover, and this thrilled her.

When they came out of the kiss, he said, 'You're so understanding, darling. I no longer feel afraid to kiss you how I always wanted to as I know you won't expect more of me and I do love how we are in bed now . . . I was very remiss in the first few months.'

She kissed his cheek. 'Aye, I love it an' all. I never knew so much enjoyment could be had without, well, you knaw.'

'I'm glad, darling. You are a lot happier and therefore I am. Shall we go now, or shall we stand here and analyse our odd marriage all afternoon as to how we've made it work?'

Trisha laughed at this. But he was right. They did have an odd marriage, but it suited them both with the problem that Walter had. Though secretly, she hoped there may be more in the future for them to enjoy as twice now she'd noticed him showing his need. He'd never tried to do anything, but then he'd probably be afraid in case it let him down. But she always had hope.

Two weeks later, with October nearly out, Betty, their new assistant, came through to the workroom just as they were tidying up and preparing to leave for the rest of the day – something they did most days now, either together or separately, so always one of them collected the girls from school.

'Eeh, you lasses, you've a handsome man called into the shop asking for you. Is there sommat I don't knaw?'

Her eyes twinkled with mischievousness.

'Ha, naw. We've naw secrets these days, Betty, love.'

Trisha had known Betty all her life. She lived at the bottom end of Enfield Road and Trisha had passed her house most days when she'd lived there. From her going to school days when a child, to going to work later on and every time she went to the shop or to come into Blackpool town.

Always a nice woman, with a cheery word for everyone, but never getting involved in anything that went on in the street, Betty was gentle-natured, short and too skinny with wiry hair that curled when wet but dried to a frizz. Her husband had passed away about six months ago and her kids had long flown the nest and lived away.

It had been a good piece of luck last week when Trisha had bumped into her walking down the promenade after not seeing her for a long time.

Always one for a natter, she'd told Trisha that she was lonely and fed up. The idea of offering her a job came out of the blue as they'd had no one call in in response to Martha's notice on the door.

Betty had jumped at the idea and, though early days, was working out really well. She was good with the customers, and didn't mind what she turned her hand to, from wrapping parcels to stitching hems while she sat in the shop keeping an eye on things.

At first, she'd been afraid to serve anyone and had called them every time the doorbell clanged. They hadn't remarked on this, but had hoped she'd take responsibility for the customers eventually. Then after just two days she'd come through to the back glowing. 'By, there's nowt to this selling lark! I've sold a baby blanket!'

They laughed at how proud she was but had both been relieved.

When they went through to the shop and saw Jack standing there, they both took a sharp intake of breath. Trisha recovered first.

'Eeh, you're lucky to have caught us, lad, we knock off earlier now,' was all she could think of to say.

Jack was smiling, which shook them, but did sound grave when he asked, 'May I have a word in private?'

Once in the back, he looked at them both, his expression one of joy.

'Well, I cannot believe I am saying this, but Jenny is in remission!'

'What? Eeh, lad, I ain't sure what you're saying, but I knaw me heart feels glad.'

'Apparently it can happen with the type of cancer she has of the blood. No one knows why and it is very rare, especially, I'm told, when it was so advanced as it seemed to be in Jenny.'

It was Martha who asked, 'And what about Peter? Has this news helped him at all?'

Jack shook his head. 'I'm afraid not. I went to see him myself to tell him, but he didn't know who I was or what I was talking about. We're all very worried about him . . . You see . . . well, he's unresponsive and worse than ever.'

'Oh no!'

Martha had gasped this out, and this worried Trisha. Did Martha still hold feelings for Peter?

'He's being watched, but nevertheless, I am concerned. I haven't told Jenny and asked the staff at the institution not to if she does get strong enough to visit as it will break her heart.'

'So, you'll naw longer be needing us then, lad. I've mixed feelings about that as I was looking forward to them coming, but more than that, I can't tell you how happy I am at why they ain't.'

'Well, the thing is, Jenny isn't under any illusion that this can last. The doctors have told me – not her – that it won't,

136

but she was a nurse, so she does know these things. Anyway, she's sent me to ask you if you could find time to visit? She is so grateful to you both and says that when the time does come, she can die in peace with the knowledge her boys will be loved and cared for, but she'd dearly love for them to meet you and get to know you while she is alive, so she can see for sure.'

Trisha saw the same hesitation in Martha that she felt herself.

'I'm sorry, I shouldn't have asked. You've promised us so much already.'

'Naw, it ain't that, lad ... Well, I'm sure Martha feels the same ... It's getting to knaw Jenny. It'll make it harder to lose her, and seeing the lads with her will make me knaw they belong to her ... I knaw they do, but, well, it was like it was just them. Now I knaw I'll take Jenny into me heart and everything will be different.'

'It is that I did have the same thought, Trish, but now that you are for voicing it, I'm thinking differently. We will be able to talk to the boys about their mammy, and it is that they will not be coming to strangers.'

'Aye, put like that, I don't knaw what I was thinking. Of course it's best. I'm sorry, lad.'

'Ha, I've always been too sad on my visits here to say how much I love being called "lad".'

His look made Trisha cast her eyes down. She didn't know why. But then, the moment passed.

'And I haven't said how very glad I am that you are the women I wanted you to be and that Jenny had faith that you were.'

Martha still seemed unsure to Trisha, but then the reason surfaced. 'May I ask one thing? I mean, well, it is that I am for holding a secret from me wee child. She isn't for knowing that Peter is her pappy. She is thinking me husband is. I will be telling her when she is older, but it is something that we all agreed to – Peter as well. It was for being his idea.'

'Of course, I will tell Jenny that, but she probably knows anyway, as obviously she's never met your child but knows of her. But knowing Jenny, if Peter told her those were his wishes, then she wouldn't have interfered with them. I'll just remind her not to let it out by mistake.'

'Ta, it is grateful that I am.'

'So, can I tell her that you will visit in the school half-term holiday?'

'Aye, you can, lad. It'll be good to meet her and, like Martha says, to be able to talk to the lads about her when we have them.'

With this, he left a few minutes after, and Trisha felt a small feeling of regret that he had. She liked Jack and would love to talk to him about his time at sea and seeing the world. It all seemed a huge adventure to her, when she hadn't been out of Blackpool – well, she had been to Fleetwood! This thought made her giggle.

'What is it that is amusing you, Trish?'

'Eeh, I'm nervous about going to Manchester, that's all. Will we get lost?'

'No, it is that we just catch the train and then be asking for a cab to take us to Jenny's house.'

'Well, you're worldly-wise, I ain't, so I'll just follow you. But eeh, in a way, it's sommat to look forward to, ain't it? I mean, it'll break the week up an' all for the girls. Though I ain't looking forward to seeing Jenny looking poorly and it ain't comfortable knowing someone so young's going to die. What will we talk to her about?'

'I know, but if it is that we can help her to die more peacefully, then it will be worth it. And for them little boys to already know us is going to help them, for sure it is.'

Trisha agreed, with sadness in her heart for the young woman. Why was the world so cruel?

ELEVEN

Trisha

The week passed and before they knew it, they were queuing up with the rest of the mothers, and some fathers too, Trisha noted, feeling that pang of loneliness she often felt. Pulling her coat around her, she slipped her arm into Martha's, felt the extra warmth of doing so, and the comfort of knowing they were in this together as Josh was away too.

Everyone was chatting excitedly as they made their way snake-like into the school hall. This was just a small room, but then there were only about thirty pupils altogether who attended Elmslie.

Once seated they found themselves looking towards beautiful blood-red drapes covering the little platform that was at one end of this room.

'Eeh, I'm that excited. I've never seen Sally look forward to sommat as much as she has this. She's had naw nerves about it. But then, maybe they're just playing a small walk-on, walk-off part, so don't have to remember much.'

Martha just grinned and tucked her arm into Trisha's. The gesture made Trisha think Martha knew something that she didn't. But then she thought this silly. Surely Martha wouldn't have a vision about a kids' show?

Trisha's mind wandered from this problem as she thought, *Eeh, I never thought I'd be sitting in a grand hall such as this.* She looked up at the ornate ceiling and the carved cornice and marvelled at its beauty, as to her it looked like a wreath of flowers and leaves around the room.

Music trickled into the air. Delicate-sounding music she knew was played on the keys of a piano. Not the clunky ones but the ones that were almost like bells. Slowly the curtain opened and there on the floor was a little girl crouched tiny with her legs crossed and her head bent over. Around her the set looked like flowers floating on water. The little girl unfolded gracefully. Trisha gasped. Martha gripped her arm.

Tears ran a silent trail down Trisha's face as she watched her Sally, dressed all in pink, dancing as if she was an elusive fairy flying around a pool of water lilies. Never had she seen anything so beautiful in all her life. Never had she realised that the way Sally always jigged about could be harnessed into this stunning, graceful, butterfly-like creature.

The room had fallen silent. Trisha took her eyes off the stage for a moment and glanced around her. Folk were mesmerised by her little girl.

When the music died, they were all quiet for a moment, but then as one, they stood, and the noise was deafening as they clapped and cheered and called out, 'Bravo.'

When the clapping died down, a gentleman behind her whispered to his wife, 'We are seeing a ballerina born, dear. Who is she? Do you know? We should find out. She needs nurturing from this very young age.'

Trisha's blood boiled. She wanted to turn around and tell him that she nurtured her Sally and was the only one that did or ever would!

But she soon forgot her anger as she was caught up once more in the magic of the show, the beautiful piano playing, and the story, as narrated by one of the older girls.

It appeared that the fairy was lost and all the girls needed to help her to get home to Ireland where she should be with the rest of the little people.

At this, Trisha felt Martha stiffen. Did she mind, or did she think that they were taking the mickey out of her folk? Trisha wasn't sure until the show ended and her little Sally somehow flew up to the top of the stage and was hidden by the valance of the curtains, with the rest of the cast waving to her.

The scene almost had Trisha crying out as it felt to her that her Sally was leaving her, but Martha moved beside her and brought Trisha's attention back to her reaction during the show. 'Are you all right, lass? Did it affect you, them talking about the little people?'

'It was that it did as I suddenly felt the pain of longing to see me homeland once more.'

'Eeh, love, it's been a long time now.'

'It has, but I've never been for even looking on the graves of me mammy and pappy or for saying a proper goodbye to them.'

Trisha didn't know why she said it, but the words came out. 'Well, if we can go to Manchester!'

Martha laughed and this reassured Trisha enough so that she felt she could talk about what she really wanted to. 'Aw, me Sally, me lovely Sally. I can't believe it.'

'She was amazing, love, but it was disappointed I was not to be seeing me Bonnie.'

'Maybe she was one as moved everything about when the scenes needed changing. You couldn't tell who they were, they were all dressed like elves with green faces.'

'No, I would have been knowing her even in that disguise. But it is that she said she was in the show, but that I would be surprised.'

Moments later the two excited girls came running through a side door with a host of others and hurled themselves at them.

'Ma, Ma, did you see me, did you? I was a fairy, and I went up, up in the air . . . Eeh, I loved it, Ma.'

Trisha bent down and picked up her glowing Sally and hugged her to her. Tears flowed down her face – they were tears of joy and love for her little girl. And pride too.

The thought came to her that Sally didn't take after her as she was a clumsy thing, though she wasn't that time when she went to Blackpool Tower, and met Sally's da.

For a moment she remembered gliding around the dance floor in the arms of Ralph. His expertise as he took her effortlessly around in a waltz. So graceful, so fluent with his steps and his body in tune with the music. And then she knew why her little girl was so talented.

'Excuse me.'

The voice directed at her brought Trisha back down to earth as it was the man who had commented about Sally to his wife.

'I don't mean to be rude, but I am Leonard Plant. I run a school of dancing in Blackpool. Is this child your daughter?'

'Aye, she is.'

'Well, may I give you my card? I would welcome her as a pupil and would take her to the top of her field. She is a ballet dancer in every sense of the word. Even as she ran to you, I could see her grace and the beautiful shape she held herself in.'

Not altogether sure what he was talking about, Trisha took the card. 'Ta. Me lass is always jigging about, but I ain't seen her like she was tonight.'

'That is because someone harnessed the beauty of her movements. She has enormous talent and potential. I would love you to bring her along to my classes. Good day.'

With that he was gone.

Sally likened him to a tall Charlie Chaplin as he had the same scraggy-looking hair that Charlie had in his films and the same moustache. Only Leonard was tall, slender and graceful.

A tugging on her arm brought her attention to Bonnie. 'It was me, Aunty Trisha! I played the piano!'

'What? Eeh, me little love. Did you?'

'Yes. I had some help from Mrs Peacock, but I played a lot of it. And it was me who played that note as Sally was winched up.'

'By, lass, that puts a different light on things – winched up? Eeeh, I thought she flew!'

Bonnie laughed. Sally joined in. Their excitement oozed from them.

Trisha turned to Martha. 'Well, it seems we have two talented little girls, lass. I've never been so shocked in me life as when them curtains went up.'

'Ha, nor is it that I have been. I was for knowing a little about what Sally was doing as Bonnie told me, but she said to keep it a secret . . . But Bonnie! A pianist – well, it is that she is a budding one. To be sure, I wasn't foreseeing that!'

'Your spirits are letting you down, love.'

They were all giggling when they left the school. 'What a way it is to begin your half-term, girls.'

Both looked a bit downcast at this. 'We don't want a holiday from school, do we, Sally?'

'No, Bonnie. We want to go every day!'

Trisha smiled at Martha. 'Eeh, that's good news. Imagine if we had to drag them there by the scruff of their necks, lass.'

Martha only nodded, but then said wistfully, 'You know, it is that Josh said he would one day take me to Ireland, but it has never happened. I'm going to be getting on at him when next it is that he is at home.'

'You knaw, it's sad that our men are missing out on these occasions. We could never explain them to them – not draw a proper picture in words. You had to be there to capture what we did.'

'You're right, Trish, love . . . Oh, how I miss Josh.'

'When will he be home, do you know?'

'I am only for knowing that last week there was an inkling that something grand to do with history was to be found. I think it was to do with a young fellow called Tutan . . . something. It is that his grave has been found and it has to be photographed. When Josh telephoned, he was as excited as a boy as he was telling me he never thought to get such a chance, but it is that there is a sickness about in London and he is for being the only one who can go. He was sailing away to Greece today.'

'Greece! By, I've heard of it, but ain't got a clue where it is. Anyroad, Walter said he won't be coming home as we're going to Manchester tomorrow, but he'll meet us at London Road station and see us safely on our way.'

Martha smiled, but there was no real joy coming from her. This worried Trisha, but she knew the feeling and knew nothing could fix it.

'Right, I reckon these lasses deserve a treat. Come here, let's do your coats up and wrap you in your scarves and mitts as it'll freeze your socks off out there. Then we'll go for some chips at Macie's, eh?'

There were squeals of delight from both girls, and Trisha thought at least they didn't suffer when their das were away as their little lives were full of good things happening for them.

Walter was waiting when the train pulled in. His smile sent a lovely warm feeling through Trisha. She ran towards him, closely followed by Sally and Bonnie. It felt so good to be in his arms. A week could feel like a year at times. His kiss was gentle but full of love. It didn't last long because of Sally demanding attention. 'Da, Da!'

He went onto his haunches and hugged her and Bonnie together. Smoke swirled around them, puffed from the train's funnel. Whistles blew as folk ran towards trains, pushing and shoving. All of it unfamiliar and exciting. Though the smell and feel of the smoke clogging her nostrils, and the sensation of being too enclosed, made Trisha want to escape it all.

Martha voiced this. 'It is that I am not for being happy on train stations.'

Walter rose and gave her a hug. 'No, they aren't the most comfortable atmospheres. Let's make our way out. This way.'

Trisha thrilled as he took her hand. But then froze as she glimpsed Carl standing outside a booth that sold newspapers. 'Eeh, what's he doing here, Walt?'

'Who?' Walter looked in the direction she was.

'I can't see anyone we know, darling.'

Carl had gone!

'It was that Carl. That bloke who was nasty to me at our wedding.'

'Carl! Really?' Walter seemed to be panicking as he looked around. 'You must have been mistaken, darling . . . He – he's away on a course . . . unless, well, he could have come back on a train, maybe?'

Again, Walter looked around. 'Oh well . . . We must have missed him anyway. Let's get out of here and on our way. Come on, girls.'

Trisha knew she wasn't mistaken but didn't bother any more about it as she accepted it must just have been as Walter said. Though why Carl seemed to hate her, she didn't know. And she had no doubt that he'd seen them. But then, he wouldn't want to approach Walter and have to speak to her, she was sure of that. She shrugged as she had the feeling that she was glad he'd just disappeared as she didn't want to see him either.

Jenny was a small, frail young woman, with bruising on her matchstick-looking arms and legs.

She had a lovely smile that shone with inner strength and Trisha loved her on sight.

'Hello, lass. I'm Trisha and this is Martha. And this is Walter, me husband.'

Jenny stared at Martha for a moment, then said, 'Come in. Ah, are these your girls? Hello, little ones.'

Trisha breathed easier. Jenny must have wondered what the woman who stole her husband's heart before she met him looked like, but the moment had passed.

Sally and Bonnie beamed at her. Bonnie, as always the forward one, said, 'I'm Bonnie and this is Sally. Have you two boys?'

'I have. Joseph is asleep. He has just drunk a whole bottle of milk and that was after he had some porridge! He's a greedy one and will grow really big and . . . strong.' Jenny's voice broke, but she took a deep breath and recovered. 'Johnny is in the scullery. I sent him there to wash his grubby face before you arrived.'

'What's a scullery?'

This question from Bonnie shocked Trisha and made her realise how privileged Sally and Bonnie were.

'It's like a kitchen, lass. Now let us get in before you ask owt else, eh? Aunty Jenny needs to sit down.'

Jenny smiled gratefully at Trisha, but as soon as she sat, Bonnie asked, 'Are you my aunty?'

'I'd like to be, love, if you'll have me?'

'Oh, yes, we will, won't we, Sally?'

Sally grinned and nodded.

Just stepping inside Jenny's house, a terraced, took Trisha back in time to the one she was born and raised in, in Enfield Road in Blackpool. Though this one was a lot posher with a bay window, giving much more room in the living room, and a gated garden in the front. Other than that the layout inside made her immediately feel at home.

Only the furnishings were different as they were more of the modern style – an armchair each side of the fireplace, with oak-wood arms and legs and an upholstered seat and back, in a grey colour, though the back upholstery was framed by the same wood. An oak table, with leaves that could be put up to make it bigger, stood under the window with a dining chair each side and a bowl of fruit sat on a crocheted mat in its centre. And there was a sofa against the back wall that matched the chairs.

Trisha knew the door facing the front door would lead to the scullery and the one in the opposite corner would lead to the stairs, and probably to two bedrooms.

Walter took charge as Martha seemed to have clammed up.

'Now then, girls, don't overwhelm your new aunty.' He turned to Jenny. 'It's nice to meet you. How are you feeling, dear?'

'I can't believe how well I am, thanks, Walter. And it's nice to meet you too. Me brother Jack tells me we are in the same profession – at least, I was before I became ill.'

'Yes, I'm a doctor – well, a specialist in neurology. I believe you nursed in the psychiatric department?'

'I did. That's how I met Peter . . . I wish more was done for the men who returned from the war traumatised as Peter was. Most are on the streets begging.'

'I agree. And I'm very sorry to hear how your husband is . . . We, well, we want to help all we can. We of course know your wishes of us. And want you to know, we will devote our lives to your boys as much as we do to our girls.'

Tears filled Jenny's eyes. 'Thank you. Thank you from the bottom of my heart.'

Sally and Bonnie looked on with wide eyes. Trisha could see that Bonnie was dying to ask a question but knew they wouldn't as Walter had been quite firm with them.

'Anyway, that's in the future, and I hope not too near a future . . . You have heard that I'm one of life's miracles, haven't you? They don't happen often, and I never thought I would be chosen. Three weeks ago, I could hardly stand. How I managed my boys, I don't know, but Johnny is a wonder. He really helped me.'

As she said this, Johnny came through the door and without a trace of shyness announced, 'Hello, I'm Johnny. I'm four, you know.'

Trisha heard the sharp intake of breath that Martha took. Johnny looked so like Bonnie, the same dark eyes and same shaped face. The only difference was the colour of their hair as Johnny had black hair like Peter's.

He stared at Bonnie and Bonnie at him. His was a confident stare, but for the first time ever, Bonnie showed signs of shyness as she sidled into Martha's coat and pulled it across herself.

Sally saved the day. 'I'm Sally. That's my ma and I'm six.'

'What's a ma?'

Jenny laughed as she told Johnny, 'It's her mam, you daft thing. Mams get called different names in different areas. Bonnie and Sally are from Blackpool.'

Sally had really found her voice. 'Bonnie calls her ma Mammy, as her ma is from Ireland.'

Johnny burst out laughing. But not in a way that could be said he was being rude, he just found it all amusing. Both girls laughed with him, and the ice was broken.

'You can come and see my baby brother if you like … Can they, Mam?'

'Yes, but be quiet and don't wake him. Do you girls want a drink? I have some orange juice … Oh, I didn't think, I haven't offered you all a cup of tea.'

'You've hardly had time, lass. But naw … well, at least not made by you. You sit a mo and I'll put the kettle on. I'll soon find everything.'

'Thanks, Trisha.'

Trisha was glad to escape and hoped with her out of the way Walter could break the ice between Martha and Jenny. It was getting awkward.

The kitchen was almost a replica of how her own had been with its deep pot sink, stove with two ovens and a dresser. Even down to having a small table in the centre.

When she went back into the living room, carrying a tray she'd found standing on the floor leaning against the dresser, Martha still sat quietly on the corner of the sofa.

Knowing her so well, Trisha knew she was uncomfortable and felt at a loss as to how to alter things.

Walter sat back with his legs crossed, not helping at all as he and Jenny talked medical stuff and about the hospital. From what they were saying they knew some of the same people.

'Here you go. Shall I pour for everyone?'

'Actually, I've decided not to have one, but if you can fetch the children down, darling, I'll take them for a walk to that park we passed not far down the road. The fresh air will do them good. They've been in that stuffy train and then the car and now indoors . . . Will that be all right with you, Jenny, if I take Johnny too?'

'It will. Poor lad doesn't get to go out, only into the backyard, unless Jack's here. He misses his dad; they did everything together.'

When this was sorted, Trisha was glad as she knew Walter's motives. As much as he would have loved a cup of tea, he would be hoping with him out of the way, Martha would relax a little and be able to talk to Jenny.

Surprisingly, this happened very quickly as Martha asked, 'How is it that Peter is getting on? Is it that there is hope he will get his memory back again?'

'There is, thanks, love. The doctor of the department is a friend of mine. He dropped in the other day and said that they had tried to get it through to him that I'm all right, and the next day he asked if he knew someone called Jenny as he couldn't get the name out of his head. That's very promising. When I first met him, he knew nothing, but after about a year he asked me one day if he knew anyone called Martha.'

'Oh? I was not for knowing.'

'I know, love. It was me who gradually pieced it all together and came and found you. I had a dilemma as I found that you were happy and by that time I was in love with Peter. But after we married and everything came back to him, it was clear that he felt so guilty about what had happened that I thought it best to bring him to you. I – I hope I didn't do wrong.'

'No. It is that my mind was eased. I'd never been for losing faith that there was a reason Peter left. But ... well, I'm in a powerful dilemma, so I am.'

Trisha sat and listened, leaving them to get everything out in the open.

'I understand. Peter told me about Bonnie, and I agreed with him when he said that she was happy and loved. We couldn't give that stability to her – I don't mean financially. Everything on that front is fine, I have an inheritance and half of this house is mine. I share the ownership with Jack. He has a bedroom upstairs. We're lucky, this is a larger than usual terraced and we have three bedrooms. But emotionally – something I am very aware of because of my past job, and being married to Peter – this isn't the best environment for kids. I worry all the time about Johnny. But he is so young. He's taken everything in his stride up to now.'

'It's sorry to the heart of me that I am. But it is that you have put my mind at rest that, for now, we are doing the right thing.'

'I wouldn't ever change that. But there is something I would like to say. When I knew about my condition and my slim chances, and how it sent Peter backwards, I had to

153

make arrangements for my boys. You were all I could think of, Martha. Peter spoke so highly of you once he remembered – your kindness, and your caring ways, that I just knew I could approach you. There is no one else. Peter isn't capable and we don't know if he ever will be, so without you, I knew it would be an orphanage. I couldn't bear that. Peter had a terrible life in one of those.' Jenny began to cough.

'Eeh, lass, take your time. You've nowt to worry about now. Me and Martha are going to step in, but I've a mind that you'll live a long time yet.'

Jenny had controlled her coughing. She shook her head. 'I don't think so, Trisha. But what I wanted to say was that I'm sorry to burden you like this . . . I mean, me kids are good kids, but no one should be asked to take on others' children. I feel that I've left you with no choice.'

Martha answered this. 'No, it isn't for being like that. When it was that Jack came and asked me, I hesitated. You see, well, me husband . . . he . . . he had news that was for upsetting him, and I was worrying that to ask him to take on the children of . . . well, of the man who was for being the father to my child would be too much for him . . . I – I was right.'

'Aw, but that don't affect things, does it, Martha? You see, Jenny, me and Martha we live just doors away . . .'

Trisha was relieved to see Jenny relax as she explained how she and Walter were going to take the children and be the main parents to them. 'But Martha and Josh will be like aunty and uncle, won't you, Martha?'

'Sure, it is that we will. So, brother and sister will be together, but it is that they cannot know they are that until they are older.'

'I understand ... How can I thank you?'

Trisha felt near to tears for the plight Jenny found herself in. 'You don't have to, lass. You're in a very sad position. We can help, so that's that ... though there is sommat else that has occurred to me. Would you consider coming to stay with me for a while? Walter would bring you on a Friday night when he comes home from the hospital. Me and Martha could give you a nice time in Blackpool, and the kids. It would be a break for them and for you.'

Jenny's tears spilled over at this.

Martha got to her first and held her close. Trisha could only pat her back and rub her hand gently. Doing so gave her the feel of how the cancer had ravaged poor Jenny's body – she was just skin and bone.

When she calmed, she said, 'I would so like that. I get so very tired. To have the worry of the children shared, even for a short time, and for me to get a rest, would be enough ... Are you sure, love?'

'I am. More than sure. We've plenty of room and you can rest all you like.'

'But you have a shop, don't you?'

'Aye, but we can work that between us, don't you worry. Look at us, able to come today, no bother. And now's a good time as the kids are off school and we've arranged things around that, so there's allus one of us able to take care of them and not have to keep them around us in the shop all of the time.'

'But what about Peter?'

'Eeh, I didn't knaw you visited him, love.'

'Just once a week. Not that he knows . . . Well, he seems happy that I'm there, but he doesn't know me.'

'Well, we have telephones, so you can ring the hospital as often as you like, lass.'

Jenny looked at Martha.

'It is that I would love you to come too, Jenny, love. My heart is for breaking to see your plight, and if we can lighten the load for you, for sure it would be a pleasure.'

'Thank you.' Jenny broke down once more, though Trisha had the notion that she was almost too exhausted even to cry. Poor soul. To Trisha, who'd nursed her own dying ma, Jenny didn't look long for this world. The very word 'cancer' meant death.

As she caught Martha's eye, she read the same was in Martha's thoughts and hoped with all her heart that Jenny had a little while longer and would make it to Blackpool. She so wanted to care for her.

TWELVE

Martha

Martha could feel her spirits sinking lower and lower over the next few days. There was no word from Josh. She knew there wasn't going to be as he couldn't telephone, and he may be home before a letter could get to her.

Every night, her pillow was wet with tears. During the day, she threw herself into her work. Even on the days when it was her turn to stay at home and look after Bonnie and Sally, she rushed around doing the housework and then worked on anything she'd brought home to do, on her treadle sewing machine that was set up in the spare room.

Today, being Wednesday, was their half-day closing, and Betty's day off. They'd brought the girls with them so that they could both work in the workroom and try to catch up on the mountain of orders that all needed to be shipped in time for Christmas.

The girls were fine with that arrangement, knowing it was only going to be for a few hours that they had to amuse themselves upstairs in the flat.

Usually, on a Wednesday afternoon, she and Trisha did something together with the girls, but Trisha was taking Sally to see Leonard Plant once they closed so Martha, not wanting to go home, had decided to try to spend the afternoon finding workers who could work at home. Something she felt sure she would succeed at as many could do with the extra money, especially at this time of year as they began to think about the approaching festive season.

It was only days since their visit to Jenny, and Martha hadn't yet settled down from it. Jenny was constantly on her mind, as were the two boys.

She sighed as she stood folding the leaflets that Josh's manager had printed for her. Her intention was to post them through the doors of potential workers in Enfield Road, where she and Trish had lived, and the surrounding streets.

She'd chosen this route because when they had lived there and had walked to the tram stop to get to work in the summer months, they'd always seen women sitting outside knitting, embroidering or crocheting, so they knew the skills were there.

She read one of the leaflets to make sure it said the right things.

The Layette Lasses shop is looking to employ workers.
We require women who can work in their own homes
and have sewing, crocheting or knitting skills.
The sewing work – stitching garments
together and sewing hems.

The knitting work – matinee jackets, baby
coats, bonnets, mittens, booties and blankets.
The crochet work – as knitting ...
Please apply by calling into the shop on the
promenade, or by a message delivered to the shop.
All work will be delivered and collected.
Rates will be discussed with successful candidates.

Satisfied with this, she donned her thick coat and bonnet
and pulled on her mitts and called for Bonnie to hurry and
get her outdoor clothes on.

'Eeh, lass, are you sure this afternoon's a good time for
you to do this? You need to rest, you knaw.'

'I can't, Trish, love. I only feel lonelier when I do.' The
ever-present tears that Martha constantly fought welled up
in her eyes.

'Aw, lass, lass. I knaw your pain. At least, I do in the weekdays ... Eeh, that it should have come to this for us both, eh?'

'I try to cope, as sure as God is in heaven I do, but it is
that I don't succeed. When I lock me door at night, I feel
that I am cut off from the world.'

'Eeh, lass. You remember how we lived together once,
eh? Why don't we do it again? I mean, during the week we
could. You knaw, we've both got plenty of room to set a
bedroom up for each other, and the girls already have a bed
at each house. By, I'd love that. We're being daft ha'peths,
both being lonely at night and us only three doors away
from each other.'

Martha could feel hope rising inside her. 'Oh, Trish, I
would be for loving that. I know we often sit together in

one house or the other, but it is for being when it is time to lock the doors, switch off the lights and go up to a lonely bed that I am feeling it most.'

'Well, you'll still have the lonely bed, lass. I ain't offering for you to come into mine!'

They burst out laughing. And Martha felt better.

Doing the buttons up on her coat, she thought how Josh had been with her when she'd chosen this winter coat and how he'd loved the rust colour with its contrasting fur collar and cuffs. She hugged it around her, trying to imagine it was him, how he had held her when she'd tried it on.

With Martha being on the small side, the length was a little longer than she normally wore her clothes, but today, as the wind howled along the promenade, she knew she would be glad of it. And of her thick Lisle stockings.

'Well, here's the lasses. Eeh, look how you've buttoned your coat, Sally. Come here, love.'

'It is that Arthur is here for us, Trish, so I'll leave the locking up of the shop to you, eh?'

'Aye, see you later. Don't go getting too cold now.'

Martha took hold of Bonnie's hand and waved to Trisha and Sally. She was pleased to see that Arthur had the hood up over the cab's seating area as this would afford them some protection.

'Jump up, lasses. By, it'll freeze you today. Can't you do your errand on another day and enjoy your half-day at home?'

'No, more's the pity, for it is that me and Trisha are desperate for help before the children go back to school.'

'Well, I don't think you'll be short of folk taking you up on your offer. It's a grand idea as many need the money but their old men won't allow them to go out to work. But this, well, he can hardly object as they sit knitting a lot of the time anyroad.'

When they reached Enfield Road, Martha's heart dropped. She'd never been really happy here. The neighbours hadn't trusted her, thinking of her and her granny as gypsies who had no right to a proper house. Some had been afraid of her powers too.

Sensing this, Arthur said, 'Eeh, lass, I'll just be at the top of the street. Don't you worry. What you're offering, them in this street'll be more than grateful that you thought of them first. Do you want to leave Bonnie with me?'

'No, Mammy, I want to come. You promised I would see our old house.'

'She'll be fine, ta, Arthur. It's good of you to offer, so it is.'

She didn't hear Arthur's reply as a voice shouted, 'Martha! Hey, it's me, Ted!'

The lad who had run a few errands between Trisha and herself when Trisha was nursing Bobby and couldn't come out of the house stood a good four inches taller than she remembered him.

'Hello to yourself, Ted. My, it's for being good to see you. Is it that you have left school now?'

'Aye, but I'm fed up to the teeth. This ain't your little lass, is it? By, you've grown from a nipper, lass.'

'I'm five now.'

Ted grinned. 'Well, add on ten and you'll catch me up.'

'What is it you are doing now, Ted?'

'I can't find work, Martha. It's with the season being over. If you can get set on at the start, they often keep you on doing winter repairs and painting and that, but it's a long wait till Easter. Mind, I do all right. I clean the cars of the posh lot and they give me a bob or two.'

'Sure, that's for being a good idea. But it is that I may be having some work for you whenever you haven't that to do.'

'Really? Aw, I never thought. I mean, you're a baby shop, so I didn't ask. I ain't got nowt about me that'll help to make that stuff. Me ma has, though. You should see what she knits. She made this jumper for me. She sends me to the jumble, and I get a bag full of owt that ain't sold at the end of the day that's made of wool that I can have for a penny. The organisers are usually glad to get rid of it. Then Ma unravels it, soaks the wool to straighten it and she makes loads of stuff. She's doing a bit better than when you lived here, now that me da's home.'

Martha was impressed by the grey jumper that had panels of cable each side. Something she knew took a lot of skill.

'Sure, that is good to hear. So, are you thinking she might have time to work for me? Here, have a look as I've a leaflet explaining.'

Ted read it. Not quite a man but too old to be called a boy, Ted had been brought up the hard way. The eldest of Martha didn't know how many kids. At the time she knew him, his father was away fighting in the war. Ted had been a ragged-arsed kid. But he'd always had something endearing about him and he still did, and a lovely nature too.

He was fair, with a few freckles over his nose and a cheeky grin, and his clothes – apart from his prized possession, his jumper – looked too small for him.

As he passed the leaflet back, he said, 'Me ma could do that easy. I'd say she were skilled enough to do the knitting of them things. She mostly knits in the evening, when all the nippers are settled down. Would that be all right?'

'Of course, whenever it is that she has time, only it is that sometimes we'll need garments for a certain date as they have to be posted off, so she will need to produce them on time ... But I am thinking, is it that you can ride a bike, Ted?'

'Aye, I can. I ain't ever had one of me own, but me mate's got one and I ride his sometimes.'

'Well, for sure I am thinking that if this idea takes off and I get me workers, I will have a powerful need for a lad like you to deliver and collect. And I am for having many other jobs as it is that me husband is working away and cannot be doing them all for me.'

'I'll work for you and gladly. When can I start?'

'You're altogether a nice young man, Ted. I'd be glad if it was you could come to the shop tomorrow ... And is it that you remember Trisha?'

'Aye, of course.'

'Well, she is the owner of the donkeys from the beach now and has some land too. I know it is that she will be needing helping hands with it all.'

'Aw, I'm glad I didn't go out now. I was on me way to take a walk to me mate's as I was bored, and to tell the truth, fed up with all me brothers and sisters scrapping all the time. By, it'll be grand to have a job to go to.'

'Well, let me be having a word with your mammy, and we'll see how it goes.'

Ted looked down at Bonnie. 'Do you want a piggyback? Only we live a way along the street.'

Bonnie just put her hands up to him and was soon perched on Ted's back.

'Eeh, you're a weight and a half. Ha, I could carry two of our young 'uns for the weight of you.'

Bonnie just hugged his neck and giggled. But Martha had a pang of sadness as she thought how Bonnie must be missing her pappy giving her rides like this.

When Ted took them into his home, his mother sat nursing a young baby. Several children of very near age sat around her feet. The room was scruffy, but clean, and very cold.

'Who you got here then, our Ted?'

'You remember Martha, Ma? And this is her little lass, all grown.'

'Eeh, I do. What's going on?'

Ted told his mother why Martha was here.

'You're that lass from up the road a bit, aren't you?'

'Yes, it is that I am.'

'By, you and Trisha did well for yourselves. A shop, and men who have a bit of money. I couldn't believe it when Trisha nabbed a doctor and you the councillor's son. Mind, I never had any argument with either of you and felt sorry for the pair of you at times. I knew what it was like not to have a man around when you had a nipper. Did you both marry the dads of your young 'uns, then?'

Martha was taken aback by this question.

'Ma, don't ask personal questions, it's nowt to do with you. You're embarrassing Martha.'

'Eeh, Ted, lad, I don't knaw where you come from. You're too sensitive for your own good.'

When Ted's mother laughed at this, Martha was shocked to see that she had most of her teeth missing, and what she had left were black. Her hair hung in lank greasy strands and her face looked careworn. But the baby looked clean and well wrapped up and the children, though ragamuffins, were clean too.

'What is it you are thinking about my offer, Mrs Randal?'

'Call me, Mandy, as that's me name and me and you ain't got a lot of age difference. And aye, I like it. I like it very much. I could do with the money, and I love to knit and sew. I'm a better knitter, but good at sewing the garments together.'

'I'd be powerfully happy to offer you work, Mandy. I'm thinking of a sample garment first. I'll be sending you the wool and the pattern. You will be paid, to be sure, but it is from that that me and Trisha will decide if we can offer you more work.'

'So, what you paying, then?'

'Trisha is for making seven knitted baby garments a week ...'

'Bloody hell, you ain't expecting that from me, are you? What's she got, mechanical fingers?'

'Ha, it is that it seems like it at times to be sure, but remember, she can work all day and often sits knitting in the evening. Anyway, what we are thinking is that if you can be sewing them together and perhaps knitting some too, we can be paying you four shillings a week.'

'Four shillings! For doing a bit of knitting and stitching! Eeh, ta, love . . . Ted, you go to the shop with Martha right now, lad, and get me that pattern and wool, eh? And if you've a garment ready to be sewn together, Martha, send that an' all. I'll soon show you what I can do.'

'Oh, I'm altogether pleased, so I am. We really do need help as our postal business is growing by the day.'

'I'm getting a job an' all, Ma. I'll be your collection and delivery lad. Though I need a bike.'

'To be sure, we will provide a bike, and keep it in running order, Ted. It will be the property of the shop but will be for your use for the business and for personal errands, so it will.'

'My! It's like Christmas has come early, lad. Ta, Martha, lass. And thank Trisha for me an' all. I tell you, if I have to work all night, I'll do you a lot for your money . . . Eeh, lad, I don't knaw about Christmas coming early, but when it does, we're going to have a smasher this year!'

'Aye, and we can order a few hundred weights of coal and wood an' all, Ma, and get the nippers warmed up.'

'We can, but we're to tread carefully, so as not to hurt your da's pride. He works hard on that farm for a pittance, but a man likes to feel he's providing for his family.'

'Aye, I knaw. But knowing Da, he'll be pleased his son is helping out. Not so much you, though, so we'll make it look as though most of it comes from me, eh?'

Martha had memories of her own pappy, and how he struggled to keep them fed and warm from what he earned working on the farm that used to belong to his granddaddy, till the English sacked it from him. She sighed, as still the Troubles in Ireland rumbled on and threatened to come to a head once more. But she also knew her fellow country-men had right on their side, they were fighting for what was theirs, and for justice, but to her, violence, death and destruction didn't help – her own mammy and pappy had died in vain.

'You've gone quiet, lass . . . Eeh, you ain't having one of your visions as I've heard tell about, are you?'

'No, sorry. It is that a memory came to me. I am for knowing the struggles you talk of.'

'Aye, I knaw. You had a few when you lived here, and in particular when this little lass was born. But, eeh, Bonnie by name and Bonnie by nature she is.'

Feeling afraid that Bonnie may pick up on something and come to conclusions, Martha made her excuses that they had to get on as she was hoping to get more workers. 'I'll meet you at the shop in about an hour, Ted, and be giving you all your mammy will need.'

Taking Bonnie's hand, Martha retreated out of the door.

Popping the leaflets through doors as she went back along, the air was suddenly filled with the rumbling of a train on the line on the opposite side of the road. Bonnie jumped, then clapped her hands. 'I love the trains, Mammy.'

'Aye, it was that we had a good journey to Manchester on one, wasn't it?'

'I can't wait for Johnny to come to stay at Aunty Trisha's. I liked him.'

'I know you were for getting on well and that's good, so it is.'

'Mammy? Why are Ted's family so poor?'

'A lot of folk are for being poor, me wee darling. They work hard, so they do, but their pay is low. But it is that Ted's mammy is having so many wee ones that it makes it hard for her.'

'Why don't we give the girls all of my old clothes?'

'Ah, that is for being a lovely idea, my wee one. I will be asking Ted if it is his mammy will accept them.'

'And they were cold, Mammy. I was in there too.'

'I know. But it is that we are going to give their mammy work, and you heard Ted say they are going to get coal.'

'But they need it now.'

Martha felt her conscience prick at this. She hadn't thought.

'Well, I'll be giving Ted an advance on his wages, so I will, then it will be that he can go to the coal yard and buy a barrow full. I was for spotting a barrow through the window that looked over the backyard.'

'And we can send him with all my old clothes too. They're all in bags, even my baby ones.'

'We will be doing that, I promise. Now is it that you are warm enough, wee one, as I'm nearly done and you can be running back to the cab if you like?'

'No. I'll stay with you, Mammy.'

'Sure, this is the house that Trisha lived in, and there, next door, is where Mammy lived.'

'Did Da live with you, Mammy?'

Martha caught her breath, unsure what to say as she'd never been in a situation where she had to directly lie to Bonnie and didn't want to.

At that moment, Mrs Higginbottom, the nasty-minded woman who had been Martha's neighbour, came out of her door. 'I thought it were you. Slumming it, are you? We ain't seen sight of you for years down here and we don't want you back, ta very much.'

Bonnie clung to Martha's coat.

'You may have risen, but at the heart of it you're nowt but a gypsy. And we don't forget . . . Is this the bastard that you had when you lived here, then? Eeh, she'll grow to be another charlatan, no doubt, taking folk's money for a pack of made-up lies. Passed her off as belonging to the councillor's son you nabbed, have you? Eeh, she's gypsy through and through.'

Martha tried to hurry away, but Mrs Higginbottom shouted after her, 'Aye, go on, and take your bastard with you. And don't come back!'

Martha didn't stop to put any more leaflets through doors but grabbed Bonnie in her arms and ran with her to Arthur's cab.

Arthur stood leaning on the door. 'What was all that about, lass? Eeh, you're shaking. I'll give that woman a piece of me mind!'

'No! Sure it is, I just want to get away from here, please, Arthur.'

'All right, lass. But you don't have to take that sort of abuse . . . Come on, Bonnie, let me lift you up, lass.'

169

Once seated, Martha hugged the sobbing Bonnie.

'Mammy ... what's a bastard?'

'Don't be saying that word, Bonnie. It is a naughty word, so it is, and only used by wicked people like that woman.'

'Am I one? Is that what a gypsy is?'

'No, you are for knowing what a gypsy is. Aunty Cilla is a gypsy and you love her. And yes, it is that we are descended from gypsies, you are knowing that.'

'But that lady said it as if it was a bad thing to be.'

'She is for being bigoted, me wee darling, take no notice. The gypsies are for being lovely and talented. It is them who make the lovely baskets and baby cradles we sell in the shop. Now, dry your eyes, me wee darling. And be for forgetting her. She's not being worthy of you thinking about her.'

'Why did you live there, Mammy? Couldn't Da afford our house then?'

'It was only for a wee while. Now forget all about it, I shouldn't have been for taking you there.'

Bonnie sat with her head on Martha's lap. Martha could see her eyes closing as the rhythm of the horse's trot rocked her gently. Her body shook every now and again with rebound sobs, tugging painfully at Martha's heart as she gently brushed a damp curl from Bonnie's forehead. Love for her daughter flowed through her, making her determined to protect her wee child from any harm – but hadn't that confrontation harmed her? *And all I did was run!*

The reason was her fear of Bonnie finding out the truth.

As if he'd read her thoughts, Arthur said, 'Sometimes the truth is very painful, lass, but hiding from it can mean it catches up with you and bites you when you're least expecting it.'

This stunned Martha for a moment, but then she remembered that Arthur was a first-generation gypsy himself and men often had the gift too.

'I am knowing this, Arthur, but it is a choice we made, Joshua and I.'

'It's a mystery to me who fathered your babby, lass, but it ain't none of me business either. It is talked of, though – gossiped about, as naw one knaws. So be prepared for someone saying sommat to Bonnie one of these days – sommat that would be better coming from you.'

'Ta, Arthur, I am for realising that now. I am hoping for her to be older and understanding more, but to be sure, every day I am regretting that decision. Sally is for knowing the truth of her birth and isn't affected by it. She still looks on Walter as her da and is for being happy, but it is that we have left it too late, and yet, it is too early. Am I for making sense?'

'You are, lass, but if I was you, I would do it soon, as the little lass will quickly get over it.'

Martha sighed. She just didn't know; it was all so complicated. Peter was still alive, not dead, like Ralph. And that did make a difference.

'Will you be taking me back to the shop, Arthur? I've to meet Ted, and then I will need to be getting home. I've a powerful need to be with Trisha and am hoping it is that she is home.'

'Aye. It was a good day when you landed next to Trisha, lass. You've been a help to each other.'

'And it is that you have been a help to us both, too, for you've always supported us.'

'Well, I promised your gran I would, love, and I like doing it.'

'Me granny! I wasn't for knowing.'

'Aye. She used to say she wasn't long for this world but I didn't expect to be there when her end came.'

Martha shuddered remembering her granny running out into the road when a tram suddenly appeared that they wanted to catch. Brushing the memory from her, she was glad to see they were on the promenade now and she could watch the sea as they travelled the last few hundred yards to the shop.

Ted was there waiting.

'Leave the young 'un where she is, Martha. I'll keep me eye on her.'

'To be sure, it is good that you are. Ta, Arthur.'

Ted stood flapping his arms around himself to keep warm. This reminded Martha of the promise made to Bonnie.

'I'll be hurrying to get the wool and pattern, Ted, but get yourself inside, it is for being warmer in there as the stove is never for going out.'

'Ta, Martha.'

'And it is that I am going to give you an advance on your wages too. I am wanting you to go to the coal yard before they close, and get yourself a barrowful of coal.'

'Eeh, Martha. Ta, I've been worrying about the little ones. They have it hard, you knaw. It were never so bad for me, as I were the only one for a while, and even when a couple more came along me ma and da coped with everything.'

Rustling through her purse, Martha found she had five shillings. 'Take that, Ted.'

'By, that's a fortune, lass . . . I mean, ta, Martha. I'll work me socks off to pay you back.'

'We'll be stopping a small amount every week from your wages, Ted, so you are not to be worrying about it.'

'I'll get a load of groceries an' all with this lot. And a jug of ale for me da, he deserves it. He's a good da, you knaw. He says it's Ma's fault, he only has to jump in bed with her and she's got her belly up.'

This shocked and embarrassed Martha, but she didn't want to show it so hurried towards the workroom.

She wasn't gone many minutes before she came back again. 'There you are. Now, it is that I was thinking to have you come around to me house, but you are having a lot to do and will need to be getting a move on before everywhere closes.'

'What're you wanting me to do at the house, then? If it's important, I can come after me shopping. I can borrow me mate's bike.'

'It is that I have a few bags of children's clothes for the wee ones. Will your mammy be accepting them?'

'She will and will be grateful. Eeh, Martha, you're like an angel. Where is your house? I'll come as quick as I can.'

As Martha travelled home, she had mixed emotions assailing her. But the one that was helping her was the feeling that in Ted, she was going to have a real helping hand, and this is what she wanted more than anything – and one who could make her laugh, because now she was out of his presence she wanted to howl out loud about what he'd said about his da.

Somehow, she knew that everything was going to get easier from now on. But she knew she had to do something about Bonnie knowing the truth and she just didn't want to.

THIRTEEN

Trisha

'Eeh, lad, let me see what your ma has done then?'

Here it was Friday, only two days after sending Mandy the wool and a garment to stitch, and she had returned both with Ted.

Ted unwrapped the tissue paper carefully. 'Ma kept the paper from what Martha sent her, clothes and stuff. Some of the frocks were wrapped in it.'

'Well, I've got stuff an' all, Ted, that might be useful to your ma. I got it ready for the jumble recently, not thinking your ma might need it. Only I'll have to sort it out another time. We're having some friends come to stay tonight.'

'Ma'd be grateful for owt. Me da were all right with it an' all. And he were all right about me bringing some money home. Me and Ma did wonder if he'd feel a bit off with it, but he's been encouraging Ma on. He told her we might get a chance of renting a bigger house if we're careful with what we do with the extra money me and her can bring in.'

'You will, lad. I shouldn't wonder, we'll do all we can to help ... My, these are perfect. Look at these, Betty, lass. Mandy Randal from the other end of Enfield Road made this and stitched this babby coat together. By, they're grand!'

Betty couldn't believe it. 'Who would have thought, eh? You should be proud of your ma, Ted, that's lovely work.'

'I am. She's the best. I knaw our house is a bit scruffy, and the kids run around ragged-arsed, but Ma's got a heart of gold and would do owt for us. I was telling Martha how talented she is.'

'Well, you were right to blow her trumpet.'

'He is, Betty. I think we who live and lived in that street owe her an apology as we haven't thought good of her. I remember making a remark to you, Ted, and when I did, you stuck up for her. Well, I said I was sorry at the time, but I'm doubly so now.'

'Naw worries, Trisha, I'm used to it. Folk judge you without knawing you. That's the way of it.'

Trisha felt ashamed. She hadn't tried to get to know or to befriend Mandy and she felt sorry about that too, now.

Martha came in from the workroom. 'I heard you all ... Oh, that is for being beautiful. And it is that Mandy made it? Well, Ted, your mammy has got herself a job. I'll be getting a couple more ready for her to knit and sew, but will let her be setting the pace of how many she can do. Though I will be pinning the date needed onto the pattern, so I will.'

'Ta, Martha, and ta for them clothes and shoes you sent. They fitted Amy and Susie. It's just a pity you ain't had any lads, as our Alf's arse is hanging out, and Eddy's toes stick out the end of his shoes, not to mention Fred, Bill, Joe and Pete. They all need stuff. And the bigger girls, Lucy, Phyllis and Daisy.'

'It's sorry we are, we both would have loved a son too. Is that not right, Trish?'

'Aye, it is.'

'Mind, our Daisy's talented an' all, you knaw. She got some frocks from the last jumble and has cut them down, but she can only sew by hand, she ain't got a machine like you've got. She's done a good job, though, of making herself a couple of nice frocks. She's going to try to make Lucy and Phyllis one each an' all.'

'How old is she, Ted?' Trisha asked.

'She's coming on thirteen. Me granny taught her. Me granny could make owt, but she died. I didn't think any of us would pick up after that, but we have. Granny had a machine, but Ma sold it to put towards Granny's funeral. We didn't want her to have a pauper's funeral, so we sold a lot of her nice things. Not her clothes, though. Ma's made many a shirt and pinny for the girls out of them.'

Trisha looked at Martha. 'What age can lasses work, lass? Have you any idea? I mean officially, like an apprenticeship?'

'I am not for knowing. In Ireland it is that they can work full time at fourteen years, but I am thinking many get after-school jobs before that. Maybe it is that we would be allowed to give Daisy some work, but not machine work.'

'But she could come here, maybe on a Saturday once she's thirteen. I had a Saturday job when I was thirteen. What do you think, Ted?'

'She'd be made up, even if it were cleaning your lav. She's a good worker, Daisy, with a good head on her shoulders. But there ain't never been anyone who'd give her a chance. That's why she made herself them frocks so she could look decent when she went around asking for a job.'

Trisha loved the sound of Daisy. She could just remember some of the girls, but not which one Daisy was. To her, at the time, they had just been kids from the large scruffy family down the road, and like most was wary of them, hearing tales that they'd stolen a purse from an old lady, and regularly lifted stuff from Mrs Philpot, the local shopkeeper. Now, she couldn't think why she hadn't offered any help to them as they were the actions of cold and hungry kids!

Shame washed over her, until she thought about the troubles she had of her own at the time and how they left her little time for helping others. The most she did was knit socks for the soldiers fighting in the war.

'Well, you tell her to come and see us tomorrow. At least Martha, as I'll be settling me guests in. Is that all right, Martha?'

'Yes, I'd be pleased to see her, and to be finding her a job. There's a pile of new garments that are wanting pressing and bagging. And it is that I am to get you on parcelling garments today, Ted. But first it is that you can put the kettle on as I'm of a mind you'd like a hot drink. Your nose is still a powerful red colour, so it is.'

'Just call me Rudolf!'

This made them all laugh.

'By, I am cold an' all. But if you've any deliveries, I'll be doing them first.'

'No, only to your own ma, lad, and you said she can't work on them till evening time, so there's naw rush. Get a hot cuppa down you, and make us all one an' all . . . You do knaw how to make tea, I take it?'

'Naw. Me ma could never afford tea. I've had stinging nettle tea. A gypsy told me ma how to make that. She called around the houses selling pegs and asked for a cup of tea but ended up giving the recipe to Ma when she heard Ma couldn't afford it . . . Mind, I can make a good cocoa, we allus have cocoa.'

Once again, Trisha felt sad that she hadn't known or even tried to find out the lad's plight, but then, affording tea used to be rare for her too. 'I'll show you. But you need to learn fast as we like our tea, don't we, girls?'

When they were in the kitchen, Trisha told him, 'At least you didn't say it was women's work, Ted. I bet your da would.'

'You don't knaw us, Trisha. Naw one does in that road. They accused us of all sorts that we didn't do. They said we stole stuff, but we didn't. I knaw who did, but naw one would have listened to me . . . I bet you never heard of us being caught red-handed, eh? Naw! So how come it were all put down to us, then?'

Trisha could have bitten her tongue off. When did she let herself get that she thought she could say just what she wanted? She had to turn this around. 'Eeh, lad. We've all done you an injustice, but what I said just now, I was only going on me own da. He were one for thinking that certain things were me ma's domain and certain things his and he never did hers and never expected her to do his. Anyroad, making a pot of tea, or whatever we had, came under Ma's work . . . I weren't meaning to offend you, love.'

'I'm sorry. I find most do make assumptions so I'm allus ready for them. I shouldn't have snapped, but aye, me da is like that an' all. He's surprised me and me ma by being all right with her working and earning . . . Mind, if she wanted to drive a tractor, I don't think he'd be keen.'

Trisha laughed and the moment passed.

'Do you remember much about the war, Ted?'

'Aye, I remember me da were away and we were scared we'd lose him. We went on our knees every night as a family to pray for him to be safe. And I remember your Bobby coming home and how the street hailed him a hero – they didn't do that for me da.'

Trisha let this go, her mind was in a turmoil of what Ted's and his family's life must have been like and she only lived along the street from them and hadn't seen it – or bothered to look. But she'd make it up to them now if it was the last thing she did.

'I was thinking, your da being a farmer, and him going, lasses would have done his job. They were called Land Girls.'

'We learned about them at school – hey up, kettle's blowing its top!'

Trisha had never been so glad for a kettle to boil. She talked Ted through warming the pot and watched him do that, and then carefully spoon in three scoops of tea leaves and pour the water onto them.

'Grand! A good job. Now, we've put the milk in the mugs and the sugar for them as wants it, so I'll leave you to

judge when it's brewed and to pour and bring it through ...
Don't forget the strainer, though ... Now, I'll just get a
brown paper bag and put some tea leaves into it and you
can take it home for your ma and da to have a treat.'

'Eeh, ta, Trisha. You're a good lass.'

Trisha laughed at him. 'Cheeky!'

His grin told her he didn't hold a grudge, but still Trisha
meant to put everything right and make sure he and his
family were cared for from now on.

When it came to one o'clock, Trisha didn't feel at all
guilty at leaving Martha. She had Betty in the shop and
Ted busy parcelling up the orders, so was well covered.
What a good feeling that was, and how free it made her
feel. For the first time, she felt certain they had made the
right decision in getting staff in. And if Daisy proved
useful too, it might be all they need. They would have to
see how it went.

At Martha's house she found Sheila asleep in the chair,
looking even more pale than normal, and was confronted
by Bonnie. 'Am I glad you've come up, Aunty Trisha! Sally's
been driving me mad dancing, showing me steps she
learned. She just seems to want to do that all the time and
not play with me.'

'Aw, Sally, that's not fair.'

'Well, Leonard said I was to practise every day, that he
wanted those steps perfect when I went next week.'

'Mr Plant to you.'

'No, Ma, he said I was to call him Leonard.'

'Eeh, what's it coming to? Though I suppose those arty types carry on like that. Well, just him. You have to show respect for all other adults.'

'Well, there's Pansy, his wife. She plays the piano, and all the pupils call her Pansy.'

'Oh? Well, just them two and that's it. Has Grandma Sheila been asleep long?'

'No, she just keeps nodding off and then waking as if something has frightened her. But she doesn't stay awake long . . . Is Grandma Sheila poorly?'

'Naw, Bonnie, love . . . Well, a bit. She has a bad chest, but she's all right.'

Trisha went over to the sleeping Sheila and touched her arm. 'Sheila, Sheila, love.'

Sheila jumped and looked for a moment as if she had no recollection of where she was or who Trisha was.

'Are you all right, lass? It's Trisha. I've come to take the girls so you can go home now.'

Sheila blinked, then yawned. 'Sorry, love. Eeh, it's cold in here. Have you just got back?'

'Aye. By, you've let the fire out, love. I'll just get it going again. Are you off straight home now that I'm here?'

'Naw, George is coming for me at teatime, he don't like me driving now. I miss it, though. I was so independent and could take meself off anywhere. I worry an' all how you girls are going to manage when the children are back at school as I won't be able to fetch them for you any more.'

'Don't worry.' Trisha was on her knees, twisting the sheets of a newspaper she'd found in the basket next to the hearth and laying them in the fire basket. She had to hurry

182

as the heat still in the embers was scorching the paper and reducing it.

Chucking a handful of kindling on, she struck a match to it all. Once she had the small nuggets of coal placed, she held a double sheet of newspaper over the opening of the fire to cause a draught under it to help the fire take hold.

'We'll sort sommat. We're getting things a bit easier at the shop now so there's allus one of us who can leave it.'

'That's a relief. I have been worrying, lass. Though George said he'll allus pick them up if he has time and bring me here with them, if you're stuck.'

'That's good to knaw . . . There, that's the fire going now.' Trisha turned and looked at Sheila and it struck her just how frail she was. 'Eeh, lass, this is too much for you. We won't ask you again, eh?'

'But I like to see them, lass. I – I don't think I would if I didn't care for them for you.'

This shocked Trisha. Why did she think that? But then, she thought, Sheila and George weren't frequent visitors. Martha had said she hardly ever saw them.

'I knaw you'd be welcome anytime, Sheila. Martha's said as much and has wondered why you don't come unless asked.'

'Well . . . it's just that . . . We, well, we ain't the real grand-parents and we didn't want to seem as though we were butting in . . . I mean, especially with how things are with Josh. We didn't want him thinking he was letting us down by not giving us grandchildren and we were using Bonnie as a substitute.'

Trisha swivelled around, afraid of Bonnie picking up on this, but she and Sally were chatting away oblivious.

'Just be careful what you say, lass.' She nodded in Bonnie's direction. 'Anyroad, I don't think it's a bit like that, and if I was you, when Josh comes home you should have a talk with him. I'm sure he'll put your mind at rest ... Now, what time is George coming?'

'He told me to give him a ring if I wanted him any earlier. Are you taking Bonnie with you?'

'Aye, I thought I would as they keep each other happy.'

'Would you phone for me then, love? Tell George to come anytime as I'm quite happy here if he's busy.'

'Are you sure? Only I can't stay, I've to get everything ready for Walter bringing Jenny and the boys.'

Sheila sighed. 'You're taking a lot on there, lass. Who is this Jenny and how come you've been asked? Me and George are mystified.'

'It's not for me to tell you. You speak to Martha. I'm sure she'd have told you if you came to see her more. She's lonely, you knaw.'

'I knaw. I almost don't want to share her pain as it makes me own worse, but I will from now on, I promise. I knaw she can't come to me with being busy and having no transport. Anyroad, I don't need to knaw, but I do get curious. It ain't like every day someone turns up and asks you to have their kids, is it?'

'Naw, you're right there. But for me and Martha, how we're fixed, it's a blessing, and yet it's going to be really hard work. And that's why we're trying to sort the shop out. We're hoping that we can take it in turns to work at home ourselves as the boys will need us here. But we've other ideas an' all. One is to make a workroom in the flat upstairs and make it nice and homely up there for the boys to be with us in the day. We're plotting and planning all day about this and the other. We'll make it work, you'll see.'

'You're a good pair of girls, I knaw that much. Aye, like me, you're mismatched to your menfolk in a lot of ways, but you've got spirit, I'll give you that.'

Trisha had never thought of Sheila being mismatched to George, but then, he was a successful businessman, having the biggest estate agency in Blackpool, and did speak posh, even though he let out the odd Lancastrian word. Then to top all of that, he did serve on the council, so yes, she supposed, like her, Sheila was out of her depth at times.

'Right, where's George's number, Sheila? Only I've to get going.'

Trisha still felt afraid of the telephone. She'd never got used to it, and avoided it if she could. She didn't trust the thing, nor the operators, feeling sure they listened in. Then there was the flipping crossed lines when you could find yourself listening to some posh bod – always posh, as the poor never had telephones. They'd ask who you were and tell you to get off the line as if they had a divine right to it!

'It's in the book next to the phone in the front porch, love. Ta for doing that for me . . . Eeh, that fire's going nicely now, and I'm as cosy as toast, so tell him he needn't hurry.'

Trisha suspected Sheila would go back to sleep the moment she left her and decided she'd pop back in an hour to see if she'd gone or was all right.

Once she got into her own home, she felt the chill of that too. 'Right, me lasses. I have to get all our fires on the go now. We'll need a warm house for Aunty Jenny and the boys arriving.'

'Ooh, we can't wait, can we, Sally?'

'Naw, it'll be grand.'

'Sally, you're to say "no" and that it will be "lovely", not "grand"!'

Trisha smiled to herself as Bonnie took the words from her mouth, but was pleased to see that Sally didn't retaliate, she just sighed, which made Trisha want to tell her to just be herself and be damned, but she knew that would undermine all the school had done, so kept quiet.

'It's all right really, Sally, if you just want to say it that way with me. I don't mind.'

Sally grinned at Bonnie. 'I do try, but me words just come out.'

Trisha laughed out loud and the both of them joined her. The tension eased. 'Come on then, coats and hats and boots into the hall cupboard while I put a match to the fires. I have them all laid out.'

This took just a few minutes as she'd laid fires in every room. But as she went around, it did give her the chance to check all was as she wanted it to be. It was, apart from getting Walter to move the cot into the spare room later, so that Joseph could be with Jenny in the guest room.

The boys' room had been completed, with two beds for the time when Joseph would need to move into there. This meant Walter no longer had an office and had everything he'd had in there moved to his flat in Manchester – a move Trisha had hated as it had felt so final.

★   ★   ★

When at last they arrived, they were all there to greet them and everything was ready. Trisha had cooked tea the moment she'd come in, making sausage and mash, the kids' favourite, and Walter's too – although he may have just said that to make her feel better about the limited dishes she could cook, all of them being what she was used to having on a much smaller budget to what she had now. He had asked once if they could have duck, but she hadn't a clue how to cook it, so had got him a nice pork chop instead.

It was times like that she felt most out of her depth and was determined to buy a cookery book one day to learn some different dishes.

All this was forgotten when she was in his arms. He held her tightly and kissed her cheek. When he let her go, he told her he'd missed his girls and then lifted Sally into the air and made her giggly. When he lowered her, she clung on to his neck.

'I'm afraid I've been claimed, Martha, so cannot greet you and Bonnie properly, but how are you?'

'Tired, but it is that is how it is at the moment. Otherwise all right, but altogether pleased to be seeing you all here safely. Jenny, let me be giving you a hug.'

Trisha was shocked at how Jenny looked much worse than she had the week before and read in Martha's expression that she was concerned too.

Everyone hugged Jenny, and Trisha and Martha did Johnny, too, but the girls, with Sally now down and by his side, just told him to come with them and they would show him where he was to sleep.

Sally showed great perception by saying, 'But if you like, you can sleep in my room. You can have Bonnie's bed, and then you won't be on your own.'

'Ta. I might, but Mam said I can get into her bed with her, then we'll all be together.'

Trisha hadn't thought that Johnny may be afraid on his own in a strange house, but could see now that of course he would be. 'Aye, that's a good idea, lad. But it's all up to you and your ma. There's naw rules here.'

Johnny gave her a lovely smile. She just wanted to hug him, but didn't want to overwhelm him.

'So, where's little Joseph, then?'

'He's still asleep on the back seat of the car, darling. He's quite safe, and I wanted to get Jenny in first so you can get her warm and comfortable. I'll go and get him now.'

'Aye, that were a good idea . . . Well, lass, do you need the lav, first?'

'I do, love, ta.'

'We have one in the yard, but two upstairs. One in the bathroom you will have to yourself, and one that leads off our bedroom. This way.'

As she followed Jenny up the stairs, Trisha felt afraid she wouldn't make it, so kept close to her to provide support if she needed it. By the time they arrived at the guest bedroom, Jenny was exhausted.

'I can help you if you like, lass. I mean, I don't wish to embarrass you or owt, but I have done some nursing. Me ma. I nursed her for months.'

'I'd be grateful, love, ta.'

When Jenny was comfortable, Trish asked, 'Would you

like to get into bed, eh? I can bring you a tray up. It's nice and warm in there for you.'

'Oh, Trish, I would. I don't reckon I could tackle them stairs again.'

'Come on then.'

The children were on the landing. Johnny was wriggling about, obviously wanting the loo. 'Eeh, me lasses, you should have taken Johnny to the lav in my bathroom. In you go, lad. Sally, show Johnny where his ma will be after, there's a good lass. Aunty Jenny's going to stay up now and get into her bed.'

'Are you very tired, Aunty Jenny?'

'I am, Bonnie.'

'Can I come and help you? I'm very good at folding clothes.'

'I'd love that. Ta, Bonnie.'

'And I'll bring Johnny to you, Aunty Jenny.'

'Well, I'm going to have a lovely time with two little helpers like you to care for me. Ta, Sally.'

'Sally, run down and tell Aunty Martha and Da what's happening. Tell Aunty Martha she can dish the tea up in about five minutes and Da to bring Jenny's bag up and leave it outside the door . . . Come on, Bonnie, lass, you're going to be a big help.'

Johnny appeared out of the bathroom. 'I'll come, Sally.'

To Trisha, he looked afraid, and her heart went out to him. He must spend a lot of time feeling unsure. His little world had changed so much since his brother had arrived.

And it was set to change even more. How would he cope? She'd have to make sure she helped him all she could.

FOURTEEN

Martha

When Trisha came down the stairs, she shook her head. 'Eeh, Walter, would you have a look at Jenny? She ain't looking right to me.'

'Of course, but I can't treat her, I have nothing with me to do that. But I can see if it warrants us calling the doctor, or an ambulance.'

'Ta, love ... I don't like it at all. Jenny's a funny colour ... Aw, Martha, look at little Joseph. He's as happy as Larry, kicking away there in the pram. Mind, he's getting a bit big for it. Have you still got that baby carriage?'

'Yes, it is that's it's in the attic. We're going to need to get it down soon, so we are.'

'I'm glad you didn't get rid of everything you had for Bonnie. Mine, but for the cot, had all gone long before me and Walter married, but then I knew I weren't going to have any more.'

Martha felt the pain of this. She knew Trisha didn't mean to hurt her, though, so let it go. 'He's adorable, and it's a shame so it is that Jenny has become ill. To be sure, we were looking forward to her coming to stay.'

'Aye, but maybe she's just tired after the journey. And she's like us, missing her man.'

'Ah, it is so. It's for being a pain that's like a brick has lodged in your heart. I am for knowing how she feels not to have any communication.'

'I reckon from what she was telling me while I helped her to undress that Peter's a little better. It was like she said before, once he'd asked if he should knaw someone, he made great strides. Apparently, he's also asked if he should knaw two children called Johnny and Joseph.'

'Oh? Maybe it's a good sign, for it was said that happened about me. But we will have a powerful dilemma on our hands if it is he does get better, as for sure he'll want the boys, and we'll not be knowing if he is capable?'

'Aye, that worried me, but we won't be able to deny him his right. Maybe someone in authority will have a say on the children's welfare as it would scare me to put them back into his care.'

'It would me too. Just look how it is that Peter can suddenly not be knowing who he is or where it is he was coming from.'

'Well, it might be that we're meeting trouble afore it's even travelling towards us, so we'll have to wait and see. Now, shall we get the kids and us fed, lass? Me belly thinks me throat's been cut.'

'Ha, Trish, your sayings will always be for keeping us going, so they will. It's all ready in the oven. Call the wee ones and at least we can be giving them theirs.'

'Aye, and then we'd better see if little Joseph needs his bottom changing once the kids are eating. He's had a long journey an' all.'

As Martha worked, she wondered if she could tend to Joseph. If she could stand the longing he'd already awoken inside her.

The telephone ringing made her jump. She heard heavy footsteps coming down the stairs and guessed it would be Walter. The phone went quiet, then she filled with joy as she heard, 'Josh, my boy, where are you? Yes, Martha is here. She's having dinner with us tonight. Look, can you ring back? It's vital I make a call. I'll explain all. Righto, speak shortly.'

Martha ran into the hall. Walter put his finger up to silence her and sombrely dialled a number. The joy Martha had felt died as her worry for Jenny increased. But mixed with that was an underlying excitement. Josh was in England. But where?

'Bonnie has more gravy than me, Aunty Martha, and I like gravy with onions in.'

'Oh, sorry, me wee one. For sure, it is that I was distracted. Here, you be having what you like. Tell me when it is I should stop pouring.'

'Now! Ta, Aunty Martha. It was all right, really.'

Martha ruffled Sally's hair while trying to listen if Walter was still talking. He was. *Oh, Jesus, Mary and Joseph, let Jenny be for being all right, and be getting me Josh back on the phone!*

'I like onion gravy, Aunty Martha.'

'Well, it is that you're a growing lad, so you are, Johnny. There you go, man.'

'I ain't a man, you know.'

'Oh, it is for being a term we are using in Ireland.'

'I will be one day. Like me dad . . . Me dad ain't well, you know.'

'I am knowing, love. Eat your tea while it's still for being warm.'

Martha paced up and down doing nothing in particular. She put the dishes, one containing the mash and the other sausages swimming in gravy, back into the oven, then asked the children if they wanted bread and butter with their meal and straightened one of the chairs, her nerves making her fidgety.

When she heard the ding of the phone going down, she rushed to the door leading to the hall. Walter looked grave, stopping her from asking about Josh. Instead she asked, 'How was it you found Jenny to be?'

'Not well. Not well at all. She doesn't want to go to hospital, and has medication with her, which she is late taking. I have called the doctor and how we go forward will be his decision, but I feel very worried.'

'We can be taking care of her. Both Trisha and I have been freeing up our time, so it is that we are ready for this week. Maybe it is that Jenny will be picking up once she is over the journey and getting ready to come here.'

'You're right. She could . . . Oh, that was Josh, by the way – the phone call that came through. He's in Liverpool, just docked, and as he has his car there, he will be coming straight home. He said he will stop if he sees a telephone box and give you a ring again . . . I'm so sorry, I just felt it urgent that I get a doctor to Jenny.'

'Oh, Walter, you could not be giving me better news.' She clasped her hands in front of her breast as excitement zinged through her.

'I know, dear, it is hard on both you and Trisha. You are sacrificing a lot so that your men can follow the paths they were meant to.'

Martha looked at Walter, then shuddered as a vision came to her.

'Are you all right, dear?'

'Yes, it is that I know the strain you are under. Leading two lives is for taking its toll on you, Walter.'

'I – I don't know what you mean! I – I, well, yes, it isn't pleasant for us men to be away from our wives and families, but sometimes it's a must ... Excuse me. I need to go and wash for dinner.'

Martha could have kicked herself. Why did she say what she'd seen? But then, she hadn't, for there was far more in her vision and she trembled at the thought of the rebound from it all. She wanted to save Trisha from the pain and save Walter the heartache he would go through due to the decision he would make. But she couldn't. She looked heavenward. *Holy Mary, why me? Why is it I am cursed with this gift? It is not and never was a gift to me, but a cross I am for having to bear.* And yet, she remembered that when she worked on the prom as a fortune teller, there were many times she saw good things for her clients. Those times were nice to remember.

They'd eaten their dinner and were sitting with Jenny by the time the doctor came. Trisha had tried to feed Jenny a little dinner, but she hadn't managed it, and in the end

Walter had suggested just giving her water. She'd taken this gladly and managed to tell them how to make a bottle up for Joseph.

But when it came to changing Joseph's nappy – not something they'd ever done for a boy – the mood lightened as they tried to master folding it, which had to be done differently for him than it was for the girls. They giggled at how he liked the fuss but then showed his appreciation by peeing in their faces as if he'd suddenly become a fountain. He was delighted with this and their reaction, and laughed a belly laugh, showing his bottom two teeth and how his top two had just broken through.

Even Jenny managed a giggle at this. 'I forgot to tell you about that happening, never lean over him when changing his nappy, girls.'

But then the giggling turned sombre as she said, 'How am I to bear leaving him and Johnny?'

Walter went to her side and took her hand. 'It will be different when it happens, my dear. You will be ready, I promise you. You are the most courageous young woman I have ever had the privilege to know. And you won't leave them, you will be by their side for ever and we will make sure we keep your memory alive for them, we promise.'

Martha, moved beyond words, swallowed the lump in her throat and went to Jenny's side. Walter moved away a little for her.

'It is that we are Catholics – we don't go to mass often, but for sure, when we are needing help and comfort we are for finding it by talking with a priest. Would this be something you would be liking, Jenny, love?'

'Yes, ta, Martha. I think I were christened a Catholic. But Mam didn't hold with it all, so I ain't ever been to church and Peter was never for religion. I – I ain't had me boys christened even, but that's been bothering me. I'd like to see that done now … It's funny, but since this happened to me, I've thought a lot about God and tried to talk to him to ask for help, and I have felt differently about things.'

'That's for being good. Tomorrow we will go along and see the priest for you.'

Martha took Jenny's hand and closed her eyes. 'Jenny, don't be for being afraid. I see a beautiful garden, the sun is shining, and sure there is a gentleman waiting with his arms outstretched. It is that he has a great love for you.'

'My dad! Oh, Martha, ask him if he is my dad.'

Martha didn't have to ask, she knew. 'It is.'

'Peter told me you were a fortune teller, Martha, and that you weren't happy seeing into the future, but you have helped me. Thank you.'

Martha felt the tears pricking her eyes. Suddenly she knew that the gift she'd never liked could be of help and had been many times. It was coping with the bad things that the future shared with her that she hated, and not being able to change them, not even when she knew they would break her dear friend Trisha's heart.

Bonnie coming up the stairs, with Johnny and Sally following her, calling out, 'Mammy, the doctor is here, I let him in,' took the moment away and gave Martha a welcome distraction. 'You're for being a wee good girl, Bonnie. Now, downstairs, all of you, and let's be leaving the doctor to make Johnny's mammy better, shall we? Sure, it is the long journey that's for making her poorly.'

As they went out of the room, Johnny said, 'Me mam's going to die. But I don't know what that is, Aunty Martha.'

Martha's heart filled with tears at this, but something compelled her to be as honest as it seemed Jenny had been with Johnny. 'It is for meaning she will go to heaven and live in happiness, while watching over you, my wee one.'

'What's heaven? I don't want her to go. Dad went somewhere. Will he come back to look after me and Joseph?'

Martha thought she would break, her emotions were so fragile, but she had to be strong for this little boy facing so much upheaval and sadness in his life.

She wanted to be honest but couldn't be. The truth was so brutal. So unfair.

'I'm sure it is that everything will be all right. You're not to be worrying, for none of us know what it is that will happen tomorrow.

Martha raised her eyes heavenwards. *If only it was that I didn't know, but my heart is burdened with all the troubles about to descend on us all. Even knowing me beloved Josh is on his way home to me is not lifting me spirits.*

Downstairs Martha decided that she would sit and read to the children and asked Sally to fetch her favourite book.

Sally came down with *Doctor Dolittle*. 'I don't know if it's my favourite, as I haven't read it yet, but Grandma Beth and Granddad Cyril sent it for my birthday.'

'Well, it will do nicely as I am hearing it talked about as a very good book. Now, there is only one position for children to hear a story. I am wanting you all to be sitting crossed-legged on the rug around me as I sit on the chair.'

They giggled excitedly at this and Martha began to feel a little relief. When she began the story they didn't seem so sure at the first paragraph of how children and animals followed the doctor wherever he went, but as she read about the animals Doctor Dolittle had in his house and garden, they giggled, and more especially at Dab-Dab the duck, Gub-Gub the baby pig, Jip the dog and Too-Too the owl.

'I'd like to have all of those animals. I love animals, and Dad said he'd get me a dog when I'm five.'

'Well, we will have to be seeing what we can do, Johnny, but what is it you are thinking of donkeys?'

'I know they go hee-haw, hee-haw.'

This had them in fits and Johnny in awe when he heard he could have a ride on the donkeys the next day and how his Aunty Trisha owned them. He was so delighted he clapped his hands. Martha felt better, thinking that when the time came, the donkeys would help him to settle.

The jollier atmosphere lifted even more when Martha read out to them that one day an old lady with rheumatism came to see the doctor and sat on a hedgehog sleeping on the sofa. This had them falling backwards as they howled with laughter. Martha laughed with them and sent a silent prayer of thanks up to the author, Hugh Lofting, for having such a wonderful imagination as she had to admit, she was enjoying the book as much as the children were.

They were so immersed in the story that they groaned when Walter came down with the doctor and interrupted her reading, though Bonnie and Sally did stand, as they had been taught to do at school, when someone of importance came into the room.

'Now, children, I know it is that you want to hear more, but it is important that you are being polite. Off you go to Sally's room, and if you are good and are being very quiet, it is that I will read more later.'

'Sorry, Mammy. Sorry, Doctor. Only we were enjoying our story.'

'That's good to hear. I think all children should be encouraged to read and there's no better way than to start listening to a story at your mama's knee. I remember doing so so well.'

The doctor ruffled the hair of all three as they passed by him.

Martha felt mortified that Bonnie had sounded as though she was ticking the doctor off with qualifying her apology in such a way!

'Martha, Bonnie has an old head on her shoulders, and is full of courage . . . I know, it must sometimes make you feel like cutting her tongue out as she is so outspoken and direct with her honesty. But she will learn to curb that as she gets older, and under your guidance. Just be glad she has the strength to know her convictions and will be true to them. That quality may stand her in good stead in the future.'

This wiped out Martha's shame and made her swell with pride. For herself, she had understood that the confidence Bonnie had made her say what she thought and that, being only five, she hadn't yet learned that could be rude or hurtful. But it was just so good to hear someone else express that they understood too, as she knew Bonnie never meant to be any of those things, she was just stating facts as she saw them … She also knew that what the doctor had said was true, her daughter was destined to do courageous acts, but didn't want to think about it or have more than that revealed to her.

'Well, now. I am not overly worried about your friend, though Walter, you did right in bringing me in. She needs rest and no stress. The journey did cause her stress, as undertaking any time away from home, even if we are looking forward to it, can. And her story is harrowing, and in a way, it must seem that the future she has mapped out for her children is more real to her with her being here.'

'Oh, is it that we have done wrong in bringing her here for a break?'

'No, it is the right thing to do. She tells me it was what she wanted, to be able to see for herself where she was planning for her children to be. But unless she is kept as stress-free as possible, her condition could take hold once more … We are so much in the dark about cancers, but the form she has has been known to go into remission, but is never cured. I have given her something to make her rest now.'

'Is it there are things that we can do?'

'Build up her strength is the most important but she may not have much of an appetite. Try high-protein foods, like scrambled eggs, and broth made from good quality bones and vegetables. Sieve it through a muslin cloth, so there aren't a lot of solids in it, but all the goodness is. And give her freshly squeezed orange juice to get vitamin C into her ... I'm sure Walter can advise you on the best nutrition. It is one of the things we learn when training to be doctors before we decide to qualify in specialities.'

'Yes, thanks, Edward, I will make sure the girls know what is best for Jenny. I know they will take special care of her.'

'Yes, and the sea air will do her the world of good, Martha – only, no taking of the waters. Never heard of such a daft idea in all my life as that. Good for the skin, but not much else! I treat more visitors for chills and colds than anything!'

He and Walter laughed at this, but Walter did concede, 'Well, the myth is good for Blackpool businesses as well as for your coffers treating them all, as I'm sure we wouldn't have half of the moneyed folk come if they didn't think they would benefit. They prefer to flock to the sun ... Anyway, Edward, will you join me in the front room for a brandy while I sort out your cheque for payment? With so many children in the house now, I have been banished to a bureau in there as my office!'

'Poor you. Us men are gradually being taken over, you mark my words.'

They went off laughing and chatting and Martha thought that she'd never seen Walter so relaxed. But then, he was with someone who thought the same way as himself and had the same knowledge, and who he held a great deal of professional respect for, so it was natural that he should be.

Running up the stairs, Martha met Trisha on the landing. Her look showed her concern. 'I've Joseph in the cot fast asleep, and Jenny's fallen asleep too now, as she's taken the powder the doctor gave her ... Eeh, Martha, lass, have we done right bringing her here?'

'It is that we have.' Martha told her what the doctor had said.

'By, that's a relief. Well, we'll do all of those things. Walter said he can borrow a bath chair from the hospital rehabilitation unit for her, so she won't have the strain of walking ... It'll be grand. We can all wrap up warm and walk everywhere.'

'Oh, and I've news I wasn't for telling you earlier as you were busy with Jenny and Joseph, but Josh is on his way home!'

Trisha grabbed her in the biggest hug. 'Eeh, lass, that's the best news ever. I'm that glad for you. It's grand.'

'It is. I haven't said anything to Bonnie, for I fear something may stop him from travelling this far, but once it is I hear from him, then I will be telling her.'

'Talking of the kids, I reckon we need to get them into bed an' all. How about Bonnie stays here the night and Josh is a surprise for her in the morning, eh?'

'Oh, that would be such a help, so it would. As it is that it may be the early hours of the morning when he is arriving.'

'Well, that'll be fine then. Let's go down and have a cuppa while the kids are quiet. Where's Walter? Is he downstairs in the front room.'

'He is for having a tipple with the doctor.'

'Then we can have a few minutes' peace, lass.'

As they sat drinking their tea the telephone rang again. Martha, taking no heed that this wasn't her house and not her place to answer the phone, rushed and picked up the receiver. 'Josh? Josh, is that you?'

When she heard his voice, her tears overflowed as if she was a river.

'Don't cry, my darling, I will soon be holding you in my arms. I'm only about two hours away, though looking for fuel at the moment and that will delay me.'

'Oh, I have been missing you so much, my darling. It is that our lives have been busy, but empty.'

'I'm sorry. I have been the same, darling, and yet pulled in so many directions as I love what I am doing. We will get used to it.'

Martha wanted to scream down the phone, *Do you love it more than you love me?* But she swallowed the words and agreed. 'Maybe it is that we will.'

'Darling?'

'Just be for hurrying home, my darling. Let us have as long as we can have together . . . For sure, it is that you are staying home for a while?'

'At least two weeks, darling. There may be an opportunity for me to photograph the King and Queen for their Christmas release to the press. But if that falls through, it depends on any news stories . . . Look, it's a bad line and very cold and my money is about to run out, so . . .'

He was cut off by a voice saying, 'Caller, if you want to continue with this call, please put tuppence in the slot and press button "A".' Then all she could hear was the drone of there being no call on the line.

Feeling like breaking her heart, Martha bravely wiped her eyes and straightened her back. Josh was coming home, wasn't he? She should rejoice, but it was the limit of the time they would have together and him not seeming to care, but already planning his next trip away from her that put a dampener on any joy she should feel. How she wished they'd never gone for those stupid tests!

'Eeh, lass, I'm sorry. So, Josh isn't home for long?'

'Just a wee while, but to see him at all will be heaven. Shall we be putting the children to bed? I need to be doing something, so I do.'

When they climbed the stairs, they were struck by the silence. Opening Sally's door, they were met with three sleeping children already in their pyjamas. Bonnie and Johnny were curled up together at the bottom of the bed and Sally snuggled into the top.

'Eeh, them two knaw they have a special connection, love.'

'It is that they do. It's instinctive and beautiful. Maybe I could be using their relationship to soften the blow for Bonnie?'

'Aye, it might help, lass. Anyroad, you leave them to me and get yourself home to get it all warmed up for Josh coming.'

Despite everything, Martha felt a thrill zing through her at the thought of Josh coming home a place that hadn't felt like a home since he'd left it. Now it would be again.

FIFTEEN

Trisha

As Trisha lay next to Walter that night, for the first time ever, after he returned at weekends, she didn't feel like cajoling him into making love to her.

She lay in his arms thinking how lucky she was to have him and how sorry she felt for Jenny, and yes, Martha, for though they both had the love of their man, it wasn't dependable, in that one could go off for long periods of time doing what he wanted to do, and the other had a sick husband. Yes, Walter went away, but she knew that every Friday night he would be home and he would call most nights to speak to her and that made it easier for her.

But suddenly, this peace of mind was shattered as Walter's body shook with sobs.

'Eeh, me love, what is it? What's upsetting you?'

Though she said these words, she was filled with the fear of uncertainty.

'Walt? Walt, me darling. Tell me what's wrong?'

Still he didn't speak, and Trisha began to dread what he might say if he did.

Getting onto her elbow and facing him, she took his hands from his face. 'Whatever it is, tell me. Don't suffer alone, me darling.'

'I – I can't ... I ... Oh, Trisha, thank you for loving me. Always know, no matter what, that I love you and Sally. That you are the only true family that I have, and that ... well, I am trapped.'

'Trapped? How, darling? If you ain't happy, surely you can come back to the Vic and to us?'

'I can't ... I – I've done things ... I can't explain. Please don't make me. Just hold me, and help me.'

Trisha was mystified and afraid. What could Walter have done? Why couldn't he tell her?

He surprised her then by pulling her to him and kissing her, but with such passion she was taken away from the frightening place that held doubts and uncertainty and caught up in Walter's demanding lovemaking, not able to believe that he'd rolled on top of her and had entered her!

But disappointment filled her. This was the moment she had longed for, but in his movements, it seemed to her that he was trying to prove something, rather than being consumed by a need to make love to her and to give himself to her.

When it was over, she lay there, not having reached her own climax, and feeling used, until Walter held her so lovingly and stroked her hair. 'I so want to be like other men, darling. You helped me to be that.'

Thinking he was referring to him not being able to make love before she held him gently. 'Of course you are, look what you just did.' Fibbing a little, she told him, 'You loved me like I've never been loved, and it was wonderful. You don't expect anything, you don't take from me, you give to me.'

In this, she felt she was only lying this once, as despite his affliction he'd always tried to help her, once he'd realised how much she was suffering with frustration, by loving her in different ways and bringing her to satisfaction.

She was rewarded with a tearful smile. And then drawn towards him to be held in a loving cuddle, that to her was worth the world.

When she woke, he wasn't beside her. She hoped what had happened hadn't made him feel ashamed. Her first thought was to run along to see how Jenny was. She met Walter coming out of Jenny's room. He opened his arms to her. When in them, he kissed her hair and told her he loved her. Her world seemed a wonderful place at that moment.

After telling him she loved him and not referring to the mystery of the night before, she asked, 'How's Jenny?'

'I've actually spent most of the night in the chair in her room. I heard a moan and came along. Jenny was sweating and very disturbed by a dream she'd had. Joseph woke too. I got Jenny to take some water and her medication for pain, and then soothed Joseph. It was lovely to spend that hour holding him with the house all quiet. He gripped my finger as if to say he knew I would take care of him.'

'Aw, that's nice. I feel so worried for Jenny, though. Has her cancer come back?'

'It never goes away, just lies dormant for a while. We don't know why. And I have no means of testing to see if it's back. But she slept for the rest of the night and woke just now asking for a cup of tea, which is a massively good sign.'

'That's grand news. By, I was scared yesterday. I'll go and put the pot on. Is Joseph awake now?'

'Yes, but Jenny has him on her bed and he's quite content, if a little whiffy.'

'Oh. Uh ... well, I'm experienced now with boys, you knaw. Maybe you'd better put the kettle on, and I'll change Joseph.'

Jenny was propped up in bed and smiling. And as Trisha thought her Walter had done this for her, her heart filled with love for him, and she prayed that whatever demons afflicted him would leave him.

'By, lass, you're looking a lot better. I'm to see to Joseph and Walter will bring us a cuppa.'

'You've a good man there, Trisha, love ... My Peter is of the same nature, but dogged by this mental illness. It has blighted our time together.'

'I knaw. You've been dealt some rotten cards, lass.'

'I'm all right now. I – I ... well, can I ask something? I mean, I shouldn't, but I – I'm scared of the future.'

Trisha sat on the bed. She caught a whiff of Joseph, but as he was content, put her arm around Jenny's bony body. 'Owt, lass, and don't think you shouldn't. You can ask owt you like. What is it, love, what are you scared of?'

It seemed a silly question, as in Jenny's shoes, Trisha knew she'd be scared out of her wits.

'You can say no, but . . . well, can I stay here till I die?'

Shock trembled through Trisha. She hadn't expected this. But her heart went out to Jenny, so tiny, and ravaged by illness. 'I'd be honoured, me darling.' She hugged Jenny to her, in a gentle way. 'Don't you be worrying any more. Everything will work out, you'll see.' Then to stop herself breaking down as Jenny's grateful tears fell, she said, 'Mind, this won't get the babby's nappy changed,' and busied herself while wondering how on earth she was going to cope.

Walter came in at that moment. 'I'm waiting for the kettle to boil and wondered if you need a hand, darling . . . Hey, what are those tears for, Jenny? Has Trisha been beating you while I was gone?'

Jenny laughed, a lovely sound. 'No, she's saved me from a lonely death.'

'Good gracious, who's talking about anyone dying? That's a long way off.'

'Naw, not dying as such, but needing care, love. Jenny wants to stay here and for us to help her through it all. I've said she can.'

'That's an excellent plan and one I was going to suggest. In fact, I have made a plan of my own to fit around it if Jenny agreed. Now that I don't have to persuade you to stay here, dear, I can put my plan into action.'

'Eeh, Walter, you're talking in riddles, lad.'

Walter laughed. 'Ah, there's the kettle. I'll see to that while you finish with Joseph and then we'll talk over what I have in mind over a cup of tea – I bagsy the chair, though. I do enough of sitting on women's beds!'

With a cheeky giggle he was gone, leaving Trisha amazed at this different, playful side to Walter.

'He's adorable, Trisha, and don't go worrying about him sitting on women's beds. He'll mean in his work. I've had many a kindly doctor sat on mine and hold my hand while they told me bad news. I can imagine your Walter doing that.'

Trisha hadn't worried at all, but just had a lovely feeling that maybe things would change in the future. Maybe, too, she should encourage Walter to talk more. Whatever triggered his actions last night seemed to have now lifted off his shoulders, and she was glad.

Over a cup of tea, he told them how nurses had to give up their career when they married, he thought Jenny had probably had to, and yet, many of them wanted to continue. He went on to say, 'I have a very good friend – she was a work colleague – and I saw her recently, she was walking along Lytham Road, and I stopped to ask her how she was. She told me she'd not been good. That her husband had left her. She said she was coping but how much she misses nursing and how she would love to get back to it. The idea came to me in the night when I first thought that Jenny should stay here that we could employ her to take care of Jenny, or at least to be on hand when you are at the shop, Trish. What do you think?'

'Aw, that'd be grand.' Trisha felt such a rush of relief at hearing of this nurse and the possibility, she wanted to hug Walter.

Her heart hadn't hesitated in offering a home to Jenny, but her head had been in conflict as she hadn't known how it would work out.

'Are you happy with that, Jenny?'

'I am, Walter. I didn't want to be a burden, now I won't be. I can pay a little towards me keep and this nurse, as me dad left me some money. But knowing I had it and owned half of a house, I've had to pay towards all me medical costs, so it ain't so much now. Jack has helped me a lot from his half, and I know he would continue to do that for me care.'

'There's no need to. You are giving us a gift of your two boys to care for and that's payment beyond what Peggy will cost . . . That's her name, by the way, Peggy Marshall. She's a very homely type of girl and I know her to be kindly and caring.'

Trisha shot a glance at Jenny to see if what Walter had said about the boys had upset her, but she was smiling a lovely smile. 'That's my gift too, to know they will be loved and in a caring, loving home. It gives me peace if a lot of sadness too.'

Walter came over to the bed and took Jenny's hand. 'It is bound to, my dear, but you are a very brave young woman, and we will make you as comfortable as we can.'

Trisha held on to Joseph tightly and felt she would break her heart at the touching scene. Life just wasn't fair.

Jenny seemed a lot better for having her future settled as they'd gone on to talk about how it should all happen. It seemed that Jack could come home whenever he needed to and had recently been given an office position on land so that he would always be able to do that.

Jenny had said that he would go to her house and bring anything she needed and would close the house. And that they had a kindly neighbour who would keep an eye on things. And even though still weak, she did manage to eat and enjoy a boiled egg for breakfast, as did the youngsters as they chatted away, dipping their soldiers in the yolk.

'I'm riding a donkey today, Uncle Walter.'

'Well, I think you'll like that, young man. You have to say, "Gee up, Neddy and take me to the fair."'

They all giggled at this.

'Though we haven't got a donkey named Neddy, so you'll have to say Daisy!'

'Ha, Sally, Daisy will never gee up, not unless she wants to!'

'I know, Ma, but she's my favourite, and I think as she is so old, she was the donkey that Mary rode when she wanted to have her baby Jesus. We learned about it and all about the story of Christmas at school.'

Trisha laughed. Sally was like her with having a soft spot for the old girl of the herd. She turned her head and smiled at Walter, willing him not to shatter Sally's imagination around the role she thought Daisy had played in the nativity.

He didn't, just smiled back at her and changed the subject. 'Trish, are you thinking of just taking the children out, darling? Only I have another idea up my sleeve. I'll ring the Vic and chase up that bath chair, then I could come too and we could all go together. And I'd like to see how the cottage is progressing.'

Trisha hadn't dreamed that Walter would want to go to the promenade. Containing her joy, she told him, 'Those builders you engaged to install a bathroom called the other day for the key. They said they would make a start, but I've had no time to check up on them. Eeh, I still can't believe I own it. It should belong to both of us as this house does.'

'No, darling, this house is ours, but there is only me on the deeds, so you must keep that cottage as only owned by you. Have you been informed that the deeds have been put into your name?'

All of this was above Trisha. She looked blankly at him.

'Never mind, leave that to me and I will contact the solicitor. I can do this while you help to get Jenny ready, and I can phone the Vic at the same time. I have no doubt it will be fine.'

When Trisha came back downstairs, all was sorted. The solicitor said he held the deeds to the cottage and they were in her name.

'Strangely, Benny has stipulated that they should remain with him. I asked if he would transfer them to my solicitor and he said that though it seemed the sensible thing to do he had specific instructions from Benny. I don't understand that, nor the clause that the cottage mustn't be sold ... Anyway, the Vic is sending a bath chair to us by ambulance! I thought that very decent of them as I was wondering how I was going to get it here, other than walking to pick it up.'

Trisha just accepted all of this, thinking that she didn't have any idea about any of it, let alone getting a bath chair here.

She was saved from having to offer an opinion by Martha popping her head around the door. The big smile on her face told her that all was well in her world too.

'Hello, Trish, love. I was for wondering how Jenny is, and what plans we have for today?'

When Trisha told her, Martha had a tear in her eye. 'Ah, that is a lovely outcome to the worry that we had. I'll be helping you all I can ... And so, it's the promenade, is it? And shall we be going to Macie's for a hot drink and a tea cake after the donkeys, as it is that knowing her, she'll have already put up her Christmas decorations and the kids will be for loving that, so they will?'

'Aye, that'll be a treat, though it could start them off nagging us and God knaws how we'll find the time to put ours up. Anyroad, we can call in at the shop and check that Betty and Daisy are all right and at least root out the box of decorations that's still stored there.'

'Well, we will be needing to wrap up well, it's powerfully chilly altogether today.'

Trisha laughed. She still found Martha's way of expressing herself so lovely, but funny at times too.

With the children wrapped up in winter coats, boots and bonnets, it was decided that Trisha and Walter would take them in his car, which was bigger than Josh's and had a bench seat in the front as well as in the back. Then, with Jenny swathed in a blanket holding Joseph in the bath chair – when they'd finally got Joseph to stop wriggling and protesting – Martha and Josh would walk, pushing her. It was quite a way from St Anne's Road and this worried Trisha, for Jenny's sake. But there didn't seem another solution, until they got to the promenade and saw Arthur.

When he asked who all the children were, and where Martha was, he said, 'By, you should have fetched me. I could easily get the bath chair in the back by folding the seats up. Do you remember me doing that with the pram once, Trisha? Well, I've done it many a time with all sorts of carriages. Which way were they going?'

'They went towards Squiresgate Lane.'

'Eeh, that'll take them way too south for here. I'll go along and find them and bring them to you.'

'Ta, Arthur, and if you do manage the bath chair, that'll be a bonus for the future for us.'

'Sure I will. Well, I'll get on me way.'

'Well, I'll just nip into the shop then, Walter. I won't be a moment. You three be good.'

Betty was dealing with a customer. She looked up. 'Ah, the very person. I'm just telling madam that she can have anything she likes in a different colour.'

'That's right, lass. You're doing a grand job.'

'Daisy is fetching the different wools.'

'You have chosen well, madam, that little outfit is very popular.'

'Thank you, yes, I love it.'

When she turned back to Betty, Trisha winked, and took her leave, confident all was in hand.

When Arthur rolled up with Martha, Josh and Jenny, they were all soon huddled on the beach, but there was no sign of Dickie and the donkeys.

'Eeh, what a daft ha'peth I am! Of course he wouldn't bring them down in this cold. Well, I'll tell you what, we'll

215

have a hot drink in Macie's, and one or two of the stalls are still open – look, Roly is! He's an old favourite of Blackpool's and nicknamed that because he is as round as he is tall.' They all giggled at this.

'Let's go and see him. We can have a go at knocking down a coconut, or fish for a goldfish.'

The children squealed with delight, and more especially when they neared the stall and a young man came cart-wheeling down towards them.

'That's me son. I ain't naw spring chicken now, Trisha, lass, so he's the one to amuse the crowd and will soon run the stall on his own. We call him Bendy.'

Trisha laughed. 'Well, with them antics, he's certainly attracting the crowd.'

Bendy twisted his body so that he was looking through his legs. The children loved it, but like her, Josh and Martha squirmed. Walter, though, went into explaining that Bendy was double-jointed, and seemed about to analyse him, but Roly saved the day by giving the children fishing nets. They called excitedly, 'Help me with mine,' and the men were summoned to guide the children.

When he straightened, Bendy told her and Martha that besides helping his dad he worked in the Tower Circus, but he was ready to give that up when his da retired. 'Come spring, you should take the nippers to the circus. It opens at Easter.'

'We will, Bendy. Ta for making them laugh.'

'And don't be too eager in making your pappy retire. It is working that is keeping him young, so it is.'

'Aye, you're right, but he suffers with the aches and pains now.'

Walter was off again at this, telling Roly that if he'd been doing the same bending and twisting antics, then he'd probably pulled muscles or strained them. They all laughed when the retort came from Roly, 'By, you think yourself a doctor, don't you?'

They didn't enlighten him.

All the children won a goldfish and had to carry them around in one jam jar that Bendy found for them. But after taking a turn each and moaning they didn't want to carry it again, Josh ended up with it.

Josh had been quieter than he usually was, and Trisha wondered if seeing the boys, he was feeling his pain all over, as he was reminded who Bonnie's father was. She sighed. He was a different Josh completely to the lovely fun-loving, do-anything-for-you Josh she'd known before he'd found out he couldn't father children.

It was lovely to get into Macie's, and as they'd imagined, they were met with a festive scene of paperchains strewn across the ceiling and looped over the window. Silver tinsel, thrown over these, glittered as the draught caught them and had them fluttering and catching the light. A holly branch stood in the corner in a tub of sand, and this too was strewn with tinsel and hung with baubles. The children loved it, as did the grown-ups. And as predicted, both girls began to ask questions as to when they would put theirs up at home.

Walter quietened them by promising that he would sort it out the next weekend he was home, when he would cut down a branch from the holly bush near to the cottage too.

This settled them and gave them all a chance to catch their breath. And, feeling warm and cosy now, gave them a moment to take off their coats.

Jenny had easily been lifted inside with them and Trisha was overjoyed to see her pink cheeks and smiley face as she looked around in wonderment. 'By, the sea air is doing you good, lass.'

'I'm having the best time, Trisha.'

Bonnie, who hadn't wanted to leave Josh's side, came over to them and put her hand in Jenny's. A gesture that made Jenny smile even wider.

'I'll help you with your tea, Aunty Jenny.'

'Ta, love, but I think I'll manage this time. Last night I was very tired after the journey. You go and sit with the others and enjoy your juice, eh?'

Bonnie trotted off happily and sat with Johnny. Trisha watched Sally to see if she was all right as she'd gone from being Bonnie's only companion to playing second fiddle to Johnny. But she was happy as Macie had the wireless on. *Music in the Afternoon*, a popular programme, was playing 'Carolina in the Morning' and Sally's little head was bobbing in time to the beat. Trisha expected her to get up and dance at any moment.

When they reached the cottage, Dickie was there mucking out the donkeys. Bonnie and Sally rushed over to him.

'Hey! By, I didn't expect company or I'd have hosed down. I'm a bit stinky.' Sally held her nose and did an exaggerated, 'Ugh,' making pandemonium break out as Dickie chased her, followed closely by Billy, the mischievous donkey, and Bonnie and Johnny.

'Don't pick me up! Don't, you're covered in poo!'

By now they were all laughing, and Josh, who seemed to have at last relaxed, laughed louder than them all.

The happiness on Martha's face at this gave Trisha a warm feeling. She didn't miss Martha snuggling into Josh and him putting his arm around her and kissing her hair.

The children were soon engaged in helping to saddle three of the donkeys and lost in a world of their own – Johnny included, who'd taken to the animals as if he'd been around them all his life, instead of these being the first he'd ever seen off a page in a picture book.

'Shall we go in and see what work has been done, darling? I'm sure they will call us when they are ready to have a ride.'

'Aye, Walt, I'm excited to see how far they've got. What about you, Jenny?'

'I'm warm enough out here, but Joseph will be stirring and needing a bottle soon.'

'Aye, well, we have a paraffin stove in the cottage. I'll put a kettle of water on it, and that will warm the kitchen an' all, so you can sit in there and feed him.'

Inside everywhere was covered in dust. 'Oh dear, I don't think the bottle idea is a good one. We can't bring Joseph in here.'

This was something Trisha would have expected from Walter, not Josh. It seemed at last that he really was coming out of his shell.

'Naw. Let's have a quick look, get the donkey ride done and then get home, eh?'

'Me and Martha will help with the saddles, then we'll be ready quicker. It's getting colder by the minute.'

'Good idea, Josh, thanks. Come on, Trish, let's get up the stairs, but go carefully in case the builders have left any obstacles in the way.'

The bathroom was really taking shape. A sink on a decorative pedestal was already in place, and piped in. And the bath, a huge sided one that looked lovely and deep, was standing where it was going.

'Eeh, it's grand. I'm going to love soaking in that bath.'

'Ha, it'll take more than a tank full to fill it and all night to heat the tank!'

'Aye, but it'll be worth it and I can top it up with panfuls; I'm used to that from before I lived in a posh house, you knaw.'

Walter grinned at her. 'Come on. I think we've seen enough, and this dusty atmosphere is getting down my throat.'

He steered her out, stopping at the doorway and smiling down at her. 'I'm so glad you have this, darling. A place of your own – a home. It puts my mind at rest.'

'By, that's a funny thing to say, Walt. I have a home with you. I wouldn't want to move from there . . . We don't have to, do we?'

His face clouded for a moment, but then he gave a little laugh. 'Of course not, darling. I only meant that everyone should have a place, and this can be your bolthole.'

Trisha didn't want or need a bolthole, but she didn't say so. Something stopped her from opening up what she thought might be a can of worms, though she had no idea why she thought that.

Outside, she was soon laughing with the others at the antics of the children on the donkeys. Johnny, especially, this being his first time, was a delight to watch as he wallowed in riding Billy, who was showing off his speed, making Dickie run along beside him for all he was worth.

But underneath all the joy and frivolity, a small flicker of fear of something, she didn't know what, still burned in Trisha.

Martha must have sensed this as she came and stood beside her. Her squeeze of her hand comforted, and yet somehow confirmed that something wasn't quite right. But whatever it was, Trisha didn't want to know.

PART TWO

Building on
Broken Dreams

1923

SIXTEEN

Martha

Christmas had passed and was just a memory now. For Martha, those memories marked the last time she was with Josh as he'd been away for weeks.

One of the highlights of the celebrations had been them all going to midnight mass, and Jenny chatting with the priest. He'd seemed to help her and had arranged to christen the boys.

This had taken place on New Year's Eve and been a lovely day. But only two days later, Jenny had taken a turn for the worse.

Martha had been feeling under the weather too. A sickness that she couldn't fathom as it was like the morning sickness she'd had when carrying Bonnie, but which she couldn't put down to being for the same reason. Though the thought did come again as she lifted her head from the chamber pot and tried to swallow to stop the spasms happening.

Her mind went over the possibility, but then, she'd had her period as normal – but had she? The last one had been late and very scanty ... *Oh, Mary, Mother of God! That is for what was happening to me with Bonnie! Sure, wasn't I five months gone when I realised fully? But it can't be ... let it be ... no, it is for being impossible.*

Happiness filled her, then ebbed, then filled her again.

How is it the doctor they saw could be so sure that Josh couldn't father children? What if he was wrong? She clasped her hands to her breast, so longing for it to be as this was her dream for herself and Josh. It would complete her happiness as she felt sure her Josh would stay at home then and take up managing his factory again to be by her side.

She counted back as to when it might have happened, if it had, and concluded that it must have been in the November when he was home for three weeks, for her to be having sickness now.

That will be making me due in June! Oh, please, please!

Bonnie coming hurtling into her bedroom stopped these thoughts. She came to a halt and stared. 'Mammy, have you been sick again?'

'Yes, sorry, darling. I will empty the chamber pot. I don't know why it is that I keep it in here, but it was for coming in handy as sure, I couldn't have made it to the bathroom.'

'You're not ill like Jenny, are you, Mammy?'

'No, my wee darling. I'm just for being under the weather.'

'Is Jenny going to die soon, Mammy? I don't want her to.'

'I am knowing how it is that you are feeling, Bonnie. But it is in God's hands.'

226

'Well, we must go to church and ask God not to let it happen.'

'Yes, it is that we should pray for Jenny. Now don't you be worrying your head.'

Martha had hardly got these words out than Trisha's voice shouted up, 'Are you up yet, lass? Come as quickly as you can. Walter has called the doctor and Jack. I'll need your help with the kids.'

Martha's heart dropped. 'Is it you have brought them with you, Trish?'

'Naw. I ain't got them dressed yet, and Joseph is fractious. I think the poor little mite is teething. I can't remember now when they get their next lot.'

With her sickness forgotten, Martha called out that she wouldn't be long and hurried into the bathroom, quickly flushed the contents of the chamber pot away and swilled her face. It wasn't until she was pulling the wool frock on that she'd hung on the bathroom door the night before that she noticed Bonnie, her face showing her fear.

'Oh, me wee darling, don't be afraid. I am needing you to be a very brave girl for Johnny. Can you be doing that?'

Bonnie nodded.

'Well, be hurrying yourself and get your clothes on. It is that we have to fetch Sally, Johnny and Joseph around to here.'

It didn't take long to get the children organised when she got to Trisha's and have them in their coats ready to go with her. Leaving them in the hall, Martha went to get Joseph from Trisha. 'I'll be giving them their breakfast.

Isn't it that Joseph has porridge at this feed as well as his bottle?'

'Aye, he can't get it down fast enough and demands the next spoonful before you've got the spoon back to the bowl. Ain't that right, Joseph, lad?'

Joseph grinned as if in triumph. Martha felt her heart warm a little at this. Joseph had got into all their hearts. But then a thought came to her. 'Is it I should go up and say goodbye to Jenny?'

'Aye, I reckon you should ... Eeh, Martha, lass, it's unbearable.'

Martha took the weeping Trisha into her arms.

'It is that you have done your best for her, me darling, and we knew it was that this day would come.'

Brave words, but Martha knew her own face to be wet with tears.

In Jenny's bedroom, she found a solace. Jenny was sleeping and gently slipping away. Her face showed no pain, just an inner peace, and it was this that gave Martha the help she needed to say goodbye.

Walter sat by the bed and shook his head, and Nurse Peggy, a lovely, homely girl, sat in the corner of the room. She smiled a watery smile. She had shown such love to Jenny and had nursed her day and night in these what seemed to be Jenny's last days. Always in a gentle way.

Martha smiled back, feeling the pain she could see in Peggy in her own heart.

'Is it that Peter has been told, Walter?'

'Jack was going there first before he comes here. He should have gone last night ... I told him that if Peter can come, he was to bring him here to Jenny. Will you be all right with that, Martha?'

'I will, of course. It is that I would like to see him and for Bonnie to as well.'

'Yes, that's a good idea. Let her get to know him gradually.'

Bending over Jenny, Martha kissed her cheek. 'Night, Jenny. I wish for you to go happily in the knowledge that it is that your sons will be loved and cared for.'

There was no response but a further relaxing of her features.

'Oh dear, that's a sign that it will happen soon. I don't think the doctor will be here in time, but there is nothing he can do.'

Walter looked drained. His eyes glistened with tears. Martha touched his shoulder. 'You did all you could. It is that you and Trisha have been altogether wonderful.'

'Thanks, Martha. It's a relief that you are taking the children.'

'Has Johnny been for saying goodbye?'

'Do you think he should?'

'Yes, it will be in his memory for ever, as Jenny is for looking so beautiful.'

Walter left the room and returned carrying Johnny.

'Johnny, it is that you are coming to mine to have breakfast, so say goodbye to your mammy, wee one.'

Johnny stared at Jenny. 'Will she wake up?'

'No, she's fast asleep, Johnny.'

'Will you hold my hand, Martha?'

'Of course. I will lift you so it is you can kiss your mammy.'

Johnny leaned over and kissed Jenny. 'Is she going to heaven now?'

Martha felt her soul tug with pain, but she managed to nod her head.

With a child's resilience that is not understandable to adults, Johnny said, 'I know me mam will stay with me, she told me. She said she will always be by my side.'

The tears overflowed, and Martha saw Walter look away and wipe his eyes.

'It is that she always will be.'

Johnny snuggled into Martha's neck. She quietly left the room with him, then marvelled how, once he was with Bonnie, he smiled and said, 'I kissed me mam.' Bonnie put her arm around his shoulder, and he put his around her waist. In silence, and with Sally hanging on to the pram, they led the way to Martha's house.

Jenny died fifteen minutes later.

The next day, as Martha took the girls to school, theirs wasn't chatter of Christmas and presents as she could hear other children talking about, nor was it about what they had been through losing Jenny, but of the day ahead. It seemed they were focusing on returning to school and using it as a welcome distraction that made the world seem normal again.

Martha called into the shop after dropping them off, and despite the cold enjoyed the ride, sitting up on the top bench next to Arthur with the sea air ruffling her hair into ringlets and biting her cheeks, making them flushed and rosy.

She found that Betty had been through the order book and organised Mandy and Daisy into making what was most needed and had got Ted doing all that was asked of him. They were coping well, and so, to help with her own and Trisha's distraction, she took home all they needed to make the three gowns and two bonnets to complete an outstanding order.

She hadn't been back long when a distraught Jack arrived and almost fell into Walter's arms.

How glad she and Trisha had been that Walter had decided to take time off work as he took the responsibility off their shoulders of all the things that had to be done quickly – the registering of the death and arranging the funeral. For the latter, Walter had liaised with Jack over the telephone and begun to put everything in motion, with the first happening being that the funeral directors had collected Jenny's body and were going to prepare her for her brother's visit.

Walter had also contacted Josh so that Martha didn't have to tell him, only be comforted by him. Of all his kind words, the ones that meant the most to her were that he was coming home.

'Come and sit down, dear man. Your heart must be breaking.'

'Oh, God, I – I don't know how to tell you ... Where's Boxie and Joseph?'

Martha stepped forward and took hold of Jack's arm. 'The wee boy is having a nap. And Joseph is for sleeping in his cot too. Is it that you want to see them?'

'No thanks, Martha. I just need to sit down.'

They were in the kitchen and Trisha, who hadn't spoken till now, pulled out a chair from under the table. 'Here you are, lad. Rest yourself while I get a pot of tea on the go. By, you must be in need of one. Have you just driven from Manchester?'

Jack nodded. 'I arrived there last night, and went to see Peter . . . Peter's dead . . .'

'What? Jesus, Mary and Joseph, how is it this has happened?' Martha felt herself sink onto the chair opposite Jack. Her stomach had turned over and she had to swallow hard not to be sick.

'When I rang the asylum—'

'It was that he was in an asylum, not a clinic?'

'Yes. I had no control over that, Martha, I'm sorry. He was moved to the asylum because he became difficult to manage. They were kind to him. He wasn't troublesome once there, nor was he with the more severe patients who cause disruptions and scream all the time – though when I visited, I did used to hear them and often caught Peter sitting rocking in a chair with his hands over his ears, poor chap.'

Martha felt her heart crying for Peter's plight, but in some ways a little relieved that he was suffering no more. 'How did he die?'

'They told me over the phone that he'd remembered a lot and was ready to have a home visit but was very agitated as he wanted to go immediately to see Jenny. Then, after I told them what had happened, they said they would leave it to me to inform him. But when I got there, he was dead! They thought he was lying down to rest before my visit, but I – I . . . there was a lot of blood . . . He'd slashed his wrists . . .

He was a trusted patient, you see, and was allowed to wash himself and so he had his toiletries. He'd used his razor.'

The room fell silent but into that came a hoarse whisper. 'Naw, not again. Naw, poor lad.'

Walter rose and went to Trisha's side. 'It's all right, darling. Memories are bound to be triggered of Bobby. Don't deny them . . . but this is another tragedy of the same calibre. Was there a note, Jack?'

'Yes . . . someone had told him about Jenny . . . though they all denied doing so, but how else could he have known? The note said . . . I – I'm sorry, Martha, but it does refer to you . . . Are you all right to hear it?'

Shocked, but compelled to know, Martha nodded.

Jack took a folded paper from his pocket.

'*Please tell my children that I love them, and I am sorry, but that I cannot function enough to care for them, nor can I stay in this world when my beloved Jenny has left it. Please take my sons to Martha . . .*'

Martha gasped, 'Oh, we didn't think, but it is that he wouldn't have known Jenny and the boys were here.'

'No. I hadn't told him. I thought it too much. And I doubt that he knew that this was Jenny's wish, but I have no way of knowing that. May I continue?'

Martha, trembling more than she had been, nodded once more.

'*She will look after them and love them and bring them up with their sister. That is where they should be.*'

'But Bonnie isn't knowing of her relationship to Johnny. Please, Jack, don't be for telling her, it is too much for her at this time.'

Trisha's hand slid along the table towards her. Martha took hold of it. With all her heart, she wished that Josh was here.

'Yes, you told me, though I never understood it. Surely—'

'Look, lad, with how Peter has been, Martha and Josh thought it best. We all did. How can you explain to a little child that the man who has cared for her and been in her life since she were a babby ain't her da, when she thinks he is?'

'If it was that Peter was well, like he was when he first found me again, then she would be for knowing now, but he wasn't, and so it was Peter himself who was asking us not to tell her. He wasn't wanting her life disrupted until she was for being much older. But it is that we sent him photos and let him know how it was that she was progressing, until we found out that he was back in hospital with memory loss once more.'

'I understand, yes, it was the right thing to do ... Peter goes on to say: *Tell Martha, it's never left me how our love was hurt, and I am for ever sorry. I die happy now and go to be with my Jenny.*'

'Ah, it was that he couldn't be for helping what happened to us. But I am heart sorry that his experiences in the war caused him to suffer how they did. For sure, that suffering reached others. Poor Jenny, coping alone with the children when sick, and then dying without him by her side.'

There was the sound of a sob. Walter moved to Jack's side. 'Let it all out, dear man. You have so much sadness in your life at the moment.'

Trisha resorted to being her usual self as between her sobs, she asked, 'Can I get you a cup of tea, lad?'

Jack shook his head. 'No, thank you, Trisha. I have to travel back. I have Peter's funeral to arrange and that entails picking up his death certificate and seeing to the registration of his death as the institution have me as next of kin. Though I am hoping that the funeral director will now delay Jenny's and let me arrange to bring Peter to her side so we can have a service and burial for them. When Peter was well, they were a devoted couple. It's a tragedy, but one that should end with them being together.'

'I hope it is that you manage that for them, Jack.'

'I will help with sorting this side of things,' Walter told him. 'So, do you want to keep it as is, in Blackpool, and to make it a double one here?'

'Yes. They should be near to their children. And I will come here when on leave to see the children and hopefully take them home with me on occasion. The house is mine now but will pass to the boys in the future, and of course I will pay towards their keep and buy anything they need for their schooling or anything else.'

Martha rose then and went over to Jack.

Her body was shaking, and she felt sick as she neared him and all the emotions he was going through mixed with her own. Hearing of Peter's death had deeply affected her, but she managed to take him in her arms and hold him in a sobbing hug.

Trisha broke this up by saying, 'Well, lad, just come and have a peep at the lads before you go, eh?'

'I'd rather not, Trisha, ta. I couldn't take it. I have to go and get myself together. Seeing to practical things will do that. But I will be the one to tell Boxie when I return the day after tomorrow ... I will ring you, Walter, so that we can liaise.'

'Of course. Have we got the telephone number where you will be as I may have to face a decision that I would want to run by you?'

Jack wrote on the kitchen notepad Walter had passed him. 'But don't worry, Walter, if that happens and you can't contact me, I will be happy with whatever you decide, so don't hold things up.' The two men shook hands, then Jack had his hand on the doorknob when he hesitated and looked back at them.

'You are all amazing, what you're doing for me and my nephews. I thank you from the bottom of my heart for taking the boys in. There was nowhere for them to go and until Jenny told me of you, Martha, I was terrified that they would have to go to a home. You see, although I could provide a roof over their heads, I couldn't afford a full-time nanny for while I was away. A lot of my money has gone on Peter's expenses, and much of Jenny's went towards her medical expenses and hiring a nurse when she was very ill. I never told Jenny, but I paid for Peter to have a lot better care than paupers get, and for profession-als to help him, too. It was a relief when she told me about you, Martha, and about your little girl, and asked that the boys be brought up by you so they knew their sister. And because she'd heard such wonderful things about you from Peter.'

Martha could only nod, but then managed to say, 'It is that we already love them.' She couldn't admit that having them herself – her dearest wish – was blocked by Josh.

'I'll always be on hand to help – except when I am at sea as I will have to return to my former job now. But every port we call in, I will contact you, if only by sending a letter. And there's always a way of contacting us. I will put you down as acceptable contacts, so any message that's urgent will get to me anywhere in the world, and the number is on that pad too.'

'Don't be worrying yourself about anything, Jack. Everything will be fine.'

'Thanks, Walter.'

With this, he said a final goodbye and left, leaving Martha feeling like she'd been punched.

But loving arms took hold of her, and she knew that Trisha had sensed the many emotions assailing her.

She didn't push her to talk about them. Some things were private, even amongst friends.

Not that much was held back between her and Trisha as they were so close, they knew what each other was thinking and also when it was that talking about their feelings wouldn't help them to heal.

Martha was trying to come to terms with the horrific news that the father of her child had committed suicide.

Trisha would know how this felt and feel her suffering and would be there for her. Loving her, caring about her. Martha knew that – they both knew it of each other.

* * *

It seemed to Martha that life had become about death and funerals as she stood with Josh, a little back from the awful, gaping double grave in which lay two coffins side by side.

She was shocked that Jack had insisted that Johnny and Joseph be here. Joseph, now eleven months old, crawling everywhere and into everything he could investigate, was thankfully asleep in the pram under the care of Peggy, a little way away from the mourners.

For herself and Trisha, they had taken Bonnie and Sally to school as normal this morning, but now she wondered, should she have brought Bonnie? Would all of this come back to haunt her in years to come? She wouldn't let in the visions that threatened. She just couldn't face them.

Josh shifted uncomfortably beside her. She knew he'd sensed her distress. He looked at her quizzically. His expression showed he needed answers. He was still such a different man to the one she'd married. Sighing, she whispered, 'I am thinking about Bonnie and how she will never know Peter.'

His face relaxed and he became once more the loving husband she knew and mourned – the man who then wouldn't have dreamed of putting a career before her but was content to keep his early ambitions as a dream only and with running his printing and photography business in Blackpool. Even talking of opening a shop selling all things to do with photography, from cameras to lenses and films to offering a portrait studio, and a developing and framing service.

How she wished with all her heart that what she thought might be happening to her was. Instinctively, she touched her stomach. This brought the sickness that she'd fought down this morning to mind and she felt her stomach swimming once more. She clung on to Josh as if she would keep him with her for ever by doing so. But already he'd told her that he'd be away for the next two weeks.

To Martha, when he was gone, it felt as if half of her was missing, and yet, Josh seemed to love it and was full of himself and the people he'd met when he came home. Life just wasn't the same any more.

Making herself concentrate on the service didn't help. Memories of Peter floated in and out of her mind. How he'd turned up at her tent, sick, homeless and hungry. How she'd cared for him and let him stay in the tent overnight, but then he'd turned up at her house at midnight and she'd let him in. How she'd fallen so deeply in love with him and had given herself to him. How could she have done that? And then to wake up a few days later and he was gone, leaving her devastated. How differently things would have been if he'd have stayed.

Josh once more squeezed her hand. 'Memories?'

This time, she nodded. She was entitled to remember today.

His arm came around her and held her close. The gesture spilled her tears.

With the service over, Jack came over to them. Johnny immediately hugged her legs.

'My mummy and daddy are in heaven now, Aunty Martha.'

His words were so precise and sounded as though he was repeating something as it had been said to him, but that he couldn't take in.

Martha glanced over to where Trisha stood with Walter. The priest had Walter deep in conversation and Trisha was looking as if she was interested when Martha knew she'd have wanted to be with her and little Johnny.

Going down on her haunches in front of Johnny, she tried to comfort him. 'It is that I know, me wee darling. And they are together and are all well again. And it is that we are going to take care of you for ever now, while your Uncle Jack is at sea.'

'Uncle Jack told me, but I like when you tell me. It sounds like you are singing.'

They all laughed at this. Martha scooped Johnny into her arms, feeling a deepening of the love she already had for him. 'I have never told you, but it is that I am from Ireland, a country that is for being across the water. But we will always live in Blackpool.'

'Uncle Jack said that my Aunty Trisha will look after me.'

Martha wished with all her heart that she could say no, it was going to be her, but she nodded and told him, 'It is that we are going to share you and your brother as we are for doing now, wee fella.'

'I'm glad . . . I love you, Aunty Martha, and I love Bonnie, very, very much.'

Martha hugged him to her, tears streaming down her face.

'Are you sad because Mummy and Daddy have gone to heaven? I am. I didn't want them to go, but they got very sick, didn't they? Will you and Aunty Trish get sick?'

'Oh, me wee fella, it is missing them that is the reason I am crying. And for you too. But it is that we will make you happy again with the love we have for you. And no, we won't be getting sick. And you are for knowing that Bonnie and Sally love you and Joseph very much too.'

'Yes, they are like me sisters and I love them, and when I am big I'm going to marry Bonnie as we love each other the most.'

This cut into Martha. She wanted to shout that Bonnie was his sister, his real sister, and they could never marry.

But she just held on to him and prayed that when the truth was told it would be softened by the love he and Bonnie had for one another.

SEVENTEEN

Martha

As Martha held on to Johnny, with the wind whistling around them and her heart breaking for him, and for herself, Josh came down to crouch beside her. 'Yes, young man, they will always be like sisters to you. And they will love you as we do.'

'Will you play football with me when you're home? Uncle Walter says he can't play football.'

Martha looked at Josh. His face registered pain, but then joy as he said, 'I will, son.'

'Am I your son?'

'Sorry, it's an expression. A lot of men will call you son. But I wish you were. You are just the kind of son I would love to have. And I will treat you as though you are. As your Uncle Walter does already. Though we are both away a lot.'

'I know, you are away for a long, long time, and Aunty Martha and Bonnie are sad, but Uncle Walter's only away for a few days, and Sally says that's all right as she knows when he will be home and can count the days.'

Josh looked shame-faced. Martha could tell that he couldn't look at her.

Johnny seemed to want to talk and talk and they all let him, as now he was saying, 'My daddy was away a long, long time, and now, he went to heaven, and I won't ever see him.'

His lip quivered. Martha held him to her. She had no words. As she looked over his shoulder at Josh, she saw that he had tears running down his face, but he reached out and took Johnny from her arms.

'You cry, son. It's all right to cry when you're very sad. I'm crying as I am very sad too.'

Between sobs Johnny asked, 'Did you love my daddy?'

Josh didn't hesitate. 'I did. I met him once and we got on very well together.'

'And my mummy?'

'Yes. And you know, they will never leave you really. They will always watch over you.'

Johnny looked intently at Josh as he listened, and then shocked them all by saying, 'I love you, Uncle Josh. Will you be my daddy?'

Josh hugged him. 'Thank you, Johnny. Your love means so much to me. But what about Uncle Walter?'

'I love Uncle Walter, too. So, it is hard to choose, but you have Bonnie and I want to stay with Bonnie for ever. And Joseph needs a daddy too.'

Josh looked at Martha, almost begging for help.

'It is that you have the memory of your own lovely daddy, and Walter and Josh are for being your uncles, Johnny. Sure, it is that that has suited you till now.'

'But I won't have anyone to call daddy, and I want to call Uncle Josh "Da" like Bonnie does.'

Suddenly, he was crying. The sound cut Martha in two. 'I want Mummy and Daddy! I don't want them to be in heaven.'

He turned his body and put his arms out to Jack. 'I want to come home with you, Uncle Jack, and be your Boxie.'

With tears streaming down his face, Jack took him. 'You will. Every time I'm home from sea, I'll pick you both up, and your new sisters too – if they want to come, that is – and we'll all go to my house to stay as that's what the house you used to live in will be, Uncle Jack's house. But your home will be in Blackpool. You'll only be visiting me and taking care of me while I'm home.'

Johnny stopped crying and looked at Jack as if this was a good turn of events. 'Like Mummy took care of you? Only I couldn't do your washing and cooking, you know?'

'Ha, no. Just keep me company and fetch things for me, stuff like that. I'll manage the washing and the rest of it, though you could help me to dust.'

Johnny clung to Jack. 'I wish you weren't a sailor, Uncle Jack.'

Jack ruffled his hair. Martha wanted to hug them both as Jack bravely kept his voice steady as he said, 'I have to be. Do you remember me telling you the story of Lord Nelson? Well, he went to heaven, so I have to keep our seas safe for him.'

Johnny wasn't impressed by this. Martha had the feeling that all of this was too much him. 'I am for thinking it is time that we all go for a cup of tea and a drink of orange juice for you, Johnny? Trisha has some ready for us, so she does.'

As they walked towards the cemetery gate, Trisha and Walter had at last broken away from the priest and joined them.

'Eeh, lass, is Johnny all right?'

Johnny dropped Martha's hand and ran to Trisha. The men fell into step behind them.

'I want to live with Bonnie, Aunty Trisha. Would you be lonely without me?'

Trisha was taken aback. Martha jumped in. 'It is that I have been explaining that we will be doing as we are now and be sharing the care of him and Joseph.'

'No! Don't want to share!'

Trisha picked him up. 'Eeh, you're a lump to lug around, lad. But now ain't the time for picking and choosing and making choices. Let things stay as they are, eh, love? You've your own room and we can move the other bed out for now and put the cot in so that Joseph can move in with you. It's grand, ain't it?'

Johnny's bottom lip quivered again. His eyes filled with tears. 'But me mam won't be in the next room any more.'

'Ah, so it is that is the reason? To be sure, it is only natural for you to be feeling the sadness of that and wanting to avoid it.'

'Aye, I remember that feeling when me ma went to heaven, Johnny. It's hard and it hurts every day. You can stay at Martha's whenever you want, lad. Both of our homes are yours and allus will be.'

Johnny hugged her. Then put his head on her shoulder and began to close his eyes. Trisha looked very grateful when they reached Walter's car. 'Eeh, he's heavy when he's awake, but asleep, he's a weight and a half!'

Martha put her arm around her and tried to take some of the weight. But then Arthur drew up to take Peggy and the pram, and Peggy called over, 'Put him in with me if you like, Trisha.'

'Aye, I will Peggy, lass. There you go.'

As the men drew nearer, Martha heard Jack talking about his home.

'Jenny and I grew up there and were left it by our father – with the proviso that if anything happened to one of us, then the other would become the sole owner. He was in printing too.'

'Really? Did he work for someone, or have his own place?'

'He had his own. He sold it when he retired as I wasn't interested in following in his footsteps. I took after my mother's side who have been generations of sailors despite never living near the sea!'

'How interesting. I would have loved to have met him. I only got into printing as an extension of my photography work, which is my first love. I don't know who I take after as there aren't any artistic ancestors on either side.'

As they drank their tea, soon after arriving at Trisha's house, Johnny climbed onto Josh's knee and snuggled into him. Martha looked over at Walter and was relieved to see that he didn't mind.

To Martha, it was as if her Josh and Johnny really were father and son as she could feel the love between them.

Once again, she touched her own tummy. *If you are in*

there, I hope you are a boy, little one, for Josh has said how it is he always wanted a boy. Though I am knowing he will love you with all his heart, no matter what you are.

Taking a sip of his tea, Jack told them that there was money in a trust for each of the boys to be used as they needed it. 'I mentioned a little the other day of how I could help out, but I have since been to our solicitor and found out a lot more. He tells me my father left it for any grandchildren in the future. It is a tidy sum, and will pay towards their keep and for their schooling and any clothes they need. Our solicitor will just require the bills. We will work it all out when the time comes. But here is his card. You only need to contact him if am away and you need something . . . And so, all that remains is for me to say thank you. Thank you for all you have done. That day I came to the shop, a stranger to you and yet you didn't turn me away, I knew I had met some very special people.'

'Eeh, lad, it's us who should thank you for trusting us and for the love and joy the boys have brought to us.' Trisha rose and turned to Peggy. 'Now, let me and you get them sandwiches you made laid out, Peggy.'

As Peggy stood, Jack did too, and took Joseph from her. 'Thanks for everything, Peggy. I know you cared lovingly for my sister.'

'Like Trisha said, it was an honour. A beautiful lady and adorable kids. So sad, so sad.'

Johnny stirred on Josh's knee. He looked up at Josh, rubbed his eyes, and said, 'Did we play football?'

'Ha, you've been dreaming. But we will, and we'll even get Walter to join in.'

Walter laughed. 'Remember my pathetic attempts when we were at school? I don't think so.'

Both men laughed.

'Uncle Jack can play.'

'Well, maybe we can stick Uncle Walter on his side and then we're bound to win the match.'

With the laughter that followed, which Johnny joined in with gusto, Martha could see a bonding going on between all the men and the little man that Johnny was.

'Well, I'd better go and fetch the girls, they'll be coming out of school now.'

'Oh, Josh, it is that they will be out, so they will. How was it I forgot them!'

'I'll come ... Please, Aunty Martha, can I come?'

'Yes, if it is Uncle Jack is not for minding.'

Jack shook his head.

'Well then, it is that you will have to hurry and get your coat and shoes on.'

Laden with a tray of sandwiches and one of pork pies, Trisha came through from the kitchen. 'Eeh, lass, what were we thinking? Mind, with how slow Sally is at getting her coat and boots on, no doubt they won't notice you're late. I'll plate some sandwiches for you all.'

In the car, Johnny sat between Martha and Josh, still chattering away ten to the dozen. He told them that he wanted to go to school too.

'Well, you're certainly ready, you're a clever little chap. But the girls' school is only for girls, no boys allowed, so we'll all have to find a good school for you.'

Josh turned to Martha and smiled. Then as he looked towards the road again, his hand reached out, crossed over Johnny, and took hers.

Johnny grinned at her. 'I like to see you happy, Aunty Martha. Your eyes twinkle. Bonnie said you cry at night and that you're sick in the mornings. You said you wouldn't get sick.'

Josh's head swivelled in her direction. The car swerved.

'Hey! It is that you will be running us off the road!'

'I – I, oh, Martha, Martha . . . We'll talk later, darling.'

'Yes, it is that we must.'

'Are you sick, Aunty Martha?'

'No, it is that I'm fine, me wee fella. I've never been better, so I haven't.'

'That's because Uncle Josh is here. That makes me happy too, and Bonnie, because we love him.'

Martha smiled to herself. Now she knew why Johnny had been all over Josh today, because Bonnie loved him and so he did too.

She could see that the penny had dropped with Josh too.

He grinned as he said, 'And I love you all.'

But Martha could tell by his voice that he was over-whelmed. She loved him so much just for being him – a kind, caring man. Today she saw that man again.

As they pulled up outside the school, Martha looked into Josh's eyes. His held such love and seemed to be trying to give her a message. She smiled at him. His was a teary smile back. 'Is it good news you have for me – impossible news?'

Martha could only nod, an action that spilled her own tears down her cheeks.

'There they are, Aunty ... Aunty? Why are you crying?'

'These are for being happy tears, my wee fella. Come on, let's go and meet the girls, eh?'

Much later, Martha could feel the stillness of her home as Bonnie, to help Johnny settle, had stayed at Trisha's. With the promise of all being allowed to sleep in the same bedroom, Johnny had gone to bed happily.

Now, having bathed and changed, she and Josh sat down to eat a supper of ham and eggs. They hadn't yet spoken of what Johnny had said about Martha being sick in the mornings. Josh had seemed unusually quiet. Now, he took her hand.

'I hardly dare ask, my darling.'

'It is a possibility that I am pregnant, Josh.'

'Really? Are you sure?'

'It's not sure that I am, but it is that I have all the signs. I am thinking that if it is so, it must have happened when you were home in November.'

Josh rose. 'Oh, my darling, my darling.'

His arms enclosed her. His body shook with sobs. 'How can I make it up to you? I'm so sorry ... I – I have been so selfish.' He lifted her hand and kissed her fingers. 'Those boys cut through my pain and stupidity. They made me see reality. I – I didn't enjoy being away, I hated every minute of it. I am a fool. I let my pride rule. I had said it was what I wanted, you had agreed, and I couldn't back down, my stupid, mixed-up brain wasn't letting me.'

'It's all right, me darling.'

'Forgive me, Martha, I missed you so much. I wanted to change my mind. I am needed, I am a man who can love and give so much. Why did I react how I did? There are so many children who need a home, I wanted to go to the orphanage and scoop them all up and say, I can be a daddy!'

'It is that you can, Josh. We are not for knowing for sure it has happened, but I feel that it has. And you are a daddy already, for isn't it that you are for being Bonnie's daddy, and you can be to the boys?'

'I can. I love them already. I wish we were having them now, but I haven't even made it possible to make a home for them. I am such a cad. I cared about one thing, and one thing only. How could that have happened? And now Trisha is so looking forward to keeping them and has got everything in place for them.'

'They should be ours, Josh. It was for being the wish of both Jenny and Peter. Trisha is for knowing that. Yes, it is that she has a bedroom ready for them, and had to, and to be sure, wanted to, but it is that she will accept that we should be the ones to be giving them a home. She was for hearing the requests of each of the boys' parents.'

'And all of this won't be on your shoulders, my darling.'

'Is it that you mean it and you will be home with me, me darling?'

'I do. I am only freelance. I only have to pass on the work I am booked for, and there are many waiting to take it on.'

'But it is for being your dream.'

'It was an escape. Something to hide behind from what I looked on as my shame. Because of that awful report putting our childlessness down to me, I found it difficult to

251

face you, darling. Before that I was looking to get Father to find a premises for my photography shop.'

Martha closed her eyes against the emotions that swamped her. As she did a vivid vision came to her. Without opening her eyes, she said, 'It is that you will achieve your dream. You will become a photographer taking important news pictures for the world to see the horror that is happening. Not for many years, but it will happen.' Her breathing became heavy as she saw her Bonnie in the dream too, surrounded by bodies and blood and fire.

'Martha, Martha! Oh, my darling, what have you seen?'

Martha shuddered. 'Hold me, Josh. Make me safe, make it not happen.'

'What, Martha, what is going to happen?'

Martha opened her eyes. 'I don't know, I am only knowing that something is, and it will involve fire, blood and death. A war, maybe? I saw Bonnie, only she was grown and was for looking like me, not Peter as it is she does now. She was amidst it, and you, you were for having your camera, and it is that I know you will be so very important, so you will. Oh, Josh, I hate it that I am having visions. I have never been for wanting to know the future.'

'I know, darling.'

Josh didn't deny them. He had never done that or called her silly for thinking she could see the future; he'd always accepted this side of her.

He held her close to him. 'We will face what we have to face when the time comes, darling. In the meantime, if things work out, we will have a family to raise, our own family that has just expanded, and we will do that to the best of our abil-ity – together, as I am never going away again.'

He kissed her then, a loving kiss that sealed all he'd said as a truth.

'I'm going to ring Walter now, darling. I'm going to talk to him about how I feel and the specific request of the boys' parents, and tell him I am ready to take on that responsibility. But I will say that if that hurts Trisha, we will work together to help her, and as now, she will share in taking care of all the children, it's just that we will be the parents.'

When he'd finished his call, he was beaming. 'Walter and Trisha agreed! They have each felt that way all along, from Jack first coming to the shop, to the time he read out the suicide note that Peter left. Trisha said to tell you that she never mentioned it because she knew the heartache you were going through and didn't want to add more to that. Oh, Martha, what have I done to you?'

His kiss this time held a reassurance, as if he was saying, *Believe in me again.* And she did with all her heart.

When they came out of the kiss, Josh excitedly made plans. He was going to decorate the back bedroom for the boys. 'We'll shop for beds for them. Oh, and they'll need a cupboard and shelves, and a box for their toys, and drawers just like Bonnie has . . . Oh, Martha, and we'll need a cot . . . a cot! And we've all that stuff in the attic . . . It's going to be wonderful.'

Martha's heart swelled with joy.

EIGHTEEN

Trisha

Trisha woke to the sound of giggling and squeals of delight from one room, and of a hungry, demanding eleven-month-old from another. And then the soothing tones of Peggy and Joseph gurgling happily.

She put out her arm, but Walter was gone. Memory came to her of him saying he would have to get up early and get to the hospital as he was worried about his cancelled list of patients not being seen.

But this wasn't the reason for the feeling in the pit of her stomach that something had hit her out of the blue. She frowned as she stretched, and then sat bolt upright. *It's the kids! They ain't going to be mine!*

Tears stung her eyes for a moment. Yes, she'd said all the right things, but she hadn't meant them. She'd loved the thought of being ma to Joseph and Johnny. And Walter had only just told her before the telephone rang that he was keeping Peggy on to help her as once Josh went away again, poor Martha had enough on her plate to be able to help her fully.

She'd known he'd meant that Martha threw herself into their business almost to the exclusion of everything to help her to cope with her loneliness.

But now me own loneliness will come back and I ain't wanting it to!

As she lay back a moment, she wondered what had changed everything so drastically. She didn't want it to.

But as she swung her legs over the bed a different thought came to her. *Eeh, I'm a daft ha'peth, they'll only be three doors away and I'll have them around here as much as Martha will have them there.*

With this, Trisha felt better about the children and tried to put it all to the back of her mind as she dressed and then helped Bonnie to get her things together.

Her nerves and fears calmed as she did and with her crossness gone, she relaxed about it all and didn't dread knowing that Martha would call to take to Bonnie home to get her ready for school.

A few minutes later, as the phone always did, the doorbell resounding made Trisha jump. Why they needed a bell that clanged like that one did whenever someone came to the door she didn't know. 'Eeh, me lasses, it sounds like the church bells. I've a good mind to cut the rope from it so folk can't use it ... Now, carry on dressing, and I'll go and see who it is.'

'I've got it, Trisha, love. I'm almost at the bottom of the stairs with Joseph.'

'Ta, Peggy. Eeh, what would I do without you?'

As she said this, the pain of the decision made last night hit her again and she felt her heart drop. *Will I even need Peggy? And yet, I love having her around.*

Peggy had slept over in an armchair so often while nursing Jenny that they'd decided to offer her the guest room now it was sadly free again and told her she could stay over whenever she liked. Trisha had been so grateful for her doing so these last days since Jenny died. In her mind, she'd seen her weekdays being so full that she'd have no time at all to think of missing Walter, as she imagined Peggy and her sitting together in the evenings when the children were in bed, instead of being lonely again. Would that happen now?

'It's Martha and Josh, Trisha. I'll see to the children as they want to talk to you. You take them into the front room, then I can feed the little ones. I'll bring a cup of tea in to you.'

Trisha ran down the stairs with her arms open. Martha came into them and she hugged her gently. 'Eeh, Martha, lass, are you all right? Aw, you both look shattered . . . and yet, you've a look of . . . I don't knaw, excitement or sommat.'

'No, love. For sure it is that I've never felt better in me life . . . It is that we have to talk to you, though, Trish.'

'If it's about your decision, it's all right, you've naw need to worry over me.'

'Well, we did want to make sure you are truly all right with it, Trisha, dear. I mean, it must have come as a shock . . . And, well . . . if you are upset at all, then we wanted to say that we will carry on as planned.'

With her arm still around Martha, Trisha felt it was time to be truthful with Josh.

'There was nowt planned really, Josh. It seemed like there was naw alternative with how you reacted to being asked to take them ... I'm not blaming you, lad. It was a shock that you'd had, and sommat no one would like to hear. I knaw more than most. Besides, you'd already taken on one love child, as we've allus called Bonnie, and to ask you to take more fathered by the same man was a massive thing for you to even consider taking on.'

'I was a stupid fool, Trisha. I just can't understand how everything affected me how it did. Yesterday with Johnny ... well, it made me realise that I needn't suffer the pain I was, being away from my darling Martha and Bonnie, punishing them and myself for something none of us could change, but that I could be a father – that I was needed and was a worthwhile man.'

'Aw, Josh. I'm glad. And for you Martha. Eeh, you've been through the mill, lass.'

They hugged again.

'Let's go and sit down. Peggy's going to bring tea. Eeh, she's a gem. I'll not need her now, though.'

'But it is that you will, love. And I will be needing her too. Things don't have to be changing much. The plan always was for us to be having them a few days a week each. I know that wasn't for happening while Jenny was alive as it was for being natural that they stayed where she was, but it is that we can be doing that now. You will be needing Peggy on those days, as we are for thinking we will have them every weekend, so it is that you and Walter can be enjoying your time together.'

Trisha wanted to say how much having the house full had helped to change Walter when he was home, but she could see the joy in Martha at this massive change in her life and nothing would let her spoil that.

'Aye, that'd be grand, though Walter does love them all, so maybe sometimes we can have weekend days with them and you two have a break together when you ain't working . . . Anyroad, it'll all pan out. The main thing is the kids have a stable place they can call home.'

They all agreed on this. But to Trisha, it seemed that everything happened to the wishes of Josh, and she began to think that was men for you, as Walter had his life planned out and she just fitted into it.

By, I think I'm getting to be a bitter old biddy! But eeh, I'm not wrong. It's said it's a man's world and it bloody well is!

'Oh, Trisha, ta. Ta, me darling. And it is that that's how it will be. But the boys are to think of ours as their home and of me and Josh as their parents.'

'Aye. It's the natural way. Bonnie is their sister, the three of them should be together. And now that Josh has accepted that and won't be going away, it's made it possible for them.'

'What about Walter?'

'He's pleased, really. He says that Jenny and Peter's wishes should be carried out and he was glad that Josh was willing to do that. He said he'd worried about the responsibility on me shoulders and that he'd only ever wanted to be uncle to them but would have taken them on fully if it had worked out like that.'

Martha looked sad for a moment. Trisha knew she could see though her and would know she was putting on a brave face. But the boys weren't to be fought over and to her, this was the way things should be.

'It is that I need a hug, me darling, before I can tell you another piece of news that is for making me and Josh so joyful.'

Trisha rose. 'Aye, well, I can see that, lass.'

'Oh, Trish, it is sorry that I am.'

'It's all right. I understand, though I ain't for understanding how things changed. I mean, how one little lad got through to you Josh when Martha couldn't.'

'I don't understand it myself, Trisha, and put like that, it makes me feel even more of a cad.'

'You and a million other men, lad. You all call the shots.'

Martha laughed. 'I am for agreeing with you there, but oh, Trish, I've something to tell you. But where is it that the girls are?'

'Peggy's watching them. Ah, here she is with a pot of tea. You shouldn't, you know, Peggy, love. Eeh, here you are a trained nurse and running after me like you're a servant.'

'I'm the happiest I've been in a long time, love. I always wanted to be a nanny, you know, but I had elderly parents so couldn't live away. Even when training I travelled home every day. There you go, I've put the milk and sugar on the tray and the children are dressed and having breakfast.'

As she left the room Trisha said, 'By, I'm going to miss her. But with just Sally to care for, I can't ask Walter to keep her on.'

Neither Martha nor Josh said anything while she poured the tea for them all, but then they gave her the shock of her life before she had time to take a sip.

'Trish, me darling, I think it is that I'm pregnant!'

'What? . . . The morning sickness! Eeh, I thought you were poorly, but how? I – I mean, not how, but . . .'

They hugged once more. Trisha had tears in her eyes. 'It's like a fairy tale, a beautiful dream. Eeh, love, I thought it weren't possible.'

Josh was smiling from ear to ear. 'We have our doctor coming this afternoon. We're hoping he will confirm it. If he does, and we hardly dare hope, then I'll seriously think about suing the one who gave us a wrong prognosis. Anyway, the time is getting on, so I'll take the girls to school.'

The moment Josh opened the lounge door he was accosted by the three older children. All wanted to hug him and have his attention.

'Eeh, he's like the Pied Piper, the kids just want to be with him.'

Martha laughed, a happy laugh, and Trisha thought things were as they should be. Yes, she was disappointed that the arrangements had been changed as she'd looked forward to being ma to the boys, but to see the happiness on Martha's face lessened that. She'd enjoy the kids when it was her turn to have them and that would be enough for her.

'Anyroad, it's a good job, and lovely to see an' all as, by, they're a handful at times and you're going to need help from willing hands, love.'

Martha was grinning again, and the glow of happiness was back on her face.

After all the kisses goodbye and Peggy saying she had to bath Joseph as he was stinking the place out, Trisha was glad to be alone with Martha.

'Eeh, lass, I can't take your news in. Have you missed your period and everything?'

260

'Sort of. It is that I was late last time, and the time before that I was not having much of a one, and now it is that I'm not knowing if I'm due, or if I am, when. But it was when the morning sickness started that I remembered that I was for being like that with my periods when I had Martha.'

'Aye, you were, I remember that, only . . . Well, don't get your hopes up.'

'I tried not to, but I was for being silly enough to tell Josh and now I am worried in case it is that I am wrong.'

'I shouldn't be. I mean, he said that it was little Johnny and the love that he showed him that made him see how selfish he was being. Well, he didn't say "selfish", naw man can see that in their actions.'

'Ha, Trish, me love, is it that you are for being anti-men today?'

Again they laughed.

'Well, stuff allus has to be done their way as you knaw, love.'

'It's true, so it is. None of what is happening would be but for Josh's change of mind.'

'Anyroad, we can't change things, and we've got two of the best going, so we shouldn't grumble . . . Now, what about the set-up of all this new plan? Don't be buying beds, you knaw, I have an abundance of them.'

'And they will still be needed. Just as it is that Bonnie has a bed in your house and Sally is for having one in mine, it will be that the boys will need one in each too.'

'Aw, that's made it all sound a lot better. As now we're alone, I can admit, I was a bit disappointed, even though I can see the sense in this new arrangement. Now they will

261

have a father figure at home all the time, which is what boys need.'

'Oh, Trish, it is that I feel life is going to be different for us all.'

'Aye, we have a lot to look forward to. I've got the cottage to occupy me an' all and to care for the donkeys. Eeh, the lads love the donkeys as much as the girls do.'

'And it is that we are already building up our business and the girls are in a good school and are for loving it, and now it is that we will be having the care of two adorable boys, a wee baby, and the donkeys too!'

They giggled at this.

'Oh, Trish, it is that nothing can spoil our lives again.'

Trish felt cold as Martha's face suddenly held a faraway look and her body trembled.

'What is it love? What can you see?'

Martha came back to being her.

'I – I saw . . . I mean, I wasn't for seeing a wee baby . . . I saw happiness, but no baby, and then . . .'

'Martha, Martha! Eeh, lass, you're trembling.'

Martha shook her head. Her eyes glistened with tears.

'Is it me, lass? Is sommat bad going to happen?'

To Trisha's relief, Martha shook her head. 'No, it's a vision of way into the future that I am always getting. It is for disturbing me and comes whenever it is I am least expecting it. All I can say is, it is that war isn't over for ever. What it is they are now calling the war to end all wars isn't so. But it is a long time away, so it is.'

Trisha didn't need to know bad news and she was certain that's what had visited Martha, and not way in the future as she was pretending. *Eeh, I hope it ain't sommat that will affect any of the kids.* As they hugged, she felt Martha's body relaxing. Whatever it was had left her. Poor Martha, this thing they called a gift was more like a torture at times.

The bell of the phone made them jump apart. 'Eeh, that thing'll be the death of me, you knaw. Between it and the doorbell, they have me nerves jangling.'

This made Martha giggle. And as Trisha giggled with her, for once she felt glad of the ringing bells.

When Trisha answered, she was surprised to hear Walter's voice. 'Eeh, lad, is owt wrong? Are you there safely?'

'Only just. But yes, I'm here, darling. It's just that I was thinking on the journey. You haven't said anything to Peggy, have you? I mean, about how she may not be needed?'

'Naw, Martha and Josh came around first thing and Martha's still here. Josh went to take the girls to school.'

'Well, I was wondering how you were, too. I know it affected you a lot with how things have turned out.'

'I knaw, but I'm fine. We all agree, it is how things should be. Them kids are family and should be together. Anyroad, Martha has said that not much will change as they'll be here as much as at hers, but what about Peggy?'

'It's just that I'd like us to keep her on. You're always busy and she can be a sort of nanny to Sally and the others when you have them.'

'Aw, that's good news. She's company for me an' all when the kids are in bed. Only with Josh home now, I reckon Martha won't be around in the evenings so much.'

'Oh, that's good to hear. All right, darling, that's all I rang for . . .'

'Don't go. I've other news . . . well, sommat that's looking very likely, anyroad.'

'Oh? Be quick with it, Trish, darling, as I haven't much time before my first appointment, and I need to visit the washroom.'

Why couldn't Walter say 'lav' like everyone else? Trisha dismissed this silly thought, and told him Martha's news.

'Really? Good gracious! Well, John Bird will be surprised, as I am. I've never known his testing to fail before. Ha, give me one over him, this will . . . But I'm very pleased and hope it is confirmed . . . Though, darling, I have to warn, there are other things that can mimic pregnancy – stress for one. And Martha has had an abundance of that with how Josh went away for weeks on end with no contact . . . As we know, as our separation is bad enough to bear, and we can contact each other, darling.'

Trisha's heart sang at this. Never before had Walter hinted that he suffered from them being apart. Before she could answer, he said, 'Have to go now. Bye, darling.'

'Ta-ra, love . . . And Walt, I love you.'

But the phone had gone dead.

Trisha stood a moment assailed by conflicting emotions – happiness at what Walter had said, but fear for lovely Martha.

When she went back into the front room, Martha and Peggy were cooing over Joseph but as she entered, he put his arms out to her and struggled to get her to take him from Martha. Trisha's heart filled with love for him. He, more than Johnny, had come to rely on her and had filled the yearning ache in her caused by knowing she could never have more babies. In this, she had felt deeply for Josh and as she took Joseph and he snuggled into her neck, she prayed that Martha truly was carrying their child.

'Sure, it is that Josh is a long time. He's been gone a while.'

Trisha looked up from making Joseph giggle and saw a worried look on Martha's face. She sat Joseph down on the rug near to a dining chair they had left in there from yesterday when they'd needed extra seating. Joseph suddenly grabbed the legs of the chair and pulled himself up to stand. 'Eeh, lad, be careful.'

'Don't worry, Trisha, he's ready to feel his feet. He's been doing this for a while in his cot, so he has confidence. If he comes a cropper, it won't be such a soft landing as his cot gives him, but he does have very strong legs.'

Despite Peggy's words, Trisha stayed close by hoping to catch him, but he dropped gracefully onto his knees and crawled towards her, grinning and gurgling.

'Eeh, clever, lad. When did you learn to do that? My, you are a big boy!'

Suddenly rolling over, he landed on his back, but wasn't at all upset by the experience.

'I would say we're going to have our hands fuller than they are now with that one, Trish.' Peggy shook her head, a lovely smile on her face.

'Naw, Peggy, lass. I'm afraid things ain't going to be how we talked of them being after Jenny died. The boys are going to be living with Martha.'

'Oh? Oh dear ... I mean, well, it's none of my business, I was just sorry to hear it ... I – I thought I would still be looking after them.'

'And it is that you will, Peggy. I will be for wanting your help. It is that me and Trish are still to carry on our business and couldn't be managing without you. I am asking you if you will come into my employ now.'

'Eeh, Martha, love. Walter's phone call was about Peggy. He asked me to ask her if she would stay on and be a nanny to Sally . . . but we could share her, if Peggy is of a mind.'

Peggy gave a little laugh. 'I don't mind at all, it's wonderful news. Thanks so much. Only, Trisha, I was going to ask if I could still sleep here a couple of nights at least? I get so lonely at home.'

'Aye, you can as you break me loneliness up an' all. I'd be glad to have you.'

'Well, it is that is for suiting us all well, Peggy, as the children will be staying here a couple of nights in the week just as always was for happening before we had the boys.'

Peggy looked relieved.

'So, how do you see my hours working out?'

'Much the same as now, love, only no nights to do as you did for Jenny. And two days off a week – probably Sunday and Monday, as Saturday is a busy day at the shop. But we'll play it by ear. What do you reckon, Martha?'

'It is that that is for suiting me. Oh, Peggy, it is pleased that I am that you are wanting to stay on. The children all love you, so they do.'

Peggy beamed. 'And I love them . . . Ah, Joshua's car has just pulled up, so I'll take Johnny and Joseph out for a walk. It's quite springlike out there. I'll catch Johnny before he takes his coat off.' With this, she scooped up Joseph and went to meet Joshua and Johnny.'

'Well, lass, your big moment will soon be on you. I thought I'd go to the shop for the afternoon and make sure all is all right. I could do with the fresh air an' all.'

'Oh, it is that I am a bag of nerves, Trish. Pray it is a baby I am carrying, me darling.'

'I will, lass.'

The door opened and Josh stood there. 'Sorry, I had a puncture! I hadn't a clue how to change it. I had to walk to the garage to get Bert.'

'I thought it was that you'd ridden off into the sunset, me darling.'

'No. I'm never riding off again, not without you on my white charger with me.'

They laughed at this.

'Well, I've to catch Peggy to tell her I'll be out for a couple of hours. So you both can ride that charger around to your own home and get ready for your big moment.'

As Josh kissed her cheek, and Martha hugged her, Trisha did pray. But as she donned her coat, after a big hug from Johnny, and with Peggy happy to take a key with her and see to the children for a while, she begged, *Please, please, for lovely Martha, make it be that she has a babby on the way.*

NINETEEN

Martha

'I'm sorry, Martha, but you aren't pregnant.'

The words cut through Martha's heart. She couldn't take them in. 'But how is it I have had the symptoms?'

'Well, strictly speaking, you haven't. You haven't properly missed a period, only had late, scanty ones, and on examination of your breasts, they are not showing any signs of the changes we associate with pregnancy. The sickness and the scant periods can both be put down to stress if that has been present, or to a possible phantom pregnancy – a very rare phenomenon but one that has been known to happen. It can occur when there is a very strong desire to have a baby. Have you been under a lot of stress?'

'Yes, it is that I have.' Martha glanced at Josh. She saw the look of shame and guilt on his face and wanted to take that away from him. 'We lost two friends lately. Then it is that my business has been more of a strain.'

'Well, those are major causes of stress. And you haven't had Joshua by your side either, I understand? Well, I strongly believe your symptoms are caused by stress. You must rest more. And I am very, very sorry that I couldn't be the bearer of the news you are both wanting.'

Josh at last spoke. 'It's all right. Disappointing, but then we knew the chances were very slim, if non-existent. We will be fine. I won't be going away again and we are both very happy to be taking on the responsibility of the children of the friends Martha spoke of who passed away recently. I'll care for Martha, Michael.'

'That's good. But if the symptoms persist, call me again. My advice to you, Joshua, is to take Martha away for a complete rest. Give her something good to look forward to as that can really help to alleviate stress.'

'Thank you, Michael. I will do all I can. I will see you out.'

When Josh returned, he took Martha into his arms. 'What have I done to you, my darling? How could I have been so selfish?'

'Hush, this isn't for being your fault. It is that you had a natural reaction to the terrible news we were given that we could not have a family. But you are all right with me not being pregnant, which is for showing you are truly better.'

'I am. I truly am, my darling. Disappointed, but yes, I am over the news we had, and looking forward to beginning our new family life . . . About that break Michael suggested, I would love to take you to Ireland at Easter, but there does seem to be unrest in the area you want to go to, so will it be safe?'

Martha wanted with all her heart to be able to say yes, but she remembered the passion with which her country-men hated the English, and the lengths they could go to.

'No, it isn't for being safe. I have married an Englishman, and so would be looked on as the worst kind of traitor. It is that terrible punishments were handed out to any girl caught even being friendly with an Englishman. And it is that you wouldn't be safe either. Sure, I can be having a break here. By Easter, Trish and I are hoping to have more workers making the garments ordered, so we are. I will be talking to her and see if it is we can take turns in having a week off each with the children.'

An excitement welled in her as she began to let the idea of taking the children away for a week take root. 'We could be for finding a cottage to rent, and just be spending our days walking, and playing with the wee ones . . . Oh, Josh, I would love that.'

'Ha, it seems that Michael was right, a holiday to look forward to is the tonic you need. But are you all right, darling . . . truly all right?'

Martha knew that she had to admit the truth. She'd wanted Josh to talk to her when he was troubled and he hadn't, now she must not do that very same thing. 'No, it is that I feel a great sense of loss. It was that I believed that I was nurturing your baby, me darling, and now I am finding out that I'm not. It's a pain gnawing away at my heart. The baby I thought we had is not for existing. I can't take it in.' Sobs wracked her body as her bravado was stripped away, leaving her unprotected and needing Josh's strength.

He held her, not speaking, but gently steering her to the sofa.

'It's a sadness we share, Martha, darling, but we can't let it define our lives again, we can't.'

270

Martha looked up. Josh's face was wet with tears, his suffering there for her to see. 'You are for being right. We are to get through this together.'

'We will. And the children will help us ... How about we go shopping right now? We need so much to make them truly comfortable.'

'I would love that, as it is that we need to settle the boys here soon. I'm for worrying about Joseph, though. He is being very clinging to Trish.'

'Hmm, maybe if he is in the same bedroom as Johnny, he will settle, and seeing Trisha every day will reassure him. And what about Peggy? Can we employ her now?'

Martha told him about how Walter wanted to keep Peggy on. 'So, we are going to share her, but it is that when she doesn't go to her home she will sleep at Trisha's. They are for being company for each other.'

'That's settled then. Come on, we have about an hour before we have to fetch the girls. We need to buy a single bed and a cot in that time, as we will leave yours at Trisha's for when Joseph sleeps there. He'll be safest in a cot until he is around two.'

'Yes, it is that we need to protect him. He crawled today for the first time!'

'Really! Ha, he'll be into everything and a handful now. Are you ready for this ready-made family, my darling?'

'I am. Oh, Josh, I am altogether ready.'

It wasn't long before they had bought a nearly new bed and cot from Second-hand Lil's shop, knowing there wasn't a stall in Blackpool that sold these items and having no time to go to Preston, a more commercial town about ten miles away. Lil promised to deliver both on a cart later, and told them of a new stall that had been set up on the promenade selling bedding. Best of all for Martha was that it was right next to Cilla's tent, so, after making her purchases for the boys' beds, she popped to say hello to Sunita, but to her delight found Cilla was there too.

'Cilla! It is happy that I am to see you. How is everybody?'

As Martha hugged Cilla, she was reminded of the gypsy camp that she hadn't visited for a long time as Cilla smelled of fresh air with a tinge of woodsmoke from log fires.

'Everyone is all right, but eeh, Martha, lass, you are for looking peaky. You've been through a hard time, but that will ease now. It is Trisha who is going to need you.'

'I know and it is that I am getting stronger and will be there for her.'

'And Joshua, it is that you will be by Martha's side from now on. And you both will prosper. But do not follow your heart, Martha. Don't go to Ireland as only heartache awaits you there. Live with your memories for now, but in the future, there will be peace there and then you can return.'

'Oh, Cilla, we had thought about it, but no, I received the same warnings.'

'Ah, you're not following your true calling. But, by, I ain't for blaming you. It ain't easy to let the spirits in. I'm grateful to have Sunita take the strain from me at times, I can tell you.'

'Oh, Cilla. I am for knowing your dilemma. You are brave to carry on. And we are so proud of how you are for progressing.'

Cilla laughed. 'Aye, I am mixing with the rich and famous now. You should see me vardo, it is the best on the camp, and eeh, I've news an' all. I'm to be married!'

'Oh, that's wonderful. Is it that I am invited?'

'You are, love, but it is to take place in me Romano's camp in Cornwall.'

'When? Oh, it is that I have never visited there.' Martha looked up at Josh, who was smiling and nodding his head. 'This could be the place for us to go on that holiday, darling.'

'I am to be wed on Easter Saturday. And you really would come? Oh, Martha, could I have Bonnie for my bridesmaid? I mean, I knaw it is to be a gypsy wedding, but I am wanting what the gorgers have and bridesmaids is one of them.'

'She would love that, but it is that we will have Sally with us too. Could you be considering having both girls?'

'Aye, I would love that. Sally is in me heart an' all. But what about these boys that I have seen on your knee when I am thinking of you? They aren't yours as that is never to happen again, dear Martha, and I'm heart sorry, lass.'

'It is for being all right. Josh and I are happy with how our lives are for turning out.' Martha told Cilla about the boys, not feeling a bit surprised that she knew of them and of the childlessness she and Josh now knew that they faced. There was very little that Cilla didn't know.

They hugged then and Cilla said, 'I'm glad you've accepted it. For holding on to heartache can ruin your life, lass. And you ain't to worry about owt else affecting your health. Your mind and heart have cured you. You will pick up with this acceptance and having Josh always by your side.'

'Well, that is for being all I need to know. But it is sad that I am that I have to leave you now, as we have so little time. Can you be writing down the details of your wedding for me? And is it that you will settle down in the south with your new husband?'

'Aye, a gypsy wife makes her bed where her man does. Sunita is to be the family fortune teller now. I hope she can call on you and that you will keep the clan busy with making your baskets and cots.'

'Oh, it is that you can, Sunita, any time you will be welcome. And I am still for wanting cots and baskets by the dozen. Arthur is loving his visits to the camp to pick them up for me. The gypsy blood that flows through his veins still draws him there.'

Sunita, looking almost lost sitting at the table and in the chair that Martha remembered her lovely granny sitting in every day as she told people's fortunes, beamed as she said, 'I'm good with needlework an' all, Martha, so if you have any work I can do in the winter, that would be good as we're packing up now to close until Easter and I ain't good at making baskets and stuff with wicker.'

'I do and would be glad of your help. What is it you like to do?'

'Crochet. Grandma taught us all, but I was the only one who mastered it.'

'But that is for being wonderful! Come to the shop anytime but Wednesday afternoon and it is that one of us will be there to show you what is needed, or it may be that you will be wanting to be doing the work in our work-room instead of taking it home?'

Martha hoped Sunita would say yes to this and felt happier when she did as she didn't relish trying to get the smell of woodsmoke from anything Sunita made. A lovely smell to her, but to others it may not be acceptable. Sunita's large brown eyes lit up. 'Eeh, you've made me so happy. If I were to stay in the camp, I'd be everyone's lackey being the youngest girl, or me da would be trying to marry me off and I ain't much for that yet.'

'The Layette Lasses to the rescue it is, then.'

Clutching the paper with the details on, Martha felt an excitement zing through her. She'd never been to a gypsy wedding, nor to Cornwall, which was miles and miles away, but both had given her something to really look forward to.

It was when they were passing Roly's stall and found him open that Josh said, 'How much longer have we got? I've a mind to try to win something for the boys.'

'Ha, it is just that you want to have a go. You are for being a boy at heart. It is three boys I am to be called on to take care of, so it is.'

They laughed together as Josh's arm came around her and pulled her close. Into her ear, he whispered, 'Ah, but one of us is your man and will be showing you the love that he has for you later.'

Martha thrilled at this, but blushed as she looked at Bendy who was leaning against the pole of his father's tent, as she was sure that his smile was saying he'd heard that. But as he went into a series of cartwheels, she laughed along with Josh and the moment passed.

Josh won a teddy bear for Joseph and a toy engine for Johnny. You'd think he was a kid who'd been given a lolli-pop he was that thrilled.

When the girls came out of school, they were both smiling happily. They ran into Martha's and Josh's arms.

'Well, it is that things will be different at home from now on, me darlings.'

They were in the car and Martha had decided to tell them that the boys would be living with them.

'What, all of the time, Mammy?'

'Yes, they are to look on me and Da as their mammy and da too.'

'Why? Doesn't my ma want them now their ma and da have gone to heaven?'

'Of course she does, Sally. But it is that before they went the boys' lovely parents asked that Johnny and Joseph be cared for by me and Uncle Josh. You see, it is that we knew them a long time ago.'

'And anyway, I love them,' Bonnie said.

'I love them as well, Bonnie.'

Josh took charge. 'We know that you both love them and that won't change, girls. Nor will you all sleeping together as you will do as you do now – a few nights at Sally's house and the rest at ours. Everything will seem the same as always to you. It is just that your mammy and I, Bonnie, were given the responsibility of them both to bring them up, and that is what we're going to do. We want you both to be happy about that and to help the boys to feel at home and loved.'

The girls looked at each other. Then Sally grinned. 'Well, I'll be happy as long as I am at my ma's on a Wednesday, as that is my dance school day and I love to come home to ma and dance my new steps for her.'

'So, is that all settled then?'

They both giggled as they nodded their heads.

Martha felt relaxed and happy by the time they all got home armed with crumpets to toast in front of the fire, which Josh soon had roaring up the chimney as he stoked the embers with kindling and logs.

'I'll go along to Trisha's, so I will. I need to be telling her what happened and see if it is that she and the boys can join us for crumpets. Shall you be coming with me to say hello to your mammy, Sally?'

'No. I'd like stay here with Bonnie, Aunty Martha.'

'Well, it is more than likely that Mammy will be coming back for crumpets, so she will.'

The girls ran up the stairs together, giggling as they went. Josh smiled at Martha. 'Well, that went well. Now, don't be long, darling. I'm starving with missing lunch.'

It was a relief to Martha when Trisha greeted her in her usual way with a hug, and there was no sign of this morning's talks having left her hurt or resentful. Martha couldn't have borne that.

'Eeh, lass . . . Well?'

Martha hadn't thought she'd cry, but she burst into tears.

'Aw, love. Come on into the kitchen. It's nice and warm in there as I have the stove lit. Are the girls round at yours?'

She nodded, unable to say anything for a moment.

They sat down at the table. Trisha took hold of Martha's hands and held them in hers while Martha poured out her heartache. It helped that Trisha knew the pain she felt and didn't try to replace not carrying a child with other things, like the children they already had, or how lucky she was to have Josh back with her, but just let her talk, shared the feelings she had and was there for her.

'It's been a long road for us, Martha, love. We've had our troubles. But we've allus got through them together and we will this an' all. You'll see ... How's Josh taking it?'

After listening to how positive Josh was and what a lovely afternoon they'd had, Trisha said, 'That's good. Really good. You have the support from him that you've allus needed, love. Hang on to that, eh? ... You knaw, it's funny, ain't it? But here we are now, not wanting for anything, money and home-wise, with a good business we've built up from nowt, and yet we're denied the one thing we want the most ... Mind, I ain't much for church and all that, but you knaw, I reckon God is still looking after us. He gave us one special child each and then sent us two more to look after. Oh, and a load of donkeys!' They burst out laughing at this and Martha felt better for it, as she realised that yes, she truly was blessed.

As if they'd conjured up one of their blessings, Johnny came bursting through the door. 'I heard your voice, Aunty Martha. Are you going to be my new mam and Uncle Josh me da?'

Martha looked at Trisha.

'I thought it best to tell him, love. As you can see, he's over the moon.'

Martha smiled. And whispered, 'His love of Bonnie is for being what is behind it all, you know!' then laughed and went down on her haunches in front of Johnny. 'Aye, it is that I am. And we have a bed coming for you and a cot for

Joseph today, so whenever it is that you are ready, you can be coming to us.'

'What, now?'

'Yes, me wee fella.'

He looked at Trisha. 'But I can still come back here to be with you, like you said?'

'Oh, it is that you will be putting us on trial, is it?'

Johnny looked mystified. Martha regretted her words and put out her arms. He came willingly into them. 'It is that you can be where you feel you want to be, me wee darling. We all love you very much, so we do.'

Trisha came down beside them. 'Aye, we do. You have a bedroom here and always will have, and Bonnie has a bed and Joseph a cot, and Sally will have one at Martha's.'

'And Nurse Peggy is still going to look after us?'

'Nanny Peggy, now, lad. And aye, she is.'

Johnny was quiet for a moment, then grinned. 'And Uncle Walter will be in goal when we play football?' They all laughed. Johnny's grin widened as he looked up at them, showing he was very pleased with himself.

They went on to chat for a few moments about how Trisha had found all at the shop running smoothly and Peggy had gone home for the night. 'She wanted to leave us to talk to the boys but will be back here to take care of them tomorrow as I'm thinking we both need to get back to work, lass.'

'We do. It is that we need some normality. And those crumpets will be toasted black if we don't go round to mine this minute!'

With Trisha carrying Joseph, and Johnny holding Martha's hand, they hurried back down the road.

The crumpets smelled delicious, and Bonnie and Sally were busy spreading them with butter when they arrived. Both were attacked by Johnny when they opened the door, who squealed his delight at seeing them and ran to them for cuddles.

To Martha, it was as if everything was put back together again, when after cuddles with the girls, Johnny ran to Josh for a hug and asked if he could start now to call him Da?

As he and Josh chatted, Joseph strained against Trisha's hold to get to Martha.

She hugged the wee fella to her, leaving Trisha's arms to Sally.

With how Joseph snuggled into her Martha felt an acceptance by him and knew a happiness fill her heart. She knew that she now had all she needed in the world. She let in the happiness this gave her, not giving space to any heartache as that was now soothed.

By the time Easter arrived, so many things were sorted, and all was running smoothly at home. The children loved the routine and always had something to look forward to. The shop was running like a small factory as well as a retail outlet as they had converted one of the rooms upstairs to a work-room and had three workers up there at any one time alongside Martha and Trisha. Though Sunita, who had made a close friend of Daisy, would be leaving within days. Already she had been working less and less on the beautiful crochet garments she made to get her tent ready for the season once

Easter and Cilla's wedding were over. After that she would do what she could for them between her readings while the visitors arrived in Blackpool by their thousands.

Lately, the workroom had been buzzing with excitement as the bridesmaids' frocks, in a lovely ruby red with sequins sewn all around the hem and with little fitted black bodices, were being made and that excitement spilled over to boiling point when the morning came that they were to set off for Cornwall.

The journey took two days but went as smoothly as it could with three youngsters and a baby. Sunita was to travel down with her clan, and they had set off many days before in their caravans pulled by the horses.

It was when they neared Cornwall that they spotted some of them on a wide expanse of grass verge. When they slowed, they caught sight of Cilla and Sunita, who waved frantically for them to stop.

Josh pulled the car off the main road next to them. As he did, Cilla's father called out:

'Be having a cup of nettle tea with us, Martha. We've been hearing all about you and your family and it is heart glad we are you're to join us. Sure, you, Martha, are a descendant of our clan.'

'I am that, sir. And it is that I would be glad of a cuppa with you.'

'We have cider for the big man, and juice for the wee ones.'

Martha loved hearing her own dialect spoken, and this was noted by Josh. 'You're with your own people, my darling, even though we couldn't go to Ireland. I'm so glad.'

Martha felt her love for him surge through her. He was so accepting of all people and was in his element when they agreed that he could take photos and throughout the wedding too. Up until now they only had pictures of ancestors that had been drawn with charcoal.

'Come away in to see my vardo, love.' Cilla said this as they came out of the hug they'd given each other. Her speech was now a mixture of the Irish brogue of the gypsies and the Lancastrian dialect she'd picked up from being with other children when little.

Martha gasped when she climbed the steps of what looked like a new vardo. Inside was draped with gold netting that had a sparkle to it. The bed at the back was covered in a blue velvet cover, and curtains of the same material with a leaf of gold printed on them swathed the opening to the bed. On the floor was a blue and gold rug. Each side of the vardo had shelves with beautiful china stood behind a wedged edge, and nearer to the door, a tea caddy and teapot. In the corner near to the door on one side was a wood stove with a chimney reaching up through the rounded wooden roof. Outside of the caravan, Martha knew that boxes that slid underneath would hold saucepans and washbasins and all that was needed.

'It's beautiful. And is it that this is your wedding dowry?'

'Aye, it is. My husband is coming from a poor family of Romanian gypsies, and this is what he wanted from me to be my groom, but by, he's worth every penny and I can't wait to have him beneath them sheets with me.' Cilla put her head back and laughed out loud.

Martha couldn't help but join her and wished her all the luck in the world.

'The heather hung at the entrance and our knowledge will bring me that, Martha, love. Happiness is made, and I intend to make us both plenty.'

The wedding was magical and Cilla looked lovely in a gold and white gown that made her look like a princess with its ruffled hem in shining gold held out with layers of stiff netting and its satin white bodice and top of the skirt. Her headdress, in the same gold, stood high on her head, with a white veil trailing from the back. The bridesmaids all did her proud and Martha felt that pride in the way Sally and Bonnie played their parts too.

After the service, held in a small village church, they all walked back to the clifftop where the vardos were parked. The sun had come out, food was plentiful and laughter was the order of the day as one after the other of Cilla's and Romano's family entertained. Especially Romano's whose family worked in circuses. There was juggling with the feet as they balanced on their hands, and a great ladder made by the bodies of five men standing on each other's shoulders, horse riding with acrobats doing all kinds of balancing tricks whilst on the backs of horses racing in a circle, and then dancing.

This is where the children had the most fun just letting themselves go. Though Sally took it more seriously and imitated the movements of the gypsy ladies who did a dance that involved bending and twisting their bodies, while their hands danced with fans spread out between their fingers and making all kinds of shapes and circles.

Soon Sally had two fans too, and a space cleared for her. Everyone stood in admiration as this little doll-like child moved with the grace and expertise of someone much older, lost in a world of her own. The applause rang out when the music ended. Sally, like a true pro, took a bow.

'We have a true professional dancer in Sally, Martha.'

'I know. Is it that you caught her on camera?'

'I did. I think I got some wonderful shots with the camp-fire in the background and the setting sun behind her in the distance too. And plenty of the wedding and the guests and of all the families ... It's been the most exciting and wonderful event I have ever been to.'

Though his face changed then as there was a drum roll and Cilla stood still looking towards an advancing Romano. Cilla looked afraid and seemed to be wanting to run, but she looked Romano in the eye.

'What is happening, darling? I don't like this.'

'It is for being a ritual and it can look very intimidating, but it is that Romano is now ready and will claim his bride and take her into the vardo. All will clap as he completes the act of making his bride his own. I think now it is the time to take the children to our cottage. Sure, it is that Cilla will be for understanding.'

They didn't have to worry about gathering the children, as they, sensing the sinister atmosphere, had gathered around Martha and Josh's legs and Joseph had been put into his carriage a little while before.

As the drum roll got louder, they quietly slipped away unseen and were halfway down the path by the time the slow hand clapping began.

Josh, holding Johnny in his arms, winked at Martha. 'Well, just as Romano is at this very moment claiming his bride, I will claim mine when the children are asleep, so watch yourself, Martha, my love.'

Martha burst out laughing, but at the same time felt the familiar feeling snake down her spine.

The cottage they'd rented was lovely. Nestling at the bottom of the hill leading to the cliff, it faced the sea, which was a short walk further along the path. Inside there were old but comfortable furnishings that looked too big for the room – big armchairs covered in a blue and green fabric that seemed to hug you when you sat in them, a sofa which the children loved to bounce on and whose old springs were strong enough for them to do so, a dresser filled with china, and a footstool all arranged around a huge fireplace, in which Josh soon had a fire roaring up the chimney. To Martha, it was heaven, as was the whole day as she'd touched her true roots.

For Martha, once peace reigned, with the children fast asleep in bed, her loving time began as Josh who had perched himself on the sofa gently pulled her down beside him and held her close. His kisses and caresses took her into a world she loved, as they slipped off the sofa and joined together in a frenzy of giving and taking to the sound of the crackling fire and in its warm flickering glow.

TWENTY

Trisha

Trisha loved it when it was her turn to have all four children, as it had been overnight and today.

She stood thinking over the last four months, about how all had worked out well and how happy they were, as she leaned on the gate that led to the paddock, watching the children riding the donkeys, their laughter ringing out across the green fields surrounding her little cottage.

Now renovated, the installation of the bathroom had left her with just two bedrooms, but one of these was large as it ran from the back to the front of the house. This one she'd made into a kind of dormitory with three beds in a line with the cot nearest to the door, as well as a play area where all the toys were stored in a box, shelves holding jigsaw puzzles, games and books – more books than any of the other items as all three older children loved books.

She smiled and waved as they trotted past her. Joseph, now nineteen months old and quite strong and tall for his age, being held on the saddle by Dickie, gave her a lovely grin as he went by.

Trisha was proud of how they were all growing. Johnny had just had his fifth birthday in July, only days after Bonnie had had her sixth.

Sally, who tried to mother the boys but had to vie with Bonnie for that privilege, was to have her seventh birthday next week, but today, being Saturday, she was having a party this afternoon.

The party would mark the end of the long school holiday too – another cause to celebrate.

For her and Martha, it would be a relief not to have to juggle their work between time off to spend with the children, though Peggy was a marvel still and took most of the strain, and after all it was hers and Martha's choice to be around as much as they could.

School term beginning was a source of joy too for the kids, as they all loved school with a passion, even Johnny, who'd so far only had a tutor at home but looked on that as his school.

Josh had put his name down for Rossall private school for boys but Johnny couldn't start until he was seven. Josh and Walter had attended there – Walter being a boarder as he lived so far away.

Thinking of where he'd lived in those days made her groan inwardly as it reminded her that Walter's parents were travelling down today from Cleator, in Cumbria, where they lived.

The thought gave Trisha an attack of nerves and she wished that Walter would turn up soon so that he was here to greet them. Her worry deepened as to why he wasn't. What could have happened to him?

Some of that worry was triggered by how she felt out of her depth with Beth – not so much Cyril, as he hadn't shown any signs of looking down on her, though both made her feel as though any kindness they showed wasn't really felt. And this went for when they sent Sally a lovely doll at Christmas time as the note with it wasn't loving, but almost curt, wishing Sally a happy Christmas, and that was that. It struck Trisha as being in such contrast to how they were at the wedding with Sally. But Walter had never given her an explanation of why they had changed.

Trisha was glad that Sally didn't see anything was wrong, as her comments were that Granny Beth and Granddad Cyril must love her to send her something so wonderful. This had settled Trisha's mind, as she'd never want Sally to feel she wasn't wanted, or wasn't good enough for anyone.

'We're here!' Josh's voice called out to her. 'Where's all the gang?'

Trisha couldn't believe she hadn't heard Josh's car, but the last bit of the drive to get to the cottage was just a track, so this had cushioned his wheels.

Martha got out and ran towards her. As they came out of their hug and Martha waved to the kids, she seemed to Trisha to be trembling as she asked, 'No Walter, yet?'

'Naw, he's late. I wish he'd hurry. His ma and da'll be here in a mo.'

'Don't worry, it is that Josh will keep them entertained for you. Have you not been having any telephone call from Walter? Maybe it is that his car broke down.'

'You're edgy, Martha. Are you all right, lass?'

'Yes, it is that I didn't sleep well, that's all.'

Trisha wasn't so sure it was all, and she began to worry about Walter and if Martha had been having one of her visions. She prayed not. She was the happiest she'd ever been in her marriage. It was now quite normal for Walter to make love to her. And he'd become a kind and gentle lover who knew what she liked. Though each time he'd acted strangely afterwards, almost as if he was ashamed, or hadn't liked it, even crying after one occasion. He'd said it was because he didn't think he was very good at it, and no amount of reassuring him helped him to think otherwise.

But she kept telling herself it was a step in the right direction and that as his confidence built, then he may get over this and be happy that he'd enjoyed it as much as she had.

His behaviour was all a mystery to her.

Trisha sighed. She was out of her depth and wished she dared to suggest that a psychiatrist might help, but she thought that would rock his confidence even more, so just continued to be patient and enjoy what they had.

'Will you just look at the children, and be hearing their laughter. Isn't that a sight and sound to be warming your heart, me darling?'

'It is, Martha, love. I'm sorry I couldn't wait for you before they had their rides, only Dickie must take the donkeys to the beach this afternoon. You saw yesterday how many kids there were about, most likely come for a treat to Blackpool before they start back at school. Trade falls drastically after that and I'm already subsidising the donkeys' keep out of me own money.'

'It's fine. I'm glad that they are having such a treat. Is it that they slept well? They weren't for keeping you awake all night?'

'Naw, after running around here and a hot bath, they were too tired to stay awake.'

'This is for being a haven for them. I'm so glad you decided to bring them here last night. It was very peaceful for me and Josh. We had a lovely evening, so we did.'

'That's grand, love. And how were things at the shop this morning?'

'Oh, they're for being fine. Betty is a marvel altogether. And Ted was busy parcelling up and addressing as usual. I was for being amazed at how much it was that they completed in the week. Betty was saying that she had been busy and had taken orders, but she was for sitting and tackling all those hems when I arrived. I told her that she should leave them for the girls when it is they are in on Monday, but she said it gives her something to do while the shop is quiet.'

'Aw, that's good. Mind, she's been with us a long time now, so she should cope. We're two fussy old biddies.'

They giggled.

'Well, it is for being our baby, so it is.'

Trisha nodded but her attention was taken by a car she'd spotted coming towards them. 'Huh, huh, here they come!'

Martha looked around her. 'Where is it that Josh is for disappearing to?'

'Ha, probably made himself scarce. Oh, there he is.'

Josh had gone through the gate and had taken over from Dickie holding Joseph, the pair of them giggling together.

'Well, looks like it's down to me to greet me in-laws. Would you put the kettle on, lass? They'll be ready for a cuppa, I'll bet.'

'I will and gladly, me darling. Good luck!'

Trisha pushed Martha playfully, then took a deep breath and headed towards where Cyril had parked the car.

Beth got out first. Without saying hello, she looked around her. 'Where is my darling boy? Is he inside?'

'Naw, he ain't arrived yet, and he ain't contacted me. I were expecting him at nine as he said he would set out at six, so he'd be here to help with everything.'

'Everything? You mean, getting the food ready?'

This was said with such disdain that Trisha cringed. 'Aye, and the children as we all stayed here last night.'

'Your "bolthole".' She looked around her. 'Well, it is looking better than I thought. But I don't understand why it was left to you . . . Was this Benny a *good* friend?'

Trisha felt her colour rising and, with it, her temper.

'The best ever, but if you're asking did I go to bed with him, then naw, I bloody well didn't, and that's swearing for you!'

'Patricia . . . Patricia, wait, dear.'

Cyril ran after her and grabbed her arm. 'I'm sorry, Beth can be – to use your own swear word – bloody awful at times. I'm very cross with her and often take her to task. That was unforgivable, but if I tackle her, she can very cleverly make it look as though I have read her insinuation wrongly.'

'Don't worry, Cyril, it ain't your fault, but I just don't knaw why she is so nasty to me. I hardly ever see her.'

Cyril sighed, then shuffled his feet and looked down at them. 'I – I wanted to ask, are you happy, my dear?'

Something about Cyril made Trisha feel unsure about whether he was trying to change the subject out of kindness or not. Or if he really needed to know as she had a sneaky suspicion that for some reason, the state of her marriage mattered a great deal to him. This thought triggered a feeling in her that Cyril wasn't genuine. She decided that no matter what his motive was for asking, she could answer him truthfully.

'Aye, I am. I've everything I need, a good, kind and loving husband. Me, Sally and the kids have no money problems, and I have me own business, and the bestest friends a girl could have. I've nowt to be unhappy about.'

'So, Walter is a loving husband towards you?'

This further put her on her guard as it seemed to Trisha Cyril didn't expect Walter to be good in that department, but she couldn't discuss that with him. 'He is, and I love him with all me heart and miss him so much when he ain't here.'

Sally came running over them, much to Trisha's relief.

'Granddad Cyril . . . Granddad Cyril! Did you see me on the donkey? He is called Billy. He can be naughty and race away, but he doesn't with me. He likes ladies.' She giggled as Cyril lifted her in the air. 'I did, Sally. I saw you galloping away. I thought you would win any race.'

'Not on me legs, I don't. Bonnie allus beats me.'

'Always, Sally, remember?'

'Sorry, Ma.' She looked at Cyril who'd now put her down. 'I'm trying to talk proper as my school likes it, but I forget when I'm happy, and Ma says all the words how I like to say them.'

'Well, it is good to speak properly, but forget all of that today as it is a happy day – a do as you please day. It's your birthday party! And we have a present for you.'

'Ooh! Can I open it today, Ma?'

'You can, me little love, as soon as Da gets here, eh?'

Sally seemed happy with this and left Cyril to run towards Beth, who hadn't moved from where Trisha had left her. Trisha thought she looked pale and frightened and felt sorry now that she'd reacted how she had, but she was so on edge about Walter and why he wasn't here yet or hadn't telephoned.

He'd insisted she had a telephone installed in the cottage so he could contact her if she was staying there and not at home. He'd called her the night before as he did every night to say goodnight and to tell her he loved her, and he'd always have a word with Sally, making her giggle and telling her how much he loved her too. Last night he'd told Trisha he couldn't wait to be home and would set out really early so he could get here in plenty of time for Sally's day.

Deciding she was wrong to speak to Beth in the way she had, she went over to her. 'You'll be needing a nice cup of tea no doubt, after your long journey, Beth. Martha's got the kettle on. I'll take your bag for you.'

'Yes, well, a cup of tea would be welcome, thank you. But I can carry my own handbag. Our overnight case can stay in the car till we get to your house. There's just Sally's present.'

'Aye, all right.'

Trisha could think of nothing more to say. It was obvious that Beth was not in the mood to relax and forget that she was slumming it.

They were sitting in the garden, the children were playing a game of catch, Dickie had left to take the donkeys to the beach and Josh, who could talk to Beth and Cyril on the same level they were used to, was keeping them happy. She heard him telling them how New Road, opposite the North Pier, was now called Talbot Road, after the Squire of Lytham's son, Talbot Clifton, and all about how the road stretched from the promenade to the family's estate at Layton, when suddenly the telephone bell seemed to cut through the air. Its loud ringing quietening everyone.

As she went to rise, Trisha saw a look on Martha's face that she'd seen many times.

Fear clutched her heart and froze her to the spot. Josh jumped up. Trisha knew he, too, had seen Martha's trance-like look. As he rose, Martha began to shake and she whispered, 'It's happening.'

Trisha remained rooted to the spot. Whatever Martha knew, she didn't want to know. Somehow, she found herself in Martha's arms. 'It is that I am here for you, Trish, me darling. I will be helping you.'

'You knaw sommat, Martha, you've known a while, I could feel it ... Eeh, what's going to happen? I ain't for standing it, I've had enough. Me life's happy now, Martha.' This last came out as a whimper.

Martha didn't answer but clung on to her. Trisha did the same to Martha, knowing she was going to need the strength she offered.

When Josh came through the door, his face was deathly pale. 'Come inside, everyone. Leave the children playing. Something dreadful has happened.'

Trisha heard her own moan, felt her knees go weak, heard a cry of anguish from Beth, then felt hands grasp her arms and guide her indoors. Josh was on one side of her, Martha the other. Cyril had hold of a trembling Beth.

'Carry on playing, children. We have things to do that you can't be involved in. Be very good, now.'

The cries of, 'Yes, Da,' from Bonnie and Johnny, and, 'Yes, Uncle Josh,' from Sally could barely be heard above a wail from Joseph, who was at that stage where he needed the reassurance of grown-ups around him. He came running towards Josh, his arms out, his little legs going ten to the dozen, shouting, 'Da, Da!'

Sally and Bonnie chased him. When they caught him, they somehow managed to soothe him just as the door closed on what Trisha felt was life as she knew it.

'I – I don't know how to say this . . . That was Carl.'

Beth's gasp and cry of 'No, no,' seemed to slice into Trisha's heart. She stared at Josh.

'It . . . I mean . . . There's, well . . .'

Trisha wanted to scream at Josh to just tell them, but then she wished he hadn't and that she could turn the clock back and for the dreadful news not to have happened.

Walter was dead!

Josh's voice droned on amidst the shocked silence. 'Carl says it happened this morning as he was driving out of Manchester and that the police caught him at Walter's flat and informed him . . .'

'Why? Why him? Why was he at Walter's flat!'

Trisha didn't know why she screamed this. It didn't make sense to her and she could see from Beth's face that she thought it a stupid question, but never in a million years did she expect what happened next as Beth ground out, 'Because Carl is the single most important person in the world to Walter – not us, his mother and father, and most certainly not *you*!'

Her voice rose then. She took no heed of Cyril crying out, 'No! Beth!'

An ugly expression twisted her face as she glared at Trisha and screeched out. 'You were just a cover for his *real* life . . . his *real* love – his *disgusting* lover! You were just someone who made his life simpler. Just so he could have the facade of being married and having a family. He came to love you for what you were to him, what you put up with. But really he used you! Why he chose you I will never know. You're a slut!'

'STOP IT! STOP IT NOW!'

Joshua made them all jump. A silence fell. Trisha felt sick. Shock trembled through her every limb. Words came to her as if they were stones being thrown at her, each one hitting their target and causing her deep pain – *loved Carl! . . . Only came to love you! . . . Carl was Walter's true love – his lover!*

Though arms held her, Trisha felt alone in the world – a frightening world where she was nothing. She could feel herself sinking, and just let it happen. She wanted to escape this horror – her Walter, gone. Truth was dawning. Her life was crashing to nothing.

Sobs penetrated the thick fog that had descended on her. Opening her eyes, she saw Martha's lovely face looking down at her. Tears glistened on her cheeks. Her eyes held love, concern and anguish.

In the background she could here Joshua saying, 'It's all right. It was the shock. The doctor is coming. He'll give Beth something and help Trisha too.'

And then Cyril: 'It broke Beth's heart when Walter told us he would never marry. He got into a temper – something rarely seen, but then even a saint gets in a temper with Beth! She was on and on at him – she even called him ugly. She said she wanted grandchildren, but that no one would look at him. It was then that he snapped. He said that he was different to other men, that he couldn't love a woman. That he loved Carl … It's my fault, all of this. I wanted to save face for Beth, and for Walter not to suffer ridicule or spite. I suggested he marry. I told him to find a widow, or some such who already had a family. I – I thought it would make his life seem more normal to others and he'd be left alone, then he could find a way to be with Carl too … I've caused so much pain … so much.'

'Don't torture yourself, Cyril. We can only do what we think is best for our children. Walter should not have done what he did … Poor Trisha. She doesn't deserve this.'

Then Trisha heard the dreadful sound of a man sobbing. Cyril had broken down. Where Beth was she didn't know, nor did she care. She wouldn't mind if she never saw the vile woman again. But, oh, God, was all this real?

Holding Martha's gaze as if her life depended on it, Trisha asked, 'Are the children all right?'

She felt the wetness of one of Martha's tears dropping onto her face.

'They are, me darling. They're still for playing their game as if all is well, so they are.'

'But it's not, Martha. It's not . . . What are we to do? I just don't know what to do.'

'I know. It is that your world has been turned upside down, me lovely Trish. I think it is that we have to tell the children.'

'Naw!'

'We will have to, me darling. What is it you can do otherwise? As young as they are, it is better that they know. They are expecting a party. Poor wee mites, they cannot be having that now.'

'How? How do we tell them sommat like this?'

'We have to be saying that Walter has gone to live in heaven. The wee boys understand that, and sure it is that Sally and Bonnie will. It is that it will break their hearts, but we are not able to save them that pain.'

'Oh, Martha, will you do it while I hold them?'

'I will, me darling. I'd be saying Josh was the best, but he is for coping with Beth and Cyril. Beth has run off somewhere, we are not knowing where.'

'What if she hurts herself, like . . .'

'Like Bobby and Peter did? Yes, it is a possibility, but then the way of it is that no one can stop someone from doing that. If it is that you stop them once, they will find a time. When life has lost all meaning, there is only one path we all see open to us.'

As if she realised what she'd said, Martha hugged Trisha to her. 'But it isn't the road that you will travel. You are for having Sally and me and Bonnie and the boys ... all of us, so you have.'

'I do. I have a lot to live for, but, oh, Martha, how could Walter have done this to me? How? It's wicked, cruel ... How?' This last word caught on a sob, and for the first time, Trisha felt herself breaking down. Her lovely Walter. How would she ever get over all she'd learned today?

TWENTY-ONE

Trisha

'Patricia, you do have your rights. You are legally the widow of the deceased. The only thing that can take those rights from you is if there is a will that gives instructions for your late husband's burial. What exactly was said?'

Trisha sat gripping Martha's hand. A few days had passed since the awful news, and she hadn't slept a wink. She felt the exhaustion in every part of her. Even her mouth didn't want to move to speak. She stared at the solicitor who had been so kind to her when Benny left her the cottage.

Martha explained what had happened.

'I do need you to affirm this, Patricia, so Walter's parents want their son to be buried in Cleator? And his friend ...' – the solicitor coughed in an embarrassed way, then gave Trisha a pitying look – 'wants to have him buried near to him in Manchester. But he is willing to give way to the parents, is that correct?'

Trisha nodded.

'But what do you want? Are you objecting to any of these suggestions?'

This time Trisha found her voice. 'I only want what's right. Is it for me to choose?'

'Well, let me make a phone call. I know Clampton and Clampton and Partners, Walter's solicitors, very well. They may shed more light on these matters. I won't be a moment.'

'It is right that you have your say, Trisha, but don't be fighting these awful folk. They are for being more powerful than we are.'

Trisha felt as though she was doing everyone's will, letting them carry her along. Telling her that as a wife she had rights. She knew they were trying to protect those rights, but none of it seemed to matter. She was so hurt, her heart felt like a heavy lump of pain. That her Walter could have treated her in this way still seemed impossible. It was as if it was all a lie, and yet it all fitted. Everything had a reason now – Walter not making love to her, and then being repulsed after he had. For yes, that was the word, she knew that now. Him wanting to live in Manchester. It seemed he and Carl shared a house there, which they had bought together – oh, how bloody Carl liked telling her that!

Carl had telephoned yesterday evening. She hadn't been able to get a word in. His voice had screeched on and on. 'And don't think you're getting anything, madam. You've had all you're having. Bled my darling Walter dry you did, wanting a posh house next to your friend, furnishing it with the best. Take, take take, Walter told me. Well, you can get your bloody arse out of your posh house as it isn't yours any longer, lovey!'

Then he'd slammed the phone down, leaving her standing staring at it.

Martha had been there to catch her as always. It was Josh who'd arranged this visit today for her. Lovely Josh, who listened to her and didn't impose a stranger onto her but allowed her wish to see the solicitor she wanted to.

The next phone call had been from Cyril. He'd seemed like a different person. The thought occurred to her that being two people ran in the family as Cyril was all businesslike, saying that the funeral had to be arranged up in Cleator, that Carl had spoken to him and told him he wanted it in Manchester, but that wasn't going to happen. 'This is his home. His mother deserves to have him back with her.'

For one moment, Trisha had thought, *Oh yes, they deserve each other – mother and son!*

The wait seemed eternal. All the while Martha held her hand. But Trisha couldn't respond. She just stared out of the window, watching a bird hopping from branch to branch on the tree outside, its head bobbing as if it had a lot on its mind: where to fly to next, or maybe where to get a morsel to eat from. *Just like me. I'm not sure what to do next. Only I haven't got wings. I can't just fly off . . . Oh, I wish that I could.*

When the door opened, Trisha jumped. She looked around at the solicitor. His face looked grave.

'Now, my dear, it seems that your late husband has set down his wishes very clearly. He is to be buried in Cleator in the family grave.'

'She won, then.'

'Who, my dear?'

'His mother. And his friend. He was happy for him to be buried there. He wanted Manchester but didn't mind as long as it wasn't Blackpool.'

'Hmm, well, I have to tell you, Patricia, that you are required to attend.'

'Required? Bloody required!'

'I'm sorry. I meant to say that you should attend. There is a will reading scheduled for afterwards. The funeral is in two days' time.'

'It's already been arranged, then? Eeh, what kind of people are these? How come they've been on and on at me, when they knew all the time? Are they monsters?'

'Yes, I think they are. I'm so very sorry . . . All I can say is, remember that Benny looked after you. Remember that you don't need them, or anything from them.'

A trickle of apprehension clutched Trisha. What did he mean? It sounded like he knew something that might affect her.

'I'm sorry, I cannot say any more. I have been told things in confidence, and you will hear them after the funeral. All I can say is that I will help you to fight the proposals if you want me to, but the cost of doing so will take all you have and more. So, try to accept it and be thankful to dear Benny. He was a good friend, who loved you like a daughter.'

Trisha could hardly swallow. She couldn't think what it was that was coming to her. She didn't want to go to Cleator. But he'd said that she should.

★　　★　　★

303

Back at her home, with Martha popping around to her own house to fetch Sally back to her as Josh had looked after the children, Trisha looked around her.

She loved this house; she'd made it a home. It had symbolised her rise in life, her being loved by someone who was of a higher class than her. It had made her feel worthy, valued. Yes, she'd chosen where she'd like to live as she'd loved Martha's house and wanted to be near her. She remembered how excited Walter was when it came up for sale. Was that a sham? Had he told Carl that she was take, take, take?

It hadn't been like that. She'd have lived in a barn with Walter.

She wandered into her kitchen. Her lovely kitchen that always had the lingering smell of her baking in the air, making it homely. And now she wondered if she would have it taken from her by the monsters. But they couldn't do that, could they? She was Walter's wife – his widow. The house would come to her, wouldn't it?

She leaned her hands on her beautiful table and lowered her head. Tears streamed down her face. She felt used. Dirty. Oh, God, how she'd played tricks to make Walter want to make love to her, not knowing he found her repulsive. Now she understood his reaction after the few times he'd managed the full act. Hugging herself, she felt her skin crawl, wanted to go and get into a hot bath and scrub and scrub herself clean. And yet, Walter had loved her, hadn't he? All of that couldn't have been a lie. She must have meant something to him.

Sally's voice calling out, 'Ma, Ma, where are you?' made

Trisha straighten. She wiped her eyes with the back of her hand and sniffed loudly.

The kitchen door opened, and Sally flung herself at her. 'Eeh, lass, me little lass.'

'I want Da. I want him. Why does he have to live in heaven and not here with us, Ma?'

Trisha looked up at Martha as she held her sobbing child. Martha shrugged; her bottom lip quivered. 'I'll be back in a wee while. I think it best you two have a chat, me darling.'

Trisha nodded. Not wanting to – wanting to cry, *Don't leave me.* But even though it was so painful to her, she owed Sally some time together to allow her to let out how she was feeling. 'He didn't want to go, me little love. He didn't want to leave us.'

'I ain't ever going to be friends with God ever again. Why did he do this to us? We ain't naughty . . . Is it because we don't go to mass?'

'Naw. We say our night prayers. Da having to leave us ain't sommat that can be explained, nor can it be blamed on owt, lass.'

'But if we did go to mass, we could pray for Da.'

'Where has all this come from, Sally, love? Who's put these ideas into your head?'

'Lucy at school. She goes to mass every Sunday with her ma, and she says she's making her First Holy Communion in May next year. She starts her lessons after Christmas. She says she'll wear a white dress and a veil like a bride.'

'Aw, and you will make yours too, lass. I hadn't mentioned it as it is a long time away, but I saw the priest when he stopped me and told me all about it. I promised him we would put you down for it. Da wanted that for you an' all.'

'But don't we have to go to mass and be good to take Holy Communion? Lucy says we do. Lucy says you can't go to heaven unless you are good and free of sin ... Was Da free of sin, as he didn't go to mass, did he?'

Trisha closed her eyes against the pain this brought. Walter wasn't free of sin. He'd committed adultery, he'd broken his wedding vows when he said he would forsake all others, but then he was human, with human failings. Had he done anything worse than she had when she was unfaithful to Bobby with Ralph?

'Da was a good man, lass. He was kind. He made sick people better. God ain't going to shut him out of heaven because he didn't go to mass.'

'We could go for him, Ma.'

'Is it what you want, me little lass?'

'Yes. And Bonnie does. We've been talking about it. Bonnie ain't old enough to make her communion, though. You have to be seven. God don't think you know right from wrong till you're seven.'

'Eeh, lass. I'm so proud of you. And I knaw Da would be an' all. I promise we'll go to mass on Sunday. But ... well, look, Sally, there's sommat I have to ask you, love. How would you like to live in the cottage and not here, eh?'

'With the donkeys? Can we? But, well, it's a long way from Bonnie and the lads and Aunty Martha and Uncle Josh ... Will they miss us?'

'Naw. They'll be with us all the time, just like now, and all will stay the same only we will have to travel further ... Only, well, I ain't much for staying here without Da.'

306

'No. And Da liked the cottage so he'd come and be there with us, wouldn't he?'

This shocked Trisha. 'Lass, Da can't come with us.'

'But Aunty Martha said he'll allus be with me.'

'Eeh, me little lass.' Trisha didn't correct Sally's speech, she needed to express herself how she wanted to. But she just held her tightly to her. 'I thought you meant ... But aye, he'll allus be with us both. We can still talk to him.'

Sally was silent for a moment, then lifted her head. 'If he heard me then, he'd have said, "It's always, not allus."'

Sally giggled. A good sound.

Trisha made herself giggle. 'I knaw, he got me into the habit of correcting you, little lass.'

'You still can, Ma. I want to talk proper. If I don't, the kids at school laugh at me.'

Once more, Trisha was shocked. Her little Sally was really opening up to her.

'But I like how you say words, Ma. You won't change, will you?'

'Naw, lass. Nowt'll change me. Shall we pack a few things and go to the cottage, eh? I don't want to be here.'

'I don't, not with Da never coming back to us. Can I take Loopy? I ain't never taken Loopy before.'

Loopy was a toy dog with long ears that Trisha had knitted and stuffed for Sally when she was a baby. She had no idea she was still attached to it. She was learning a lot about her little girl today.

'Aye, you can take whatever you like. Though if we do move to live there, you'll have to choose favourite things only, as we ain't got a lot of room.'

'But what will I do with all my other things? They ain't all my favourites, you know.'

'I know. But they could be for other kids. We can take all that you don't want to the children's ward at the Vic, or to the orphanage.'

'I'd like that, Ma. Da told me about poor children. He said I should sort out all my toys and give some to those less fortunate. I'll do it for Da.'

'Good lass. There's lots we can do for Da ... we need to go to Grandma Beth's and Granddad Cyril's for Da, me darling, as that's where Da will be laid to rest.'

Sally clung on tightly to Trisha's waist. 'I don't want to lay Da to rest, Ma.' A sob escaped her. Trisha went down on her haunches. 'Naw, neither do I, little lass, neither do I.'

They held on to each other and cried together. But then, it was as if Sally became the adult. 'Don't cry, Ma, I'll look after you now.'

'Aw, me little lass. I knaw you will ... How about you make a start, eh? Go and pack a few things so Ma doesn't have to. And I'll get my few things together. I'll pop round to see if Uncle Josh'll take us to the cottage, eh?'

As she walked to Martha's, Trisha thought to herself that she must make herself say goodbye to the house as she was certain the solicitor had news on it, and it was news he didn't like. She would make this stay at the cottage as if it was for ever and see how it went. She'd only ever stayed there overnight. A lot would be different. Travel for one. It wasn't in walking distance for little Sally, and she'd have to get back and forth to work herself. *Mind, I'll have Arthur to call on. I could book him for regular*

times. Aye, it'll all work out. It might have to if I'm right about
them taking me house.

This thought made her heart feel heavy. She sighed.
She'd got through worse; she'd weather that storm if it
came.

It was while she was in the car with Josh that the idea came
to her. 'Josh, I saw a woman driving a car the other day and
your ma used to. Eeh, lad, it would help me if I can do that
if I have to live in the cottage.'

'It won't come to that, Trisha, I'm sure. I think you're
worrying unnecessarily over a feeling you had that the
solicitor had bad news that he couldn't give you. I think it
was just that you'd lost your wish to have Walter buried
near to you . . . I still can't take it all in, you know.'

'I knaw. It's like we didn't knaw him . . . Hadn't you any
idea, Josh?'

'No . . . at least, now we know about it, I have thought
about things that happened in our school days. There were
rumours about the boys that boarded. I've thought for years
that it was boys' talk, but they did involve Walter. It goes on
in such environments – experimenting, mostly, but . . . Oh,
I don't know . . . I – I'm just so sorry, Trisha. If I had any
idea, I would have spoken to him about it, but I didn't.'

'Don't worry. I didn't and I were married to him.'

'Look. I don't know if it will help or not, but you did
save him from the possibility of going to prison.'

'What? How? Eeh, he weren't in danger of that, was he?'
Trisha glanced back at Sally and was relieved to see she'd
dropped off to sleep. She always did in the car, but the poor

little mite was exhausted from the shock and all the crying she'd done.

'Well, if caught, he and Carl would have gone to prison. It's called engaging in homosexual activity and it is against the law, punishable by a hefty prison sentence. Being doctors and having no family home in Manchester, they could get away with living together as both are married men.'

'Carl is married an' all?'

'Yes, Walter told me once. I don't know whether he thought I would get suspicious. I mean, he knows you and Martha have no secrets and, well, Martha and I don't either, so he may have guessed that if I knew he had supposed difficulties in that area . . . I'm sorry, Trisha, I never thought, you don't mind me speaking so openly, do you?'

'Eeh, naw, of course I don't, lad. You're enlightening me. So, there's another poor lass just like me, struggling with feeling unwanted and, well, unattractive to her husband.'

'Yes, though, well, I am a bit more worldly wise than you are, my dear, and I do know that some married women who also have the same tendencies.'

'Women! Eeh . . . you mean, they don't like men?'

'Yes. It goes on, Trisha. Myself, I think live and let live, unless it causes pain to others, which it has to you. Not his parents so much. Walter was honest with them, it seems from what was said on Saturday, but how many other women are going through what you're going through?'

'Well then, the law should be changed to let folk live how they want to. Eeh, I'm feeling sorry for Walter now. He were a decent bloke, Josh. It seems stupid laws forced him to do what he did, but he tried, you knaw. He tried his hardest to make me happy and he did keep everything private from me and anyone who knaws us. The strain on him must have been awful, poor lad.'

'I'm glad you think of it like that, Trisha. It will help you in the future to cope with it all ... Now, what you were saying about learning to drive. I'd be glad to teach you. How about we get that old truck at the back of the cottage going, and we can drive around the paddock to get you used to it?'

'Eeh, lad, you're scared to get me out on the road, ain't you? Well, we women can do just as well as you men. But, aye, that's a good idea. It'll show me if I can handle driving.'

'Right, I'll get my mechanic, Bob, to come and have a look at it for you. In the meantime, if you want my help with anything, you only have to shout. I can come and pick you up for work and drop Sally off to school with Bonnie. It's not a problem.'

'Ta, love, that'd be grand.'

They'd reached the cottage.

As Trisha looked at it, she thought how lovely it looked, and how much she loved it, but she couldn't believe that it might have to be her permanent home.

'I'll go and have a look at that truck while I'm here, Trisha. I haven't had a proper look at it.'

As Trisha opened the door the heavy-hearted feeling stayed with her, but then Benny's words came to her as if he was sat there in the corner of the kitchen where he loved to be next to the range:

Men talk about different stuff to women. You knaw, your Walter can't help being like he is. He shouldn't have married. But that said, he's made your life better, lass, and little Sally's, so try to make yourself content with that and just in case, I need to see that solicitor, lass.

Did Benny know? But how? Her mind raced. Every word of what Benny had said now rang true. And him leaving her this cottage! It all added up. *Oh, Benny, me lovely Benny. Ta, lad. Ta for giving me and Sally all of this. We might have landed in the workhouse, who knaws? 'Cause I feel certain I've a lot to face where me home's concerned. I'm preparing meself for that, Benny, and with your help, lad, it ain't such a worry.*

The sound of Sally chatting to Josh surprised Trisha, then. She'd left her asleep in the car for a few moments while she tackled coming into the cottage with maybe having to look at it in a different light.

She went out and around to the back of the cottage. Here was a garden, a bit overrun but it could be made a nice spot, and a barn, which Sally had never bothered with. The stables were in the paddock, opposite the barn, and by the whiff of them they needed mucking out. This surprised her as she trusted Dickie to do it regularly. She'd make sure he did tonight when he brought the donkeys back from the beach.

The truck stood in front of the barn. 'Any luck, Josh? Eeh, it looks a bit clapped out.'

'No, I reckon I can get it going. I've cleaned the plugs. It's whether I can crank it as it might have rusted, though the bonnet was well covered with sacking.'

Trisha grinned. The truck looked on its last legs. 'I've never explored the barn, never had need to, but I'll take a look while I'm here.'

The door opened surprisingly easy. Inside, though, was a bit creepy as spiders' webs hung everywhere like net curtains. The interior was well lit with plenty of windows, though if they were cleaned, it would improve things, Trisha thought. She tentatively went further inside. Lined with shelves that were weighted down with everything from tools to saddles and harnesses, she spotted some fuel cans in a corner of the shed. Picking one up, she could tell it was almost full. One whiff told her its contents. 'Josh, there's petrol in here if you need it.' But then she jumped as the engine of the truck roared into life.

It was as she was on the way out that she noticed the chest. It was a huge, beautifully decorated chest and had a padlock on it. She remembered she found some keys in one of the drawers when she'd been clearing Benny's things and had put them on a hook on the back of the kitchen door, just in case they were needed for anything. Now she wondered if one of those would fit the chest.

Josh appeared at the door. 'Come on, Trish, I've got it going.' He was like an excited schoolboy. 'Let's have a trial run around the paddock, eh?'

'What, with me driving? Eeh, lad, are you sure about this?'

'Come on, you'll never make a driver if you're scared before we start.'

He looked around him then. 'Hmm, an Aladdin's cave. Be interesting to root around in here for half an hour …

Just look at that chest! That'll be worth a fortune. Would you mind if I have a good look around, Trish?'

'Naw, help yourself. Most of it means nothing to me. Though those items for the donkeys look special. Not the sort of thing they would go to the beach in.'

'No. I wonder if Benny put them in any shows at one time. Arthur might know. Weren't they great friends?'

'Aye, and both descendants of a gypsy clan, like Martha.'

'This is really interesting. Let's have a trial in the truck first, then I might have a mooch round.'

With Sally sitting between them on the bench that went the full width of the truck, Josh drove onto the paddock. But then stopped. 'Right, in the driving seat, Trisha.'

Trisha was shaking with nerves but determined to have a go. She listened carefully to Josh's instructions and set off. Sally squealed with laughter as the gears grated then they lurched forward and then backwards before coming to a halt.

But Trisha soon mastered it and drove them forward, the uneven ground throwing them all over the place and setting them off laughing their heads off. Trisha began to feel better. She hadn't imagined herself ever again giving a belly laugh like she was now, and it felt good.

'Right, pull up, Trisha.'

When she did, Josh told her, 'Off you go on your own, I'll have a look in that barn.'

'Eeh, let's do it, Sally, lass. By, I'll soon be taking you to school at this rate.'

'In this old truck?!'

Her indignation made Trisha smile, and yet saddened her. Many a kid would love to have just a ride in this truck, let alone be taken to school in it. For a moment, she worried that Sally was getting different values to herself, but then she thought, that's what she'd wanted for her, wasn't it – a better life than what she'd had herself – and she was going to do her best to see that happened.

When she started off, though a bit smoother, she still rattled their bones and had them laughing till the tears streamed down their faces. But these were good tears and for now that was all that mattered.

TWENTY-TWO

Trisha

Trisha clung on to Martha's hand. It seemed that was all she'd done these last few days – that and hug Sally – as they'd travelled north to Cumbria and since they'd arrived.

Words of comfort and kindness had come in abundance from Martha and Josh. But no words could console her.

Now they sat in the cold church, the priest's words echoing around the few folk who were here to mourn. Walter's coffin stood like a lonely symbol to a life that had been a lie.

Feelings within Trisha had been a constant turmoil of loving Walter and wanting him not to be dead, and hating him and wanting to be able to beat him with her fists.

At this moment, she stared at the coffin, tried to imagine him inside, still, not breathing, no longer able to hurt, or to love . . . or to deceive.

She'd almost shouted the word out. But bit her tongue.

The priest droned on about Walter's childhood. Had he ever had one? She couldn't remember him talking to her about it – but then, he was rarely with her to talk. He was with *him*! One of the monsters who stood with Walter's parents, head bowed, sobbing his heart out. Trisha wanted to cut his rotten heart out. He'd stolen her Walter. He'd enjoyed his company, his love and had known the completion of that love without having to strive for it, coax it, take the lead and almost beg for just a little act that would give him release. Not like she'd had to do at times.

Shame washed over her to think about those times now when she'd lie beside Walter, so wanting him to touch her, and accepting for so long him not making love to her properly, but just giving her a release of her pent-up frustration by caressing her only.

Now it seemed those times were just a doctor doing what he knew would help her, while all the time, she'd thought he suffered some condition and by getting him this far, she'd raise his desire and cure him. Now she knew why that had been so difficult to do so.

When he did make love to her, was he able to because he was thinking of Carl?

As the service ended, everything happened after that without her really feeling it and taking her thoughts from her. The long walk behind the coffin to the bleak graveyard, the burial, the sound of sobs around her, the sight of Carl almost collapsing onto Cyril as the coffin was lowered. His moans of 'I don't want him to be dead!'

Now they sat in Beth and Cyril's front room – a cosy, but dowdy-looking room with dark red furniture and carpet, a mahogany dresser and occasional tables, and thick velvet

317

curtains that shut out most of the light, even though it was a warm, sunny last day in September.

It suited them, this room that had no feeling, no comfort – functional, but not really fit for purpose. How two people could hide their true colours for so long beggared belief. Poor Sally was bewildered as twice since coming into this room she'd tried to go to them and had been crossly told to be a good girl and stay quietly with her mother.

This second time as Sally came back looking lost and rejected, Beth's whisper could be heard all around the so quiet room. 'If they must be here, why can't they just keep out of our way?'

Cyril glared at her. 'For goodness' sake, keep some dignity for us, will you?'

Beth looked mortified but didn't retort.

Cyril caught Josh's eye. 'I'm sorry, she's overwrought. It's all too much for her. Of course you are all welcome.'

Welcome! Trisha wanted to spit in his eye. She hadn't wanted to come, knew she would be humiliated, but her own solicitor had insisted.

What she'd seen of Cleator when they'd arrived here was beautiful. Mountains in the distance, hills surrounding the small town, and they'd come over a bridge to a river running not far away, with its picturesque views. But, oh, how she wished they hadn't come. None of it was how Trisha would have liked it, and she didn't seem able to mourn her Walter. As he had been that too – hers. Hers and Sally's.

The solicitor, who sat to the side of a bureau with his papers spread out on the desk, formed by the lid being open, cleared his throat. 'We are gathered for the reading of the last will and testament of Walter Kenning. May he rest in peace.'

He cleared his throat again and then, in a very formal voice, read Walter's words:

'*It is my wish and intention that the assets of my estate shall be distributed as follows . . .*' He paused and lowered the document he was reading from. 'Well now. Before I progress, I believe we have Walter's widow amongst us.' He looked around with an expression on his face as if something unpleasant was about to show itself to him.

'That's me, sir.'

'Yes, well, I'm afraid there isn't much in the last will and testament that is of interest to you, Mrs Kenning.'

A noise like a disdainful smirk sounded from across the room. Trisha looked in the direction of where the sound came from. Carl sat in the opposite corner to her; his arms folded, his face scanning her, Martha and Josh with a look that said he thought them scum.

Trisha cringed. Martha's hand tightened on hers.

Josh, who sat on the other side of Martha, stood and picked up the dining chair he was sat on and moved it to the other side of Trisha. Sally, who'd been sitting on his knee, followed him. As he went to pick her up, the solicitor's drawl directed at him. 'Is it necessary to have that child in here?'

'I believe so, sir.' Josh had that tone in his voice that brooked no argument. 'I cannot leave to care for her elsewhere as I need to stay to protect Walter's widow. He wouldn't expect anything less of me in this hostile environment. He would be appalled that Trisha is being treated in this way.'

'As you wish.'

Carl looked aghast at Josh. His face had reddened, and it was obvious he was using all his self-control not to retort.

Suddenly, Trisha seemed to find the strength she'd been lacking. Standing, she glared at each one in the room. 'I knaw what you're all hinting at, so you needn't keep making snide remarks, and you, Carl, eeh, how you can sit in the same room as me beggars belief. I don't need owt of Walter's, ta very much. You can share the spoils of his life between you for all I care.'

Martha stood. 'Trisha, love!'

'Naw, Martha, I'm going to have me say. I were deceived – used – but I ain't without me pride, or me memories of how Walter played the wonderful, kind and loving man. They're tainted now by his true character coming to light. And, aye, at times I hate him, but I hate you more, Carl. You can have what you want of what's left of the man who didn't deserve mine and Sally's love, and should never have made it that we suffered this indignity. I just don't care any more!'

When she sat down, she was shaking from head to toe. Martha's arm came around her and held her to her.

But she could not protect her from the vile Carl or any of these folk as humiliation clothed her with Carl's retaliation.

'Kind and loving, huh? He had to work hard to achieve that. You repulsed him, as you do me. The way you speak, the way you pawed him, he felt sick to the stomach at having to be with you and your brat!'

'That's enough! How dare you speak like that to Trisha? How dare you? You will apologise now!'

Josh looked like a giant as he towered over Carl. Carl shrunk back.

'I'm sorry, I'm sure, but she should apologise to me too.'

'Shall we all calm down, please. This is very upsetting for everyone, especially the deceased's parents. Please show them a little respect and compassion.' The solicitor's face was bright red as he said this. To Trisha, he looked afraid, and yet he had set the atmosphere and to her mind was ultimately to blame.

Everyone settled down again. Trisha dreaded what was coming but hoped she had prepared herself.

'To my wife, I leave my thanks for all she added to my life and the sum of one hundred pounds. For my stepdaughter, who enhanced my life beyond words, I have set up a trust fund to pay for her schooling and a sum in the amount of one hundred pounds when she reaches the age of twenty-one.

'To my parents, I leave the sum of three hundred pounds, and I wish them to go on that world tour they have always dreamed of. If in the event they do not outlive me, then the sum left to them is to revert to my main estate.

'After these legacies I leave my beloved Carl the balance of my estate, to include all property and personal effects, and I thank him for the happiness he gave to me and for giving my life – my very existence – a meaning.'

Carl's smirk sickened Trisha. Her heart felt like lead. Tears stung her eyes, but she hung on, keeping her pride intact. Rising, she kept her voice steady and looked straight ahead. 'Thank you. I am leaving now. Come on, Sally, lass.'

Sally wriggled off Josh's knee and ran towards Beth and Cyril. 'I have to go now, Grandma Beth.' She put up her arms for her hug.

Beth turned her head away.

'Grandma?'

'I am not your grandmother, child. Not any longer.'

'I know you ain't my proper one, but you still can be my grandma, if you like.'

'I don't like. Go with your mother.'

Sally stood her ground, staring at Beth.

'Come on, Sally, love. Don't worry. Grandma Beth and Granddad Cyril are very upset. Let's leave them for now, eh?'

The solicitor stood as if he would stop her leaving, but he just said, 'Erm, before you go, there is a letter for you, Mrs Kenning. Your late husband lodged it with me to give to you in the event of his death being untimely.'

'He did what?' Carl glared at the solicitor. 'He said nothing about this to me. I think I should be allowed to read it first. Surely it can be classed as being part of "the rest" of my Walter's estate?'

'No, I'm afraid it isn't, sir. This was lodged specifically for Mrs Kenning and is her property and her property alone.'

'Well!' Carl's head bounced on his shoulders as he looked from the solicitor to Beth and Cyril as if they could do anything, which alarmed Trisha. Had they colluded in all of this? They'd seemed to hate Carl, but all day they had been hanging on his every word, comforting him. The thought came to her that they must have known he was to inherit everything, and so needed to butter him up – to have him as a friend to keep something of Walter near to them. With this thought a small amount of pity for them entered her, but then, did they deserve that from her? Sighing, she didn't know what to think any more and was glad when Josh rose and took the letter for her as she only had enough energy to leave the room with her head held high as she was so near to collapsing point.

'How is it they can feel that they can humiliate you like that, me darling? I just want to be hugging you.'

'I need a hug, love, ta.'

As she held her, Martha said, 'I am not for believing what I heard and witnessed. It was as if Walter was for being a stranger to us.'

'He was. If I'd have known the real him, I'd never have fallen in love with him, but then, there were many times you hinted. You knew, didn't you?'

Martha hung her head.

'Don't feel guilty lass, we had a pact. I made me own decisions, but then, how was I to know? That ... that man they portrayed wasn't like Walter showed himself to me. I'm trying to let go of what I thought was the truth. How could he have done this to me as if I was nowt?'

'I am not thinking that it is right that you should let all of it go, Trish, love, not all of it was a lie.'

'How much did you know, Martha?'

'It is that I had a powerful feeling came to me that you were both to be suffering heartache. But it was too late by the time I was realising what was Walter's true life. I was for being as shocked as you when he died ... Trisha, I did not see that coming. Nor could I tell you of my premonitions as I would have been going against your wishes.'

'Aye, I knaw. And I knaw you try to hint to me, but allus I've said I'll face what I have to face when it hits me. I will with this an' all.'

Josh joined them outside the house then. He was shaking with temper. 'How dare they? I've a good mind to report that solicitor for bad practice. He was to blame for that shambles.'

'Naw, I want nowt more to do with them, Josh.'

'I know, Trisha, and I don't blame you. You deserved none of that. If Walter wasn't dead already, I'd kill him myself! He's insulted you and us. He's thrown your love and our friendship back in our faces, and when we can do nothing about it. I'd like to go back to the churchyard and spit on his coffin before the grave diggers cover him up!'

Trisha had never seen Josh so angry. 'Don't be worked up on my account, Josh, lad. I'll get over it. I'm used to knocks. This one has kicked me in the stomach, but I'm trying to find some understanding after what you said of how the threat of prison hung over Walter.'

'I wish now that they had been caught – the pair of them. I would relish knowing they were rotting in prison . . . Come to think of it, I might just have a word with someone. That will is evidence of their relationship, not that I believe it should be criminal to love how they did, but I so want my revenge on that spiteful Carl.'

'I'm not for thinking that it is the way we should go, me darling. The will was expressing Walter's love for Carl but nothing in it would be incriminating to Carl. And you are right, they shouldn't be persecuted for loving one another, but for how they were for using poor Trish to be able to do that, then, yes, I too am feeling that I want revenge.'

'I know, Martha, but I am incensed and would so love to get our own back on the pompous idiot. God, if he comes to live in the house, I won't be able to bear having him that close.'

'Josh, don't do this to yourself. It's not worth it. He ain't worth it. Let's forget them, all of them . . . I knaw it ain't easy, and I feel like clawing them all to death, but I ain't going to let them spoil the rest of me life. Walter's left me well off, and me Sally is taken care of an' all. I ain't asking for owt more. Revenge ain't worth having to stay in their lives a moment longer than I have to.'

'You're right. And it's all done and dusted. I have the letter and a cheque for you from the solicitor. He's given me the details of the trust for Sally, too. You are the trustee of the account, so you can draw Sally's fees and any money you need to equip her for school. He will have regular statements from the account so he can keep an eye on it. But I doubt you will ever hear from him again.'

'Ta, Josh.'

'Now, shall we go back to the inn and collect our things and get out of here? We can stop at that inn in Keswick and have a bite to eat.'

They agreed with Josh and left it to him to go into the inn and to bring their overnight bags out to the car.

'Let me knaw how much the bill was, Josh, and I'll pay it.'

'No, that's all right. It's been our pleasure to bring you and to help you through today . . . Though, of course, not much else has been a pleasure.'

Trisha nodded at this. 'Would you mind if I read me letter now? Only I don't want to be on me own when I do.'

'To be sure, that's fine, me darling. I'll be coming to sit in the back with you before it is we set off. I can hold your hand then and be near to comfort you.'

'Ta, I don't knaw what I'd do without you, Martha. Both of you.'

Trish recognised the note paper as soon as she opened it. They were sheets out of the writing box that she had bought for Walter for their last Christmas. She'd thought the case so beautiful. Shaped like one of those sloping desks, the outside was inlaid with a pearl-effect picture of a quill pen. The box opened to provide a pad lined with velvet to rest on while you wrote and a compartment for writing paper and envelopes. Each crisp sheet was embossed with the same quill pen design. Walter had loved it. She remembered his hug, and his kiss. A tear plopped onto Walter's letter. When she wiped it away, it smeared the first word, 'Darling'. *How appropriate*, she thought. *Like the love he gave me – smudged.*

Darling Trisha,

This is the hardest letter I have ever had to write, but if you are reading it, then it means that I am no longer with you.

It also means that you now know the truth about me. I want to apologise – not for who I am, but for hurting you so badly.

It will be hard for you to believe, but I have never loved another woman like I love you. And it truly was with all my heart. For the love you have shown me has been unconditional. You took me as I was from what you saw – I was under no illusion, as by any means I was not pleasing to the eye.

Then you accepted when I couldn't make love to you. Although lately we did, and that was through your gentle coaxing and patience. Please do not believe Carl if he says anything bad about it.

I know Carl very well, and he will put words into my mouth that aren't true. It suited him to make me say I was repulsed by you. I wasn't, darling. I loved loving you. I was just a weak person, who couldn't believe I was loved by him, and so did everything he asked of me.

Trisha gasped as confusion sent her into a whirl.
'What is it, me darling?'
Trisha could only show Martha the letter and point to what she hoped was the truth. Martha didn't comment. Trisha read on.

If I seemed strange after we'd made love, it was the shame I felt. It washed over me after each time – the shame of my deceitfulness towards you.

As much as I love Carl, he can be controlling and often used emotional blackmail. He did that to make me leave him my property. I didn't want to, I wanted to leave it to you, but I did have a large sum of money, left to me in various legacies, which he knew nothing about. This I have left to you and Sally and my parents.

I am choosing to be buried near to my parents so that you will not be subjected to meeting Carl, because wherever I am laid to rest, I know he will visit. I don't think you will unless I am in Blackpool. So, this decision was made to save you further hurt and confrontation, for no matter how much I counsel Carl not to insult you or hurt you, I know he will. He is innately jealous of you and what you mean to me. He will seek to discredit you and crush you.

I want to thank you, darling, for allowing me to be a father to our precious Sally.

May I ask if you can find it in your heart to keep her love and respect for me and not taint it by telling her about the real me?

You see, the real me is also a man capable of great love and I gave that to you to the best of my ability.

I am not making excuses when I say I cannot help being me. If I could have done so, I would. I, and men and women like me, are made differently to you. We didn't make ourselves – we were made. Why? No one knows. Maybe one day they will.

But ignorance led to branding us criminals and throwing us into prisons for an indeterminable time. Therefore, we build a life that shields the life we desperately want to – no, need – to live to be true to ourselves.

What I have done to you to enable me to live this life is despicable. And as I write this, I am desperate to find a way out. I will. And when I do, you will read this. For death is my only sanctuary. I cannot bear to leave you and Sally and to carry on living in this world without you. The end of us must be the end of me.

I want you to go forward, I hope with a little of the love you gave to me still in your heart even though you now know who I am, as then I will rest easier.

I love you, Trisha, despite all the complications that I am. I love you deeply. Once again, thank you.

Your loving Walt xxx

'Eeh, God! He killed himself. Naw ... naw ... naw!' Trisha found it hard to pronounce the words as her mouth was stretched with the agony of crying and talking.

'Trish, Trish, me darling. Oh, Trish.'

'It's ... it's happened again, Martha! Bobby first, now Walter. Naw ... naw ... naw!'

'Stop the car, Josh. Be helping me to help Trish.'

As the car slowed, Trisha heard Josh say, 'Is Sally all right?'

This jolted Trisha. She looked down frantically at Sally who had her head on her lap. Seeing she was asleep was a huge relief.

The car came to a halt. Martha gently took hold of Sally whilst Trisha felt strong arms wrap around her and help her out of the car, then hold her close.

'What is it, Trisha? What has Walter said to make you think his death wasn't an accident? Oh, God, what a mess.'

'I am for having the letter, Josh ... Oh, Josh, it is as Trisha was saying. Poor Walter could no longer cope with his double life. He loved Trish very much, and yet knew that what it was that he was doing was going to cause her so much pain. He says he couldn't continue in that way. God love him.'

'I can't believe it. My God ... Walter! He always seemed so level-headed.'

'It was for being an act of love, Josh.'

Josh read the letter. 'I can't take it in ... Walter? But then, Trisha, in this letter, I think Walter is trying to help you, not only in shielding you from whatever the hateful Carl might say, but he states that he really wanted to leave the house to you! We should take this further.'

Trisha clung to Josh, her mind a turmoil at this moment. She didn't care about winning the house back ... *How am I going to bear it? Two men died for the love of me. Am I some kind of monster?*

But then she thought, *No. I didn't make Bobby or Walter what they were. I only loved them. And yes, I will continue to love them both despite their failings – we all have those. Me more than most.*

With this thought, Trisha felt stronger. She came out of Josh's arms. 'I'm all right, ta, both of you. It was a shock, but I'll do as Walter told me to and go forward with me life. And yes, I will fight for what Walter wanted me to have. I have to, for Sally. And aye, I'll do the other thing he asked of me, I'll allus keep Sally's love for him alive, though it may take me a long time to accept all I've been put through and me marriage being a sham – made so by the man I loved, and who said he loved me.'

With these decisions, Trisha felt she could face the future. *I'll give it me best anyroad, I owe that to Sally.*

TWENTY-THREE

Martha

Martha couldn't believe it when after a week of settling Trisha into her cottage, she peeped out of the curtain at the sound of a horn beeping and there Trisha was in a car and sitting behind the wheel grinning.

Running to the front door, she stared at the car. It was obviously not new, but it was amazing all the same to see Trisha at the wheel and Sally giggling through the back window.

Trisha opened her door with a creak, then had to hold on to it as Blackpool's renowned October winds almost flung it open out of her grasp. 'Eeh, lass, what do you think, eh?'

'Where is it you got it from? . . . How is it you are driving it? Josh said it was that you'd driven the truck, but—'

'Ha! Aye, I drove the truck around the field every night after you left, then once I felt confident, I asked Arthur to find one for me. He were shocked an' all! But he came up with this! I love it.'

'You weren't for saying.' Martha looked at the white car with a black roof and swelled with pride that her Trish had actually driven it. 'Oh, Trish, it's lovely and it is proud of you that I am. Are you knowing how to fill it with petrol, and how is it you can turn that handle thingy to start it?'

'By, that's the hardest part of it, but I'm mastering it. Though Arthur came this morning to get it going for me.'

'Haha, you'll be having muscles like a man, so you will.'

They both giggled, but then were surrounded by a herd of excited kids as Bonnie came out followed by the boys, Joseph bringing up the rear.

'Jump in, me lads and lasses. Your car has arrived!'

When they were all seated and Martha had fetched Bonnie's school bag, she waved them off with her heart in her mouth, but Trisha reversed the car out smoothly, and went on her way, tooting the horn as she did.

The distraction of the phone ringing took her mind off her fears as she ran back in to answer it.

'George! Is it that everything is all right?'

'No, Sheila isn't well. Is Josh there? I've tried his shop, but no answer and the factory manager says he hasn't seen him yet this morning. I thought he left home around seven.'

Martha's heart skipped a beat. 'No, it is that he left for work. He was a lot later than is normal for him. Maybe it is that he didn't hear the phone. How badly is Sheila?'

'Very. She's in the hospital. They are giving her oxygen.'

'Oh, Holy Mary, Mother of God, what next is to befall us? Poor Sheila. It is that I thought when she was here just a few days since that her health is deteriorating, so I did.'

'Well, she collapsed this morning. I am worried sick. Please try to get hold of Josh. I'm at the Vic, women's ward. Thanks, Martha, goodbye.'

Martha looked around frantically, then jumped as the letter box flap lifted and letters spewed through. Calming herself, she picked up the receiver and dialled 'O'. The operator's voice came down the line.

After giving the number of the shop, she came back with, 'Eeh, everyone wants that number this morning, you're the third. Is there someone special at the end of that line?'

'No, it is for being my husband's shop. Please be putting me through.'

As had happened for his dad, Martha didn't get a reply. The operator cut her off after a few minutes.

Picking up the post, Martha ran for her jacket. The sun was shining on this late October morning, but there was a nip in the air.

By the time she got to the door, Trisha was back. Not letting her get out of the car, Martha ran out to her and grabbed the passenger side door. 'Take me to Josh's shop, Trisha. And it is that you must hurry, love, something is happening to my Josh, I am for knowing it.'

'Eeh, lass, are you acting on a vision then?'

'No, strangely it is that I didn't get a premonition, but . . .' Martha brought Trisha up to date with what had happened.

'By, lass, it never rains but it pours. I'll soon have you there.'

Trisha slammed her foot down and the car shot forward. It was only Martha's quick reactions that saved the children from harm as they too shot forward in the back seats, but Martha was able to get her arm in front of them, even though it bruised her badly. 'Trisha, it is that you need to make movements that are less jerky. Johnny and Joseph were for almost coming to harm then.'

'Aye, I haven't mastered some things yet and it is a bit like riding the roller coaster at times. Sorry, lads, Aunty Trisha will be more careful.'

With her arm sore and her heart still beating ten to the dozen, Martha sat back and prayed her Josh was all right.

When they reached the shop on Waterloo Road, below where Josh used to have a flat, the door was open.

'It all looks in order, lass. Come on, let's go and see.'

'No, it is that the lights aren't on, and that is for being strange as you cannot work in there without them.'

'Eeh, I can see that all the window is blocked in behind the dis ... Naw! Martha, look, lass, half the cameras have gone out of the window and the shelf is broken.'

'Be staying there with the kids, Trisha, I'm going in, so I am ... Josh! Josh!'

The small light that splashed in through the doorway and beamed through the broken backing of the window didn't light the shop enough for her to see inside. 'Josh!'

Reaching for the light, Martha switched it on. The sight that met her made her scream. Josh lay unconscious on the floor, blood seeping from a wound on his head. Trisha came running in.

'Naw! Josh, lad ... Martha, telephone for an ambulance and the police! Hurry, lass. I don't knaw where the phone is.'

As Martha ran to the counter, she registered the chaos around her. Expensive equipment lay strewn around the floor. The glass front of the counter was smashed and all of the cameras that had been displayed had gone.

Frantically she picked up the receiver, dialled the operator and asked to be put through to the police station. They answered immediately and took charge, saying they would organise an ambulance and send someone round to the shop.

With the relief of help coming, she went over to her beloved Josh. 'Is he still unconscious?'

'He is, love. But he's breathing all right, and his heart is ticking strongly. I reckon he's had a bad blow to the head.'

Martha had the urge to shout that she could see that, but stopped herself. She knew that Trisha was in shock too.

The sound of bells clanging gave a sense of help being on hand, but didn't settle her frightened and desperate mind. 'It is that he is here!'

The policeman ran forward and knelt beside Josh. 'Poor lad, he must have been jumped as he opened the shop. We've had one or two burglaries lately. Sharpe's the jeweller's was done over last week. Same thing, a blow to his head just as he let himself into the shop. But he's all right, lasses, so don't be fretting. The hospital will soon get him round and but for a bad headache for days, he'll be fine.'

Distant bells interrupted him. 'That'll be the ambulance now. Is that your car with the nippers in, eh? Get it moved so the ambulance can park near, and look after them kids, they're screaming their little heads off.'

This did more to make them both jump into action than any kind word could. Trish was soon zooming towards the promenade in reverse gear!

'Stop! Jesus, please stop, Trish. It is that we'll be run into if we get to the prom.'

The stopping was a sudden jerk, but luckily apart from bouncing on the seat, the boys were all right.

Martha jumped out. 'See to the boys, Trish. It is that I must be with me Josh.'

Running for all she was worth, on shaky legs she didn't think would carry her, Martha arrived at the open doors of the ambulance, just as they stretchered Josh out. His eyes were open.

'Josh! Oh, Josh, me darling. Are you for being all right?'

A little moan and a nod of his head reassured her. His hand came out to her. 'Hop in with him, lass. It'll reassure him.'

Martha turned and saw that Trisha had driven up close again. 'It is that I need me friend to be following us.'

'All right. I'll tell her, you get in with Mr Green. That's his name, isn't it? The copper said it was, as he knaws him.'

'Yes, Josh. He's my husband, so he is.'

Once in the ambulance, Martha took Josh's hand. 'Oh, Josh, me darling, what is it that happened?'

'Don't ask him a lot of questions, lass. He'll feel confused. Just sit with him and let him knaw you're here, eh?'

Martha's heart raced as she looked at Josh's ashen-white face. His eyes closed, then his throat retched.

'Eh up, he's about to throw up. Mind yourself, lass.'

Josh threw his heart up into the tin bowl the ambulance man held under him.

'Eeh, I'd say he's got concussion. That might take a bit

336

longer to sort out. Bloody thieves. There's a gang of them and the cops can't catch them. No one ever sees owt. But we've had some in here who knaw who they are but won't tell. I reckon they're a violent lot because of how they use brutal force on the shop owners and how folk are afraid to give out knowledge on them.'

Martha shuddered as she thought of Betty opening up the shop, but then she thought this gang wouldn't be interested in a lot of baby clothes. She almost wanted to giggle at the thought, but knew if she did, she wouldn't be able to stop. As it was, she wanted to scream and scream such was the fear and panic inside her.

At the hospital, she was made to sit down in a waiting area while Josh was whisked away.

At last Trisha came through the door carrying a distraught Joseph and with a crying Johnny holding her hand. Johnny broke away and ran to Martha. Holding him steadied her a little. 'It's all right, my wee one. Da will be fine, it is that he has banged his head. Now, you are for doing that often and you're all right, aren't you?'

'Yes, but I saw blood. And Da couldn't walk, he – he was on a bed.'

Martha could sense his fear. His little world was still so fragile.

Sitting him on the chair next to her, she encouraged him to lay his head on her lap while she took Joseph. Joseph stood on the bench and hugged her neck.

'Shush, my wee ones. All will be fine, so it will. Da is to have a cut on his head seen to, then it is he will come home with us, so he will.'

'Is there owt I can do, lass?'

'It is worried I am about George and Sheila. Can you be finding out where they are?'

'Aye, I'll ask at the desk and see if they can contact George. He's in the women's ward with Sheila, is that right?'

Martha nodded as she stroked the now quiet Johnny's back and patted Joseph gently. He gradually quietened, and this made Martha feel a little better.

When Trisha came back she said that they had rung the ward and Mr Green was coming down.

'I brought your letters in, Martha. I thought you'd be sat here. I wondered if you wanted to flick through them to see if there was anything important.' As Trisha handed them over, she pointed to the top one. 'We knaw who that one's from, don't we?'

Trisha was smiling. It was then that Martha saw the navy stamp. A letter from Jack, at last. She looked up at Trisha. 'Oh, thank goodness. It's been for being a long time. Will you be opening it for me, love?'

After a moment, Trisha gasped. 'He's coming home! Eeh, he wrote from Gibraltar, five days ago. He'll be in Portsmouth now. He asks if you can put him up, but by, that'll be a bit of a bind now, love. We don't knaw what's happening with Josh and his ma yet.'

'We'll be sorting something out. He can have my guest room and it is that he'll be a help with the kids.'

'He could stay at mine, but it wouldn't be right with me not . . .' Trisha took a deep breath. Her eyes filled with tears.

'Oh, me darling. I want to be hugging you.'

'I knaw. For all he did, I miss Walter. We were good friends an' all. His coming home was the highlight of me life.'

Martha felt the tears pricking the back of her eyes but dared not give way to them. 'It is that we all miss him, me darling.'

Trisha sat down. 'But it's like I've got to forgive him to get right with meself, but for what? Being who he was made to be? . . . Do you knaw, if he'd have told me, I'd have gone along with it to help him . . . right in the beginning when he first courted me . . . Aw, Martha, was all that a sham – a set-up?'

Martha didn't think she could deal with this right now, and yet she had to. 'Sit next to me, love. It is that I cannot move for having the boys.'

When Trisha sat, Martha could feel her shaking. 'It is that grief hits you when you are least expecting it, Trish. Be letting yourself grieve, don't always be stopping it because of what happened. You are to remember the happy times. I know you are for understanding Walter now, and it is that you know that he suffered because he loved you so much. Don't think it is that you aren't allowed to grieve for him.'

'It's seeing me house an' all. It's so unfair what that man did and got away with. I knaw from Walter's letter that he were forced to give our home to that beast. I wouldn't be able to bear seeing him in the garden.'

Martha was at a loss. Trisha had stopped crying, but her voice showed her distress. Johnny caught on to it.

'I feel sad when I think of me mam and dad, Trisha. I cry into me pillow.'

'Eeh, I knaw, lad, it hurts, don't it? Well, me and you could cry together. If ever you feel sad, you get Martha to ring me, and I'll take you in me car to where we can cry with each other. 'Cause you feel lonely if you cry on your own.'

'I do. It makes me cry more. If I was with you, I'd be able to stop.'

Martha felt the pain of this. She hadn't known Johnny cried on his own.

'And if it is for being in the night hours, come and wake me up, me wee darling. I won't make you stop, I'll just be for holding you until you feel better.'

'What, in your bed with you and Da?'

Martha grinned. Little Johnny always had a way of getting what he wanted. Josh had never allowed the children into their bed, except on a Sunday morning when they came in and jumped all over them. 'Well, if it is that you are really sad, I'll lie with you on your bed, how is that?'

The conversation ended there as George came through the swing doors, his face ashen. 'How is my boy? Where is he?'

Martha went to rise but found that Joseph was asleep on her shoulder. His legs had buckled and he perched on her bruised arm.

'Oh, George, I'm not for knowing . . .'

George cut her off by turning towards the desk and demanding in a loud voice from the terrified-looking young girl behind it to know where his son was.

'He will be in the assessment ward, sir, but you cannot go in there. The doctor will fetch you when he is ready.'

'Ready? Well, I want to know now, not when *he* is ready. What's his name? No doubt I know him and once he knows it's me, he will let me in.'

Martha had never known the lovely George to behave like this before. She wondered just how Sheila was as this behaviour was of a distraught man pushed beyond his limits.

'Will you be taking Joseph, Trish, love?'

Once Trisha had Joseph in her arms, Martha rose and went to George. 'Come and be sitting yourself down, love. They are for saying that Josh may be concussed. They are taking the best care of him possible. How is it that Sheila is for being?'

'She's not well, Martha, dear. I woke up in the night and she was sweating. I cooled her down and she went back to sleep, but then this morning, I woke to her leaning over the bed unable to get her breath. She's asking for Josh.'

'Oh dear, that such a thing should happen to Josh.'

'Now, now, dear, you were being strong when I came in. You must be so now for me too. Trisha, is there a way you could take the boys home? I think it would be best for Martha not to have the worry of them. '

'Aye, I'm driving me own car now, George!'

'Really? Well, good for you.' George shook his head. 'When I think of the two ragamuffins you both were when you came into my estate agency that first time, I feel very proud of how you've progressed. I – I was sorry to hear of Walter's passing, love. He was a good man, and I know you were very happy.'

Martha was glad now of Josh's decision not to tell his parents about Walter. They'd known him a long time due to his association from school days with Josh and were sad not to be able to go to his funeral. She watched Trisha closely, ready to go to her side.

'Ta, George. It was a shock. I – I'm doing all right now, though. I've got to, for me Sally.'

'If you don't mind me asking, what happened to your house? Are you just unable to live there? Josh didn't seem to know. I mean, I'm not being nosy, but I said to Josh that if you wanted to sell it, we would handle it for you.'

Trisha blushed. But then surprised Martha as she answered, 'It wasn't left to me. Someone had a hold over Walter, he was bullied into leaving his estate to them. But I have a letter from Walter that tells me all about it and so I ain't letting it worry me.'

Martha thought about what Trisha had said not ten minutes ago about seeing her home and knew the pain behind this denial.

'That's preposterous and illegal! Leave it with me, my dear, I will talk to people I know. Don't worry, I won't mention names, but I'll see how you stand in that.'

Martha saw Trisha go to protest and then stop herself. This shocked Martha. If there was a chance of winning the house back, would Trisha go through with it? She'd have to talk to her, make her realise that it might mean the whole story coming out and Walter being disgraced and already she'd been warned that the cost of contesting the will would break her and could leave her homeless. But then, it might mean justice for Walter as Trisha was right, he was bullied. Poor, lovely Walter. If only he'd talked to Trisha.

At last, a nurse appeared. 'Mrs Green?'

Martha stepped forward, glad that Trish hadn't left as George had suggested.

'The doctor would like to see you, dear.'

'Can my father-in-law come too? He's Josh's ... I – I mean, Mr Green's father.'

'Yes, of course.'

The doctor, an elderly man, smiled as they entered the room where he sat behind a table with files stacked on one side of him and papers laid out in front of him.

'George! I didn't realise that Joshua was your son.'

George shook his hand.

'Good to see you again, Andrew, though I wish it was under better circumstances – my son and wife both being in this hospital at the moment.'

'Well, you have no need to worry about your son.' He turned to Martha. 'So, this is your daughter-in-law? Pleased to meet you, Mrs Green.' He shuffled the papers in front of him. 'Now, Joshua is not well, but then the poor fellow has a nasty gash on his head suggesting a heavy blow with an instrument. The position of the wound, though, leads us to believe that he will make a full recovery. We are going to sedate him to make him comfortable and give the injury time to heal a little. But I'm confident that though he will have a nasty headache and two black eyes, he will be well on the road to recovery in a few days' time.'

Martha sighed with relief. 'Thank you, Doctor. Is it that I can see him?'

'I think you should leave him to the nurses, my dear, and come back in the morning.'

Martha stood her ground. 'No, I am wanting to see him to be putting me mind at rest, Doctor.'

'Very well. I will fetch a nurse to take you to him. Now then, George, you say Sheila is in here. Is it anything serious?'

'Yes. She's very ill . . . I am afraid I might lose her.'

'Oh, my dear fellow. I'm so sorry.'

Martha felt shocked to the core. Yes, she'd known Sheila was not well, but she hadn't thought it was this serious. It just hadn't registered with her worry over Josh. 'Doctor, is it that Josh is already asleep?'

'I'm not sure, but most likely. I left a sedative to be given to him when he'd been transferred to a ward after his wound had been cleaned and my junior had stitched it.'

'He should see his mammy . . . Oh, George, it is sorry that I am. Is Sheila for being awake?'

'She's drifting in and out of sleep. But, yes, I agree. If it is possible, Joshua should be taken to her.'

'I will arrange it. You two go to Sheila and someone will bring him along in a wheelchair.'

When they left the office, Martha no longer felt that Trisha should wait for her. She told George she would be along very soon, but had to sort the children out.

Trisha sat on the bench. Joseph was still asleep, and someone had given Johnny a pencil and he was happily scribbling away, reminding Martha of his tutor who would be at her house by ten o'clock. On seeing her, he stopped what he was doing and ran to her. 'Is Da all right, Mammy?'

Sweeping him up, she told him, 'He is. But, me wee darling, Da's for having a sore head, and needs to be staying here for a couple of days for the nurses to look after him. But it is that someone else is coming soon – your Uncle Jack.'

Johnny cheered and clapped his hands. 'When? When?'

'It could be later today, but we aren't for being sure. It is that it might be tomorrow.'

'It's always like that with Uncle Jack. He's gone and then he comes back!'

'So, it is that we have to wait and see . . . Oh, Trish, can I be asking you to take the boys home for me, as it is that Johnny's tutor will be waiting for him?'

'Aye, I was going to suggest that. And I'll pop into the shop and make sure all's well there, then I'll stay at yours till you come home.'

Martha put Johnny down and then quickly whispered to Trisha, telling her what was happening.

'Aw, well, don't worry about a thing, love. You do what you have to do and I'll see you later. Hopefully Jack will make it today.'

Martha waved them off with a heavy heart and turned to go to the women's ward, praying as she did that they wouldn't lose the lovely Sheila.

TWENTY-FOUR

Martha

When she arrived on the ward, Martha found that Sheila had been moved to a private room.

There she found Josh sat in a wheelchair, his face ashen, his head swathed in bandages. She ran to him, stood behind him and gently took him in her arms.

His shaking hands covered hers. A sob wracked his body. Sheila lay, unmoving and unresponsive, ready to leave this world.

'My darling . . . I – I feel so lost.'

'I have you held safely, me darling, it is that me love will be with you. Is it that you have said your goodbyes?'

'I have. It breaks my heart. Such a lovely, funny and annoying mother. I couldn't wish for a better one.'

'Is it that you have told her that?'

'I have. Oh, Martha, I'm in such pain, physical and emotional.'

'I am knowing your pain, me darling, Now it is that we should get you back to your ward and let the doctors start their treatment of you.'

'Yes, my darling. Will you see to my shop?'

'I will. I'll be checking with the police as to how everything is there and seeing to it being secured.'

Martha turned to the nurse. 'Can we be taking Mr Green to his own ward, please, Nurse? I will be coming with him to see him settled.'

'Yes, Mrs Green.'

Martha went over to Sheila and kissed her cheek. 'Ta for everything, me lovely lady. I love you and will be remembering you always.' To George she gave a hug. Then with Josh saying a final goodbye, she followed the nurse, holding his hand and with tears streaming down both of their faces.

Once in a bed, the sister gave him the draught prescribed. Still holding her hand, Josh fell into a peaceful sleep.

'You can visit whenever you like, Mrs Green. Mr Green is to be kept asleep for two days, to rest his brain while healing takes place as there is a lot of bruising, which can be worrying when it is on the head.'

'I am for understanding, and ta for all your patience and kindness. I'll be resting well knowing my Josh is in your hands. And yes, it is that I will visit later and most of tomorrow.'

As she went to leave, the nurse caught hold of her and hugged her. 'I just wanted to comfort you, lass. You've a lot on your plate. But don't you worry about Mr Green, he'll be looked after.'

Martha sobbed on the shoulder of this kind stranger and found a release she couldn't burden Trisha with, as she was still so delicate, so hurt.

'Ta, that is for meaning the world to me.' Martha managed a tearful smile.

When she got back to George she found him sitting with silent tears running down his face, holding the hand of a still, lifeless Sheila.

He looked up when she neared him.

'She's gone. It was peaceful, she just slipped away.'

'It's heart sorry that I am, George. Will you look at how beautiful she looks in her peace. A lovely lady. We will miss her so much, so we will.'

'She loved you, Martha, and the children. And Josh was her world.'

'Well, it is that our hearts go with her as we were for loving her too. Are you wanting to stay longer, George?'

With him saying he did, Martha told him about how Josh was now, then left to make her way home.

Once she'd walked past the area that was to be cleared to build a park – something all were excited about – she caught sight of Arthur and waved frantically at him.

He came to a stop next to her. 'What are you doing up here, Martha, lass?'

She told him what had happened.

'Well, I don't knaw how I missed that, there's not much happening here that I don't knaw about. I'm right sorry, lass. Are you wanting to get home?' At her nod, he told her he'd a fare to drop off at the hospital and would come straight back for her. 'You wait here and I'll be along in a mo.'

Martha hadn't noticed the woman sitting in the back of

the cab as Arthur had the roof up, but she felt so grateful she could have hugged him.

At home, all was quiet. Martha had passed Trisha's car in the driveway and couldn't wait to be held by her. She prayed that Trisha felt strong at this moment.

Trisha greeted her with her arms open. 'Eeh, lass, you don't have to tell me. Come here, love.'

'Oh, Trish, it's like everyone is being taken away from us.'

'I knaw. Walter, now Sheila, bless her. A lovely woman. It's knocked the stuffing out of me. So how you feel I cannot imagine with Josh an' all.'

'Oh, it is that I have to telephone the police . . .'

'Naw need, love. They called around. They said that the shop was secured, and they had made progress. They were asking after Josh, and I told them what I knew. It seems they are close to arresting the gang responsible as there was vital evidence found in Josh's shop that conclusively pointed to a specific person and he is spilling the beans to save his own skin.'

'I am hoping they rot in hell!'

Joseph came toddling over to her, his arms up in the air. Trisha picked him up. 'Ma's tired, me darling. There, that's right, give her a kiss, but she can't hold you just now.'

As Martha accepted Joseph's sloppy kiss, Trisha asked, 'So, you had no inkling that trouble was coming your way, love?'

'No, it is as I have said, that we don't get visions about ourselves, so we don't. And it is glad that I am.'

'Aye, it's bad enough that you get them about me! So, what do you want to do now, love? Are you hungry?'

With Trisha asking this Martha realised that she was, and so she became aware of cooking smells.

'Well, I found some lamb chops and cabbage. I've potatoes on to boil and the chops in a gentle oven, but they will be done for when Johnny's lessons are finished. I've just to boil the cabbage and make the gravy. 'Oh, and I found some apple pie, so that's in the warming oven.'

'Me pie?'

'Yes, little man, you can have pie, though you're to eat your dinner first.'

Joseph grinned at her and wriggled down out of her arms. Once back on the floor he toddled off to where he'd left his toys and plonked himself down beside them and began playing happily once more.

Johnny was full of everything when his tutor left. Asking them how Josh and Granny Green were, and then chatting about his lessons.

He took everything in his stride and went off to wash his hands.

'Eeh, poor little lad, he can't take it all in.'

'He will be having a shield around him, but I expect that will be cracking when Bonnie comes home and she is told. How can we protect them from all the bad things that happen? It is for being part of life, so it is.'

'We can't. We can just be there for them. In a lot of ways, they're lucky, they have the love and support of more than just one set of parents . . .'

Martha jumped in as Trisha's voice trailed off, afraid that she would cry again. 'It is that they do. And Peggy too. Is she for coming in today?'

'Aye, she is. She'll be here soon as I asked her to get here for when Johnny's tutor was finished ... Ah, here she is now.'

Peggy came in puffing and panting. 'I'm sorry I'm late, love. Thank goodness you're here. I had visions of that tutor standing here with her arms folded ready to tear a strip off me. Funny, but it doesn't matter how old you get, you always remain scared of teachers. Anyway, the bus was late. The driver said he had a puncture and there wasn't another one to relieve him and ... Oh dear, has something happened?'

'Aye, love. Let's have a cuppa. Have you eaten yet?'

'No. I got all behind today. It seems there's some days you shouldn't bother to get out of bed as the gods are against you. Now, please tell me it isn't anything bad.'

Martha told her what had been going on.

'Oh dear. I don't think I have ever come across a family like this one, as I do think of you all as one family ... Poor Sheila. God rest her soul. I thought last time I saw her that she hadn't got long. Such a lovely person. I'm so sorry, Martha. She was your mother-in-law, bless her. And Josh too ... What is the world coming to?'

'That question is for wondering about, love. Anyway, you're here now.'

'Yes, and I'll be the one to put the kettle on and finish getting that dinner ready for you. You both go and sit down, you look all in, Martha, love. And leave Joseph to me.'

Neither of them argued with her. As they went into the front room, they heard Johnny come down the stairs and Peggy call out, 'In here, lad. I need my hug first, and Mammy and Aunty Trisha need some peace.'

Johnny came back with, 'Granny Sheila has gone to heaven now!' in an almost exasperated voice.

Martha couldn't help but smile.

They listened a moment and heard Peggy saying, 'Yes, love, and it's a kind act of God for taking her. She was weary and very sick, now she has her rest in a beautiful garden. No more pain and she's smiling and waving. Shall we wave back and then she can rest for ever?'

Martha and Trisha peeped around the door at this. They saw Johnny waving like mad.

'There, I think that will do the trick, love. Now, you get your plate out and one for me, and we'll sit and have dinner together, eh?'

'Can I wave to me mam and dad, oh, and Walter, or is it too late, Nanny?'

'Yes, you can wave to them. If you haven't, they may not be resting well. That's it, give them a good one . . . There, I feel it in me bones that they've all gone to sleep peacefully now.'

'I did that, didn't I?'

'You did. I've never seen anyone who can wave as well as you just did. Good lad. Right, I'll just take this tea through, then we can get on and get the dinner sorted.'

'I can't make dinners, Nanny, I'm too young.'

'There's a lot you can do, though. You can put the salt and pepper on the table and lay the knives and forks out. Come on now, lad, you don't get off that lightly.'

Martha sighed. 'He seems to be all right now. Peggy's a marvel.'

'Aye, she is. And a whizz at cards. I'm warning you, don't ever play her for buttons – she'll have you bankrupt and your button tin empty in naw time.'

Martha couldn't help laughing at this. Trisha joined her and, like always, they ended up in giggles.

'Eeh, I remember me ma allus saying when I was full of beans and giggling that it would all end in tears. For us, if we're crying and howling, it all ends in giggles.'

'Ha, it does. And it's good so it is that we can still see a funny side in it all, or it is that we'd be going mad.'

When they were sipping their tea, Trisha said, 'Martha, I ain't going to get upset or owt, but what do you reckon to me fighting for me home, eh?'

Martha swallowed. She had guessed that this might come up.

'I think it is that you have to follow your heart but be remembering what was said about the fight costing you so much. It is that you could lose your cottage. And what if you lose the fight?'

'But if I have right on me side?'

'I am thinking that you do.'

'George isn't the only one to say it, you knaw. That solic-itor that Arthur knaws and I got for Benny before he died, he suggested it an' all ... Eeh, Martha, if I could only have me home back, I'd be just up the road from you again. It's lonelier than ever up at the cottage. Except for having the donkeys, of course. It's like the world has forgotten you on the nights that Peggy don't stay and once Sally's in bed.'

'Oh, Trish, I'm for being so sorry …'

A knock on the door interrupted them. Peggy answered it. But it was Johnny's squeals of delight that told them who the caller was.

'Uncle Jack! Uncle Jack!'

Martha breathed a sigh of relief. She knew Trisha was troubled by the loss of her house and more so the loss of Walter, but she had such a lot on her own plate.

When they reached the hall, Jack was smiling down at Johnny and about to pick him up when he caught sight of Joseph. 'My, you've grown, lad.'

As if he recognised him, Joseph giggled.

Picking Johnny up, he asked, 'So, how are you, Boxie? Have you been good?'

'I have, Uncle Jack, only people keep going to heaven and …' Johnny burst into tears.

'Oh dear, lad, what's happening?'

Jack looked from Johnny to Martha to Trisha.

Martha felt so silly as she, too, burst into tears. Trisha was strong, though. 'Come on in, Jack. There's too much to tell you on the doorstep. Come on now, Johnny, lad, didn't you just wave to them in heaven and knaw they are resting nicely, eh?'

'I did, Aunty Trish, but I want them to be here with me.'

Martha dried her eyes and went to him. He ran into her arms. 'Mammy, it hurts.'

'I am for knowing that, me wee fella. We were saying earlier that you can cry when it hurts. Now be letting Uncle Jack come in and you can be telling him all about it while you sit on his knee, so you can.'

Jack, looking concerned and mystified all at once, bent and picked up Joseph, kissed and cuddled him and then followed them through.

'I'll hold dinner a mo, don't worry. You all get on with what you have to . . . Here, let me take Joseph, I can at least get him fed. Poor little mite hasn't a clue what's happening.'

Martha thought how lucky he was and wished at this moment that she didn't know either.

With the resilience Johnny had always shown, he was soon giggling and listening to tales of Jack's adventures.

Martha's tummy rumbling reminded her of dinner and brought the tales to a halt by asking if Jack wanted to eat.

When they all sat around the table, Johnny fell asleep eating his pudding and Joseph began to look heavy-eyed.

'It's been a long day for them. I'll see to putting them down for their afternoon nap, love.'

'It's grateful I am for you every day, Peggy, love, ta. That would be a big help.'

After listening to all that had happened and showing his shock all through, Jack gasped, 'Oh, my God! Walter! I can't believe it. And I'm sorry to hear about Josh's mum, and about Josh, Martha. It's all so sad and shocking. Remember, I did tell you that you can write to that address I gave you, and I will try to get a message back to you.'

'Well, it weren't nowt that we could call on you for, Jack. It ain't like we're family.'

'No, but if Johnny is involved, as he was very much so with Walter, and to a lesser extent, I imagine, with Sheila, then there might be something I can do . . . Anyway, should-haves don't help. Is there anything I can do now? I'm so sorry, Trisha. You were such a happy couple and I liked Walter very much.'

Martha held her breath, willing Trisha not to tell all to Jack at this moment. Her head was bursting, and she just needed peace. But thankfully, Trisha just said, 'Ta, Jack. That's kind of you.'

'It's just words, but if I can do anything, I will. I have three weeks' leave before my ship sails again, so call on me for whatever.'

'You can be staying here if you are wanting to, Jack. Johnny will love that, so he will. It is that I have the guest room kept ready, so if you want to be taking your things up, there's a bathroom for your use too, so there is. Trish had already been for saying that she will stay here with me, so we'll all be together.'

'Thanks, Martha. I will take your offer up for a couple of days, but at the weekend, if you will let me, I'd like to take all the children to my home. I've kept Boxie's room as it was and can soon put a bed in it for Joseph. There's a put-you-up bed in a wardrobe that we didn't use, I can have that, and the girls can be in Jenny's double. What do you think?'

'I am thinking that is a wonderful idea. Everything here is sad and frightening again for the little ones and that will be giving them an adventure. What are you thinking about Sally going, Trish, and you staying here with me?'

'I think it a grand idea, ta, Jack, and aye, I'd love to stay here, love. I might not go home until Josh is better. Dickie will bed down the donkeys and feed them, I'll go every day to visit them, on the beach if it is warm enough for them to work, or up to me cottage … So, Jack, will this mean that you'll stay up there after that for the rest of your leave?'

'No, I want to be near the boys, so will go into a B&B during the week, then if this weekend goes well and you are both of the same mind, I could take them for the next one after that too.'

'That'd be grand. Sommat for them to look forward to.'

'So, you're really involved with your cottage now, Trisha? I knew you'd been left it and the donkeys, but does this mean you have started the renovations?'

Martha held her breath. But then realised that it wasn't possible to keep everything from Jack. She just wished it hadn't to be tackled now when she and Trisha were so fragile.

'It's a long story, Jack. And I ain't up to telling it at the mo. Maybe later when the kids have all settled down. I've to take Martha back to the hospital now, and then pick the girls up from school.'

Once more, Martha breathed a sigh of relief. There was so much to face in the near future, and she didn't want dear Trish to have to keep dealing with the awful things she had been through.

Jack nodded. But you could see that he knew things weren't as they should be. 'Well, point me in the direction of where I am to stay, Martha, and I will go up. I might take a nap myself, it's been a long drive. And I really hope you find Josh improved.'

★　　★　　★

357

When she got back to the hospital, it was positive news on Josh. All his signs were good, and X-rays hadn't shown any real damage. In light of this, the doctor told Martha that they didn't plan to keep him sedated any longer. 'I think he coped very well with saying goodbye to his mother, and that was a sign that all was functioning well. I was so against that happening, but now realise it was the best thing for Joshua going forward.'

'Ta, Doctor. That's a great relief, we are all needing Josh.'

'I can understand that. I am so sorry about what has happened. I liked Sheila very much. Salt of the earth.'

'Is George still by her side? It is that I'm not for knowing what to do for him.'

'No. He has gone home, and Sheila was picked up by the undertaker's. They will take care of her now.'

As she sat next to Josh, Martha held his hand. Already she could see his eyes blackening. That this should happen to her lovely Josh . . . A tear trickled down her face.

Josh's eyes flickered, then opened as best they could as the swelling restricted him fully opening them.

'Martha?'

'Yes, it is me, me darling. Who else is it that would hold your hand?' Martha giggled, trying to show Josh that all was well.

His smile rewarded her. But then his face stretched. 'Did Mother . . .'

'Yes, me darling, it is that she has gone to heaven.'

A tear trickled out of Josh's eye. Martha didn't try to stop him crying but cried with him as she held him the best she could. When he calmed, he said, 'I want to come home. Will you speak to the doctor for me?'

'I will. It is that we have Jack as an overnight guest, but tomorrow he is taking the children with him to Manchester, so it is that it will be quiet at home for you for a couple of days.'

With Josh home, Martha felt she could cope. George came to stay for the weekend and together the two men cried, then comforted each other, before coming to a place where they could make all arrangements for the lovely Sheila to be laid to rest.

It was Sunday morning that they learned that the gang responsible for the robbery and for wounding Josh had all been rounded up and were in prison awaiting trial. The relief to Martha to hear this made her feel she could cope once more. Josh could rebuild his stock and continue with his business.

That evening, whilst sitting eating a tea of sandwiches followed by a Victoria sponge that Trisha had made, George talked to Trisha once more about her house. Martha felt ready to give this new twist of events her attention and to support Trisha. But all of that went into the excitement of the return of Jack and the children and the adventures they'd had.

By the time she snuggled into Josh's tired body, Martha's feelings were of how all was upheaval again – Josh to support, a funeral to face, goodbyes to Sheila, and then, to top it all, Trisha seeming to be about to enter a legal battle that may take all she had if she lost. Sighing, Martha took some deep breaths, but rest didn't come as she asked herself, how were they to cope with it all?

But as she closed her eyes, a vision came to her that told her all would come right. The deceitfulness Walter subjected them all to would be known. Deceit in not only what he did, but how he made them all love him and think him a kind man when all the time he was using them to stop himself going to prison – had he have trusted them, they would have saved him from that fate. Trisha would have too. But now, all they had thought him to be was tainted.

Martha sighed. The outcome of it all worried her, and yet she knew if Trisha could get through this, happiness awaited her. With this knowledge, rest at last came to her weary body and mind.

PART THREE

A Caged Heart is Released

1930

TWENTY-FIVE

Trisha

Trisha knelt beside Daisy and stroked her shiny mane, tears trickling down her face. 'Ta-ra, lovely lady. You've been a good 'un ... Eeh, the kids you've given fun to, and the loyalty you've shown to me. All second to none. I'll miss you, me love.'

'The cart's here, Trisha. Am I to tell them to take Daisy now?'

'Aye, Dickie. But you and Ted should take the others to the beach, lad. They shouldn't have to watch Daisy being hauled away ...Where is Ted?'

Dickie grinned. 'Where do you think, eh? Sally were crying and needed comfort. Johnny's looking after Bonnie. Inseparable them lot.'

This set up a worry in Trisha. Not that she minded Ted taking a shine to Sally. She'd seen he did so in a brotherly way and no more than he did with Bonnie, but Johnny and Bonnie, though only thirteen and fourteen years old, seemed to have a bond that went further than the brother and sister one they should have. This was confirmed and sent a fear through Trisha with Joseph saying, 'Well, Johnny does want to marry Bonnie when they are older, he told me so.'

Trisha stiffened. She had to speak to Martha. This couldn't go on, and yet she knew that Martha's biggest fear was having to tell Bonnie the truth.

'Joseph, tell them all to get into the car, will you, lad? And tell Ted to come and help Dickie.'

Kissing Daisy once more, Trisha straightened. Her eyes fell on the cottage. No longer big enough to house them all, she rarely had them all stay over with her now.

Soon, the ten years binding her to it would be over – what she'd do with it then, she didn't know, though did know she could never sell it. Her greatest wish was that Dickie would find someone to love and rent it from her and continue to look after her beloved donkeys, but he just didn't seem interested in chasing girls. Ted did, though. A proper ladies' man, he always had some great love, or heartbreak. This made her smile as the four of them came into view and Ted helped the girls to get into the car. But she frowned as he was particularly attentive to Sally. At fifteen, she was beautiful. Her figure was graceful – made that way by her love and devotion to ballet and tap dancing. Both suited her. Ballet for when she was in one of her quiet periods and seeing the world as a beautiful soulful place and tap when she wanted to express the fun side that was never far from the surface.

Sally's and Bonnie's giggles drifted over to her and she

was glad that the tears they'd shed over Daisy were over and they'd lifted their spirits.

'Well, old girl, I'll get the kids home, eh ... Eeh, they don't seem like kids any more. Shame you won't be here to see them grow into young men and women, but we'll never forget you, love.'

Turning away, Trisha saw the truck from the abattoir. She shuddered to think of Daisy being turned into food for other animals, but knew it was the way of things and that she had to accept it.

To no one in particular, she said, 'Come on, let's get home.'

As Trisha turned into the drive of her home she saw Carl standing by her gate. This shocked her as she'd thought never to see him again. This house was hers now, she'd won it back from his clutches three years ago, due to the contents of the letter stating that he'd used emotional blackmail to force Walter to leave him all of his property.

She shivered at his stance – he stood with arms folded with a look of sheer pleasure on his face.

Coming to a halt, she sat a moment watching him through the mirror of her car. His expression changed to a sinister glare. Getting out, Trisha looked towards him. 'Get off my property. You've naw right to be here.'

'Still haven't learned to speak properly, then? Well, let's see if you can put a sentence together when I tell you I know everything about you, you slut.'

'By, you've nowt to call me a slut over, when you're the biggest one going. Just leave us alone will you, or I'll call the police.'

'Ha, I think you should. You've stolen my house and money and I'm sure they'll be very interested in that.'

'You heard the verdict. The court gave the house to me as me right as the wife of Walter.'

'Yes, all based on a letter he wrote to you. Well, dear, I have found another letter that he wrote to me.'

Trisha watched as he waved a paper at her. Saw the glee in his face as he said, 'Yes, after all this time, it turned up. Walter had a way of hiding things. He loved to play games. But you would know that, he played the biggest game of all pretending to be your husband, darling.'

Trisha swivelled round. The kids all stood staring at Carl. Sally looked devastated.

'Go inside. Ma'll be all right. Bonnie, love, take Sally and the boys in, there's a good lass.'

'Yes, Bonnie, you and Sally should be friends, and look after one another as you're both bastards born of different men and not to the ones your mothers were married to.'

'Shut up! Shut your mouth!'

'Oh? They don't know? Well, well . . . Hey, Bonnie, didn't you know that the man you call Da isn't your real da, eh? Didn't you know that these two boys are your brothers? And you – Sally, isn't it? Your slut of a ma went with a man she met while her poor husband was away fighting in France and it is this stranger that's your father! . . . Now you know why I call her and Martha sluts.'

Trisha froze. A sound like a strangled animal came from behind her. She turned to see Bonnie, her eyes wide open and staring at her. Her bottom lip quivered, tears brimmed in her eyes. Johnny went to take hold of her, but she snatched her arm away and took off.

Trisha tried to grab her as she went by, but Bonnie viciously thrust her out of the way, her voice screeching, 'I hate you!'

Johnny and Sally chased after her. Joseph stood still, unsure, his head shaking from side to side.

Knowing that Martha would be at the shop for an hour this morning as Betty, now their manager, wasn't able to get there till later, Trisha called over to Joseph, 'Go and fetch your da, lad. Hurry.'

As he passed Carl, Carl caught hold of his collar. 'Joseph, eh? Well, I don't expect you remember your real father. Poor bloke killed himself. Didn't want to stay and look after you, but palmed you off onto his mistress, and this slut.'

'Let him go, you rotten pig!' Trisha flew at Carl and clawed at him. 'You swine!'

Grasping her wrists, Carl put his evil face next to hers.

'Think you won, don't you? Well, my letter, which was among the love letters Walter and I sent to each other – a place I haven't been able to touch until now – tells me that he sent a letter to you to try to ease your hurt, but if ever you were to use it to take what he wants me to have, this is proof that it is me – *me* – that he wanted his estate to go to. Well, let me tell you, I have already filed a case and have been told that if I win – which there is no doubt of – I will also be able to sue you for seven years' rent and maintenance of the property! So, madam, I hope you haven't caused any damage to *my* house! Or I will take all you own to pay for it, *and* my legal costs! Good day!'

Letting her go with a shove sent Trisha reeling back-wards into the gatepost, taking the breath from her lungs. When she gasped it back in, her body shook and tears of frustration, hate and fear tumbled down her face as she watched Carl get into his car.

Josh caught her.

'Trisha, are you all right? Oh, Trisha, was that Carl I saw get into his car? Oh, God! Why? Why has he come back after all this time and done this? Joseph is distraught. Peggy is with him . . . Oh, my dear, what is it all about?'

His strong arms held her. She clung to him as he guided her inside. 'He – he's going to take it all . . . Eeh, Josh. Everything I've got in the world, he's going to take it!'

'Calm down, dear. Try to tell me all about it. Nothing is like it seems. We'll fight whatever rights he thinks he has.'

Once she'd managed to tell him what had happened, Josh gasped. 'He told Bonnie? . . . Christ! Where is she? Joseph couldn't tell us anything, All he said was that his real da had left him, and that I had to look after you.'

'She ran, Josh. Bonnie ran. Johnny and Sally went after her, but I ain't got a clue where she went.'

Josh ran his hand through his hair. More used now to coping with the falls in life than he'd ever been when they'd met him, he seemed to regain his strength as he took charge. 'Go around to our house to be with Peggy, Trish, and calm

Joseph. Reassure him that his dad loved him very much. But don't tell him everything. We'll do that together when we get the others back ... Bloody Walter must have told that cad, Carl, everything about us!'

Once more his fingers brushed his hair back off his face. 'Why didn't we tell Bonnie years ago? How stupid and selfish we were.'

'Naw, lad. You did it for Bonnie. You all thought it best, even Peter. He didn't want her to knaw till she were older. Now she is, he's no longer here. None of us could have predicted that. We'll make Bonnie understand.'

'I hope so. Now, do you feel able to care for Joseph?'

'Aye. I'll do me best by him. You go and find Bonnie, lad. She needs you, and I'd start in Our Lady of Assumption Church.'

'Yes, she would make for there. She has an uncanny affinity to the Church and religion.'

'As does Sally. Though I reckon for her, it's the pageantry of it all.'

'I suppose we all need something and Bonnie's Irish ancestors were all devout from what Martha tells me. Though I have to say, I've found a peace myself when I've gone to mass with Bonnie and Martha ... Let's hope that's where she is. Are you all right now, love?'

'Not all right, but I'll do what has to be done for the youngsters. What the future holds, though, I hardly dare think.'

'One step at a time. We'll look after the youngsters, then on Monday we'll see your lawyer. Don't be scared by any of Carl's threats. Even if he has right on his side now. When

369

you went to court you had rightful claims. There was nothing stolen. You were given the entitlement and that took you a long time to gain. What you have or haven't spent of the money left to you in that time cannot be reclaimed. In the eyes of the law, it was yours to spend. No challenge to that can turn the clocks back. But be prepared. It does sound like Carl can win the house back as that is still a tangible asset. But you have your cottage, love. No one can take that from you.'

'Aye, well. We'll see. Right now, me heart's breaking for our lovely Bonnie, and at possibly losing me lovely home for a second time. But the kids are the most important thing ... Go carefully, Josh, and get Martha from the shop. I reckon Betty should have been there an hour since.'

Joseph sat next to the window with his head held in one hand.

'Eeh, lad. I'm sorry you had that happen. That man's a nasty man from me past. He wants to hurt me. He's using you to do that.'

'Well, he's hurt me too, Aunty Trisha. I've got a pain in my heart. I was going to tear up that picture I have of me real dad. I just want to punch him.'

'We'll explain everything, lad. It ain't like that Carl said it was. It ain't like that at all. Your dad was a lovely man who loved you very much. He didn't want to leave you.'

'Well, why did that man say that Bonnie is my sister? I know she's like a sister, but that ain't real.'

'I can't answer all of your questions, love. Not yet. Wait for your mammy and da to come, eh?'

Peggy came through the door at that moment. 'Here you are, Joseph. I've made you the hot milk you asked for. Drink it up and you'll feel a bit better.'

'Thank you, Peggy . . . Peggy, will you go now there's no little ones to care for and you're not our nanny?'

'No, love, whatever gave you that idea? I've the job of caring for you all, your mothers and fathers too, with all they have to do. And you'll still need care for a while yet, as you all do.'

Trisha told him, 'Peggy's part of the family, lad, and will always be. I couldn't do without her, none of us could, so don't be worrying yourself on that score.'

For the first time, Joseph grinned. 'She's part of the furniture . . . We've been learning the meanings of old sayings at school.'

Peggy laughed, 'Well, I can give you a few of them if you want them. "Never spend a penny when a ha'penny will do" and "A bird in the hand is worth two in the bush".'

'Aye, and, "Not all you read or hear is the truth." A good one to hold on to right now, lad.' As Trisha turned after saying this, she saw Joseph's drawing book on the side of the dresser. Wanting to change the subject, she picked it up. 'Eeh, lad, you've allus had a talent for drawing. Can I have a look, eh?'

'Yes. Though I have a surprise in there for you, Aunty. I'll show you.'

When he opened the book, there was a picture of Daisy. It was so lifelike that Trisha's eyes filled with tears. All that had happened had taken her lovely old Daisy out of her mind. Now she was back and her heart felt sore at her loss. 'It's grand, lad. Dear Daisy. Eeh, we're going to miss her.'

'Da said he'd frame it for me to give to you. Would you like that?'

'By, I would, lad. It'll have pride of place on me dresser. Ta, love, that were a kind thought.' Knowing she had his attention away from everything else now, she asked, 'What else have you been drawing, then?'

Joseph became animated once more as he showed her the airship he'd drawn and told her that it had flown all the way to Canada and how the British Empire Games had been held there earlier.

Her heart went out to him. He was being so brave when underneath she knew he was confused and upset. At this moment, she hated Carl more than she thought it possible to hate anyone, and Walter, who she'd always held dear, was beginning to join the same ranks.

How dare they take her life and that of these children and destroy them, just so that they could live the life they wanted to live?

She'd thought that she'd forgiven Walter, but he had destroyed her and was now reaching out to destroy those she loved, and all for his own selfish need. *I would have saved him anyway. I loved him enough. If only he'd told me. If only he'd trusted me instead of using me. That I cannot forgive Walter for, and never will. As now I know that all the kindness he showed to me was a means to an end. Yes, I understand that he couldn't help who he was and who he loved, but he made a decision to cover that* up by finding himself someone to marry: me – an unsuspecting, individual desperate for love, with a ready-made family and grateful for every morsel of affection he gave me. Walter, you weren't a nice man. I know that now.

TWENTY-SIX

Martha

Martha proudly folded the christening shawl she'd crocheted and loved how the silver thread shone as it caught the August sunshine that beamed through the shop window.

Feeling unsettled, but not knowing why, she let in the painful feelings she'd felt so many years ago when she'd discovered she wasn't carrying Josh's child and never could.

Laying the shawl on the tissue paper ready to wrap it, she sighed. For all her happiness and having her lovely, happy Bonnie, she still held a yearning deep inside of her. *Bonnie! Oh, God, me feelings are to do with Bonnie!* Praying all was well, she closed her eyes, saw Bonnie running, crying, but didn't know why or where she was running to. Until the crucifix came to her and she knew it was the church. Relief clothed her as she assumed it would be over Daisy dying. They'd all been to say their goodbyes with Trisha. They would be upset ... Why had she panicked?

This explanation didn't quell her fears.

Her hands shook as she carefully folded the wrapping around the shawl and her earlier thoughts came back to her. 'Go and make a mummy very happy and proud and look beautiful as you wrap the wee baby in love.'

'Did you speak, Martha, love?'

Martha smiled at Betty. 'Och, it's me talking to meself, so it is. Take no notice.'

The shop bell clanging in an urgent way made them both jump. Martha swivelled around and was shocked to see Josh standing there. 'Bonnie! Me Bonnie!'

Josh nodded as he came towards her. His face held anguish.

'She knows, darling.'

He didn't have to say what. 'No! Holy Mary, Mother of God, how is it that happened?'

Josh caught hold of her and turned her towards the office that now took up the corner of the shop that had originally been hers and Trisha's workroom.

'Excuse us, Betty.'

Betty nodded, her face showing her concern but asking no questions.

'How? How is it that Bonnie is knowing? . . . Oh, Josh, Josh, is it that that has sent her to the church?'

'You know where she is?'

'Yes, it is that I saw her running there – well, not saw as it were. I thought . . . I thought Daisy . . .'

'Oh, I see. No, darling, it isn't Daisy. That Carl . . .'

She listened to the destruction that had been caused amongst their darling children and Trisha. 'Oh, Josh! Josh!'

'We'll have to handle it, it's all we can do, darling. Be strong. Bonnie is going to need us to be, and so are the boys.'

Martha gasped in horror as Josh told her what the spiteful Carl had said to Joseph.

'But Johnny too. He must be wondering about everything and where they all fit into what they have been told. But as far as I am aware, he and Bonnie are together, and they have Sally with them. She will help them, I'm sure.'

'But it is that we have to go to them.'

'Yes. We will and quickly, my darling.'

The church door opened with a creak. Martha peered round it. Father O'Hannigan was knelt in front of Bonnie, his voice gentle, his manner one of someone who loved and really felt for the children's hurt.

He looked up and raised his hand to stay them.

'Bonnie, it is that you have had a powerful shock, but that you are to look on yourself as especially chosen by the Baby Jesus, so you are.'

'Chosen for what, Father?'

'For many things, but for this in particular. God knew a boy. A special boy. He was to grow up without a family, so he was. But it was that he was brave and fought for his country when hardly old enough to do so. What it was he saw and went through upset the balance of his mind and shut it down from the outside world. But it was that God had one more job for him, and that was for him to be bringing children into the world. Those children were you, and you, Johnny, my boy, and young Joseph, so they were.

Now, it was that God knew of another wee boy, whose illness was going to make it impossible for him to father his own children. And so it was that He thought he was the one to grow up strong and to look after these wee children for Him, and love them and be doing all he could for them, because it was that the first boy was to suffer too much to stay on in this world. So, my dear Bonnie and Johnny, you are for being very special children. You are to make Josh happy. Without you all he wouldn't be having children to love, so he wouldn't.'

'But he didn't tell me, Father, and neither did Mammy . . . I am Mammy's child, aren't I?'

'You are. The young man I told you about was for finding your mammy, so he was. And he was for loving her with all his heart until his mind broke away again and tortured him with not knowing her any longer, or who he was. Your mammy had to struggle to keep you, and to be bringing you up, so she did. But she did it, and then Baby Jesus was for sending her Josh and the story is almost complete.' He turned to Johnny. 'God had a big job to do, as it was that he needed your mammy to be with him in heaven to care for your pappy. And so, he was for putting the idea into her head that the woman who had loved her Peter would love her children. And a beautiful story is complete as it is that the lonely boy whose mind got lost is in the arms of the woman he loved, who was for caring for him through his troubled times, and they knew that the children they were for loving dearly would be happy with a wonderful couple that God had chosen for their sons.'

A sob, and Johnny moved forward and put his arm around Bonnie. Martha held her breath. Then Sally, young for her fifteen years, said, 'Don't cry, Bonnie. We're more like sisters than ever now as God did all of that for me too. And he made it that my ma and your mammy would be friends so that you and I would always be together and connected.'

'That's for being right, Sally,' Father O'Hannigan confirmed.

Bonnie looked up into Sally's face. Then they were in a hug with Johnny trying his best to hug them both.

Martha slowly let out her breath and thanked the Holy Mary that she'd once confessed all to the lovely Father O'Hannigan and had been absolved from her sin of lying with a man out of wedlock. He hadn't broken the confessional vows as they had talked many times outside of the confessional box and he'd counselled her to forgive herself, giving her much the same scenario as she'd just heard him give to Bonnie but always telling her to talk to Bonnie now she was old enough to understand. To her shame, she hadn't found the courage.

'Ah, it is that your mammy and da are here now, Bonnie. Time it is for you to show how it is that you love them and how lucky it is for you that God chose Josh to be your da.'

Bonnie turned. For a second her face showed that stubborn look that Martha knew so well and she had insight enough to know that it was a spirit that Bonnie would need in the future. She shuddered against what that future might be, but let it leave her for now as she went forward with her arms open.

'Why didn't you tell me, Mammy, why?'

'Peter wasn't for wanting us to, me darling. When his memory came back and he found us, he saw how happy and settled it was that you were and what a good man Josh was. Peter was for saying that he didn't want that disrupted . . . Then it was that the time never seemed right. I am heart sorry, me wee darling, that it is that you should find out in this way.'

'But I want Da to be my real da.'

'I am, Bonnie, darling. In everything, I am. I couldn't love you more, even if I had fathered you. Nor could I love the boys more. But that love was misguided in making me want to shield you from the truth. Can you forgive me?'

Bonnie stood still. She looked from one to the other. 'It hurts.'

Sally hurried forward and held her hand.

Martha hadn't yet put her arms down. 'Is it that you will let me help it to hurt less, me wee darling?'

'Oh, Mammy.' With this, Martha knew a joy as Bonnie came into her arms.

Johnny was just behind her. Like before, he hugged Bonnie. Martha could see he was suffering for her and knew that it must be a shock for him to realise that Bonnie was a half-sister to him and not someone who had become like a sister.

As they walked to the car having thanked Father O'Hannigan and said their goodbyes to him, Bonnie clung on to Martha. Sally held Bonnie's hand as if she would protect her and Johnny walked in front with Josh. It was as if Bonnie had forgiven her, but was unsure now how to treat Josh. Martha was glad he'd seemed to have decided to give her time.

It was as he was parking the car that Josh called Martha over and whispered, 'I think this has happened just in time and may be a blessing in the end. Johnny told me he was planning on marrying Bonnie when they were older.'

Martha smiled, though her heart had flipped. 'It is that it would have fizzled out – a crush, I think it is that it is called now, that happens amongst youngsters. But it is good that it has been thwarted, so it is.'

'Yes, but extra care with Johnny till his heart mends, darling.'

Martha nodded. It seemed Josh had taken it seriously, so she must too.

It was three weeks later with school term beginning that things improved for them but worsened for Trisha. Martha had prayed and prayed for Bonnie to make a move towards Josh. His heart was breaking as he thought he'd lost her for good and had come out as the baddy in it all.

Joseph had accepted everything well, only taking a short while to see the truth and not believe Carl. This time it had been Josh contacting Jack, who had got in touch with the doctor who'd treated Peter. A meeting was arranged, with Jack splitting the cost of it with them, for the doctor to explain their dad's illness to both boys and how it was an act of love for them that had made him go with their mother. He hadn't ever wanted to be a burden to them.

The boys seemed very settled after this and loved their time with Jack, who had taken leave pending his retirement from service and had accepted their offer of using their guest bedroom. He took them shopping for all the uniforms and school items they would need for Rossall School. And to his delight, the school ran military groups and both Joseph and Johnny had joined the naval force. It was with great pride that Jack helped them to shop for the uniform they would need and taught them to salute smartly, something they did whenever he entered a room.

Both she and Josh found this very funny but didn't show it to Jack as to him it was deadly serious, as was his own salute to his boys. 'Naval personnel always salute each other, and in particular lower ranks salute higher ranked officers and the officer returns that out of politeness,' he told them. They never questioned it again but still giggled over it when alone in their bedroom.

'It's like living aboard a ship!'

'Ha, he'll have them scrubbing the decks next, so he will.'

'We shouldn't laugh, it has been his life. I'm not sure how he will cope in civvy street.'

'Is it that he is for having plans?'

'Yes, he intends to sell the house in Manchester and buy a small one here.'

'Hmm, that is for making sense to be near to the boys, but, well, I am wondering if there is an ulterior motive? In fact, it is that I know that there is.'

'Oh, have your powers been at work? I know that look, darling.'

'What I've noticed is more than a feeling, and has been for triggering a premonition, but all I'll be saying is that Jack might be hoping to get a little closer to Trisha, so he might.'

'Ha, you're incorrigible! That's probably more wishful thinking than a premonition . . . Anyway, there's something else I didn't know, and that doesn't seem to have visited you either, which is that after getting to know Bonnie, Jenny left her a small legacy to be taken from her half of the estate their father left to her and Jack!'

'Oh, but that is so kind, so it is. And her not for being a relation of Bonnie's.'

'But technically she was, as she was stepmother to Bonnie.'

'I wasn't for thinking like that, but still it is a kind act, so it is.'

'It is, my darling. And I'm glad that the boys are settled in their minds now.' Josh sighed. 'If only Bonnie could be.'

As if he'd conjured her up, a knock came on their bedroom door. 'Mammy, Da, are you awake?'

They shot apart from the cuddle they were in. 'It is that we are. Is there something wrong, me darling?'

'I just want to be with you.'

Tall, slender, beautiful Bonnie opened the door in response to Josh calling out, 'Come on in, darling.'

With her slight frame and long legs she looked like a frightened, delicate fawn as, taking small steps, she came in.

Martha sat up and held out her arms to her. As she kissed her their glorious red hair intermingled. 'I love you with all my heart, me darling. Everything will be all right, so it will.'

Bonnie looked up and smiled, and then twisted her body and put her hand out to Josh.

Josh took it, not speaking, but with tears filling his eyes.

'I love you, Da. I'm glad that God chose you to care for me.'

'Oh, my darling daughter. Let me give you a hug.'

And that was it. A huge relief settled over Martha and her heart felt topped up with love once more.

It was as Martha, Josh and Jack were sitting down – the men glad of the peace and the huge breakfast Martha had prepared of eggs with potato and bacon lardon cakes after having suffered complete chaos as Bonnie, Johnny and Joseph had finally left for school – that Trisha burst in, her obvious anguish and recent tears clear to see.

'Oh, Trish, what is it that has happened?'

'Eeh, Martha, I've received an order to attend court! I'm to answer the counterclaim of the ownership of me house and a sum of money that is to be settled on the contestant who is proved to be the legal owner of me house!'

Martha hugged the distraught Trisha to her. 'It is that you are the rightful owner. That pig is not for taking it off you ... Oh, me darling, be strong. It is that you have right on your side, so it is.'

Both men had risen. Jack moved forward first. 'Come and sit down, Trish, love. Martha has told me all about it. Is there anything that I can do to help?'

Martha noticed that Trisha's anguish seemed to lift a little as she looked up into Jack's face. Her thoughts went to her premonition and her heart sang with the knowledge that things would get better for her dear friend, but for now, it seemed there was a more pressing matter bothering Trisha.

'Eeh, I wish that there was, Jack, but I think I'm just going to give in. I've naw fight left in me.'

'You can't do that, Trish.' Josh looked appalled. 'You must fight for what is yours. We'll all support you. You still have the letter Walter wrote, don't you?'

'Aye, I do. But Carl says that he has one that makes mine null and void, and someone must believe him for this court case to take place.'

'That's not the case. Anyone can bring a case in front of the courts. I know Carl has strong evidence – well, I don't know, but for his case to be heard, he must have – but then, so have you. You were given the letter on the day of Walter's funeral and by his solicitor. Carl has only just happened to find one to him all these years later. Look, let's speak to a solicitor and get you protected, eh?'

'Ta, Josh. Aye, I want to feel that someone with authority is on me side.'

A month later, with a shaking Trisha by her side, Martha entered the imposing interior of Preston Court. Jack, who had now sold his house and was renting a cottage while he decided what he was going to do, and Josh, were just behind them.

It was a shocked quartet that left the courtroom two hours later, with Trisha once more losing the right to her home on St Anne's Road. She had been given a month to vacate it, but was not called upon to return the one hundred

pounds that had been the sum of cash left after all the legacies Walter had bequeathed.

'Just get me away from here. By, I'm filled with hate,
Martha, that I feel I'll hurt someone if I don't get out. Me
pain is that deep, I'll never knaw peace again.'

Before Martha could answer, her heart suddenly lifted as
Jack stepped forward and took Trisha's arm. 'I'll take you
for a drive, love. I'd like to see Pilling Sands that the boys
have been telling me about.'

'Aye, I'd like that. Ta, Jack.'

As Martha hugged her, she told her, 'Don't be worrying
yourself over the youngsters. It is that we will collect them
and give them their tea. And it is that Josh will take me to
the shop first so that I can be getting an update on how it
is the orders are flowing.'

'Ta, Martha.'

To Martha, it was as if Trisha had died inside, as if she was
an empty shell, and she wondered if she could ever pick her
up again. She prayed that she could and, if not on her own,
she willed that Jack could as she'd noticed Trisha relying on
him more and more of late. But oh, how she hoped that
Trisha would see his love for her soon, as her lovely Trisha
seemed sliced apart by pain.

TWENTY-SEVEN

Trisha

For September, it was a lovely day, but the sun did nothing to lift Trisha as she stepped out of Jack's car on the roadside next to Pilling Sands.

They'd driven in silence, something she was glad that Jack had allowed. But then, his kindness was something she'd come to rely on a lot lately, that and his friendship. Often they had laughed together as he'd helped her with some task or other that involved lifting or heavy work. And always she'd noticed that he never intruded on her, letting her feel free in his presence. Though she had to admit there had been times when she'd hoped for a little more. Now wasn't one of those times. She needed to absorb the pain of Walter's words as they went round and round her head:

My darling Carl. The love of my life. How am I to leave this world without you? But I must. I cannot bear the pain I am causing. You will know to what I refer. Please be kind to Patricia, none of this is her fault.

After an initial intake of breath, showing the shocked feelings at the opening of the letter, the court had fallen silent. Not a paper had rustled.

Josh had squeezed her hand. The lawyer had read on:

I have left her a letter too, telling her my usual lies, but I owe her that much.

Trisha's heart had felt as though it had split open.

Patricia is innocent in all of this. But I feel I have left her with enough money for her to live comfortably in her cottage, besides doing it up for her. And so, I meant every word of my will. It is you that I want to leave my estate to. You who I owe so much to, my happiness, my life.

It must be today that I go. And so, I am writing you this final love letter. You know you have my heart for ever. But I have told Trisha things or put things in such a way that only a coward would. I regret that now but cannot stop to take the letter I left for her back from my solicitor. I have to leave this morning; it is the only way I will find peace.

I realise now that these things may lead to her contesting the will, so it is vital that you show this letter if she does. Though I doubt she will as she is of limited intelligence and may never even think of using what I have said as a weapon.

I love you with all my heart and thank you for the time we spent together.

Your Walter x

The silence that had followed the reading was broken by the lawyer giving out the date the letter was written as the date Walter died. And then reading out a sworn statement of lies by Carl that though he was very fond of Walter, he hadn't had feelings for him or ever engaged in sexual practices with him. That they were friends, but Walter had wanted more. It was this that had led him to take his life. Carl's statement had finished by him saying, 'I am an eminent specialist in medicine and have been married to a wonderful woman for many years.'

Trisha had wanted to scream out, 'Liar!' But she'd sat still, her hurt at Walter's words so deep her throat couldn't have released any words.

This statement was accepted, and her home rubber-stamped as no longer belonging to her. The final twist of the knife being Carl's smirk as he left the court.

They had climbed the fence, Jack taking her hand to help her, before he spoke for the first time. 'Can I give you a word of advice, Trisha?'

She nodded.

'Come, let's sit on the sand.'

Once they were sat, Jack leaned back on his hands and gazed out to sea. 'Let go of it, Trisha. At the end of the day it's bricks and mortar that you made a home inside of. You can do that with your lovely cottage – you have done. I love it so much more than your house.'

'It's not the bricks and mortar, but aw, the pain, the words, the feeling of being used. I feel like I'm nowt.'

Jack's hand came over hers. She didn't pull away. A strange but familiar feeling fluttered in her heart. One she knew she harboured but had denied.

'You're not "nowt", as you call it. You're beautiful.'

Trisha almost gasped at the tightening of her throat. How could she feel like this? She mustn't. This wasn't what Jack was feeling. He was just being kind.

'Trisha?'

Her name sounded like velvet on his tongue.

'I love you, Trisha.'

His hand brushed up her arm and down again. Shivers trembled through her.

'Can you learn to love again? Could you learn to love me?'

Still unsure, Trisha stared out to sea as she tried to control and slow down her breathing.

'Trisha? Trisha, please listen to me. I have loved you for years, since I first met you in the shop when I came to tell you about the boys needing a home. You were so kind. Then when I went back to sea, I found I couldn't get you out of my mind. And then after Walter, well, I thought that with my lifestyle it was unfair to ask you if you could love me. But I have been afraid that you would meet someone. But now I am home for good, and I can make a new life. I want that life to be with you. You have occupied my every waking hour for years. I'm sorry if I shouldn't have spoken or have chosen the wrong day, but for me it was now or never as I so want to support you through this terrible time.'

The silence hung over them, seeming to strangle Trisha as she felt any words she wanted to utter were locked inside her.

'May I hold you?'

He stood and took her hand. She didn't resist as he pulled her to a standing position. Nor when he took her into his arms and she leaned into his strong body. For it was as if all pain lifted from her and floated up towards the sky, leaving her free to love again.

And she did. She knew without doubt that she loved Jack with a love far more intense than any she'd ever felt. She looked up at him. Accepted his lips descending on hers. Tasted his sweet-smelling breath and lost herself in his deep and yet tender kiss that awoke feelings in her that she couldn't remember feeling as her heart soared towards the sky.

She had happiness, right here in her arms.

Martha's secrets, given to her by her gift of being a fortune teller, had all played out. The pain coming to her was over. Martha didn't speak of any more impending doom and hadn't done for a long time. Only that all would come right.

And there hadn't been any doom, not even from the court case. For now, it wasn't a thing to cause her pain, but to bring her love. The love of a good man.

It would be her that would have the secret. The secret of unlocking the cage that could hold you trapped with guilt, with hurt, and with despair. She had unlocked it with letting love in. The love offered by Jack. She would never let it go. She would never cage her heart again.

A LETTER FROM MAGGIE

Dear Reader,

Hi.

I hope you enjoyed reading *The Fortune Tellers* and this sequel, *The Fortune Tellers' Secret* as much as I enjoyed writing them.

Thank you from the bottom of my heart for choosing my work to curl up with.

And so, you have begun Martha's and Trisha's stories, and lived their courageous fight back from poverty to rise and fall and rise again. Their losses, their heartaches, and their joys.

Our next journey will be through the pages of *The Fortune Tellers' Daughters*.

This will take us to Bonnie's and Sally's lives, besides Johnny's and Joseph's. All are now grown men and women, who once life settled down for them had a wonderful upbringing surrounded by love – but this is 1939 and the war years are facing them. We will cry as we lose some, feel anxious at the experiences they go through, and want to hug them and save them – reading this next instalment will take you on the journey they took.

And you will continue to walk with Martha and Sally through their lives as all seems to come tumbling down. How they find the courage to care for the evacuees they have taken in whilst agonising over the fate of Bonnie, Sally, Johnny and Joseph, but also Josh and Jack, who are still young enough to play their part in beating Hitler.

If you have enjoyed this second book in the trilogy, I

would so appreciate you rating the book and leaving me a review on Amazon or the online bookstores you buy from, and on book groups, you belong to such as Goodreads, TikTok, Facebook and Instagram.

Reviews are like I'm being hugged by the reader, they encourage me to write the next book and they further my career as they advise other readers about my work, and hopefully whet their appetite to also buy the book.

If you are new to my books and would like to read more, my backlist is listed in the front of this book. There are two trilogies available, and two standalone books for you to choose from. These are available from Amazon and other online stores.

I am always available to contact personally too, if you have any queries or just want to say hello, or maybe book me for a talk to a group you belong to. I love to interact with readers and would welcome your comments, your emails, and messages through:

My Facebook Page: https://www.facebook.com/MaggieMasonAuthor

My Twitter: @Authormary

My website: www.authormarywood.com/contact

I will always reply. And if you subscribe to my newsletter on my website, you will receive a three-monthly newsletter giving all the updates on my books and author life, and many chances of winning lovely prizes.

Love to hear from you, take care of yourself and others,

Much love
Maggie xxx

ACKNOWLEDGEMENTS

Many people are involved in getting my book to the shelves and presenting them in the very best way to my readers – my lovely Commissioning Editors, Rebecca Roy and Ruth Jones, who work tirelessly, advising on structure of the story, besides overseeing umpteen other processes my book goes through. The editorial team headed by the wonderful Jon Appleton, whose work brings out the very best of my story to make it shine. The publicity team who seek out many opportunities for me to showcase my work. The cover designers who do an amazing job in bringing my story alive in picture form, producing covers that stand out from the crowd. The sales team who finds outlets across the country for my books. My son, James Wood, who polishes my work before submission and works alongside me on the edits that come in. And last, but not least, my much loved and valued readers who encourage me on as they await another book, support me by buying my books and warm my heart with praise in their reviews. My heartfelt thanks to you all.

And a special thanks to two Blackpudlians: Vicky Gordon, the granddaughter of Arturo Naventi, an ice-cream vendor on Blackpool beach many years ago, for allowing me to base one of my characters in the first of the series on her grandfather and giving me wonderful snippets about his life and his work. All served to help me bring my Arturo to life.

And to Steve Cross for helping my research into the streets of Blackpool I wanted to use as setting, and if they existed during this era.

Thank you both very much.

But no one person stands alone. My family are amazing. They give me an abundance of love and support and when one of them says they are proud of me, then my world is complete. My special thanks to my darling Roy, my husband and very best friend. My children, Christine Martin, Julie Bowling, Rachel Gradwell and James Wood, my grandchildren, and great grandchildren who all light up my life. And to my 'Olley' and 'Wood' families. You are all my rock and help me to climb my mountain. Thank you. I love you with all my heart.